Seoul
survivors

Seoul
survivors

Naomi Foyle

Jo Fletcher

BOOKS

First published in Great Britain in 2013 by

Jo Fletcher Books
an imprint of Quercus
55 Baker Street
7th Floor, South Block
London
W1U 8EW

Excerpt on page 365 from "Europa and the Pirate Twins"
Courtesy of Thomas Dolby, Lost Toy People, Inc.

A CIP catalogue record for this book is available
from the British Library

ISBN 978 1 78087 598 9 (TPBO)
ISBN 978 1 78087 596 5 (HB)
ISBN 978 1 78087 599 6 (EBOOK)

10 9 8 7 6 5 4 3 2 1

Typeset by Ellipsis Digital Limited, Glasgow

Printed and bound in Great Britain by
Clays Ltd, St Ives plc

For John Luke Chapman

Contents

PART THREE | GROOMING

PART FOUR | KEEPING MUM

PART FIVE / MISCONCEPTIONS

PART SIX / ROYAL JELLY

'How should it be sown? How should it dawn? Who will fatten the sacrifice?'

The Popol Vuh
The Sacred Mayan Book of Life

Part One

NEW ARRIVALS

1 | Long Day

'Ni-suh, Sy-duh-nee – *Omhada* – look at camera – thank you – better – pro-*fesh*-ional – Now, play with Hot-Cold, plea-suh!'

A shock attack of Nu Destruction beats was battering her body, the studio lights were melting her make-up – melting her *face* – and the scent of her own fried nerves still lingered in the air, but Sydney was on fire now and this was a war zone she never wanted to leave. Jutting her hip toward the camera, she slithered her palms up the black GrilleTex™ jacket. Beneath its slashing neckline, a tight contraption of silk, wire and pump-foam was pushing her tits out beyond maximum volume. Fuck, this outfit was a knife-free boob job: she'd never had such amazing cleavage in her *life*. But that wasn't all the OhmEgo designers could do. Tossing her hair, she pinched the metal button stitched over her heart and twisted it all the way round to the left.

Big mistake.

The music hit a disco vein and she made a stab at vogueing, but as she cocked and sliced her arms at asymmetrical angles to the world, an oven of heat bloomed through the jacket.

'This is *brutal*, Jin Sok,' she panted, fumbling for the dial.

'*No!*' he ordered. 'Go wi-thuh. Go *wi-thuh.*'

He was totally crazy. But so was she. She reached off-set, grabbed a bottle of water from a white designer stool and, facing front again, squirted the cool liquid down her neck and chest. *Ahhh.* The photog-

3

rapher stomped in applause and she chucked the bottle aside. Bending low enough for the camera to practically capture her navel, she pouted and traced the glossy circle of her lips with her tongue. A dark blush tingled in the pit of her stomach. Johnny would *kill* for her to do that at home.

Jin Sok jumped on a chair. 'Loo-kuh up. *Now,*' he commanded.

She raised her chin and he zoomed in on her chest. Beneath her mask of gold make-up her cheeks flared. For a breath-taking instant she imagined scooping her wet tits out of the bra and thrusting them into the shot.

A gush of fear soaked her panties; her bare legs trembled and she thought she might stumble. *Fuck.* What was she doing, getting *turned on* at her first major league shoot? What if she stained the OhmEgo shorts?

If Jin Sok noticed her panic, it only aroused his approval. 'Okay! Ye-suh! Baby – smi-luh!' He hopped off the chair and kicked it away into the corner of his studio where it sent an orchid pot flying. She threw back her head and laughed out loud. 'Beauty!' he roared. 'Now kissing, Sy-duh-nee – ki-suh please!'

Crisis past, the GrilleTex™ heat now just bearable, she smacked the air noisily. Her blonde braids tipped with metal cones knocked against each other with empty precision as she strutted to the front of the set. Arms crossed, she toyed with the OhmEgo logo warped into the jacket's left shoulder. Peeping at Jin Sok from behind a web of storm-proof mascara, she turned to display the puckered omega. What felt like a bucket of sweat sluiced down her spine.

'No, really, I'm *too hot!*' she complained, louder this time. Jin Sok couldn't expect her to keep going under these blazing lights, not with the GrilleTex™ temperature cranked up to the top. No wonder her body had zoomed out of control.

4

Jin Sok's shaved head gleamed above the lens and with his free hand he jabbed the air, keeping the momentum of the music moving through the room. 'Cool it, baby – i-suh cream option – chill out!' he called.

Thank fuck for that. Sydney twisted the dial round to the right. An icy shiver ran through the thermo-threads embedded in the jacket and goosebumps pinged up on her arms. Shit, that was no good either. Even in a sauna of a studio, who wanted to be cold and clammy inside full-blast air-con clothes?

She shrugged off the jacket and let it slip to the floor. Her abs were still a work-in-progress – okay, non-existent – but the bra was fringed with silky black tassels that hid her puppy fat and felt lovely and swishy against her skin as she moved. Johnny hated them – 'Fringes? What are you, a lampshade?' he'd sneered when she'd showed him the MoPho files – but he wasn't here, so fuck him. Shaping her hands into pistols, she sprayed the room with bullets, picking off all-comers before merging the guns into one and pointing the barrel directly down towards the camera.

Jin Sok urged her on in Korean and as she wiggled and winked, blew kisses and blinked, her heart finally dared to dart all its little silver arrows up into the music, up up up to the high white ceiling of the studio. Was it really true? Was she really posing for a leading international techno-fashion photographer, not being told just to 'look pretty' by some dork in a tacky suit? Thank fuck Jin Sok had spotted her in that cheap lipstick campaign. *This* was where she was supposed to be. Johnny could go find himself a new girl scout: she didn't need to sweet-talk his stupid clients any more – maybe she didn't even need to suck his big cock any more . . . *Please*, she silently groaned, closing her eyes, *please let this never stop, let this feeling never end, set fire to my clothes, let me die now, please . . .*

'Eye-suh open!' Jin Sok whooped, blasting the music until it rattled

5

the roof. She hurled herself back into the room with a flying Taekwondo kick. Right now, everything was Ohm-E-Go-Girl-*Go*.

The truck jerked to a halt, slamming Mee Hee's head into the corner of the box. Tears stung her eyes, but she swallowed hard and forced herself not to cry out. The doctor had said, *No matter what happens, don't make a sound.* She licked her cracked lips and, as silently as possible, took a deep breath. The truck engine died.

Bu-ung, bu-ung. Bu-ung, bu-ung. Mee Hee's heart hammered at her ribs, in her ears, right down in the pit of her belly: *bu-ung, bu-ung; bu-ung, bu-ung,* louder and faster, until her whole body was booming, until the truck itself must be shaking like the lid of a rice *sot* left to boil over by a bad, foolish wife. Oh, why must her own heart betray her? Why couldn't her heart be small and quiet and still?

A tear slid down her cheek. The pounding in her chest subsided just enough to remind her that her head was throbbing, her neck bent at a sharp angle to her shoulders. But she didn't dare shift or stretch, not even a finger or toe.

Was this it? Would she hear men barking at the doctor, the back of the truck rattling open? Would the empty crates and sacks piled above her be flung out, one by one, onto the road; would boots clump across the metal floor that was her roof; would the trapdoor heave open and flood her sweating, aching body with light?

No. The truck belched and lurched forward, and a thick shudder ran through her. Stifling a whimper, she pushed herself back onto the blanket the doctor had given her. If only she could sit up – but the box was so small, she could only lie flat, or curled up like a foetus on her side. Try to sleep, the doctor had said – but who could sleep sweltering in this heat, afraid that, at any minute, petrol fumes might start seeping through the air-holes poked into the walls of the box?

Beneath her, the tyres crunched over something on the road. She tried to imagine what had just been flattened: not a rabbit or a magpie, she hoped, but a tin can, perhaps, or a farmer's tool, dropped off a tractor or cart. It was important to picture the day outside, not to lose herself in the box; to remember she was travelling, going somewhere far away. But they were so many miles from her village now that she didn't know how to think about the land blurring past. She could imagine smudged mountains, beautiful as the ones she had left behind, or terrible scenes of parched paddies and swollen-bellied children lining the road: either way she might be creating a false world in her head, one that could never prepare her for where she was truly going.

A large drop of condensation splashed onto her forehead. She wiped her face with a corner of the blanket, then groped around until she found the water bottle. She took a small sip. The water was as hot as soup, and there wasn't much left. Maybe soon – *oh please soon* – the hatch behind the driver's seat would open again and a cool bottle would rumble down and hit her shoulder with a thud. Would the doctor push another bag of *kimbap* down as well? Three or four hours to the border, he had said, then eleven or twelve hours to Beijing. It was the longest day of the year, she knew. The longest day of her life.

Oh, how many more hours until she could eat? Mee Hee crossed her arms and squeezed the water bottle between her breasts like a doll. She must stop thinking about food. She'd had two meals today already, a whole bowl of *ramyon* in the medical tent before dawn and then, later, the eight pieces of *kimbap* the doctor had given her. She should have saved them, like the water, but once her lips had closed around the first perfect chewy circle of rice and *kim*, stuffed with thin, crunchy slices of *kim chi* and cucumber, she hadn't been able to stop eating until the very last piece had vanished. That was not so long ago; she shouldn't be hungry now. She shouldn't be tormenting herself with thoughts of dried squid, warm from the coals, smelling like a man, or soft and heavy *dduk*, dusted with sugar powder and filled with a dollop of sweet red-bean paste.

Her guts curled like the noodles in the *ramyon*, sending heat corkscrewing through her body. Her skin was grimy and slick, her lungs were burning, her head hurt. If only she could get a message to Dr Tae Sun, tell him to stop the truck, to let her get out and breathe, paddle in a stream, shelter in some pine trees from the midsummer sun. If only she could ask him to tend to the new bruises she could feel stealthily blossoming beneath the old ones; soothe them with the ointment he had used in the medical tent the day before, his quiet hands smoothing the milky lotion into her skin, not asking how her body had come to be a lumpy porridge of yellow and purple flesh. If only Dr Tae Sun could lay his hand on her forehead now, smear his sweet-smelling herbal cream along her ribs – but even if he could hear her from his seat beside the driver, she couldn't cry out, couldn't scream, couldn't beat the insides of the box. She was tired, so tired, and her throat was dry as tree bark, her belly bloated, her skin shrinking and tearing . . .

Then, just as she thought she would split open, her whole body began to simmer like a stew. It was almost beautiful, that feeling: her muscle, bone and skin melting into the hot, humid air, until, warm and weightless, she was floating on a greasy pillow of steam, rising up into a golden light, up and far above the stinking cauldron of the truck.

It was a wonder he had any room for lepidoptera, what with the wall-to-wall cargo packed in his guts, but the butterflies in Damien's tummy were flapping so wildly a fucking mountain range in China had probably collapsed. He was also bursting for a pee. The second the seatbelt sign went off, he frogmarched himself down the gangway to the loo.

The tang of antiseptics in the cubicle hit his nostrils like a pinch of cheap coke. Christ, he was so keyed up he could have wanked – but he mustn't disturb his system, Jake had written: for twenty-four hours before the flight, no spicy foods, no coffee, no sex. Besides, he thought, watching his urine swirl down the stainless steel bowl, who'd want to masturbate in a fluorescent-lit cell, stifling every gasp, and keeping your elbows tucked in like you were eating school dinner? Of course he wanted to join the Mile High Club – but he wanted to do it properly, not with himself.

The relief of an empty bladder was almost as good as an orgasm. But his stomach was still uncomfortably, unignorably, *there*. He splashed his face with water, ran his fingers through his lank black hair and grinned dementedly into the mirror. He didn't look like an international criminal: same annoyingly boy-band lean cheeks as always; same sky-blue eyes and bloodless white skin. Though there was a tad less stubble on his chin – Jake had said that the clean-shaven look was the best policy. Jake had said a lot of things, and because Damien was flat-broke, legally fucked, shit-scared and a fool, he'd listened.

No. Raising one eyebrow, he fixed himself with a stern, Gregory Peck meets Alex Ferguson, half-time bunker pep talk sort of look. Not a fool. There was another reason – an unimpeachable, winning season kind of reason – why he was flying by the seat of his Asda boxers out of yet another wet Sussex summer into the biggest, daftest gamble of his life. He was out-manoeuvring Lucifer's Hammer. And he had to keep his eyes firmly on the prize: Plan Can.

As pepped as he was going to get, Damien returned to his aisle seat. The Korean beside him, a bloke in a blue Lacoste shirt and Prada specs, was tapping away at his laptop, filling the screen with rows of tiny circles and squares. What had Jake called the Korean alphabet?

Anyway, it was easy to learn, apparently – especially if you were locked up for ten years with fuck all else to do.

Damien shifted in his seat. When was the in-flight entertainment going to start? He'd had to sell his own laptop and iPod to help pay for the carbon tax on the flight, and it didn't look like his neighbour was going to be striking up a friendly chat to distract him from thoughts of acute THC poisoning or imminent lengthy imprisonment. Though according to Jake, Korean jails weren't so bad – not malarial mosh pits like in Thailand or the Philippines, anyway. He'd also said the whole country ran on a well-oiled system of bribery and corruption, though Damien suspected that young foreigners could probably only pay their way out of stuff like getting pissed and thumping random strangers, or teaching ESL without a work visa. And besides, you needed money to bribe someone and he was on this plane in this condition precisely because he had less than none of that.

Christ. His brain was whirring like a stuck DVD drive. He had to stop thinking about the future – actually, to stop thinking entirely would be best. In an attempt to focus on his immediate surroundings, he stared at the seat-back video screensaver: *Han Air: Treating Our Customers Like Nature: With Attention and Respect.* Corporate eco-speak was the new opiate of the masses, but it wasn't nearly as effective as crap 3D vid-games. He craned a look down the aisle. Thank fuck: a trolley-dolly was tripping towards him with a plastic sack of headphones and Digi-IMAX glasses. He sat up straight and pushed his hair out of his eyes.

Jake always boasted that Korean women were the hottest in Asia. This stewardess was petite and heavily made-up – probably a Han Air's executive's wet dream, but she wasn't Damien's type; still, when her creamy fingers brushed his, he felt his face rush beet-red like some gangly schoolboy. Mortified, he busied himself with the headphones. Apart from a gut full of drugs, what was *wrong* with him today?

At least Han Air delivered a good range of games. Laptop guy closed his lid and logged straight on to the in-flight *Starboarders*. He was clearly at some ultra-high level of frequent flyer galaxy-building: within seconds of slapping his 3D glasses on over his Pradas he was zooming around, checking up on all the planets he'd colonised, punching the air as he racked up new points. Just watching him made Damien feel spacesick – though doubtless the ballooning sensation in his gut had a more immediate cause. He dug in his pocket for the Imodium tablets Jake had recommended. He'd taken two already, but a couple more would set his stomach like cement. He washed them down with the last of his duty-free water then, jittery again, got up to dispose of the box in the loo. There should be nothing suspicious on his person at Customs.

Ahead of him, the stewardess laughed: a high, girlie tinkle with a throaty catch. Damien blinked – and for a jolting moment, the blue-grey chairs were all tilted tombstones, and the giggle was a small, sharp fist: a punch from the past, landing right between his ribs.

He grabbed his seat-back. His mouth was parched, his vision swimming and that god-awful feeling was back in his stomach – not the anxious clamping and squeezing of the last eight hours, but that old, vast, burning emptiness, that scalding feeling of having been ripped open, torn in half, of dying to puke or sob or throw breakable things at the wall. A Jessica flashback – why now?

'Are you okay?' The stewardess touched his shoulder and he realised a small circle of Koreans in Digi-IMAX specs had interrupted their conquests of Andromeda to turn round and peer at him.

Guy Debord would have been proud, but Damien was in no shape to mentally compose Situationist Tweets. Resisting an urgent desire to clutch at his stomach, he muttered 'I'm fine,' and slid back into his seat. He was running hot and cold now; he was trembling; his whole body was blistered with sweat. Jesus Christ, why was this happening? Did one of the condoms split? Was dope leaking into his system? If he did vomit, would the hash baggies come up too? Fucking hell . . . what would Jake 'Godsend' Lee tell him do?

2 | Johnny Boyfriend

'Fin-ish-ee.' Jin Sok set his camera down on the long white studio table. 'Super-fantastic work, gentlewoman, thank you.'

'Thank *you*,' Sydney croaked. Jeez, she sounded ridiculous. She was parched, that was why: she needed some water, but she'd squirted all hers down her cleavage. A towel would help too – the sweat was pouring off her like Niagara Falls. 'Jin Sok,' she tried again, but the photographer placed a finger on his lips.

'Shhh.' From the back pocket of his NoChi jeans Jin Sok produced a pink hanky with a flourish. He patted her forehead and cheeks with the cloth, which exuded a light yet beguiling aroma. When she opened her eyes he was offering it to her in the formal Korean manner, one hand outstretched, the other supporting the opposite elbow. 'Present for top new Canada model in Seoul.'

'Me?' she squeaked. Was she ever going to act normal in front of Jin Sok?

'Okay, top new Canada *mousie* in Seoul!' He guffawed as Sydney took the hanky.

She was pleased she remembered to bow slightly and to place one hand at her elbow. It was a square of traditional Korean linen, spritzed with perfume – and now smeared with gold make-up. She twisted it into the shape of a flower and buried her nose in the folds. Sun-warmed peach? And a drift of vanilla?

'It's beautiful,' she whispered.

'Is "Summer Passion", classic aroma from Yi Min Hee, Korean movie star. Heliotrope and many secret fruits. I recommend for you.' Jin Sok saluted her, then picked up the GrilleTex™ jacket and folded it carefully over the back of a chair.

She gasped. 'Oh please, let me do that.' Her first time modelling ultra-expensive thermo-tech gear and she'd been throwing it all over the floor.

'*Oxi, oxi*. You go crazy in photo-shoot, you need relax now. Sit, have water!'

Obediently, Sydney perched on a stool and took a bottle of IceCap from the bar. Jin Sok was absolutely by far the nicest person she'd met in two months in Seoul, and super-sexy too, with his rock-solid buttocks, bossy roar and simple black T-shirt-and-jeans style. So what if he was camp as a sequinned tent? She didn't need a new boyfriend, she just needed a *friend*, not to mention, please *please*, a six-month high-end modelling contract. Still, glugging her water, she couldn't help but admire Jin Sok's biceps as he packed away his Leica.

Briskly, the Korean snapped the case shut. 'Sy-duh-nee, you know today longest day?'

'Longest day? No?'

'Yes, is summer eating party day. Come to Stack Bar. Lots of models, nice girls, dancing. You wear day-glo wig. I promise.'

An eating party? She so wanted to say yes, and for a moment she almost did, then her stomach contracted and something like a chill whistled through her. 'I can't,' she muttered. 'I told Johnny I'd go back to Itaewon straight away.'

'Ah, yes, Mr Johnny Boyfriend. He come too. Tell him no funny stuff, I very good boy.' He gave an exaggerated wink.

She smiled, but didn't laugh. 'I'm sorry. He wants me to meet some, umm, friends of his. Another time, I promise.'

Jin Sok threw her a mock-stern look. 'You *promise*? Good! Tonight Itaewon is lucky, Apkuchong must wait.'

'Shiteawon, Jin Sok, is where I have to go.'

'Shiteawon! I *like*,' he roared. 'Thank you. Thank *you*.' He bowed three times, and now she did laugh, not so much at her own joke as at the photographer's clowning determination to cheer her up. 'But I am think for you, gentlewoman, Apkuchong is better,' he continued, wagging his finger at her. 'I want you move to Apkuchong.'

Apkuchong was heaven in concrete: designer shops, cafés, rooftop terraces . . . Jin Sok's studio. But Johnny hated it – he called it Fag Central – and there was no way she could afford a place here on her own.

She sighed. 'It's so expensive, Jin Sok.'

'Okay, yes, and I am think so. Shinch'on, Hongdae better for you. I show you, north of Han River, old city. Night-life, my friend bar, I take you. In location van. Soon.'

'Yeah?' For a moment, Sydney dared to believe she might do it: go out dancing with Jin Sok, without Johnny; get her own apartment, be a famous model in Seoul.

Heading for the changing room, she squeezed the pink hanky in her fist. What right did Johnny have to tell her what to do?

A bus pulled up beside the Caddy, its engine rumbling like the guts of a North Korean farmhand. Elbow resting on the wound-down window, Johnny Sandman raised the volume on his MoPho ear-clip and placed his middle finger into 'Fuck off' position against his cheek. Longest day of the year, a cool breeze cutting the heat: perfect weather for cruising with the top down – and he had to get a call from that nitpicker Kim.

'Sorry, Doc. Say again?'

'The girl has been here for two months,' Kim repeated tightly from some white-cube 'environment' high above Seoul. 'GRIP is on schedule. We need to know that the Project will be put to her as soon as possible.'

Johnny patted his jacket pocket. Where were those OxyPops? He might need them. 'Look, Doc,' he replied suavely, 'she's coming along nicely, but like I said last week, now is a delicate phase.' The light changed and he stepped on the gas, though not nearly as hard as he felt like. It was rush-hour in the glass heart of Seoul and bumper-to-bumper Hyundais and Kias were nudging through the shadows of corporate HQs. 'She's still complaining about the pollution. And the food,' he improvised as he fumbled in the glove compartment for the Oxys and chucked the bottle onto the passenger seat. 'We both agreed she'd have to fall in love with Seoul before we scooped her into the deal, did we not?'

'Fall in love with Seoul, or fall in love with you, Mr Sandman?'

Johnny scowled. A minor point had been scored. *Breathe*, he reminded himself, *breathe deep. Don't sweat the small stuff; paint the big picture. Don't fight the losing battle; win the war.*

In his ear-clip Kim started ranting on about unauthorised operations, inexcusable delays. For the next five minutes he concentrated on negotiating the swankiest crossroads in the city, a grid of space-age towers yoked together by four-lane ramps full of morons watching flocks of 3D starlings swirl out of vidboards instead of where they were going. In any other country that would be illegal, but Korea had invented CGI Skylife, and its good citizens had decided they were going to fucking well watch it, even if a busload of school kids was killed in the process. Johnny's knuckles were bloodless and his fingers practically indented into the steering wheel by the time he exited the intersection.

But at least he was out in the open now, floating past the central flower bank of the boulevard down to Namdaemun, catching some rays. At last Kim paused. Johnny smiled his broadest milk-and-cookies smile – you could hear a smile, Beacon had said – and crooned, 'Doc, baby, calm down. The more Sydney digs me, the more likely she is to say yes to the Project. As far as the night shift goes, she's a natural, and she likes the spending money.'

'There is absolutely no need for her to be entertaining your private clients,' Kim hissed. 'You are well aware that once she signs she could be independently wealthy in a matter of weeks. GRIP insists that you make your overtures immediately.'

GRIP insists? GRIP *insists?* Johnny nearly put his fist through the dashboard. If it weren't for Johnny Sandman, GRIP would still be splicing the stem-cells of aborted poodles into the livers of rich drunks. Not only had *he* sourced the clinic, *he'd* convinced the head honchos in Cali to invest in the Doc's own personal Whacko-Jacko wet dream. He'd been telling ConGlam for months that post-Fukushima, post-Arab insurrections, post-Alpine snow-melt, Korea – with its cherry blossoms, spicy food and luxury ski resorts – was primed to become the globe's top tourist destination: the new Japan, Egypt and Switzerland rolled into one. Yeah, ConGlam's top South-East Asian trend-spotter and fixer had backed the Doc's 'creative contribution' to the Project down the line – for a cut and benefits, of course – but you'd never guess *that* from the way Kim talked to him now.

'Sandman? Are you there?'

'Just turning a corner, Doc.' Fuck Andrew Beacon; it was time for some chemical assistance. He reached over and grabbed the OxyPops bottle, flipped open the cap and tipped a couple of pills under his tongue. The concentrated oxygen fizzed up into his cerebrum cortex, clearing his brain of tension. Almost instantly, his shoulders relaxed. These things worked like magic. A shame you could only take them every four hours.

'Good. Now can you assure me that you'll speak to Miss Travers this week?'

This week? Johnny sucked his teeth. Obviously he was going to have to talk to Sydney about the Project at some point, but the last thing he wanted to do right now was give the girl any leverage. She'd been such a pain since old Stinky Gym Sock asked her in for that test shoot: bitching about everything, leaving her shit lying around the apartment, criticising his favourite DVDs, even forcing him to watch that bizarre catwalk channel while they were having sex. It had all been getting to him, and last night he'd reacted. Not in a good way, in the old Black Label Johnny kinda way.

But as Beacon said, you shouldn't dwell on the occasional back-slide. Right now he needed to play *softly softly catchee Sydney* again. Not hand her a twenty-year ConGlam contract: do that, and the girl and her candy-apple ass were likely to swing right out the door.

'Look, Doc,' he cajoled. Now he was relaxed, it was so much easier to try the Beacon approach: mirror back your opponent's feelings; assert your authority in a calm, inclusive manner; posit a win-win scenario. He'd practised it a hundred times on the course. 'I know GRIP's all ready to go. I know you're anxious about deadlines. But LA trusts me on this one, and I'm sure it would help build ConGlam's confidence in GRIP if we at least appeared to be working together out here.' Another bus farted a cloud of concentrated smog in front of him. Fuck, when were they going to go hydro in Korea? He'd have to dry-clean his suit tomorrow, and get the Caddy washed – not to mention buy a whole new pair of lungs.

'All right.' You could almost hear the tooth enamel disintegrating. 'So when do *you* suggest we talk to her?'

Yo: re-*sult*. The almighty Doctor Kim was backing down; chalk one up for the guy in the vintage convertible. And Andrew Beacon and the OxyPops parent company too, natch.

'After I get back from China.' Revving the engine, Johnny overtook the bus.

'*China?* That's weeks away.'

'No point getting her all excited until Beijing is sorted, and LA agrees.' He was coming up to the night market now; time to merge and swerve. He'd bring Sydney here soon; a little underground bargain shopping at two a.m. was sure to turn her on. Yeah, all he had to do, now he'd bought a little time, was spoil the girl rotten, get her all loved up again.

'There's been far too much excitement already, Mr Sandman,' Kim spat. Johnny let the poison run off him. *Ya di ya da.* The Doc sure needed a fuck. 'If you don't approach her the *day* you return from Beijing, I'll go over your head so fast the Venturi Effect will rip your hair out by the roots.'

Johnny frowned. Who knew what the Venturi Effect was – and who cared? No one, but *no one*, threatened the Sandman, or his fine head of hair. 'Now, now, Doc,' he replied coolly, 'there'll be no need for Air Force One.'

'I sincerely hope not. Now, what about your appointment with Rattail? Don't tell me that's been delayed too?'

'Heading there right now.' A girl on the back of a scooter gave him a cool once-over; he adjusted his balls and returned the favour, clocking the crack of her ass cheeks, just visible above her belt. *Nice.*

'Did you get my message about the vital stats?'

'Sure, sure: female, five-four to five-five, skinny. Mid- to late-thirties. Nice tits.' He couldn't resist.

'Not essential,' Kim snapped, 'just the height and ballpark weight. That's one hundred and ten pounds. Perfectly average for a Korean woman.'

'Whatever you say, Doc; whatever you say.'

But Kim had already rung off. Johnny jammed his MoPho back

into its holster and chucked it hard onto the passenger seat. The Doc being rude, issuing warnings, trying to muscle in on his patch? All *Not Good.* ConGlam, he was aware, practically venerated their new Korean-American scientific genius, and that was a potentially big problem he should have foreseen. Right now, though, GRIP could go fuck itself with a broken test-tube because *he* was still in charge of Sydney Travers. Who had a big date with her boyfriend tonight, and she'd better not forget it.

At the next red light he sent Sydney a text and a photo, then, prodding his Gotcha Watch, he buzzed her EarRinger – three times, meaning 'Urgent: check MoPho'. Sydney hated it when he did that; she called it Communication Accessory Overkill. But he didn't want her to miss the humdinger he'd snapped earlier: Long John Silver and pearls, if he said so himself. That would inform her last night was to be wiped from the hard drive.

Keeping one eye on the road, he browsed his MoPho playlists and sent Sinatra to the car stereo. 'Between The Devil and The Deep Blue Sea', that's what he wanted to hear, something jaunty before his meeting with the body-snatcher. Rattail – what kind of street-scum name was that for a GRIP subcontractor? Though knowing Konglish, the guy probably thought he was Dean Martin.

That was a good line; he'd have to remember it. Snickering to himself, Johnny swung a left, cut up a Porsche and powered into Namsan Tunnel Number Three.

As Sydney closed the dressing room door her EarRinger vibrated three times. She started; it still shocked her every time Johnny buzzed. And it was beginning to piss her off, too: what the fuck did he think he was doing, bugging her during her shoot?

At least it wasn't a call, just a quick prod to let her know to check her MoPho. How many times had she told him not to use the EarRinger and Gotchas like that? The matching jewellery sets were supposed to be *intimate* – a way for couples and best friends to exchange private messages, not boss each other about. She should stop wearing the twisted hunks of platinum – a twisted hunk, just like *him*, she'd yelled at Johnny once. They'd laughed, but the joke was starting to wear thin.

The MoPho was in her bag, on the chair in front of the make-up mirror. She tossed the pink hanky down on the counter and checked her inbox; maybe he was cancelling and she could go to the party.

Fat chance. There was a text, all 'baby' and 'dollface', reminding her to meet him at the *kalbi* place and be ready for a big night with the suits – as if he hadn't already told her a hundred times before she left. Plus he'd sent a photo. 'Thinking of You'. Which she ought to look at, if only to avoid the hassle of explaining why she couldn't be bothered.

It was his cock. *Again*. A sideways view this time, spurting cum all over a picture in a magazine. She peered closer. It was one of the lipstick ads: her small, glossy face half-covered with a big white blob of Johnny juice.

Sydney recoiled. What the hell was he playing at? Was *this* his way of saying sorry for last night? Or . . . was it some kind of *threat*? The last thing she needed was for a money shot featuring her face to get onto the wrong MoPho. And what if she'd opened it when Jin Sok was around? No, no, *no*! Her stomach flip-flopping, she deleted the photo and stuffed the MoPho back into her bag. She unclasped the EarRinger too, and jammed it in the pocket with the Gotcha Watch she'd taken off earlier, when Jin Sok was deciding which of her own jewellery she could wear. He'd been impressed that she owned such high price-tag bling, but right now she never wanted to wear the devices again. She was going to have to seriously set some *boundaries* with Johnny tonight.

First, unfortunately, she had to take all these gorgeous clothes off. She unhooked the bra and carefully put it back in its box with the foam pump equipment. Unscaffolded, her breasts deflated at least three cup sizes, and the bruises near her armpits Johnny had made last night were exposed. Well, he wasn't going to do *that* again, either. She slipped out of the OhmEgo shorts and draped them over the back of a chair, then examined herself in the full-length mirror by the door.

A gold-plated punk goddess snarled back, clad in thigh-high boots and metallic panties, a hundred spiky braids blazing from her head. Okay, so she could still pinch at least an inch around her waist, and she'd never done a catwalk show. But beside her was a rail of thousand-dollar clothing and a table cluttered with hundred-dollar lotions. Things had changed since she'd got off that plane from Vancouver. She sat down at the make-up table and pulled a bottle of cleanser and a jar of cotton wool balls towards her. As she wiped her forehead a faint frown-line emerged from beneath the layers of gold paint. *Jeez.* Was that a *wrinkle*? Just as she was starting to get somewhere in life, some *dork* was ruining her looks. She scrubbed at her nose and narrowed her eyes. It was definitely time to review the Johnny Sandman situation.

It was hard to believe now, but Johnny had been totally sweet to her once – when they'd met in Vancouver he'd been funny and caring and generous, a snappy dresser from LA who'd taken her to fancy restaurants. And unlike the other agency clients, he'd really made her laugh. Offering GFE, she had to giggle at every client's jokes, and ooze sympathy and compliments all night, but Johnny had seen through that *shtick* right away: he knew he looked great, he'd said, so why didn't they talk about something else – how about her favourite stuff to do on her days off? She'd told him the usual, really: she ate out a lot for work, so she liked to eat Pot Noodles at home and watch

DVDs. Or go out shopping and dancing with the girls. He'd started talking about Korea then: the nightlife was insane, he said, and the department stores were twenty storeys high – serious shoppers took nap-breaks in capsule hotels on the tenth floor. That had got her giggling. She'd asked him all about Korea then, and the dinner flew by. It was almost like she really *was* having a Girlfriend Experience.

Later, at the hotel, Johnny had even tried to make the money part seem romantic. He'd laid the envelope on the dresser, and while she checked the bills, said gruffly, 'Do me a favour, babe? Think of this as a present. Buy yourself something nice with it – even if it's just groceries, promise me you'll get them from the best deli in town?' She needed the money for a massive overdue gas bill, but the word 'present' was way better than the usual 'donation', which often led straight to stupid jokes about sperm. And the sex had been surprisingly okay. She'd provided her usual package: French Kissing, Hugging, Bare Back Blow Job, Cunnilingus, and Full Service, of course; but rather than lunge at her, slobbering and grabbing, he'd taken his time – and he'd proved to be pretty good at muff-diving. He hadn't even whinged about the condom. Like her laughter at the meal, her orgasms weren't fake. And *he'd* cuddled *her* afterwards, too.

In the morning he'd told her he was in town for a month, on a training course, and he'd asked if he could monopolise her attentions for a month? She'd thought yeah, why not? The agency had urged her to agree, and when she'd added up the figures, it was the best offer she'd had in a long time. The extra money meant she could take that modelling course sooner than she'd planned.

It had been a great month, too. Johnny had taken her to the mountains in his rented sports car; he'd bought her lingerie, jewellery, and one day a stupid teddy bear she hadn't wanted to admit how much she liked. The best thing was that she didn't ever have to pretend she was in a good mood. She could bitch about stuff – her

23

boss, the weather, other clients – and he'd just laugh. She'd told him stuff about her family – not *everything*, of course – and one night she'd even confessed that escort work wasn't really her thing: she was saving for the modelling course and once she started getting fashion jobs she'd quit the agency.

He said she was definitely too cute and smart to be working as an escort – and he'd asked her to come back to Korea with him. He'd said that Seoul was dying for blonde models, she wouldn't need a course; he could use his contacts to get her an employment visa, and some starter jobs, no problem. He'd even shown her an email from a friend of his saying sure, bring her into the studio, they could use a blonde in their lipstick campaign. *But hey*, he'd said when she frowned and passed his MoPho back to him, *don't worry*. He wasn't one of those clients who thought the escort was falling love with him. He just liked her style; that was all. They could have fun, nothing serious, just see what happened. If the worst came to the worst, she'd have some international fashion shoots under her belt. *Just think about it, babe? Promise me that?*

Korea was too far away, and her girlfriends had told her not to trust him. She'd said she couldn't leave Canada, but the next night he'd sung that old song, 'My Way', to her. It was his philosophy of life, he'd said. A naked man using a pink dildo as a mic would have made anyone laugh, but as the song went on and he closed his eyes and really got into it, she realised Johnny could actually sing. His deep crooning had reverberated throughout her body as she lay twisted in the Egyptian cotton sheets, the words almost thrumming up her spine.

'*Wow.* That was amazing,' she'd said sleepily when he'd done. 'Sort of like a massage.'

'Excuse me?' He'd pounced on the bed and started to tickle her. 'Was that a *compliment* from Little Miss Sour-Puss?' She'd squealed and denied it, wriggled in his arms as he enveloped her in a massive bearhug. She'd thought he'd want sex again, but instead he'd murmured, 'Aww, baby's tired,' as she drifted off to sleep. 'Big bad Johnny's all worn her out.'

The next day over breakfast she'd told Johnny he could pay for her passport and an open return ticket to Seoul, but there were two conditions. First, he would have to pay for her rent and bills until she got enough work to support herself. And second, she wasn't going out with him as an escort. Instead, it would be a *real* girlfriend experience. Like he'd said: just to see what happened. *Absolutely, babe.* he'd agreed, holding her close, *That's exactly what I want too.*

Sydney removed the last of the make-up. Her exposed face looked pale and gaunt in the mirror. She'd been right to trust her gut instincts; she was modelling now, wasn't she? But living with Johnny was starting to exhaust her. Though he'd promised to help her get her own career off the ground, she was spending most of her evenings buttering up his dumb clients when she could be out dancing or shopping or meeting people she actually liked. At home, he was a neat-freak: he was all about his spick-and-span kitchen, toxic household air fresheners, precious hardwood floors, while his obsession with Frank Sinatra was like some kind of aural prison. And then there was the porn.

All guys watched porn, of course. Most of the agency clients had wanted her to do stuff just like the girls in the films on the hotel pay-per-view channel. The channel was softcore – one reason the agency recommended that hotel – so the requests were just goofy stuff really: sticking her tits out in a certain way, or putting her hair up in bunches. If they got weirder than that, she'd remind the client she only offered GFE, minus anal; other agency girls did PornStar.

But Johnny hadn't turned on the TV in Vancouver. He'd turned her on instead.

Once they'd settled in to Seoul though, he'd started wanting to watch the satellite TV on the ceiling screen over the bed. The stuff he chose was pretty ordinary to begin with: women with big hair and drag queen nails, or Korean girls playing with each other. She could take it or leave it, really, but he always asked her what she liked, so she said the girls together were pretty, and she didn't mind big hair if the cocks were big too.

Then last week he'd taken a couple of DVDs out of a drawer. He'd said he used to watch them on his own all the time, wishing there was a girl he could share them with, so they'd put one on. It was different than the others. The light was grainy, the sex rough, right from the start, and quickly moved from hair-yanking and fake rape into dungeon-style bondage. When Sydney had said the film wasn't working for her, they'd tried the next one. It was worse: garishly lit to highlight every pimple, and there was a gun in the first scene. She'd made him stop it too.

'The girls look frightened, Johnny,' she'd said.

'Ah c'mon.' He'd sounded annoyed. 'They're *acting*, babe.'

'Well, *doh*. But I don't *like* it. And the men are butt-ugly.'

Then he'd got all patronising about it. 'That's the whole point,' he'd lectured. 'This kind of film's about flirting with danger, breaking taboos. I thought you were a risk-taker, Sydney.'

He was being such a dickhead. She hadn't felt like explaining why she didn't like violent porn. 'The *girls* aren't ugly!' she'd retorted. And they weren't. Their bums had a few spots, and they weren't wearing a ton of make-up, but their faces and bodies were standard fare. The men, though, were barrel-bellied and ham-fisted, with squashed-up, greedy faces – probably just like the losers who bought deviant porn. You were supposed to feel sorry for them, but if they stopped watching that shit and learned how to hold a conversation they'd get a girlfriend, for sure. Women married ugly guys all the time.

Johnny was pissed off, she could tell, but he had put the films back in the drawer, so she'd tried to make it up to him with an extra deep-throat BJ. That had done the 'trick', LOL.

The next night she was in a playful mood so she'd told him that since she had *tried* to watch the DVDs, he had to *try* watching the fashion channel with her. Johnny thought that was insane, of course, but the ramp shows all had good soundtracks – techno-trance, Bolly-bhang, power ballads – and he could look at her if he wanted to see a naked girl, couldn't he? He'd done it, though eventually he'd fucked her so hard she had to stop watching. It had been a battle, and even though she'd sort of won, she'd known the war wasn't over.

That had been proven yesterday. She'd been so excited about the OhmEgo shoot, babbling away about it on the street, until out of nowhere he'd shouted at her to *just shut up about the fucking job, will you?* He'd totally exploded. It had been almost frightening, seeing his face get all red like that, but she'd stared him down until he'd stomped off to the Caddy instead of shopping with her like he'd promised. When she'd got home, he was drinking whiskey. And when they got into bed, for the first time since they met, he couldn't get it up.

She'd asked if he wanted to watch the porn channel, but he'd growled 'You don't like porn.' Then he'd punished her breasts, grabbing and squeezing them hard with one hand, with the other trying to force his flaccid cock inside her. *Why did guys do that?* She'd told him to stop and pulled away and curled up on the other side of the bed, swallowing back the tears. After a few minutes he'd started to snore.

In the morning he'd hugged her and touched the bruises gently

27

and said, 'Did I do that, baby? Oh, Johnny's sorry.' He sounded like he meant it – but sorry didn't matter, did it? These tits were her *job*. They couldn't *ever* be black and blue.

Sydney screwed the lid back on the cleanser. Beside the bottle, Jin Sok's pink hanky lay crumpled on the counter like a used party napkin. Like her whole fucking *life*. Tears welling in her eyes, she opened the Oxytoner and dampened another cotton ball. Why had she been dumb enough to think Johnny might really be into her? He had turned out like all the rest: a selfish, controlling jerk with a jealous streak as cold and deep as the Atlantic. So much for the Boyfriend Experience.

But as she dragged the wet cotton ball over her cheek, the clean seaside scent of the toner fought with her misery. No. She hadn't crossed an ocean to be forced to do anything she didn't want to any more. She wasn't going to let Johnny scare her, not his control freakery or his porno MoPhotos: he was just another no-neck Yank with a borderline personality disorder, and one day she was going to tell him so. Savagely, she threw the wodge of dirty cotton balls into the bin, where they hit the plastic liner with a thump. Her chin throbbed with a buried zit she longed to squeeze – but she wouldn't, no; she'd moisturise properly and tomorrow she'd have a facial, the full works: clay mask, steam and extractions. She had to look after herself now she was a model – the top new Canada model in Seoul.

'You ready go, Sy-duh-nee?' Jin Sok yelled from the studio.

'Two minutes!' Furiously, she dotted concealer over the bags beneath her eyes and applied a quick brush of colour to her cheeks.

'I want lock up! *Palli palli*, plea-suh. Leave clothes on rail.'

'Coming!' Sydney tugged off the boots and wriggled into her mini-skirt and strappy top. She'd have to do her make-up in the taxi. Johnny would freak about her hair. *So let him*, she thought as she pushed her feet into her shoes. Shit: the OhmEgo shorts. She slipped them onto a hanger and slung them back on the rail; then she stuck her tongue out at her reflection, grabbed the pink hanky from the make-up counter and turned on her kitten heels to go.

3 | Seeing Double

'Lee Mee Hee – are you awake? Lee Mee Hee?' Soft and clear as a mountain stream, a familiar voice was murmuring her name.

Slowly, Mee Hee opened her eyes. Dr Tae Sun was sitting by her bed. And Dr Tae Sun was standing at the foot of her bed as well.

She must be dreaming, not yet awake. She blinked in the gauzy light and the cracks and stains in the ceiling swam into focus. So she was no longer in the box – she could stretch, sit upright. With an effort that reminded her body how much it hurt, she pulled herself up against her pillow.

She was in a bed high off the floor, and a blue nightdress was gently brushing against her bruised skin. There was a tender spot on her forearm where a tube was taped against her skin. She followed it with her gaze: it was attached to a plastic bag hanging on a frame as tall as a person beside her. Was she in a hospital? The room was small, with faded yellow walls. There was a chest of drawers beside her and next to that an empty bed with a green blanket, just like hers, standing neatly made beneath a single window hung with thin white curtains. From outside she could hear beeping, roaring and tinkling: the noises of vehicles of all sorts, cars and buses and bicycle bells. And there were indeed two doctors here, mirror images of each other, except looking more closely now she could see one was slightly stockier, a little fuller in the face. That one, the stranger, was resting a clipboard against the iron bedstead, observing her with concern.

'Don't be afraid,' said Dr Che, *her* Dr Che, grinning broadly as he smoothed the corner of her sheet. 'This is my brother, Doctor Che Dong Sun – my *twin*. He's thirty-three years old, like me, and a graduate of Yonsei University, the top medical school in Seoul. But he wants you to feel at home with him. Please, you may call him Dr Dong Sun.'

Dr Dong Sun tried to look humble, but he seemed to grow half an inch as his brother spoke and his chest swelled slightly beneath his white coat. Mee Hee shrank back on her pillow. Was she supposed to introduce herself now? She opened her mouth, but nothing came out except a dry squeak.

'Shhh,' Dr Tae Sun said quickly, 'don't try to speak yet.'

'We were worried about you,' Dr Dong Sun said, kindly. He ticked something on his chart and slipped his pen back into his breast pocket. 'You were delirious when you arrived, so Dr Tae Sun prescribed this IV drip to replenish your fluids and electrolytes. The nurses washed you and made you comfortable, and you've been sleeping peacefully all afternoon.'

'Now it's time for you to eat.' Dr Tae Sun nodded at his twin, a barely repressed note of joy in his voice. Oh, he must love his brother very much – and all the good family feeling was contagious. The last time she had smiled so widely was when her baby was born.

The thought brought a lump of coal to her throat. Her smile wilted and she dropped her gaze to her hands. They were rough and scratched: a peasant woman's hands. What was she doing here in this iron bed, attached to a plastic tube, surrounded by the complicated music of a Chinese city?

There was a rap on the door and a woman in a blue uniform – a nurse? a guard? – entered the room, carrying a tray with four short legs. The doctors parted to make room and she carefully placed the tray over Mee Hee's lap, not spilling a drop of the soup in the bowl balanced at its centre.

31

Small chunks of *tubu* and slippery green pieces of *hoba* were floating in the soup. A delicate scent like the sea on a warm summer breeze wafted up with the steam from the bowl. Tears flooded Mee Hee's eyes: the room, the food, the doctors and the plump nurse all swam together in a blur before her. 'Eat, please, you must eat, Lee Mee Hee,' Dr Dong Sun gently urged. 'The *hoba* is full of minerals, and the *tubu* will give you protein. It's very good for you.'

She couldn't – she *mustn't* eat it. Anything but *hoba* soup—

'Lee Mee Hee, you need to eat. This is good food, simple for your stomach to digest. Please try it.' Softly echoing his brother, Dr Tae Sun handed her the spoon.

She wanted to say no, to tell them why, but the words were trapped inside her, while the fragrance of the *hoba* curled around her like a cat demanding to be stroked. Helplessly, in silence, she ate, her tears dissolving in the soup. The doctors and the nurse beamed and chuckled as if she were a child. Finally the bowl was empty and the warmth in her stomach was spreading through her aching limbs. The nurse picked up a folded piece of white linen from the tray and held it out to her.

'It's a napkin.' Dr Tae Sun smiled and pointed at his chin, just at the place where on her own face she could feel a spot of soup.

A linen napkin. It was far too beautiful to make dirty, but everyone was looking at her, waiting. Gingerly, Mee Hee dabbed at her mouth as the nurse removed the tray and bustled from the room.

'Thank you,' she whispered.

'It is our honour to feed you.' Dr Dong Sun bowed low.

'I didn't know you had a twin brother,' she said to Dr Tae Sun, her voice gaining in strength. 'And a doctor, too. Your parents must be very proud.'

The two brothers exchanged glances. Dr Tae Sun cleared his throat, and Mee Hee crumpled the napkin in her hand. She must have said entirely the wrong thing – what made her think she knew how to speak to doctors?

But when Dr Tae Sun spoke, his voice was quiet and kind. 'If our parents were still alive, they would be very proud and happy to know we are together at last.'

Boldly, she dared to meet his gleaming eyes, but it was his brother who continued the story.

'We were separated as infants, you see, when our uncle escaped from the North.' Dr Dong Sun leaned against the bed frame with the air of a man accustomed to attention. 'He walked across the frozen Yalu River, with me bundled underneath his coat. Our father had died, and our mother—'

'—who was very ill—' Che Tae Sun piped up.

His brother nodded briskly. '—begged him to take us both—'

'—but he couldn't carry two babies—'

'—as well as everything he needed to survive.'

'Uncle walked all the way to Seoul with Dong Sun and when he got there, he brought him up as if he were his own son.' Dr Tae Sun swept on. 'All his life my twin was determined to find me and now, by a miracle, we have been brought together again.'

'But . . . how—?' Mee Hee gaped at the doctors, so caught up in the story she almost forgot to cover her mouth with her hand. Of course she knew of countless people who yearned to be reunited with their families in the South, but she had never before heard of it really happening.

Dr Dong Sun brandished his clipboard in a gesture of triumph. 'Our mother recovered, and she lived long enough to see my brother became a doctor – and such a good doctor that one day he was permitted to attend a conference in China. Because of this, his photo was put up on a website, where Dr Kim, my employer, saw it. When she told me, I was so happy I thought my heart would burst, and Dr

NAOMI FOYLE

Kim was nearly as excited as I was. She has many friends in the medical world, and so she arranged for my brother to be invited to another conference, one that she could also attend.'

Website. Conference. Mee Hee scrabbled for a thread of meaning. 'Did you go too?' she asked Dr Dong Sun.

'Of course I wanted to. Desperately. But that would have alerted my brother's colleagues; they would think that he would surely want to leave them. So I had to be patient. But Dr Kim was on our side and I knew that if I waited, I would soon have my brother with me for ever.'

The doctors' faces were glowing, and for a moment Mee Hee was a little girl again, being told a story by her grandfather. But at the same time it was difficult to believe that anything – the room, the two identical doctors, the miracle of their reunion – was real. If she fell asleep and woke up again, she might be back in the box, or shivering in her hut in her village. She tugged the sheet up to her chest.

'Dr Kim is the woman who has brought us all together.' Dr Tae Sun leaned forward, his round face suddenly looking anxious. 'I mentioned the scientist to you in your village. Do you remember what I said? What I asked you to do for Dr Kim?'

Mee Hee nodded. 'Yes, I remember,' she whispered, and her heart trembled briefly, as it had in the rice paddy behind her hut when she was showing Dr Tae Sun the graves: the fresh mound covering her mother-in-law's shrunken body, and the turtle stone above the tiny sack that held her son. There, out of sight of the village, he had explained about the food-aid truck, and offered her the chance to come away, to help him and his employer, Dr Kim. She hadn't exactly understood what he'd wanted, or even really believed him, and yet her heart had stirred for the first time since her baby had died.

'I know why I am here,' she said in a louder voice.

34

'Good, good.' Dr Tae Sun patted her hand, and when she remained motionless, he awkwardly withdrew and fiddled with his watch.

'Dr Kim was very brave at the conference,' Dr Dong Sun continued vigorously.

Dr Tae Sun nodded in agreement. 'She passed me a note saying she worked with my brother, and she told me to be patient, that she would communicate with me somehow. Later, while we were standing in an elevator, she slipped her name-card and a satellite handi-phone into my pocket.'

'A what phone?' Mee Hee whispered.

'A handi-phone – the best in the world.' With a flourish, he drew a small silver object out of his coat pocket. He did something to it and it opened up, displaying buttons on one side and a colourful screen on the other. 'Made in Japan, powered by solar energy. With it you can call anyone you like, from anywhere in the world.'

'Ah.' She didn't dare touch it. He deftly snapped it shut again and replaced it in his pocket.

'My brother has also been extremely courageous,' Dr Dong Sun announced, standing up as straight as the Wise Young Leader awarding a medal. 'He smuggled the handi-phone back into North Korea and for the past two years, he has been calling Dr Kim and me from Pyongyang. Just owning the phone is illegal, so he took a great risk, and endangered his own life many times to bring you and all your sisters into China. We can never repay him.'

Dr Dong Sun regarded Mee Hee expectantly, as if waiting for her to break into applause, but she was barely listening any more. She closed her eyes as she leaned back against her pillow. Did she really know nothing at all? First, in the rice paddy, the doctor had told her that the *ramyon* he had brought to the village in the truck was not a gift from the Wise Young Leader but food-aid from the South and other Western nations. Now he had shown her what he said was a telephone, but looked like a metal clamshell, and he had happily told her it was made in the land of the kidnappers, the rapists of Korean women, the *colonisers*. A damp chill stole over her body. Who had put her in this nightdress? Why hadn't they given her a *yo* to sleep on instead of this dizzying metal bed? And how did she even know where she was?

Fearfully, she peeked up at the doctors, half-expecting them to be grinning with the sharpened teeth of the Japanese soldiers in her schoolbooks, but instead they were nervously exchanging glances, with identical – almost comical – expressions of dismay. She loosened her grip on the sheet.

'Am I in Beijing?' she whispered weakly.

Dr Dong Sun made another note on his chart. 'She's tired,' he said sternly to his brother. 'We mustn't strain her with our stories.'

'Yes, you are safe in Beijing,' Dr Tae Sun declared. 'You are in a small hotel, which we've rented entirely for you and your sisters and your caretakers. You are sharing the room with another woman from your province. You must sleep now, we'll return later.'

Exhausted, Mee Hee slid back beneath the sheets. She was asleep before the doctors had closed the door.

4 | The White Line

All Damien wanted was a stiff G&T, but Jake had warned him on no account was he to get pissed. He had to breathe deeply instead: *breathe deep*. That counsellor, years ago, had once said: *Jessica's still connected to you, she's part of you: like oxygen, like all the atoms that make up the universe.* He'd done visualisation exercises in their weekly sessions, which, amazingly, had eventually worked. He'd started to be able to nip his flashbacks in the bud, and one day he realised they just weren't tripping him up any more. Now, when he thought about his sister he imagined her just floating out there, like some black hole he'd one day get sucked into but didn't need to worry about now. He hadn't felt this burning, bottomless fear for a long time, not even when Dad died.

Gradually the lungfuls of stale cabin air diluted his panic and the memory emerged: hide'n'seek in the cemetery after church, Jessica in a blue dress, hiding behind a tombstone, laughing, just a bit of her blue dress visible. He hadn't remembered any of that before. No, that wasn't exactly true: he remembered the graveyard clearly, and he knew they used to play in it, but only because Dad had talked about it once. But he'd forgotten so much of what happened before Jessica disappeared.

Dad. Jessica. Was he thinking about them because of the argument he'd had with Mum before he left?

'You want me to pay your airfare to Korea?' she'd asked, incredulous. 'Damien, you're thirty-five years old and you've done nothing but drift around your entire life. When are you going to grow up?'

He'd held the MoPho away from his ear and tried to keep his cool. 'Mum, once I get there I'll be earning good money – I'll pay you back before Christmas. Plus, I won't be on housing benefit any more, so you'll have one less thing to complain about, okay?'

'That's what you said when Gordon and I paid for that sound engineering course. A year later you were on the dole again.'

He couldn't stop himself then. 'Christ, Mum, I graduated at the start of a fucking world-wide economic collapse – which, frankly, Gordon helped cause!'

'Oh, Damien.' Here it came again: the heavy sigh, the catch in the voice, the tears and then the simmering incrimination rising to a crescendo to finish him off: 'Why is it always like this? What happened to you? Where did my lovely, talented, bright little boy go? I can't just keep giving you money, Damien – I'm not helping you, really I'm not. You need to stand on your own two feet, make something of yourself, to honour Jessica if nothing else. What would she think of you now? Wasting all your precious gifts.'

She'd never gone that far before. 'Shut the fuck up about Jessica,' he'd demanded, and hung up without saying goodbye.

Damien opened his eyes. There was a reason he spoke to his mother twice a year and thought about his family as little as humanly possible. At least his temperature felt normal again now, and his stomach was back down at Quease Level 3. But Christ, no *Tomb Raider*, no *Spore*, no spirits, no lager; plus his dead sister haunting him, six double-bagged condoms of hash in his guts and a cement-filled case of self-inflicted constipation. This was going to be a fuck of a long flight.

'You like water?'

The stewardess had reappeared with a bottle of IceCap and a

corn-plastic cup. He didn't like the fact he was drawing attention to himself, but water was a good idea. He nodded thanks and took the cup – desalinated Atlantic, not his favourite H_2O, but they all had to do their bit to lower sea levels.

The stewardess poured the water. 'Thanks,' he mumbled as she twisted the cap back on the bottle.

'Why you come Korea?' she asked.

Afraid he would blush again, he avoided meeting her gaze – but hey, maybe a little special attention from the female of the species was just what Dr Jake would have ordered.

'I'm visiting a friend,' he told her. Good rehearsal for the passport officer.

'Friendship flower of life,' she informed him, gravely. 'Is Korean saying.'

He risked a smile up at her. 'I'll remember that.'

Her hand flew to her mouth. 'Uh!' she gasped, 'you look like *Hu-gee Grant*!'

Hu-gee Grant? Who the f—? Oh, right: *Hu-gee* thanks. So all his organic eco-nonsense metrosexual skincare routines had done nothing then. From beneath his floppy fringe, Damien beseeched her, 'You do mean his son, don't you?'

She giggled, just a normal laugh, nothing to freak out about. 'Oh yes, you very young look.'

'Thank you.' Emboldened, he ventured, 'So do you.'

'Oh no, I very old,' she said, a look of distress sweeping over her face.

He'd managed to upset her with a compliment? Christ, what was he supposed to say now?

To his relief, she recovered her composure. 'You need anything, press button,' she told him.

Actually, there *was* something he wanted – something that would answer a few questions and take his mind off his fucked-up family. 'Do you have a Korean newspaper? In English, I mean?'

She gasped again. 'You want read Korean news?' So he'd made up for his disastrous attempt at flirtation, then. 'I bring, right away.'

He watched her lovely bottom sway back down the aisle. She tripped back moments later with a copy of *The Korean Herald*. He unfolded it with pleasure – fuck iPads; reading foreign papers always made him feel like a le Carré spy, an 'old hand'. And today he even had a proper covert agenda.

At Heathrow, the UK papers had all devoted their front pages to the news that the global rise on pre-industrial average temperatures had now reached one point two degrees Celsius. *The Times* had predicted that the World Cup would be swamped by a British monsoon; the *Independent* had warned of a world dominated by hurricanes, disease, crop failure and mass extinctions; the *Guardian*, to celebrate Summer Solstice, had sent a lifestyle journalist to interview a Druid. Damien had avidly scanned this article and bingo, there it was: 'What about Lucifer's Hammer?' the journo had enquired. 'Is a two-mile-wide meteor really hurtling towards Earth as we speak? And if so, will it land at Stonehenge?'

To give the beardo his due, the Druid hadn't risen to the bait. 'Let us hope not,' he'd replied. 'Our ancestors built Stonehenge after the period of global darkness that followed the Australian Ocean meteors of six thousand years ago. They needed to know that if such a catastrophe were ever to re-occur, they would be able to gauge from the stars the right time to plant their spring seeds. If for whatever reason – meteors, mega-volcanoes, nuclear catastrophe – human civilisation has to start again from scratch, we're going to need those stones.'

This bloke obviously had his solar-panelled yurt all kitted out in Wales. Damien had put the paper back in the stand, wishing the Druid luck when half the population of Liverpool and Greater

Manchester arrived, ripping up the crops with their stilettos and crashing their Chelsea tractors into the wind turbines. Or whatever they called Chelsea tractors in the North – Chester tractors, probably. Though they'd be more like armoured tanks when survivalist Britain's long-simmering tribal warfare finally kicked off. Which, even if the Hammer hit the Moon instead of Earth, was going to be soon. Globally, a new drought, flood or economic crisis was reported practically every week.

What freaked Damien out though, was that hardly anyone in the UK seemed to be taking the situation seriously. The broadsheets loved an alarmist headline, but after reading the average Sunday paper one would be forgiven for thinking global warming was a cunning plot to force people to buy Fair Trade chocolate. Even the *Indy* believed that at worst the great British public might have to accept fewer baths and obligatory candlelit dinners. And all of them scoffed at the Hammer theorists. *Is this complacency confined to Europe?* he'd wondered as he'd waited to board the plane; how was South Korea preparing for the coming eco-apocalypse?

In a leisurely manner, it appeared. The front page of *The Korean Herald* boasted a photo of Seoul office workers sunning themselves during their lunch-break, secure in the knowledge that their country was building eight new nuclear reactors, despite national riots against them. Snorting to himself, Damien scanned the article: a government minister deplored Korea's alarming expenditure on carbon credits from Sierra Leone; an environmental campaigner warned of torrential rains, coastal flooding, another Fukushima, vats of radioactive waste already sitting for years above ground because no one wanted them buried in their own backyard. In other words, Korea was a complete policy mess, just like everywhere else.

Damien stretched his legs beneath the seat in front of him. Plan Can was definitely the only game in town. When the Hammer hit and seven billion people all stampeded for safety at once, the chance of finding somewhere reasonably stable to live would be zero; cool dudes needed to take action well in advance. He still had to convince Jake to help him, but the fact that Korea, climate change-wise, was a big fat sweating duck would only make his case more persuasive.

Do they eat duck in Korea, he wondered? And what else did Koreans worry about apart from the cost of banging up thousands of environmental protestors? He flipped through the rest of the paper. In contrast to the UK news, there was very little coverage of the NATO bombardment of Pakistan; instead there were long articles on the new famine in North Korea, the Russian invasion of Estonia and the Chinese take-over of Taiwan. The famine, the worst since the nineties, had been intensified by the new leader's rejection of international relief, while the Americans were using the two putsches as excuses to build new military bases in Poland and Pusan, on the south coast of the Korean peninsula – Pusan? That rang a bell. Didn't Jake go there once for a film festival and end up sleeping with a Russian hooker by mistake?

Damien stuffed the paper into the seat pocket. The smell of microwaved tomatoes was invading the plane. The last thing he wanted to do was eat, but Jake had said it would be suspicious not to. He'd better get rid of the pill packet now, before he forgot.

He managed to get to the loo without fainting this time. On his way back to his seat another pretty stewardess batted her eyelashes at him. Was she also confusing him with a washed-up film star? To take his mind off this deeply worrying possibility he tracked through the music channels – rubbish as usual – then waited for his dinner, rice with hake in tomato stew. After the meal, he wrapped himself in his blanket and began to compose a soundtrack in his head: a peaceful skull-space of ambient industrial disintegration, a clicking abacus and the chiming of grandfather clocks. Throw in some

Meshmass and the latest Noise Merchant mix and it was almost a lullaby . . . apart from the anvil and Hammer . . .

Light was pouring into the cabin. People were stirring, chatting in their long, drawn-out, sawing language. Damien groaned. His mouth was as dry as a stale Hobnob and his stomach felt like he'd swallowed a bag of cricket balls. Where was that bottle of water?

At least no one was looking at him any more. Like happy robots, everyone was going through the routine of preparing to land: filling out boarding cards, queuing for the loo, lowering their seat-back trays, eating cardboard bread rolls and yoghurt.

Landing – oh fuck, here it came: *sheer terror.*

He shut his eyes and returned to counting his breaths, which had no effect on his thumping pulse, but at least stopped him from attacking the emergency exit and throwing himself out of the plane. Though he willed the pilot to circle the airport for ever, landing was accomplished with the usual wobbly roar. Blood slithering around like mercury in his veins, he lingered as the other passengers jostled for space in the aisle. Thinking it wouldn't be smart to be last – and aware of Laptop Guy waiting behind him – he finally managed to push into the wake of a Korean woman dressed in long grey linen robes. This was it, possibly his last walk as a free man. And it was a knock-kneed shuffle, hemmed in by a Buddhist nun and a *Starboarder* zombie.

The stewardess greeted him at the doorway. 'Goodbye! Thank you!' she said brightly. Then she tugged at her colleague's sleeve, and suddenly two beautiful women were covering their mouths with their hands and tittering at him. 'You be very famous in Korea, we think,' his new friend finally plucked up her courage to declare.

He gave the women a sick rictus grin. Yup, the mugshots would be in the paper tomorrow. As he disembarked into the landing tunnel, a combination of the heat and pure panic set off every last sweat gland. Christ, his face was sopping wet. Didn't he have a Kleenex? He stuck his hand in his jacket pocket and pulled out a hanky.

A hanky? Oh, right, from Mum's wedding – is that how long it had been since he wore this suit? She had beetled over with it at the reception, he remembered, freaking out in case he blew his nose on a grotty tissue in front of Gordon's *Tatler*-editor sister. He shoved the cloth back in his pocket and wiped his face with his hand. If Mum had lent him that money instead of having a go at him about Jessica he wouldn't now be teetering on the verge of this deep shit-filled abyss.

Stomach in spasms, legs on autopilot, he let the herd nudge him into the passport control hall. The queue of foreigners was short. Whatever happened, it would be over very soon.

Buddhist Lady was ahead of him, an American passport in her hand. His heart hurling itself at his chest now, he inched forward, compulsively flicking the edge of his landing card with his thumbnail. For Occupation, he'd wanted to put Deconstruction Worker, but had settled on IT Consultant. An IT Consultant with no laptop: what the fuck had he been thinking? Well, it was too late now. Anyway, the big test was going to be his passport. It expired in exactly six months, the precise length of the visa, not to mention the day all the most reliable websites were predicting Lucifer's Hammer would hit.

In making his decision to leave Britain, Damien had contemplated his own petty problems in the context of the vast spiral of time. In the process he had come up with two solutions to the dilemma of his passport: a bureaucratic quick-fix, which he had found on the internet and printed off and stuck in his jacket pocket, and a long-range, eco-sustainable and cosmically attuned plan he needed to discuss with Jake. Now, though, with his damp hand clutching his battered old passport with its stamps from India, Thailand and Morocco and his hash-packed colon just a laxative away from discovery, he wasn't sure he was ever going to see Jake again.

Buddhist Lady put her passport back in her saffron bag and an officer with a face like an Easter Island statue waved him forward. His armpits were as wet as a rainforest. His feet were dead weights, cinderblocks. His mind was back in Brighton, tearing up that letter from Jake. But as in a Francis Bacon sweatbox of a dream, the scuffed toes of his green high-top Converses were stepping over the dirty white line of tape at the head of the queue.

5 | Shiteawon

The evening sun was bulging in the sky like an egg yolk in a rock glass of Jack. Johnny pulled the Cadillac onto the greasy strip winding round the foot of Namsan. After the gasoline fumes in the tunnel, Itaewon's brew of stale GI sweat, cheap perfume and fast food smelled like victory, all the sharper for his triumph over Kim. He took a deep whiff, as he always did when he re-entered the 'hood: Itaewon was a little chunk of America in an overcrowded land of dog-eaters and rice-lovers. The army base was right round the corner from Burger King, and up there on the mountain's flank, just below the Hyatt Hotel and the New York Deli, the trashiest trailer-park blonde in Seoul shook her tail-feathers just for him, on the biggest, baddest bed in town.

Last night's dip in performance had just been a blip. Could happen to any guy. Pleasantly horny now and still glowing from the OxyPops, Johnny trawled slowly through Iteawon like he was in a John Woo movie: past stores overflowing with cheap shoes, suitcases, bed-linens; street stalls dripping with leather belts and wallets, knock-off watches, MoPhos, fake Chanel, and anything from mugs to teddy bears that it was possible to emblazon with the Korean national flag. There were Korean restaurants everywhere, of course, oodles of them, and black market alleyways crawling 24/7 with *ajummas* in stained aprons ready to exchange huge wads of cash, no questions asked. At the foot of the road to Johnny's apartment a clutch of antiques dealers lent a veneer of class to the street, selling brightly polished brass deer and turtles, and *memento mori* from medals to bomb casings. Not that the war was over, mind. In this churning sea of Asian tat and guile, it was good to know that Itaewon was full of US soldiers, all keeping up their strength on burgers and fries.

He parked on the main drag outside the Hamilton Hotel, a hunk of concrete clad in orange fake brick. A fat bitch at a tanning salon, Johnny always joked about the place. Sydney didn't think it was funny, but it still made him chuckle. He slammed the car door shut, feeling good, and pushing through beer-bellied tourists, hippy English teachers and flat-topped GIs, he headed to Hollywood's, Itaewon's premiere 'leisure lady' night spot.

Rattail was a civil servant, with access to all sorts of secret files. He had said he would be on the third barstool from the left. *Could you possibly get more anal*, Johnny thought as he thrust open Hollywood's padded red door. A Korean man blowing smoke rings at the bar turned and nodded. *Yup, third barstool. Sigh.*

Otherwise the place was virtually empty. Ignoring the auto-smiles of bored hostesses, Johnny crossed the worn crimson carpet, negotiating the cheap Formica tables arranged haphazardly around the room. Without the late-night crowd of smokers, a sickly-sweet stink permeated the club. What did they pump the place full of, female underarm deodorant?

Johnny had pictured Rattail as a regular, squat Korean schmoe, but in fact he was tall and thin and fragile-looking, in his late thirties, with a bony jaw and bad skin. Despite the warmth he was dressed in a beige Aquascutum trenchcoat. At least he smelled of tobacco.

Johnny pulled up a stool.

'Please to meet you, Mis-tuh Joh-nee.' Rattail's handshake was dry, almost scaly, and there was an affected, melancholy air about him that set Johnny's teeth on edge. He ordered a rye and coke, sticking to a single. Hey, the Sandman had willpower.

'Let's get to the point,' he growled in Korean. After ten years he knew enough of the language to haggle with any Seoul shyster – though of course sometimes he pretended not to speak the lingo; contacts could give away vital information thinking he didn't understand.

Rattail's glasses were too big for his nose and he kept pushing them back up to the bridge when he talked – or nodded, mostly. He showed no surprise or distaste when Johnny outlined what he wanted, just took another drag on his cigarette.

'Sure. Two place I can get you that,' he said in English. Koreans always liked to practise. 'Accident ward, sure, sure – but has to be body no one claim. No family. No friend. Don't come in every day.'

'When, then?'

'One week, one month. *Molayo*.'

Molayo, molayo. Who knows? The all-purpose Korean evasion phrase. Rattail tapped open a new packet of Marlboro Golds, and offered him one. Johnny shook his head. The longer it took to get the body, the better. All the more reason to keep stalling the Doc. And ConGlam. Pleased with the results of the meeting, he laid a fat white envelope on the bar. 'I'm waiting for your call, Rattail,' he said in Korean. 'Have a good night.'

'*Ye, ye.*' Rattail waved him on absently, pocketing the envelope as a hostess in a white satin blouse moved over to take Johnny's stool.

The taxi pulled up in front of the *kalbi* place. Sydney checked her Gotcha. Forty-five minutes late – well, so what? The cabby handed her his Pay-dock. Nearly *sa man won* – fuck. She didn't have enough cash on her, and her bank account was getting dangerously low. The lipstick company paid its pittance once a month, and OhmEgo wouldn't make its deposit for another six weeks. In the meantime, she was stuck with Johnny and his greeby part-time work. She inserted her MoPho in the Pay-dock and entered her PIN.

Fare paid, she climbed out of the cab and eyeballed the restaurant window. The place was full of Koreans sitting cross-legged around low tables. Johnny, of course, would be in the back, at a table with chairs.

'Way-tuh!' The driver was waving a white-gloved hand.

'*Sa man won* – that was the fare!' she protested, but he opened his door and walked smartly round to the back of the taxi. She stood there, jostled by shoppers and soldiers, and prepared for an argument. These Korean cabbies in their blue uniforms, you'd think they were cops sometimes, the attitude they gave you.

'*Anneyo, anneyo.*'

No? No? What was he on about? Shaking his head the cabbie opened the trunk and took out a small Grace Department Store bag, primrose yellow with silk handles. Bowing, he presented it to her.

'You very beautiful!' he announced. Plucking at his own buzzcut black hair, he nodded proudly. 'Sun-shi-nuh. Very pre-tty.'

She peeked into the bag. *Omigod* – nestled inside, amongst some dainty packages, enclosed in a peach and sky-blue box of its own, was a bottle of 'Summer Passion'. '*Kamsahamnida, ajashi!*' she gasped.

'Los-tuh an-duh foun-duh!' His weathered face radiating self-congratulation, the *ajashi* marched back to his taxi and drove off. Jauntily swinging the bag, she pranced into the restaurant. Yup, there he was, the only guy in the place sitting on a chair. At least he'd ordered already: a yummy *kalbi* meal was sizzling on the hotplate in the centre of the table.

'You call this six o'clock?' Johnny demanded as she sat down. 'You couldn't even text?'

'Don't be such a girl, Johnny,' she retorted. 'Last time we went out for dinner you spent half the time on your MoPho.'

'Yeah, and last time I was late for a date *you* threw a shit-fit,' he snapped.

Sydney glared at him across the table and his small, pale blue eyes narrowed into mean little slits, like his mouth. How could she ever have enjoyed kissing a guy with no lips? 'So we're even, okay?' she replied, brightly.

Johnny took a deep breath and slowly exhaled. She knew what he was doing: counting to ten. She'd timed him.

'Fine. We're even,' he agreed, tightly. 'I just wanted us to have a nice meal, that's all. The clients are waiting. And now we'll have to go home first so you can take that shrapnel out of your hair.'

How come he always knew what to say to cut her down? 'Jeez, Johnny.' She heard her voice slide up the register again. 'I just had my hair done by a top stylist. Can't you even say it looks cool?'

Johnny rolled his eyes. But his voice softened. 'Hey, babe, c'mon – you look great, okay? Your hair's just too punky for the clients, you know that. Relax, eat something. Look – I ordered your favourite *banchan*.'

He pushed the dish of spicy little fishes across the table and poured her some mineral water. Okay, he was trying, at least.

'Sorry I didn't text,' she muttered as she filled her plate from all the small *banchan* dishes. 'I had to take my Gotcha off for the shoot and I lost track of the time.'

'Hey, whatever – I missed you, that's all. It's not often I spend all day without my sexy baby.'

Yeah right. He didn't want her to have her own life, more like it. 'I was just working.' She tossed her head. 'Everyone's got to work.'

'Sure, but you don't want to overdo it. You've got plenty going on with the lipstick contract and the night job – plus I might have a big money number for you in a month or two. I'm driving a hard bargain with the client right now.'

'Big money?' That sounded interesting. 'How big?'

He leaned over the table. 'As big as that hard-on I sent you today,' he whispered. 'Did you like that, huh?'

Now was her chance.

'No, it was *gross!*' But he was twinkling and winking at her, wagging his eyebrows, and she knew he wasn't listening. 'I'm not a porno star, Johnny,' she persisted. 'I'm a fashion model – a soon-to-be top fashion model, Jin Sok said so.'

A shadow passed over his expression. 'Is that right? But you're *my* private turn-on, aren't you? My little porcelain doll-face?'

'Don't keep calling me that!' she blurted out. 'I've told you, it bugs me!'

'No need to snap,' he said, coolly.

Neither of them spoke for a little while. Sydney picked up her chopsticks and turned over a piece of beef sizzling on the circular grill. Nearly done. Glancing enviously at Johnny's lager, she took a sip of her water. Across the aisle, a lone goldfish was swimming aimlessly in a huge aquarium. Otherwise, the restaurant was buzzing with Koreans: big groups of office workers flashing metal chopsticks and slapping their knees; families squabbling; little kids roaming unchecked between the tables, playing 'stick 'em up' and Grand Prix racing, making the Korean versions of 'pow pow' and 'vroom vroom' noises.

'It's not suits tonight; it's soldiers,' she said finally, 'so what's the rush? They always stay out 'til dawn on their nights off.'

'In fact, it's soldiers in suits you'll be dealing with: top brass. And they will want to get their beauty sleep.'

'Great. Leaving me fighting off the farm boys. Johnny, I am getting so tired of ass-wipes slobbering all over me at two a.m., telling me about their dead mothers and their dope-addict dads and how the army gives them self-discipline – I mean, talk about a bunch of losers. No wonder America isn't running the world any more.'

Johnny slammed his fork down on the table. It skittered across the laminate surface and clattered to the floor. 'What the fuck has got into you tonight?' he demanded, his cheeks scarlet. 'Do you want to pick the mother of all fights, or what? I'm telling you, Sydney, you don't want to make Johnny Sandman angry!'

Her own cheeks blazed, her stomach dropped away and suddenly, scarily, she thought she might piss herself. Fuck, what was happening to her? She clenched her pelvic floor muscles and stared at Johnny over the grill. There was no way she was going to let some guy who talked about himself in the third person freak her out. Deliberately, she turned her attention to the table, picking up a piece of lettuce with her fingers and squishing a spoonful of rice into the leaf. Then, with chopsticks, she plucked a nicely curling strip of beef from the grill and thrust it into the rice. This she followed with a grilled garlic clove and a big slab of *kim chi*: a gorgeous hunk of pickled cabbage dripping with raw garlic, ginger and red pepper sauce. Finally she wrapped the furly lettuce leaf around the tasty bundle and popped the whole thing into her mouth. She met Johnny's gaze again.

Now he looked a little hungry himself – and not for *kalbi*, either. 'Look, babe,' he said in a low voice, 'I don't like getting mad at you, but believe you me, when an army of gooks from Pyongyang comes pouring over the border to shoot and rape their way across the forty miles to Seoul, you're gonna be glad of a few good old boys and dumb-luck niggers to stand between the yellow peril and your diamanté panties.'

Chewing methodically, she gave him a withering look. There was no point telling Johnny to shut his racist trap. He'd only come out with something worse next time – and if he mouthed off like that around Jin Sok or one of the designers she would just *die*. She had to ditch this guy, and quick.

Johnny took his bottle of OxyPops out of his pocket.

That was a relief. He was always calmer after he'd chugged a couple of those. She maintained her aloof silence as he downed his dose and the oxygen kicked in.

'Sydney, I'm sorry you're upset with me,' he said at last. 'I'm sorry I raised my voice. I just wanted us to have a nice meal, and then a fun night in the club. It's not hard, the work, is it? And it pays good. The soldiers – they're just kids. You deal with 'em great.'

Johnny's apologies were as wooden as bannisters. He just used them to get down into her pants. But oh – why fight? She just had to be patient until she could get more work of her own. 'Forget it, Johnny. I'm tired, that's all.'

The waiter brought another fork over and Johnny started to make himself a *kalbi* morsel, skipping the *kim chi*, the wimp. 'I know, babe, but it won't take long, I promise. The head honcho tonight, I want to know where he's flying to next: Japan or Shanghai. Get him talking about the places you want to visit in Asia, all the knick-knacks you want brought back. Might only take half an hour. And if you squeeze it out of him, I'll buy you a brand-new MoPho, one with 3D TV and SatNav, so you won't ever get lost again.'

Sydney rolled her eyes. Just because she had once called his Gotcha in tears from the most confusing train station ever built. Soon enough she was really going to get lost, disappear into Hongdae, maybe, like Jin Sok had suggested: get a secret launch pad of her own. But it would be nice to watch 3D-TV during the long taxi-rides to her shoots. And it didn't sound like tonight was going to be tough – maybe it would all go down in Hollywood's, with its cheesy Barry White sound-track and giggling hostesses, and she wouldn't have to wind up in King Club, with that deafening monster rap and those scary Russian hookers baring their rotting teeth at her whenever she went to the toilet.

She treated Johnny to her most winsome smile. 'Plus my regular pay, right?'

'Hey now, I wouldn't let my little girl run out of pocket money, would I? Here, open up: longest day of the year and you're working double time – you got to eat.'

His snake lips parting in his version of a grin, Johnny lifted his chopsticks to Sydney's mouth. She bit the piece of crispy beef and pulled it slowly into her mouth, letting a trickle of grease slide down her chin. Beneath the table, Johnny grabbed her calf and pressed her bare foot against his groin. His cock was rock-hard. She glanced around the restaurant, squeezed once with her toes, then wrested her leg away.

He laughed, and took another swig of his beer. 'Hey—' he lowered his voice, 'let's finish up here and I'll take you home and lick you out, how's that? I've been thinking about the taste of that sweet blonde pussy all day.'

He didn't get it, and he never would. She was a top model now. He couldn't talk to her like that in public. But he held her gaze, breaking it only to rake her chest with his eyes, and despite herself, she felt her panties dampen.

It had been such a wild day. It might be good to lie down and get some of the excitement out of her system. Not to mention keep Johnny sweet until she figured out her next move.

'Yeah,' she replied in her best kitteny voice, 'let's go home for dessert.'

6 | *Hoba* Soup

It was dark outside when Mee Hee woke. A thin young woman was sitting on the opposite bed, sewing by the light of her table lamp. As Mee Hee sat up, she put aside her needle and thread.

'Are you thirsty?' Her room-mate leaned across with a glass of water from her bedside table.

Careful not to stretch her feeding tube, Mee Hee reached over and took it gratefully. The water was so fresh and cool. 'Thank you,' she whispered.

The other woman had a sharp, glinting sort of face. She was wearing pink lipstick and a flowered blouse and her hair was pinned back with a sparkling brooch. She regarded Mee Hee intently, appraising her face and her figure.

'You'll get plump again.' She smiled, and her pointy face became pretty for a moment. 'Look at me!' She pulled back her sleeve and pinched a tiny roll of flesh on her upper arm. Mee Hee's eyes widened. She flushed and looked down at her water. It was rude to stare.

'Ack!' The young woman clucked her tongue, sounding very annoyed. Mee Hee glanced timidly at her again, ready to apologise profusely for upsetting her, but the woman placed her hand on her heart and inclined her head towards Mee Hee. 'Excuse me, please,' she said. 'I have been very impolite. My name is Moon Su Jin. I am a pig farmer's daughter from North Pyongan-do. It was my birthday last week and now I'm twenty-two.'

Flustered, but relieved, Mee Hee bowed in return. 'My name is Lee Mee Hee. My father was a rice farmer in South Pyongan-do. I'm twenty-two too.'

'Same same!' Su Jin clapped her hands. 'We're the second-youngest here.'

Here. This small, plain room. 'I've never been in a hotel before,' Mee Hee said wonderingly. 'It's very cool, isn't it?'

'Air-con.' Su Jin pointed at a vent in the ceiling. 'It's a cheap hotel, but it's nice enough. I've been here nearly four months. You were the last to arrive. I helped the nurses change your clothes. And I put ointment on your bruises.'

'Thank you.' Mee Hee fingered the lace trim around the bodice of the nightie. The garment was buttoned up to the top. Beneath it her bruises were humming.

'You'll like Younger Sister. The Older Sisters, well, *most* of them are all right.' Su Jin raised her eyes to heaven and made a face. Mee Hee wanted to giggle, but it would be terrible to make fun of women she didn't know, so she didn't let the bubble of sound escape. 'They'll come and meet you soon,' Su Jin continued, 'and when you're better we can all go to South Korea. Like Dr Che promised.'

Mee Hee shook her head. 'I'm so tired. I'll hold you all up.'

'Don't worry. We were all exhausted when we arrived. In a week or two you'll be much better. They feed us very well.'

Mee Hee paused. 'With *hoba* soup, every day?' she asked, her voice quavering. Tears welled up in her eyes.

'The iron in *hoba* is good for the blood,' Su Jin said softly. 'That's why women must eat it for one hundred days after giving birth. Our grandmothers always knew what the doctors tell us today.'

Mee Hee nodded helplessly as the tears streamed down her face. Su Jin slipped down from her bed, climbed up next to her and began to stroke her hair. 'Tell me, Mee Hee,' she urged. 'Tell me what's wrong.'

Though she knew Su Jin's arms were around her, she couldn't feel their warmth. The sobs echoing around her came from somewhere else, not from her own throat or her drooling mouth. Like fists pummelling her from inside, the words rose up, the words she had been trying to bury in her heart.

'I only had it for *two days*,' she cried out, clasping her knees to her chest and rocking herself back and forth. 'Only two days – there wasn't enough *hoba* in the village. *There wasn't enough!*'

'I know, I know. It was the same for all of us,' Su Jin murmured.

But no, it wasn't, it wasn't the same. 'I couldn't get strong again – I couldn't *feed* him. My breasts were dry, no milk, no milk inside me, and he *died*. Song Ju died! I had no milk – I couldn't feed him – and he *died!*' At last she howled, howled like the wind in the fruit-less *gom* trees behind the hut she would never see again.

'Shhh, shhh.' Su Jin held her close. 'Shhh.'

But Mee Hee only cried harder, tears soaking her face and Su Jin's thin shoulder. Su Jin's hands were pressing into her bruises, pain was flaring across her ribs and her heart ached as if it would any moment crack like a branch in the night. This was the punishment she deserved, the pain she should feel forever, like hunger and shame, not the sad comfort of this bedroom and the terrible kindness of the doctors and the nurse and this stranger, Moon Su Jin. How could she tell them all that she should have stayed behind, that they should take her back, let her die and be buried next to her son? The son she couldn't feed, the son her breasts had failed.

Furiously, Mee Hee began to bang her fists against her thighs. Her husband had been right to hit her, right to beat her with a stick, right to tear her hair out of her head. She had deserved every single blow he had rained down upon her as she crouched, screaming, in the corner of the hut.

'No!' Su Jin gripped her wrists, pinning her fists to her sides, stopping her. 'I'm so sorry, so sorry, Mee Hee. Everyone was so hungry, so many people died.'

Like a black cloud swallowing up a mountain peak, an enormous heaviness drifted across Mee Hee and she slumped back against the sheets. Su Jin lay beside her as she shuddered quietly, her breathing torn, her bruises burning. She could hear the traffic outside, and the gentle ticking of Su Jin's watch.

'It was worse than when the Great Leader died,' she said quietly. There: now she could be really punished. Now the doctors could come and take her away to be shot, to be put out of her misery at last. 'At least we knew that the Wise Young Leader was there to protect us. But when my baby died, I had nothing left.'

Su Jin snorted softly. She sat up, dangling her legs off the bed. 'And did the Wise Young Leader protect any of us? Not in my village. Or in yours.'

A cold wave sluiced through Mee Hee's veins. She sat up hurriedly and fixed her clothes. 'May the Wise Young Leader and the spirit of the Great Leader please forgive my feeble woman's words,' she said in as loud a voice as she could muster. 'Moon Su Jin, may you also please forgive me.'

'Me forgive you? What for?' Su Jin sounded almost amused.

'For being so selfish – for crying over my sacrifice to the nation when others made far greater. Did you lose your baby too?'

Su Jin shook her head and examined her painted fingernails. All of them except one, the little one on her left hand, were chewed down to stumps. 'No, I was never married. I was only sixteen when the hunger came, and there were no more weddings in our village after that. But I helped my sister give birth and I fed her *hoba* soup for three days, until it ran out. Then I helped her bury her daughter, two months later. And now my sister is dead too, and my parents, or I would never have left my village.'

Su Jin put her fingers to her mouth. But Mee Hee reached for her hand and clasped it tightly. It was a small, bony hand, but very strong. They were silent for a moment.

'It happened,' Su Jin said crisply. 'Now I'm here. And so are you.'

7 | Soft Landing

'Ugh. What's cooking?' Damien uncurled from his foetal position on the bed-mat. The studio room was suffused with a ghostly light and the stealthy scent of cinnamon. He squinted at his watch: two in the afternoon. Christ, he'd slept for twelve hours.

Jake was lying on the sofa with his electric bass, quietly running through a riff. 'The cake!' he cried, flinging the guitar down on a cushion and bounding out into the galley kitchen. Jake was chunky, but he moved with fluid speed.

'I thought you didn't have an oven.' Damien raised his voice above the rattle of the fan blowing over his chest. It was, as promised, bloody hot in Seoul in June.

'Ancient Korean-Canadian secret,' Jake hollered back. 'I made it in the rice cooker. No fuss, no muss, no microwaves! Aha: perfection!'

'Great, I'm starving.'

Jake chuckled. 'You don't wanna explode, buddy, you better get your mitts on that hash first.'

Damien groaned. The great bowel evacuation was still ahead of him. Jake had taken him for a barbecue last night to get things moving, but while the *kim chi*, a fiery garlic pickle, had stripped the roof of his mouth, the 35-proof *soju* had just sent him to sleep as soon as they'd got back to the flat. It had been good to chat with Jake, though, reminisce about India, catch up on the last couple of years. After Mumbai, Jake had gone back to Toronto to run a market

60

stall, do a few dope deals, and save enough money to come out to Korea and connect with his roots. He liked it so much here he was going to invest his own share of the dope dosh in a bar in Shinch'on, with his Korean cousin Sam. Sam was in Canada at the moment, doing a course towards his MBA, but when he got back the cousins were going to move into a penthouse flat further up the hill. Jake was lugging his stuff up there in a couple of days.

Damien – well, Damien had left one or two things out of his account of Brighton life. It hadn't been the right time or place to ask about the passport either. First things first.

'Better make me a coffee,' he called out. Hopefully the four Imodium tablets had loosened their grip on his intestines by now, or else he'd be taking some senna pills too.

'Coming right up, buddy. Coming right up.' An espresso-maker hissed in the kitchen, then Jake appeared with two cups of java. 'Whay-hey. That's my Dames. Looking alive again, dude. You were whiter than my iBook when you came through that gate yesterday.'

'Ta, mate.' Grinning weakly, Damien sat up and reached for the coffee. The airport had been excruciating. The visa officer had pored over his passport for an age, practically the whole Anthropocene.

'December twenty-one. You need new document soon.' The man had sounded troubled, as if this were a situation he couldn't quite remember how to deal with.

Clearing his throat, Damien had taken the printout from the British Embassy website out of his pocket. 'Yes, I know. I was told I can renew it here.'

The officer had stared at the sheet, the rusty cogs of his mind had ground into place; his chipped face had reset itself in stone. Then he'd told Damien to look into the camera, stamped his passport for six months and waved him on.

One ordeal down, one to go. The baggage carousel had taken for ever to get moving, but finally his grubby backpack had thumped onto the conveyor belt. It contained mostly summer clothes and CDs; as far as luggage went it was light and entirely blameless. He'd hoisted it onto his shoulder then, with knees wobbling like blanc-manges, joined the customs queue. Even if the officers took a routine peek, there was nothing to worry about. Nothing at all.

The officers hadn't even glanced up from their white-gloved perusal of Laptop Guy's bags. With sweat streaming down his back, Damien had floated into arrivals, straight into Jake's combo bear-hug and clap on the back. To the lo-fi trundle of suitcase wheels and the random space-talk of the Tannoy, his friend had whisked him out of a revolving door, then through the glare of sunshine and hot stink of petrol fumes into a taxi outside.

Now only Jake knew where he was: safe in a ropey little rooftop flat above a labyrinthine Seoul neighbourhood – a flat that would soon be all his.

After just one more not-exactly-salubrious experience.

The caffeine got to work with a sharp twist in his gut and Damien groaned. 'Here she comes, special delivery, down the night tunnel.' He put his cup down and rolled to his feet.

Jake was at his desk, shuffling through papers. 'What doesn't kill you makes you stranger, Meadows.'

The bathroom was a tiled cell containing a toilet, sink and shower, not even a curtain. Jake had left a pair of rubber gloves, some deter-gent; a plate and a plastic basin on the floor. Damien pulled down his boxers, crouched over the basin and farted. It was a wet, wheezy fart, but produced not a dollop of solids. They were coming, though, in their own time: three meals and six latex hash bombs painfully inching their way down his rectum. Christ, it felt like he'd swal-lowed his laptop instead of auctioning it on eBay; like an SAS squadron was elbowing through his colon. He gritted his teeth and pushed.

A pellet of shit hit the basin, its propulsive exit tearing the rim of his arse. Fuck. He felt his anus, gingerly. A swollen nodule wibbled under his finger. Great, a haemorrhoid. *Remind me never to give birth.*

The next push hurt more, but – voilà! – produced a hash packet. Then, with a big ploppy rush, three came at once. Number five emerged slowly but relatively smoothly, but six was a fucking bugger. At last, though, with the help of some judicious prodding, probing and cursing, the job was done.

Damien washed his hands and wiped his arse. The tissue was scarlet with blood and his anus was stinging, no doubt shredded inside and out. He grimaced. If there was permanent damage, he'd demand Jake pay him extra. But first, part two of this particular unpleasantness.

He pulled up his boxers, and examined the basin. For some reason, as he'd discovered on that hike in Nepal, your own shit didn't actually look or smell so bad. There, he'd buried it, digging shallow holes in the earth with twigs. Here he put on the rubber gloves, fished out the hash baggies from their excremental stew and rinsed them off in the sink. Give or take the odd fleck of faecal matter in the folds of the latex, you'd never know where they'd just been. He arranged the parcels neatly on the plate, then he flushed the contents of the basin down the loo and filled it and the sink with detergent, leaving the gloves to soak too. As he picked up the plate of hash lumps he felt a quirk of pride. Howard Marks he wasn't, but he wasn't 'son of Hugh Grant' either.

'Yo, bro!' Jake had arranged a knife, a roll of Clingfilm and a set of electronic scales on his desk. He saluted as Damien re-entered the room, plate aloft.

'For the pleasure of Korean youth, and the profit of us both.' Damien set the plate of hash on the desk and pulled up a chair.

Jake handed him a pair of scissors. 'I'm not touching that latex, buddy.'

'A drug mule's job is never done,' Damien tutted. He snipped open the parcels, and their rich, peaty aroma was a reward unto itself. Jake crumbled off a pinch of the hash and rolled it under his nose.

'Umm *ummm*. The buyers are gagging for it. Now what do you say to a little quality control?' Jake took a packet of Rizlas from his pocket and rolled a Canadian-style skinny toothpick joint. He took a drag, coughed, and passed it to Damien. There was an appreciative silence as they finished the joint, then Jake started to giggle.

'What?' Damien stubbed out the roach in an ashtray made from a woven beer can.

'Buddy,' Jake gasped, 'I can't believe you just fucking did that!'

Was there tobacco on his face? Damien wiped his mouth. 'Did *what?*'

'Carried this dope to Korea shoved up your ass! Man, if I'd got a letter asking me to do that I'd have fucking burned it!'

Now they were both howling with laughter and Damien's stomach was aching for all the right reasons. 'Friendship flower of life,' he spluttered. 'Ancient Korean saying, yeah?'

'Our friendship?' Jake shook his head. 'Must be a hydroponic skunk bud.'

'Skunk-buddies!' they shouted in unison.

Damien was wiping the tears away when Jake slapped his forehead. 'Dames, you done your part of the deal; time for mine.' He rifled through the papers on the desk and handed Damien a brown envelope. Inside was a thin sheet covered in the Korean alphabet, Hangul. He had tried to explain it last night in the restaurant, but the letters were still a complete mystery to Damien. Still, he could see the paper was a contract of some sort.

'The tenancy agreement.' Jake was serious now. 'Tomorrow I'll take you to the 'lord and you can sign me off. He'll give you another six-month lease and when you go, he'll give you back the key-fee – two point five million won, see? If you leave before then you gotta find another tenant to take over or you lose the deposit, get it?'

The hash was obviously firing Jake's synapses. It was having the opposite effect on Damien. He peered at the contract. At least he could understand the numerals. He nodded; that's what they'd agreed. Tomorrow he'd have half the selling price of the hash to his name – on paper, anyway.

'And this' – Jake passed him another sheet of paper – 'is your teaching schedule.' He pointed at the top of the list. 'The kinder-garten is two hours every morning, it's a blast. These are a few privates, after-school stuff with kids, a pain to get to, but good cash. And there're always more jobs coming up. With the current situation, people aren't staying as long as they used to. The social scene ain't what it used to be. Still, you can rack up some won pretty quick if you want to.'

Damien gazed at the numbers. Maths had never been his strong point, especially when stoned, but according to Jake's figures, it seemed he'd be working twenty hours a week for about two thousand pounds a month. 'Looks great to me.' Slowly, his mind worked back through the conversation, the way it often had to do after a puff. Something was puzzling him. Oh yeah. 'What do you mean: "the current situation"?'

'You know' – Jake yawned – 'climate change. All that Hammer mumbo-jumbo. Some people think we only got until December; they want to travel, not teach Korean businessmen how to place an order at McDonald's.'

The dope rush had subsided, leaving Damien with goosebumps and a slight case of muscle tremor. He rubbed his arms. 'So what do you think?'

'About what?'

'You know, the Hammer.'

'Ah, yes, the mighty Lucifer's Hammer.' Jake eyed up a chunk of hash, sliced it neatly in two and placed the larger piece on the scales. 'Do I believe that a dense metal asteroid is currently travelling towards us at enormous speed from the Oort cloud, at an angle to the sun that makes it invisible to even the most sophisticated astronomical instruments?' He removed a pinch of hash from the lump he was weighing and shrugged. 'Nah.'

'But what if it were true?'

'It ain't true. The world was going down the drain at the Millennium, and the 2012 Solstice too, as I recall. Sheesh, they couldn't even pick a new date.'

Damien's teeth were starting to chatter. Man, this stuff was strong. 'The websites go over all that, Jake. Maybe the Mayans got the year a bit wrong. Or we miscalculated their calendar.'

'Dames: the whole scene's just a bunch of freaks waving *The World is Gonna End Tomorrow* placards. Tomorrow comes: world still here. Still, at least they can re-use the placard.'

Damien sat up. Some people needed a little persuading. 'Jake, meteors have slammed into Earth over and over again during its history. We're due a big one, and we're not prepared. The Hammer would make the 2004 tsunami look like a spilt paddling pool. Only people way up a mountain or deep inland would stand a chance. The astronomers were all talking about it until four months ago, then the head of the Royal Astronomical Society got the sack. The government didn't want her to tell us the truth, because—'

Jake cut him off. 'Because there'd be nothing they or anyone could do about it. So why freak out until it happens? Or *doesn't* happen.'

Damien gave up. If people didn't want to face the truth, you couldn't make them. 'Okay, so there's no Hammer. But what about global warming? Every year we get more hurricanes, floods, earthquakes, epidemics. I mean, how long before bird flu takes off?'

'Life's a gamble. So long as I'm living high up a hill, I'll take my chances.'

Damien's muscles were shivering now. He reached over and rummaged in his backpack for a sweater.

'You cold, buddy?'

It was now or never. He pulled on his V-neck. 'No – kind of. Look, Jake, I gotta ask you something.'

Jake put the knife down. 'Shoot.'

'Your contacts here . . .' Christ, there was no point pussyfooting about. '—could anyone get me some Canadian papers?'

'Canadian papers?' Jake raised one eyebrow, a neat trick. 'You mean *The Globe and Mail*?'

'No. I mean a passport. And a SIN card.'

Jake raised both eyebrows now. 'Okaaaay. So why would you be in the market for those, exactly?'

Damien took a deep breath. 'Britain is fucked, man. Police state, rains all year round, stabbings on the Tube every week, no room to move, and everything costs a fucking arm and a leg. If there's going to be floods and plagues, it'll get way worse.'

Jake shrugged. 'So go live in Europe. You Brits are lucky, you can teach English there.'

Damien shook his head. 'Europe's just as crowded. Any diseases, they'd spread like wildfire. And Russia's got nukes pointing at every major capital. I'm telling you, it's no time to move to Poland and drink cheap beer.' Jake opened his mouth to protest, but Damien rolled on, 'Look, my UK passport expires soon. To get a new one, I'd have to virtually sign my DNA away – isometrics, eyeball prints, blood test, face-scanning. I don't believe in that shit.'

Jake flicked a bit of tobacco out from between his teeth. 'Me neither, buddy, but it's not up to us peons to decide these things, is it?'

'Canadians don't have to give blood to get a passport, do they?'

Jake made a mock salute. 'Land o' the free, buddy, home o' the brave. Unless you're a First Nations brave, of course. Then it's the reservation for you, second-class citizenship, fracked land and nuclear waste.'

Damien ignored the history lesson. 'Well, I'd rather have a Canadian passport. And a Social Insurance Number. I've done the research, Jake. If the oceans keep rising, or the Hammer hits and there's another tsunami, central Canada's going to be one of the safest places on earth.'

Jake snapped his fingers beneath Damien's nose. 'Dude-ski, wake *up*! How many times do I have to tell you? The Hammer is a magnet for internet loonies, that's all. So basically you're saying that you wanna live in Armpit, Saskatchewan to avoid getting sneezed on in the odd queue for the off-licence? Not sure you've really thought this through.'

How to explain without explaining; that had always been the question. 'Look, there's some personal stuff going on for me too,' he muttered. 'I could do with some space to chill out after Korea. I just thought you might know some bloke who could sort me out.'

Jake held his gaze. 'Dames: are you in some kind of trouble?'

Damien ran his hand through his hair. 'Not really – I mean, not yet. I don't want to go into it, Jake, it's not important. I just don't want to go back to England, okay?'

'Not even for the World Cup? I thought you'd be sprinting right back for that.'

Damien snorted. 'Especially not for the World Cup. We barely qualified, remember? We're going to get knocked out in the group stages and the whole country's going to sulk through the knockouts and disgrace ourselves as hosts, then we'll spew up spite and recrimin-ation for the next four years. No thanks.'

'Hey, don't be so negative, Dames. It's a common coping mechan-ism to deal with fear of failure, but it deprives you of the healthy chance to hope. You guys got a good team this year. You just had injury problems in the run-ups. But with the schedule re-jigged to July now, you've had extra training time. Best chance since '66, I reckon.'

'Germany and Brazil have also had extra-training time, Jake – and it's *always* our best chance since '66, but we never do better than abject humiliation in the quarter-finals – or semi-finals, if we're extremely unlucky. Please don't kid yourself on my account, okay?'

Jake narrowed his eyes. 'An Englishman who doesn't want to watch the World Cup at Wembley: this has got absolutely nothing to do with kiddie-fiddling, right?'

'Jake,' Damien exploded, 'fuck, *you're* the one working at a bloody kindergarten!'

'Whoa!' Jake flashed him a grin. 'I'm just winding you up, buddy, relax. Look, your business is your business. You wanna live in Canada, that's great. I'll talk to Sam when he gets back, he knows everyone. Just don't mention this conversation to anyone. *Comprendo?*'

'*Comprendo.*' Damien was exhausted. He pushed his chair back from the desk, got up and flopped down on the sofa. 'Thanks, Jake.'

'Anything for a skunk-buddy.' Jake pulled open a drawer. 'Look, here's my agent's business card. Takes ten per cent for the first six months, but he's always good for a morning job. Wish I could give you the *hagwon*. That was ideal.'

Damien placed his arm across his eyes. His brain felt like it was squeezing itself out of his head through his sinuses. He had to make an effort to stay in the room. 'What's a *hagwon*?' he asked.

'Cram school – early mornings and late afternoon. I got caught in the office by immigration. Luckily I was just doing some photo-copying, or I coulda been deported. Jeez, that was a pisser to lose, thirty thou an hour. Still, you got a good week there. Especially for a kiddie-fiddler.'

Jake chortled, but Damien could barely hear him. Somewhere in the darkness in his head a little girl was sobbing, desolate, fright-ened, alone. *Where's Damien? Where's my mum?* But he didn't have to listen. He rubbed his face vigorously – he was rubbing her out and she was fading away. She wasn't crying any more. She was silent now. And his eyes were wet and his stomach felt like it had been vacuumed into an enormous black hole.

'Damien, you okay?' Jake sounded sharp, anxious. 'What's the matter, buddy?'

'Huh?' Damien jerked to attention. Christ, he had to snap out of this. He hauled himself back up to a sitting position and reached for his jeans. 'Fuck, I gotta get up. Can I check my email?'

'Sure. Help yourself to cake.' Busy again with the hash and his scales, Jake nodded at the laptop.

Damien powered up and accessed his new Hotmail account. He'd shut down the old one before he left, and his Facebook and Twitter profiles too. Three emails. Spam, Hotmail admin, and Mum, replying to his apology. He'd bet his first month's wages in Seoul that she wasn't worried about him.

Yup, no 'how are you', no 'I'm sorry I couldn't help you with the money'. Just a memo to say she and Gordon were going to Paris for a week. He was about to click 'Delete' when something stopped him. Sure, she was a shit mum, but she'd already had one kid disappear.

Mum,

Arrived safe. Will let you know when I'm back.

Dx

He pressed 'Send' then headed to the kitchen for some cake. Now he wasn't a missing child any more, maybe Jessica would leave him alone.

Part Two

CONTACT

8 | Naked Brunch

'Hey, Johnny.' Sydney padded up behind him at his desk and tickled his ribs. 'Can I have my pay for last night? I want to go to the gym.'

'The gym?' Johnny swivelled round, his face scribbled with annoyance. 'C'mon doll-face, I told ya three times: I'm going to China tomorrow, today's Independence Day, and I'm taking you to Seoul Land to celebrate. You need to have some fun, go on a few rides, eat a little junk food for a change.'

For fuck's sake. Sydney put her hands on her hips and stuck out her chin. 'I'm not *American*, Johnny. And I have to stay in *shape*. I can't spend the whole day pigging out. We can go when I get back. Now, can I have my money, *please?*'

Johnny lifted his right eyebrow. Not a good sign, she had learned. 'Of course, baby,' he crooned as he fished his wallet out of his pocket. He pulled out a crisp *man won* note and she stuck out her hand, but he waved it aside and tossed the bill on the floor. 'How's that for starters?'

Her heart racing, her hands balled into fists, Sydney glared down at the note, inches from her bare feet. Did he want her to hit him? Would that give him the excuse to punch her out he'd obviously been looking for ever since she signed that six-month contract with OhmEgo?

'Never mind. I'll use my card. Then I think I'll take *myself* out to lunch,' she sneered as she kicked the bill away with her toes.

His face morphed like a rubber mask: one weird expression after another. His breathing was shallow; his eyes glinted like chips of glass in his head.

Jeez, this was getting freaky. She turned on her heel and stalked out of the room.

'Ah, baby, it was just a joke,' he called after her, but she had grabbed her jacket and gym bag, slipped into her sandals and was halfway down the stairs.

Out in the July sunshine she marched up the road, glancing over her shoulder as she reached the corner. No, he wasn't coming after her. Feeling light-headed, almost dizzy, she stopped for a moment, sitting down on the brick banquette surrounding the New York Deli. Everything was happening so fast: first the fantastic news about the contract, then the trip to Hongdae with Jin Sok to celebrate. The place was a revelation of twisty back alleys filled with nightclubs, groovy art galleries and cheap student apartments: before she knew it she was toasting her decision to move there. It had barely taken a week to find a studio apartment. Like a total hero, Jin Sok had lent her the key-fee; she'd signed a lease yesterday, and she was moving out tomorrow, as soon as Johnny was safely on his flight.

She couldn't wait. Johnny had been all over the place lately: half the time shouting or pulling mean stunts like the one with the money; the other half whistling to himself, chucking her cheeks – which she hated – and bragging about taking her to Thailand when he got back. He'd said the other day he knew he'd been distracted lately, he hadn't been making a fuss of his little girl and he was going to make it up to her, show her the five-star treatment: fancy hotels, jewellery shopping, the works. It would be just like it was in Vancouver again. Maybe a month ago she'd have given him a second chance, but right now she'd rather shove toothpicks under her toenails.

Today was the last day she would ever have to spend with him – and she wasn't going to do it on his schedule. She stood up and headed up the hill to the Hyatt Hotel. She'd been using the health spa there religiously since meeting Jin Sok – she was blonde, and she'd soon discovered that in Korea that meant she could be bouncing with puppy fat and still get work, but if she wanted the big contracts with the sexiest designers, her stomach had to be flat as a pancake – and not a buttermilk one, either.

But after her battle of wills with Johnny she couldn't summon up the energy to work out. She got undressed, stuffed her bag of gym clothes into the locker and passed through the smoky glass doors into the women's *mog yuk tan* instead. It was nearly empty: just the two matronly, half-naked *ajummas* cleaning off their massage tables. Both wore only black bras, big flowered panties and flip-flops. One had the physique of a *Ssirûm* wrestler, with large breasts resting on her swollen belly and narrow eyes sunk in a fleshy face. The other, slightly younger, was almost as generously figured, but softly pretty still, her tightly permed hair tied up in a ribbon. She often spoke or giggled to the other, who responded in monosyllables with an air of great finality. They both knew secrets about green mudpacks and the cosmetic benefits of mashed hardboiled eggs that Sydney kept meaning to explore, but she couldn't be bothered today.

She squatted gratefully on a wooden stool in the shower chamber, directing streams of hot rushing water over her head and down between her shoulder blades and breasts. Koreans sure knew how to design showers. The mirror on the tiled wall fogged over, obscuring her puffy-eyed reflection. Soon, just keeping the nozzle aloft was too tiring; using the abrasive green mitt she'd bought at Tongdaemon Night Market, she made a half-hearted attempt at the obligatory exfo-liation required before entering the sauna – it would be the height of folly to use the shared facilities under the watchful eyes of the mighty *ajummas* with your outer dermis intact. Only dirt held it together, after all – that was evident by the thick globs of black sludge the *ajummas* scraped off people with their strong-arm technique. There was even a special word for this gunk in Korean: *doh*.

Every so often Sydney indulged in the *ajummas'* full-length *doh*-elimination treatment, but today she was afraid she would slide off the massage table and break with a tinkle on the floor. Leaving her shampoo, soap and shower mitt in the little plastic basket by the showers, she took her towel into the sauna.

The cedar-panelled room was empty, so she took two of the beaded head rests for her head and her feet and stretched out on her towel. Privacy was heaven at first, but without the breeze of other women to-ing and fro-ing the dry heat soon parched her lungs and her brain began to shrivel up like a walnut. She'd hit her limit.

Sydney lurched for the door. She thought she was fine until she hit the vapours coming off the cold pool, then, bewilderingly, her vision chequered like the tiled walls, the whole bathhouse tilted crazily and the floor rushed up to meet her as she fell.

Her right knee was throbbing, and someone was splashing her face with cold water. Blinking, she tried to sit up, but her hands slipped on the wet floor. The *ajummas* were looming over her, grabbing her arms. She groaned. At least her head was all right. The rubber hoses by the pool must have broken her fall.

'Oh my goodness. Are you *okay*?' The voice was American; it belonged to a naked Korean woman who was hovering near the sauna door. She must be a *kyopo*, Sydney realised. 'I think so.' Sydney struggled to her feet, helped by the two stout and formidable *ajummas*. Plastic sandals flapping sharply against their heels, they led her through to the locker room, where they sat her down at a low table and fetched her a mug of cool water.

The *kyopo* woman was there too, joining in the general fluster of sympathy. She was middle-aged and petite, with small breasts and just a wisp of pubic hair, and she spoke Korean as if the language were a strange, hypnotic music. Listening to her, Sydney wished again that she could understand more than a fleeting word or two. As if sensing her awkwardness, the *kyopo* turned and winked. *Let the grandmothers have their way*, her smile seemed to say.

'You like *makkoli*?' The younger *ajumma*'s soft moon face bore the sweetest expression.

'Oh, no, not in the morning, thank you,' Sydney stammered; she hadn't enjoyed the cloudy rice wine the first time she'd tried it. But the *ajumma* had already taken a white plastic bottle from the locker room cooler; beaming proudly, she shook out Sydney's water mug and filled it to the brim. Bracing herself, Sydney took a tiny sip, but to her surprise, the *makkoli* tasted delicious – much sweeter than she remembered, creamy and refreshingly spritzy. She downed the mug in a couple of swigs. The woman refilled it, and fetched out three more mugs.

The *kyopo* politely refused. 'I've got my own drink,' she told Sydney, then bowed to the *ajummas* and padded over to the lockers.

'My na-muh Myo Hae Gee.' The *ajumma* patted herself on the chest.

'Myo Hae Gee,' Sydney repeated. '*Irrem* Sydney.'

'You eat lunch?' Hae Gee asked.

'No, no food, no sleep, very weak,' Sydney explained. The *ajummas* exchanged puzzled glances, so she flexed her biceps and her meagre store of Korean: '*Kang!*' That meant strong, didn't it?

'No strong girl,' Hae Gee contradicted, patting the table 'You eat lunch here.'

Here was where the *ajummas* always sat in the locker room, counting money, watching TV or tucking into the feasts they prepared with the rice cooker and microwave in the corner by the door. Right now, the smell of stew was hanging in the air, and suddenly, Sydney was ravenous.

'That's a good idea, Sydney.' The *kyopo* had returned with her purse. 'I'm Dr Kim Da Mi – please call me Da Mi.'

Da Mi's purse was the latest Prada, Sydney noticed with a twinge of envy as the nude doctor sat down and launched into a spirited exchange with the *ajummas*. As surreptitiously as possible, Sydney took a professional gawk at her new friend. Da Mi sure looked great for her age: her heart-shaped face was framed by a glossy bob, and had only a faint whisper of creased skin around her eyes. Her neck was slightly more wrinkly, but her breasts were still firm, though too small for her to have had surgery. Unlike most Korean women, she had a bit of muscle tone in her arms. She was clearly what Jin Sok called a 'Super Power Lady'.

The *Ssirûm* wrestler held out her bowl to Hae Gee, who filled it with rice and ladles of *dwen chan chigae*. Sydney tried not to giggle. It was pretty funny, eating spicy tofu stew with two *ajummas* in their underwear and a woman wearing only gold earrings and a jade bracelet. But in the bathhouse Korean women, whether young or old, saggy or scrawny, Botox Betties or Silicon Sallys, were relaxed about their own bodies – and other people's bodies, too. Once, a teenage girl had sidled over to Sydney as she sat on the edge of the hot pool and gently stroked her thigh. It hadn't been a come-on; she was just amazed by the way Sydney's legs turned strawberry pink and clotted cream in the heat. Gentle touching between Koreans of the same gender was common, Jin Sok had told her that. *Skinship*, it was called. Even straight men sometimes held hands in the street.

The older *ajumma* passed Sydney a bowl of stew. Da Mi made a regretful face and patted her tiny belly, saying something apologetic in Korean, and Hae Gee nodded wisely and fetched a cup of hot water.

'I have a delicate stomach.' Da Mi took a small vial out of her purse. 'This is my medicine.' She opened the vial and sprinkled a dash of amber powder into the water. The concoction fizzed up with a sweet, light, flowery smell.

'Is it an Oxy-product?' So many people were into that now. Johnny practically lived on the stuff.

'Those products can be dangerous, Sydney, very over-stimulating. This is effervescent pollen, rejuvenating for us older folk.' Da Mi lifted the cup to her lips. 'I have something else that would be good for you, but eat your lunch first.'

Hae Gee brought over some *banchan* dishes from the fridge: *kim chi*, sweet radish and green beans marinated in sesame oil with little dried fish. Sydney ate obediently until Hae Gee tried to pour her another mug of *makkoli*. Alarmed, she put her hand over the top.

'Go on,' Da Mi urged, 'it's raising your blood sugar levels. I couldn't have prescribed anything better myself.'

So Sydney had another half-mugful of wine. As the meal ended she admired Da Mi's Buddhist bracelet, and Hae Gee asked excitedly if she meditated.

She shook her head. 'But I love the temples,' she added brightly when she saw the *ajumma*'s disappointed face. She did like the Buddhist chants and lanterns, the colourful temples and the sexy monks, but meditation seemed a real time-waster. Why would you want to blank your mind when life was so full of things to do and see and say and think?

'No more hot box,' Hae Gee said firmly as the *ajummas* heaved to their feet and began clearing the table.

With a stab of alarm Sydney realised that she meant the sauna. 'But I love—'

'Don't worry,' Da Mi soothed. 'You'll just have to promise to eat properly in the future.' She took a small corked blue bottle out of her purse. 'Now. This is honey, a blend of rare Himalayan orchid and Australian poppy – it's just the thing to calm fragile girls.'

Sydney glanced at the clock: noon. What the fuck, let Johnny sweat. 'Wow. Sounds ace, Da Mi.'

The doctor rose gracefully and took her mug to the sink, rinsed it and filled it with hot water. In the light from the soft drinks dispenser, Sydney could see slight furrows in Da Mi's forehead. They made the doctor look more intelligent, she decided.

'Not the purest water, but it'll do.' Da Mi sat back down and drizzled a teaspoonful of pale runny honey into the mug, then she passed it to Sydney in the formal Korean way, holding her right elbow with her left hand.

The subtle flavour of the honey blossomed in Sydney's mouth. She sat quietly, feeling her throat, chest and stomach glow as the drink slipped down her body.

'That's magic.'

'Yes, in a way, it is.'

Behind them, the drinks machine softly rattled. The *ajummas* returned to the *mog yuk tan*, letting a warm billow of moisture into the locker room. Da Mi wiped the lip of the honey bottle with a tissue, re-corked it and returned it to her purse.

Everything seemed strangely normal, more than it had for months. 'So you're from the States, hey?' Sydney asked.

Da Mi set her cup gently on the table. She had perfectly manicured, taupe-coloured nails. 'I was brought up in Los Angeles. But I've been living in Korea for the last fifteen years.'

'That's a long time.' Sydney toyed with her mug, trying to think of something to say next that wouldn't be too dumb. Jin Sok had told her that *kyopos* had different reasons for returning to Korea: some were second-generation immigrants wanting to explore their roots; others were orphans who had been adopted by foreigners. Even

though the term meant 'one of our own', they often found it difficult to be accepted by native Koreans. Jeez, she didn't want to get
into all that. 'So you don't miss America then?' she ventured.

'Not at all – but what about you, Sydney? Is that a Canadian accent
I detect?'

'Yeah, I'm from Vancouver. Well, near there, anyway.' Sydney
relaxed; Da Mi was so nice. And whether it was the *makkoli* or the
honey, she was starting to feel a bit chatty. 'I was working in Vancouver
and met a modelling agent. He got me a contract here.'

'I thought you looked familiar – you're in that lipstick advertisement, aren't you?' Da Mi almost purred with approval.

Sydney rolled her eyes. 'Yeah, that's me: flavour of the month just
because I'm blonde. *Ajummas* in the subways pull my hair out sometimes, you know.'

'Don't take offence,' Da Mi chuckled. 'They'd tuck your bra strap
in too, if it were showing. Your hair is in wonderful condition. It's
just so unusual here. The colour is natural, isn't it?'

'Well, with highlights.' Sydney stroked her hair. She had an appointment with the stylist tomorrow. He'd probably scold her for not
patting it dry the way he had told her to. 'To be honest, Da Mi,' she
confided, 'modelling's really hard work. I love it, but I have to look
after every little bit of me, and I have to stay super-thin. That's why
I didn't want to drink that *makkoli*.'

Da Mi tilted her head. 'You look lovely. I wouldn't want to see you
get much thinner. It was good to see you have a healthy appetite.'

'Oh, I love eating! It's the one thing I have in common with my
boyfriend – my soon-to-be-ex-boyfriend, I mean.' Sydney blurted out
a laugh, and the warmth in her chest flared like a sunburn.

Da Mi didn't smile. There was a small, stiff pause. An unexpected
lump swelled up in Sydney's throat.

'Things aren't going so well?' Da Mi voice was cashmere-soft.

Sydney scowled down at her lap. Her right knee was throbbing, and her heart was juddering weirdly in her chest. What was wrong with her? She'd been wound up tighter than an OhmEgo halter-top for ages, and now she'd fainted. It was because Johnny was such a jerk. Like this morning, trying to bully her into going to Seoul Land. He thought she didn't have any friends, didn't he? Thought she couldn't make it here on her own. But she *could*. Koreans were amazing: it was never any trouble for them to look out for her – to take *care* of her. Not like him.

'Hmm?' Da Mi prompted.

Sydney shrugged. 'We got on okay at first,' she muttered. 'He helped me start out here and stuff. But now I have the money for my own place, and my Korean friend is going to help me move. It's just that I work for Johnny too, and he'll be pissed if I go, so I haven't told him yet. Plus some days I hardly eat, and I've got insomnia, and I look like *shit*.' Her lower lip trembled. Embarrassed, she wiped the tears away with the back of her hand.

'Oh, dear.' Da Mi's small breasts rose and fell as she gave a sympathetic sigh. 'It sounds very stressful. Here' – she picked up Sydney's mug and pressed it into her hands – 'have a little more of the honey drink. It's very soothing.'

Sniffling, Sydney took another gulp of the mixture. Who cared about the calories? She did feel less tense now, warm from the honey, and the ache in her knee was subsiding.

'Sydney,' Da Mi said firmly, 'I'm not a GP, I'm a research scientist, but I'm telling you, you must eat sensibly. Don't worry about putting on a pound or two.'

'But if I want to get work I have to fit into Korean sizes, and they're all so tiny.' Sydney heard herself whining, but Da Mi shushed her kindly.

'Oh now. Your look is very exotic here. I'm sure the designers would alter the clothes for you. And there's plenty of other work available for foreigners in Seoul.'

On the wall behind Da Mi there was a poster of a Korean palace, its tiled roof framed by cherry trees in blossom beneath a bright blue sky. Sydney stared up at it. *Blue sky thinking.* That was one of Jin Sok's top English phrases. Why couldn't she just relax and enjoy being made a fuss of here?

'I'm sorry, Da Mi. I'm just on edge today,' she confessed.

'Have a little more of the honey drink, sweetie. And do talk about it, if you want. I know it can be lonely when you're new to a country.'

Sydney tipped back her mug, draining the last slither of the warm liquid. The humming in her body rose like a chorus. *Go on*, it seemed to be singing, *you know you want to.* 'The thing is, Da Mi—' She hesitated, but then it all poured out of her: 'This is just about the most important day of my life. I've never really had a proper job before, y'know? I was a waitress for a bit, and then I got into – well' – she tossed her head – 'escort work, which is how I met Johnny. I know that sounds sleazy, and I guess it was, kind of. The other girls were nice, and I never got into the drugs, but most of the guys were real losers, and I don't want to go back to that kind of work ever. So now I've got this amazing chance, an exclusive contract with *OhmEgo*, and Johnny's being totally horrible to me.' She felt the tears rising again, and with them a hard tinny voice in her head. *What the fuck did you do that for?* it berated her. *Now Da Mi knows you're a slut, she's going to pick up her Prada purse, make some lame excuse and leave.*

But Da Mi was still there. 'Oh *dear*,' she tutted. 'What's been going on, sweetheart?'

Sydney rubbed at an invisible spot on the table with her finger. The doctor couldn't possibly understand her life. She was just being nice to her because she'd fallen. But at the same time, Da Mi was listening to her like no one had done in months. Jin Sok was great, but all action and jokes. Annie and the other agency girls hardly even said hi any more. Yeah, even if she never saw Da Mi again, she needed to talk now. What did she have to lose?

'We had a fight before I came out,' she whispered. 'It was scary, actually. Since I got the contract, it's almost like he wants to hit me sometimes.'

'Oh, now, that is *not* good. No, I don't like the sound of that at all.'

Sydney looked up, surprised. Da Mi actually sounded mad. She was frowning and *tsking*, her eyes flashing, her lips pursed. Then, with a tiny shake of her immaculate bob, her expression melted into one of pure concern. She reached out and placed her small hand on Sydney's wrist. 'Darling, do you need a place to stay?'

'No!' Sydney jerked her arm away. Jeez, what *was* she doing, spilling her guts to a total stranger? 'We're definitely breaking up – I'm leaving tomorrow when he's on a business trip. I don't *care* if that's mean. I don't *care*.' It was such a relief to have finally said it, she was buzzing. She set the mug back down on the table. The echoing ring lingered in the air.

'He'll get over it,' Da Mi said briskly. 'He must meet lots of pretty girls in his line of work. And your future should be yours to choose. Goodness, it's actually all very exciting, isn't it? OhmEgo's a *very* up-and-coming label. You'll be a Korean celebrity in no time!'

Da Mi still liked her. Was on her *side*, even. Wow. For a moment, she felt light and wavy, a silk scarf blowing in a breeze.

Nice as she was, though, the doctor wasn't an industry prophet. Sydney wrinkled her nose and shook her head. 'It's just a foot in the door, that's all. I'm taking a big risk, really. What if I fall flat on my face?'

'Don't worry, Sydney,' Da Mi said firmly. 'I'll help you, no matter what happens. Here, let me give you my name-card.' She opened her purse again and handed Sydney a glossy business card.

Fuck Johnny. She'd made another amazing new friend. 'Thanks, Da Mi,' Sydney said eagerly, examining the card. It was embossed with a glowing green spiral and lettering in English and Hangul. 'Genetic Research International Productions,' she read, slowly. 'So, what do you do there?'

The scientist snapped her purse shut. 'Mainly I help people have children, but we also have more general research interests – some of our projects require test subjects or donors, and we pay well. You'd be very welcome to take part if you ever have time between your contracts.'

Sydney fingered the edge of the card. 'I dunno . . . you're a really smart scientist, you don't want some dumb street kid hanging around. I mean, I never even finished high school.' Even as she said the words, she wished she could swallow them back down. *What was getting into her today?* Was that honey drink some kind of truth serum?

'Sydney, look at me.' Reluctantly, Sydney obeyed. The scientist's voice was calm, her eyes mellow. 'You've had some hard times, but they're over now,' she said. 'You're smart and ambitious and lovely, and you're clearly doing well for yourself. But you're also a guest in my home country, and we Koreans, we look after our guests. Okay?'

Sydney flushed. Da Mi was super-nice, so why was she being such a dolt?

'Okay.' She nodded. 'I mean, *for sure*. I'm sorry, I'm just totally stressed out today.'

'I know – and one of my jobs is to find a cure for stress, so how lucky is that?' Da Mi smiled. Then she popped Sydney's empty mug into her own and got up, her black wisp of pubic hair level with Sydney's face for a moment. 'Now I'm afraid I have to get back to work. Are you staying?'

'No, I should get going too.' Sydney scrambled to her feet and followed the doctor back to the lockers. As she slipped back into her clothes, she realised how relaxed she felt – warm, floaty, even a bit taller. It must be good for you to be totally pathetic and unburden yourself to a stranger every now and then.

Da Mi did up the top button of her gorgeous Icinoo tunic. 'Goodbye for now, Sydney,' she said. 'And don't forget to invite me to a top fashionhouse party!'

'Sure!' Sydney giggled, and leaned down to kiss the doctor goodbye. An electric shock sizzled between her lips and the doctor's smooth cheek. Both women jumped.

'Koreans say that's the sign of destiny bringing two souls together,' Da Mi said.

Sydney fingered her faintly burning mouth and watched the scientist pad to the door in her stockinged feet. What kind of shoes would she slip into outside in the hall: Manolo Blahniks? Jimmy Choos? Oh, she *so* had to introduce Da Mi to Jin Sok.

9 / The Hotel

For the first week in the hotel, Mee Hee lay curled up on her bed, almost too tired to breathe. She opened her eyes only to sip at her *congee*, gratefully swallowing the thin slices of vegetables swimming in the thick rice porridge or slowly chewing the shredded morsels of chicken or pork. The food was so delicious she could never speak while eating. Su Jin ate reverently in silence too, and it became their habit not to disturb each other for a long while after each meal.

As well as *congee*, the nurses also brought them fruit: apples, mandarin oranges, watermelon slices, and after Dr Tae Sun removed her IV tube the cooks started adding *banchan* to her tray – little side dishes of *odang*, potatoes, bean sprouts, *kim chi*, seaweed. The nurses were Chinese, but the cooks were Korean, Su Jin said. Chinese food was very good, and *congee* was excellent for people suffering from malnutrition, but as they got stronger, it was important to keep their meals close to home, so they would not confuse their stomachs or their spirits.

When she wasn't eating, Mee Hee slept, waking only to let the nurses wash her and change her sheets, or to see the doctors, who visited twice a day. Dr Tae Sun came in the mornings, when Su Jin was out socialising or exploring the neighbourhood. He would tend to her bruises, daubing them with ointment as she lifted her night-dress up over her ribs. He also gave her acupuncture to calm her nerves and improve her circulation, teasing her when her veins twitched. Once, he gave her a hand massage to finish off her treatment, kneading her palms and pulling her fingers, joking that he was going to take them away with him. Soon, his footsteps in the hall were a signal to sit up straight, plump the pillows, smooth her hair.

In the afternoon, Dr Dong Sun took her pulse and examined her throat and ears. He prescribed pills to help balance her energies, and clove-oil for her gums. He advised Su Jin to use the oil too, on her fingertips, to help her stop biting her nails, and when she showed him some noticeable growth he brought her a South Korean fashion magazine, all the way from the train station. She barely said thank you, but she stayed up late into the night reading and re-reading it, the glossy pages snapping and sighing as Mee Hee drifted off to sleep.

Gradually, Mee Hee grew stronger, and as the days passed, she was able to eat more often, without making her stomach feel so bloated and sore. She couldn't tell if she was putting on weight, but her bruises were fading and shrinking, and her gums had stopped bleeding when she brushed her teeth. She was still too weak to walk, but as soon as she could sit up in bed for a few hours at a time, the other women began to visit her. They would arrive in groups of three or four, bringing their own chairs; the metal legs scraped against the tiled floor as the women clucked and exclaimed, telling stories of the suffering in their villages, the deaths of their children and husbands. The most frequent visitor was Older Sister, who had lost three sons in six months and was now eating so much she had begun to look almost stocky.

'Women from the Diamond Mountains are built to survive,' she would say gruffly as the others admired her thick arms. Apart from Mee Hee, the thinnest woman was Little Sister, whose quiet modesty made her seem much older than nineteen. Following the deaths of her parents, she had become a devout secret Christian, like her mother.

'Jesus fasted for many days in the wilderness,' she said to Mee Hee at their first meeting. 'I thought of his beautiful strength whenever my stomach cried out.'

Six of the other women were Buddhists. Two had always meditated, they said, despite the Wise Young Leader's orders not to worship false prophets. The others were only now beginning to learn about the religion, praying with bracelets of beads they had bought in the markets outside the hotel. Two more women wore crucifixes around their necks, but neither spoke about Jesus as if they knew him, like Little Sister did.

The visits were full of kindness and noise, and Mee Hee soon began to look forward to them. None of the women pressed her to speak, and if they did dwell on the subject of their lost children, a warning look from Su Jin had them quickly fussing over Mee Hee's health, before her room-mate shooed their sisters away.

At last, Dr Tae Sun said she was allowed to try to walk. A nurse brought slippers and a dressing gown and Mee Hee sat on the side of the bed, slipping her arms into the sleeves, her feet into the blue flannel. She thought the nurse would help, but Dr Tae Sun himself stepped forward and put his arm around her.

'I'm all right by myself,' she whispered, embarrassed, but her knees were weak and she let him help her stand. As they walked together across the room she clutched at his hand around her waist. In the morning she walked to the bathroom with Su Jin, who washed her hair and scrubbed her skin in the steamy shower stall. When they came back, Mee Hee asked if she could sit on Su Jin's bed and look out of the window.

'Of course!' She helped Mee Hee kneel on the blanket. They peered out between the curtains into the roar of the traffic, the loud pop music of the cassette salesman on the corner and the harsh cries of the street vendors.

'Oh!' Mee Hee clutched the sill and raised herself higher. She hadn't known there could be so many people in the world, so many different kinds of clothes: young girls in school uniforms; gentlemen in suits with silk ties; women in flowery blouses. And look – 'People are selling food on the street!'

'Smell it.' Su Jin reached up and opened the window and a fragrant gust of burnt sugar billowed up from the doughnut stand outside the hotel. Across the street a man was ladling out what looked like stew; beside him a woman was frying grasshoppers.

Mee Hee's mouth watered. 'The Chinese must live to eat,' she whispered.

'The bean cakes are delicious. I'll buy you one later.' Su Jin said. But Dr Dong Sun wouldn't let her interfere with Mee Hee's diet, so she arrived back with a brooch instead, a glittery blue bird.

'The messenger of the Gods.' Mee Hee stroked the enamel. *He can send my love to Song Ju*, she thought.

'For us, yes, the blue bird is a spy.' Su Jin took the brooch from her hand. 'But in Russia, the blue bird means hope. I read it in a magazine.' Su Jin pinned the bird to Mee Hee's blouse. As she did so, Mee Hee coughed and the sharp point of the pin pricked her breast. She flinched.

'Oh! I'm sorry!'

'No, it was my fault.'

'Don't be silly. Here, look at how pretty you are.' Su Jin passed Mee Hee the mirror. Almost frightened, she peeked at her reflection. The brooch was beautiful, but behind it, she saw a plain, ordinary woman, with broad cheekbones and a snub nose. There was flesh on her face now, but she would never be pretty like Su Jin.

'Do you have hope?' Mee Hee asked timidly.

'Of course.' Su Jin frowned. 'Don't you?'

Mee Hee laid the mirror down. She knew she couldn't give the right answer. Hope meant wanting things to get better. But she prayed every night that her life would stay exactly as it was now.

'You must have hope, or you wouldn't have come in the truck.' Su Jin's voice was determined, almost giving her an order. Mee Hee thought back to that moment in the rice paddy when her heart had fluttered in her chest.

'Dr Che,' she whispered. 'Che Tae Sun, he gives me hope.'

'Well, I've seen more handsome men, but those two are worth recovering for, I suppose.'

Mee Hee paused. 'Which do you prefer?' she asked, terrified of the answer, but desperate to know.

'They're as alike as two soy beans!' Su Jin laughed. 'Well, Dr Dong Sun is a little more muscular. Yes, I think I'd have to take a honeymoon with him.'

Mee Hee felt a surge of energy run through her. Was this hope? 'Oh no, they're very different,' she insisted. 'Dr Tae Sun is very gentle and sensitive. And his looks are . . . more refined.'

Su Jin flashed her sharp little teeth. 'If you're feeling well enough to fight over the doctors you should come downstairs for supper tonight. You can't just lie here mooning over your Doctor Prince!'

'I do not!' Mee Hee protested, a blush sweeping over her face.

'You mustn't brood over the past either. Come downstairs and watch TV while supper's being made.'

So that evening, holding tightly onto Su Jin's arm, Mee Hee tottered down to the lobby of the hotel, where a dozen women sat crosslegged on the floor, their faces bathed in the spectral light of the television. They applauded Mee Hee's arrival, and Younger Sister plumped up a cushion for her. Then the women began to squabble over a shelf of slim plastic boxes with colourful sleeves.

'They're dee-vee-dees,' Su Jin explained, pronouncing the foreign word slowly. 'Like books for television.'

'It's my turn to choose,' Older Sister announced, and she deftly lifted a golden disc from a sliding drawer below the TV screen and replaced it with another, making a coarse joke about how easily the drawer slid in. Mee Hee sat silently. She had seen televisions before, of course, and even videocassettes, when Education Units had come to the village to inform them of the Wise Young Leader's latest achievements. But she had never seen a dee-vee-dee casually glinting in the callused hands of a peasant woman.

'Oh good, *Castles and Queens.*' Su Jin murmured knowledgeably. A rapt hush settled over the room as the television sprang alive with swirls of golden light and a fanfare of trumpets. Older Sister, sitting beside Su Jin, pressed a button on a black rectangular unit ("It's a remote control,' Su Jin whispered) and a Korean woman's face filled the screen. Her make-up was flawless, her skin smooth, her gold jewellery tasteful and discreet; she was older than any of the women in the room, but more beautiful than anyone Mee Hee had ever seen. Despite the immense care that had obviously gone into her appearance, however, there was nothing distant or artificial about her expression. Her face was so tender that for a moment Mee Hee felt as if she were looking up into the face of her own mother.

'Hello.' The woman's voice was as full and creamy as her lips. With her lush, painted mouth and soft brown eyes, she smiled into Mee Hee's soul. 'My name is Dr Kim Da Mi. Welcome to *Castles and Queens.*'

Mee Hee gripped Su Jin's arm. 'Is that—?' she asked in disbelief.

Su Jin nodded as a woman in front of them turned her head and whispered, 'Shush.'

Mee Hee needed no further instruction to sit still and watch, entranced, as Dr Kim's heart-shaped face dissolved into a scene of rolling green hillsides. The camera zoomed in on a stone castle with round turrets and fluttering triangular flags. There were more trumpets, and then Dr Kim's warm, melodious voice began narrating a story about Queen Eleanor, who lived in the top rooms of the castle, ruled over two different lands and had given birth to three kings.

Queen Eleanor was brave and wise. She wore long, brocaded robes and presided over lavish banquets. Her trestle tables strained under great platters of food: roast beef, peacock and lamb, massive pork and pigeon pies, enormous wheels of cheese, trays of honey-glazed vegetables, mountains of fruit, huge bowls of rich, creamy puddings, and flagons of wine made from wildflowers and berries. Seeing the king and queen lick their fingers as they ate the lamb was shocking – how could anyone eat a baby animal that had been so cruelly taken from its mother? – but still, as she watched the feasting, Mee Hee longed to taste from every plate. And in the tournament scenes, when Queen Eleanor's knights jousted for her favours, she gasped and gripped her cushion, cheering with the other women when one rider toppled the other and cooing over the beautiful ornate dresses of the ladies of the court.

The film didn't really have a story, but it didn't have to. It was pleasure enough just to marvel at these rich, splendid images, bask in the stately music, lean against Su Jin and giggle over which knight was the most *refined*. When the film was over, Dr Kim's peaceful face appeared again on the screen. She thanked them for watching and said she hoped they had enjoyed the programme, and all the others in the series. Immediately, the women began arguing again.

'Queen Son Dok!'

'No, the one about Seoul!'

'Yes, the restaurants in Seoul!'

95

Mee Hee sat shyly, still enveloped in the television's luminous glow. Her heart was aching, a sweet ache that reminded her she was still alive, was still the same girl who had sat on the mountainside staring at the sunset, hoping and longing to wrap its red and orange ribbons around her waist and fly into another world.

10 / First Night Out

Damien sauntered down the concrete steps that cut through his new 'hood: Tae Hung Dong, or Well Hung Dong, as Jake called it. It was amazing how good the Dong looked after dark, especially if you'd just smoked a quick joint. The daytime monotony of apartments and rubbish was now overwritten by a maze of neon signs and eerily illuminated windows; the cop box on the corner was a cube of sterile incandescence, and the butcher's, hung with flayed carcasses, burned like an Amsterdam brothel. Next to the video store, its postered window glowing like a paper lantern, the late-night open market gleamed with food: fish, meat, poultry on ice trays; mountains of nectarines, plums, cherries, watermelons; crates of *pak choi* and eggplant, plastic bags full of bean sprouts, peeled garlic cloves and brown, holey slices of what Damien now knew was lotus root. Everything was shimmering; even the pools of vomit on the steps were almost throbbing with light.

It was stupidly hot, though. His damp shirt clinging to his skin, Damien emerged onto the main road at the foot of the Dong, turned left alongside eight blaring lanes of traffic, and made an effort to speed up. It was the opening night of Azitoo, Jake and Sam's bar, and Jake's band, Mama Gold, was due on at half-ten. Also, Sam would be there. Jake had sent an enigmatic text, giving the impression that his cousin had some news about the passport. As Damien headed towards Shinch'on traffic circle, all the underlying anxiety of the

97

last two weeks started churning in his stomach. It was hard to feel Zen when his entire future probably rested on the outcome of tonight.

It was also hard to get anywhere quickly. *Dukbogee* stands blocked every pavement corner, their stoic vendors hawking rice noodles and hot sauce to queues of nightcrawlers. Trendy boys in trim jackets and drainpipes, spiky hair gelled forward, sideburns neatly trimmed, elbowed past him; gaggles of girls in tight dresses and rhinestone jewellery teetered in front of shop windows, clutching each other's arms for support. Sucked in to the swell of the crowd, Damien kept pace with the bare legs of a mini-skirted belle. She was on her own: Jake would have tried to catch up, chat her up, but he kept his distance. He did a lot of looking these days, but he was pretty sure talking – especially the kind which might lead to touching – would not be a good idea.

He had quickly realised most Korean girls were afflicted with a fatal fondness for sentimental gifts, not to mention dreams of wedding shops. Soft-skinned and dewy-eyed they might be, but most of the girls lived at home, didn't do one-night stands and at heart were little kittens you could crush with just one flippant remark, never mind an inevitable decision to leave the country. Plus, no matter how good their English was, they didn't understand the word 'over'. Jake had dumped his latest ex in order to concentrate on his band and bar, and for the last two weeks she'd been messaging him twenty times a day.

Of course there were loads of Westerners in Seoul, but most of them were Canadian – and after just a fortnight in Seoul, Damien had realised that the only problem with his climate change-savvy, international terrorism-conscious survivalist life plan was that he just didn't fancy female Canucks. The ones he'd met at Jake's friends' parties were card-playing, skinny-Minny, PC intellectuals who hung out in packs, discussing nuclear power, racism and their grade-school teachers in Elbow or Cold Turkey, or wherever. Even if one was cute – okay, the redhead – there was no getting close to her. And if by some minor miracle you did manage to peel her away from her game of Kaiser, she'd force you to listen to Arcade Fire or Joni Mitchell all night, and then hold a conference call about the contents of your bookshelf the next day. There was no mystery or edge to Canadian girls, that was the problem; though to be fair, the Americans and Ozzies were worse.

What he needed was some moody French bird. Or a quirky Icelandic maiden. But then again, in Damien's experience even the simplest of holiday flings had the potential to turn into long-drawn-out battles for emotional supremacy. Sometimes even that was worth it for the sex and general sense of drama, but he had other priorities here in Seoul, and tonight's was meeting Sam.

He reached the traffic circle, a massive roundabout overhung by the technicolour hoardings of the Grand Mart Cinema. Opposite stood Grace Department Store, its pristine façade tied up in a neon red ribbon. Behind it, Shinch'on jigsawed out into a pell-mell, hugger-mugger zone of night spots: Hofs for beer, smoked fish and peanuts, *norebangs* for Korean Karaoke; jazz rooms; coffee shops; Web Space Cafés; theme bars named after such luminaries as Kenny Rogers, the Eagles, Coldplay, Rolling Stone. And now there was Azitoo, which, according to Jake, didn't mean anything at all.

Damien headed down into the underpass. As he crossed the concourse, a blonde girl covered in gold make-up, her hair a Medusa tangle of metal-tipped braids, glowered at him from a VidAd screen. The camera zoomed out as she tweaked a button on her GrilleTex™ jacket and her face and hair turned a cool silvery blue. *Chill out . . . with OhmEgo* the slogan urged before the girl's sly grin faded and a tofu ad took her place.

He emerged in front of Grace slathered in sweat. If he could afford temp-control clothing he'd've got himself a whole new wardrobe, but his wages were accounted for already. What he really wanted to find out tonight was that the passport and SIN card would only cost a few million so he could get to Canada as soon as possible. Then he'd be well chilled.

Her black crêpe dress slicked to her skin, Sydney pranced up the street. *Her* street. In *her* new neighbourhood.

'Freedom!' She waved to the night sky, then spun round to hug Jin Sok. 'Yeee haaaa!'

Jin Sok's deep laughter echoed off the buildings. 'You never stop moving, Superwoman. Come, now I show you Gongjang, best late nightclub in Seoul.'

She put her hands on her hips and cocked her head. 'I thought that was the club we just left?' Everywhere Jin Sok took her was the best of its kind in Seoul. Tonight they'd started at a Japanese restaurant in Apkuchong after the shoot, then gradually crossed the city back to her home turf.

'No, Smartie Girl, that best club in *Shinch'on*.' The photographer grabbed her waist and guided her past a dim strip of closed boutiques and restaurants. A few brightly dressed clubbers were eating fish sticks at an *o-dang* van on the corner, steam from the hot pots blurring their faces. Otherwise, the neighbourhood looked deserted. It was nearly two a.m., after all.

'Are you sure—?'

'Shhh. *Politzi.*' Jin Sok placed his finger sternly on his lips and she rolled her eyes, but let him lead her silently past a row of walled houses, their demure gardens just visible behind iron gates. They crossed a quiet road and he pulled her around an island of discarded electronics and a broken fridge towards a grey building: offices or apartments, it was hard to tell. A sickly pool of light spilled through the glass doors of the lobby.

A young Korean wearing an earphone headset materialised from nowhere. Jin Sok slipped him a couple of *man won* bills and after glancing up and down the road, the bouncer ushered them inside. Sydney's heels clicked on the steps leading down to the basement.

'Gongjang mean factory,' Jin Sok told her. 'Music factory. Art factory. Sex factory. You like.'

She grinned at his imperious tone. 'Is that an order?'

'Wha—?'

'Never mind.' Some things just took too long to explain.

Jin Sok held open the metal door at the foot of the stairs and Sydney stepped across the threshold into the finger-pattering thump beats of the summer's top Afro-dustrial dance track. The intertwining rhythms tugged her into a small room crammed to capacity; her hips already in synch with the music, she inhaled the warm, close crush of flesh. The DJ was scratching on a stage beside the bar; a cluster of girls perched on a cable bobbin beneath a dead tree twitched painted toes in time to the music. Beside them, a group of Korean guys were banging their beer bottles against the top of a red metal barrel. Everywhere drinkers and dancers were haloed by blue bulbs, blue candles, the glow of the drinks cooler and a blank green television screen. Around them all, wispy white, spray-painted clouds drifted between the pipes and metal plates that bulged from the sky blue walls.

'You dance, I get drinks.'

His palm between her shoulder blades, Jin Sok pushed her into the bubbling vat of bodies. Fans blew over her from every corner of the room; the DJ began dispensing an aural massage of electronic pings and whistles. Jin Sok was right: Gongjang was blue heaven, the best nightclub on the planet, a compact box of elation, sweat and sound.

Azitoo was a windowless basement, packed solid with Koreans, Westerners and young Japanese, all grooving to the mellow harmonies of Mama Gold. Damien ordered a beer from a bloke who might have been Sam and leaned against the bar, watching Jake in action.

The trio of bass, guitar and synthesiser ran smoothly through a repertoire of songs about the ex-pat experience, from the jaunty licks of 'I Guess You're Going to a Nori Bang' to 'I Love You, Lee Sung Hee', a ballad in honour of the legendary Korean-American soft porn star. 'Lee Sung Heeeeeee, do you like *kim cheeee*?' the lead singer crooned.

Finally the band took a break and Jake sidled behind the bar.

'Hey, Day.' Jake's mid-western drawl was as fake as his sideburns. 'Great to see ya. And congrats on the footie. Going well, hey, buddy?'

'We won our first game one-nil – against *Japan*. Now there's only, oh, Argentina and Portugal to go.'

'*Dames*. You could still top the group. So, you gonna join us on back-up for a number, give us some of that old Brit-pop cool?'

Damien shook his head. 'I don't sing, mate.'

'Shame – with your looks you'd be a major hit with the girlies. But here, lemme get you a G&T. Some James Bond fan might go for you then.'

His gold lamé shirt winking in the lights, Jake reached for a bottle of Gordon's. 'So, I talked to Sam,' he said quietly, mixing the drink and nodding at the other bartender who was standing sentinel at the till. Skinny, with a square jaw and conservative brush-cut, Sam looked nothing like Jake, until he threw his cousin a conspiratorial grin and above his wire-rimmed glasses, his eyebrows rose in that same wicked ghost of a Groucho Marx wiggle

Damien cast a sidelong glance down the bar. Beside him, two Korean girls were swapping photos on their MoPhos; behind him the crowd chattered and guffawed.

Jake cracked open a beer. 'Hey, relax. Sam and me, we know everyone here.'

Damien took a sip of his drink. It was a strong one. That helped. 'Okay. Shoot.'

'Bad news is,' Jake said softly, 'the price is sky-high. There's a big demand right now for Canuck papers. Guess you're not the only one thinking ahead. And to work in Canada, you're right, you'll definitely need a SIN card as well as a passport.'

Damien nodded. He had done the research online, and this was not unexpected news. All Canadians were assigned a social insurance number and issued a SIN card that wasn't nearly as fun as it sounded. You couldn't open a bank account without one, and employers needed to report the number to the tax department. Some hotels and minicab companies hired illegals without cards and paid them in cash, but he didn't want to be hanging out with dodgy folk, always looking over his shoulder. Plus, a SIN card also entitled you to government benefits if things got tight.

'That's okay. I knew that.'

'So. You have two options,' Jake continued. 'You could get a fake birth certificate and apply for the SIN when you arrive, or, for a slightly higher price, my guy here will ask his hacker contact in Canada to find you the name and number of a deceased personage whose relatives have not informed the SIN registry of their loved one's passing. My guy will then make you up a SIN card, and a passport with the same name.'

Damien's online researches had indicated that these were two secure routes into the SIN database. The Canadian government hardly ever checked it for fraud, apparently. He didn't want to have to jump through hoops when he arrived, though. 'Option two, definitely. How much does your guy want?'

'Going rate is twenty million.'

Damien wished he could whistle better. 'Fucking hell.'

Jake shrugged. 'It's a good deal. Option one is eighteen point five. I guess he pays the hacker the extra.'

Damien jabbed at the slice of lemon in his drink with his straw. 'I'm going to need some set-up money too.'

'No problem. The passport comes with a visa stamp, any date you want. Just overstay, and buy it when you can afford it.'

As always, there was something reassuring about Jake, with his solid build and dark, hush-puppy eyes. But Damien needed to be in Canada before the Hammer's big date with Earth. And even if Jake was right and the Mayans were wrong, overstaying didn't exactly appeal.

'I dunno – what if I got picked up after my UK passport expired? I'd be fucked.'

Jake took a thoughtful slug of his beer. 'Sam?' He turned to his cousin. 'Five months: you gotta save four million a month, plus live. Possible?'

Sam nodded. 'Sure, top earner in Seoul make six million a month. Okay, no sleep, but OxyPops cheap. We keep eye open for jobs for you.'

'You've got your key-money too,' Jake reminded him. 'That'll tide you over when you get there. Rent's cheap in Winnipeg.'

Damien clunked his glass down on the bar. 'All right: I'll give it a go.'

Sam stuck his hand out. 'Damien, Jake very rude. I Sam.'

'Great,' Jake cut in, as Damien shook Sam's hand. 'Now you're all cosy here. When you've got the cash, give me a photo. Turnaround is pretty quick, three or four days.'

'If you need,' Sam added, 'I get you University London MA. Help you get good jobs, very quick. Small investment; big profit. Think about it.'

The Korean girls were poring over a magazine. Jake lit a cigarette and took an order from a beefy Aussie in a Hawaiian shirt.

The knot in Damien's stomach loosened a fraction. 'I got a line on a *hagwon* job,' he told Sam. 'How much is a CELTA certificate?'

'For you, two hundred thou. Come tomorrow with cash, I get by Wednesday.' Sam gave him a thumbs-up and returned to the till. Damien raised his glass to Jake, who toasted back, draining the rest of his beer.

'And now, if you'll excuse me, Day,' he said, checking his hair in the mirrored tiles behind the bar, 'my public awaits.'

The Korean girls screamed and whistled as Mama Gold launched into a rocking rendition of 'Ajumma's Umbrella'. Sam put another G&T in front of him. Damien reached for his wallet, but the Korean shook his head.

'Jake buy tonight. Don't worry, me and Jake, we look after you.'

Sipping his drink he scanned the crowd, checking out the talent. Beside him the Korean girls tittered and he made out the words 'Hu-gee Grant.' Christ, was he going to have to pretend to be an ageing ponce to get laid here?

No, what he needed in Seoul was not sex, but a fifty-hour work week. In fact, he decided as he finished his gin, it was time for a little self-discipline. Time for a personal vow. Until he got that Canadian passport in his hand, Damien Meadows was flying solo. No chat-ups, no snogging and definitely no shagging. There would be strict limits on alcohol and drug intake too, both of which had in the past led directly to serious cash flow crises and the inadvertent acquisition of mentally deranged girlfriends.

The crowd was going crazy for Mama Gold's big number: 'Are You Married? Why Not?'

Sam leaned over to him. 'Damien, you want some E?'

'Nah, thanks, Sam. Taking a break from the old chemicals for a while.'

Sam looked disappointed. 'Is present – I bring back with me from Canada. Good times. We go Hongdae after, dancing.'

A bit of clubbing, one last E for the road. Why not?

'Okay,' he agreed. 'If you're having one too.' He could start that new austerity regime on Monday.

11 / The American

At the end of Mee Hee's second week at the hotel, a *weaguk saram* arrived. He was the first foreigner she had ever seen. His hair was not quite yellow but a sandy-brown, and his eyes, Su Jin reported, were blue like the sky on a spring morning. She had just returned from the market as he arrived, and was soon sitting cross-legged on Mee Hee's bed, telling her and Older Sister exactly what had happened.

'His name is Mis-tuh San-duh-man.' She enunciated the English words slowly but proudly. 'Dr Dong Sun told me. He's a friend of Dr Kim's. He's American but he speaks Korean. And he's a born capit-alist.'

'What does that mean?' Older Sister harrumphed. She had made it clear that she thought Su Jin talked a lot about things she didn't know much about, and maybe Su Jin did. But Mee Hee liked that about her.

'I'm telling you,' Su Jin hissed, 'after he got his keys, he went through the hotel register to see how many rooms were being used. There was one empty, and he's asked Dr Dong Sun to rent it out as storage space.'

She flicked her hair triumphantly, but Older Sister pursed her lips. 'Sounds like common sense to me.'

'It must be costing a lot to feed us,' Mee Hee offered shyly. 'If he helped the doctors bring us here, he must be looking for ways to pay the bills.'

'We're going to be making his fortune!' Su Jin glared at Older Sister. 'He's come to inspect his merchandise, that's what I think.'

And indeed, over the next forty-eight hours the American poked his big nose into every aspect of the hotel operation, from the kitchen to the laundry to the medicine dispensary. None of the other women had ever seen a *waeguk saram* either, and they chattered about him endlessly behind his back: how old was he; was he Dr Kim's lover; did you see the way he reprimanded the cooks for idling when there was work to be done? In his presence however, even Su Jin was struck dumb by his beaked profile, his sharp gaze and his basic but snappy command of Korean.

Finally, with the occasional help of Dr Dong Sun as translator, Mr Sandman gave a short talk in the lobby. He introduced himself as the Company Director of VirtuWorld, the project they had graciously agreed to be a part of. He explained that Virtu meant goodness and innocence, and expressed the hope that their terrible experiences in the North would help them embrace the close-knit life of caring and sharing he and Dr Kim had planned for them all. He now wanted to play for them a special *dee-vee-dee*, narrated by Doctor Kim, to explain the ideals of VirtuWorld.

A new *dee-vee-dee*? Nothing could have excited the women more. Hushing and shushing each other, they sat enthralled as Dr Kim's familiar face appeared on the screen, welcoming them all, at last, to VirtuWorld. Mee Hee watched with her hand over her mouth as Dr Kim took them on a guided tour of this magical land, all castles and towers, silks and fine foods, fairies and princesses. VirtuWorld would be like an island in Seoul, she told them, where people would go to escape from the stresses and pressures of life. It would be a place of peace and plenty, where nothing evil ever happened, where all suffering would be eased. On this island lived special, fairy children who would enchant the people and soothe their fears. Of course the children were not really fairies, but flesh and blood humans, growing from babyhood to adults as the years went by – and this was why they, the sisters, were so important. They had all been hand-picked by Dr Che to be mothers to these precious fairy children. So that the boys and girls wouldn't have to work every day, and would have time for a real childhood, there would be many of them, at least two sets of twins for each woman, born three years apart. Although everyone would grow up together, of course, each mother would always be able to see and to hold and love their own children.

Of course they could choose not to be a part of this wonderful opportunity, in which case, jobs would be found for them in China's South Korean communities, but Doctor Kim very much hoped they would all want to stay. She would come to meet them all in their new home in the mountains of Kyonggido Province, south of Seoul, where she would explain the simple – painless – scientific proce-dure by which they all would become pregnant with their first sets of twins.

'Please,' she implored, 'come to South Korea. Let me take care of you.'

As the screen filled with an image of Dr Kim's gentle face, the quiet sound of restrained weeping spread throughout the room. Her own yearning lodged in her throat, Mee Hee turned to her sisters for reassurance: this paradise being offered to them – was it really real? Would someone please hold her hand, embrace her, say *yes, we are saved now, truly Mee Hee, saved*. But Little Sister, her eyes closed, was clutching the cross she wore around her neck. The Buddhists were chanting inaudibly, their lips moving in time with their nodding heads. Su Jin sat behind them by herself, an expression of fierce concentration on her face.

Her sisters had suffered so much, as had she. Mee Hee gazed again at Dr Kim's noble features. This fine lady had saved their lives, plucked them like grains of rice from the mouth of death. Perhaps there was a God, as Little Sister said, who called some people to him early and asked others to keep living, to keep trying to be strong. Or perhaps, as the Buddhists argued, it was her karma to have left home, to start afresh with all her sisters, to help Dr Kim. She couldn't say if she believed any of these explanations; she just knew she was alive, not buried in a shallow grave beside her son. And if she didn't keep living, who would care that he had ever existed? *No*, she thought, as she sat in the darkened room, *I have to have more children now, to tell them about their older brother Song Ju, to make sure he will not be forgotten once I myself have gone.*

Mr San-duh-man clicked the lights back on and passed around a photo of the village in Kyonggido. The women gasped over the picture: a place they already knew in their hearts, a plateau between two green mountains, on which stood a large hall with a tiled roof, surrounded by clusters of small thatched houses. The sisters would be moving there as soon as they were well enough to travel, Dr Dong Sun announced.

Then Mr San-duh-man held up a black booklet with South Korea stamped in gold on the covers: their new passports. Their own photographs would be inserted beside false names. Mr San-duh-man said they must be sure to memorise these names – this was a private enterprise, so no one in the government knew of this project.

Finally, as a special gift, he gave each of them a framed, signed photograph of Dr Kim. As the women were exclaiming how beautiful she was, Mr Sandman said goodnight and they applauded loudly as he and the doctors left the room.

Her sisters sat discussing the village – how cosy it was, how much like their old homes in the North, what a perfect place it would be to bring up children. Mee Hee fingered the carved wooden frame of her photograph of Dr Kim. One of the houses was for the doctors,

Mr Sandman had said; they would be living in the village, staying forever, to help the women with their pregnancies, and to give birth, and then to look after all the children as they grew. She tried to catch Su Jin's eye. Perhaps they could share a house together too.

But Su Jin, a stony frown on her face, was scratching a mosquito bite on her ankle. A droplet of blood rose up beneath her one long fingernail and as it smeared darkly across her leg, a sharp, bony fear nudged Mee Hee beneath the ribs. Why wouldn't Su Jin look at her? Why did she argue so much with the others? Why was she the only one who wasn't happy?

Then Su Jin looked up, stuck out her tongue at Mee Hee and started chatting to Younger Sister. Mee Hee exhaled, and pressed the photograph of Dr Kim to her chest. Why did she have to worry so much about everything? She needed to be calmer, more accepting and peaceful. She was going to place the framed picture on her bedside table, she decided, so that the doctor's tranquil face was the first thing she would see in the morning, and the last thing at night.

12 / Gongjang

Sydney danced until she was gasping for a drink, then she stepped up, panting, to the bar, where Jin Sok was talking to two stylishly dressed Korean men.

'Sy-duh-nee my new model,' he told his friends proudly. 'She live in Hongdae now. Soon be very famous. Sy-duh-nee, this Park Song P'il, owner Gongjang. This Han Jae Ho, very big artist in Korea.'

Song P'il was a wiry man with a deeply etched face and bright eyes. He was wearing a tight purple top and natty leather braces, and moved oddly, like a bird. Jae Ho was more solid and composed. Over a white T-shirt flecked with black paint he wore a blood-orange linen shirt, the sleeves rolled up to reveal strong, smooth forearms. Beneath his thick, spiky hair his dark eyes openly roamed over her.

'*Pangapsumnida*,' she said. *Pleased to meet you.* She offered her hand to Jae Ho. The artist lifted it to his lips and kissed it. The gesture was arch, but his mouth was full and sensual.

'Ooh, gentleman,' Jin Sok teased. Flustered and flattered, Sydney pulled her hand away. Song P'il peered alertly at her then, with a fetching grin, he reached behind the bar and began rapidly flicking a light switch. The blue bulbs above the DJ broke into a strobe, sending the dancers into audible convulsions. The bouncer appeared at the door. Song P'il bowed, and ducked out of the club.

'Same same,' Jin Sok said. 'Police come, need talk to. But Jae Ho buy you drink.'

'Yes, what you drink?' Jae Ho enquired. As he reached to get the bartender's attention, his linen sleeve brushed her bare arm. He was a little shorter than she was – most Korean men were – so she pulled up a stool to even the difference. His eyes exploring her face and breasts, he passed her a vodka and soda.

'Blonde hair: nice. Look green in light,' he said.

Jin Sok laughed, and she playfully punched him in the arm.

Jae Ho nodded appreciatively. 'Very violent girl. I like. How old you, Sy-duh-nee?'

It was only the nine hundredth time she been asked that since she got off the plane from Vancouver. 'Twenty,' she replied pertly, as if rapping his knuckles with a fan.

'Ah, so young. You married?' Totally boring Korean question number two.

She shook her head and waited for the inevitable cry of, 'Why not?'

But Jae Ho only raised his eyebrows, then said, 'You brave girl come Korea all by yourself.'

Sydney wrinkled her nose. 'Oh, no – I came with a friend. Then I met Jin Sok.'

'I saw her photo. Lipstick poster. Pow!' The photographer punched the air and Sydney wanted to hug him again. Just a week ago, celebrating her move, she had got pissed and tried to kiss him, but he'd just tucked her up on her bed-mat and gone to sleep beside her as if nothing had happened. In the morning he'd told her he was gay-celibate. 'I had many boyfriend, Sy-duh-nee, many years. But now I want be monk: clean inside again.' She'd never felt so safe with anyone.

'So, are you a house painter, Jae Ho?' she asked, plucking lightly at his spattered T-shirt. The fabric was thick, the best cotton, and a little damp with his sweat.

'House paint?' he frowned. Jin Sok translated, chuckling, and poked his friend in the ribs. Jae Ho got the joke, and cuffed his hand away.

'Oh, Sy-duh-nee get even! Good, good. No. Not house paint. This shirt famous in Gongjang. Is shirt I wore when I paint this.' Reaching under her, he swivelled her stool until she was looking at a square blue canvas on the wall behind her.

The painting's churning surface was divided in half by a thick black horizontal slash. Above and below this dividing mark there was something delicate, almost brocaded, about the texture of the paint that made Sydney want to reach out and trace its details with her finger. She stood up to take a closer look. Mingled within the blue brushstrokes were the imprints of long hairs, fragile wings of insects, dried petals and scraps of what looked like Korean hand-made paper, the kind Jin Sok had used in a shoot last week.

Still thinking hard, she returned to Jae Ho. 'It's amazing,' she said. 'It's like . . . a trapped soul.'

He turned to Jin Sok. 'Sy-duh-nee very intelligence girl. Very beauty too.'

She reached out lightly, fluttering her hand along his sleeve. '*Komapsumnida*, Jae Ho.' That was the formal way to say thank you. It suited her, now she was a professional model, out meeting artists in Seoul.

It was nearly four o'clock when Damien and Jake got to Gongjang. Hailing a friend, Jake pushed onto the tiny dance floor. Damien bought a bottle of water and sat down on the sofa beneath the violent, inedible jam stain on the wall. Staring at that painting would really do a number on his head tonight. He was already half-regretting his decision to take Sam's E.

The music, however, was sublime: an insinuating mix of techno-trance and battery-acid jazz. The crowd was throbbing like a blood-blister, but thinning enough to let the dancers shine. As another wave of his E high warmed his sternum, Damien rose and sidled over to Jake. A blonde girl was dancing in front of him. He tried to side-step her and she turned to face him for a moment. The impact of her smile nearly knocked him off his feet.

The room was wobbling, his head was spinning. It was like the girl had sucker-punched him, right back into that black funnel he'd spent years trying to scrabble out of. His dad was there too, gazing at a parade of blonde girls swinging by, saying sadly over and over, *That could have been our Jess, couldn't it, Damien?*

NO, NO, IT COULDN'T, DAD, Damien had always wanted to shout. No girl Damien had ever met or seen – on telly, in a magazine, in real life, wherever – none of them could ever have matched Jessica; she was peerless. And she was never going to grow up either. She would be a little girl, always. If he did manage, on occasion, to pull her image out of that black hole he kept her in, she was unchanging, but ever-shining. Like a crystal. A hard star that would never burn out.

But now, here, in front of him, Jessica had blossomed back into flesh.

Her face fixed in a tight expression of private intent, the blonde slowly rotated her hips. Her hair was streaming down her naked back, and an alto sax cajoled sweat and honey from her limbs. Then, as the music built up momentum, she started head-banging and her glinting hair filled the air. She was Jessica, grown up; Jessica concentrating; Jessica dancing; Jessica shutting out the world.

As Damien stared, a Korean skinhead moved in close to the blonde and raised his sculptured arms above his head. As if feeding off each other's energy, they twisted and touched, grooving, shimmying, shaking, bumping hips.

A dancer pushed past Damien to the bar, jolting him out of his trance. He reached into the sea of bodies, wrenched Jake off the dance floor and pressed his mouth to his friend's ear. 'Jake, that girl, right there, see her?'

'Yesh, mate, I shee her, oh by Jove, I shertainly do,' Jake slurred.

'Do you know her?' Damien tried not to shout.

'Good grief! Itsh my maiden auntie!'

'No, really, is she a friend of anyone's?' He didn't care that he sounded desperate.

'I wish; I can but wish.' His eyes rolling around like marbles, Jake beamed down the cleavage of a girl in front of him.

Feeling ridiculous, Damien let go of his friend, but Jake moved in closer. 'Looksh like she's got a boyfriend, old chap. Shome of them do go native, y'know.'

'She just looked familiar, that's all,' Damien muttered.

Jake clapped him on the back. 'She'sh a model, goofus. She'sh on all the VidAds. In gold make-up? You must've sheen her a million times.'

He peered at her again through the crowd: yeah, Jake was right, she was the GrilleTex™ girl. He just hadn't recognised her without the gold leaf plastered all over her face.

Fuck it – minor celebs, who needed 'em? And what was the point of meeting her, anyway? Why risk getting himself wound up over Jessica all over again? Since he'd got into the swing of things in Seoul he'd had just one dream about her and then nothing, nada, no more screaming in his head, no more vast empty feelings in his gut . . . And really, he was happy to let things stay that way.

He let Jake pull him back onto the dance floor as the model and her Korean boyfriend hugged and headed over to the bar.

As the night wore on the music segued from Nu-Destruction tinged with soul to disco dipped in cream. All Damien wanted to do was lose himself on the dance floor, but it felt as if he were hypnotised: he just couldn't stop watching the blonde model flirt with her Korean friends. Okay, she was younger than Jessica would be now, but she was his sister to a T: everything from the tip of her nose to the angles of her elbows. That was Jessica bossing the boys about; Jessica singing along to a pop song; Jessica hugging the huge white teddy bear on the stool underneath the speaker. Like a record stylus skidding out of control, Damien's mind lurched between the nightclub in front of him and a distant place he'd once called home.

With a start, he realised he was crying. *Crying?* This was too much – this wasn't normal. He was on *E*, for fuck's sake; he was supposed to feel *ecstatic*. But he was sweating now, a burning, freezing sweat that dripped sour sizzling droplets down his chest and into his stomach. *His stomach.* Oh no – oh yes—

Damien barged into the men's bog, elbowed aside a Korean surf-punk and spewed up into a sink. The jet of vomit seared the back of his throat, but instantly his head felt clearer and his stomach light as air. He rinsed his mouth out, then the sink, and stared at himself in the mirror. *Christ, Day, don't go psycho on me now. Breathe. That's better. Take a chill-pill. Breathe.*

Back in the club, the skinhead and his friends were propping up the bar by themselves, watching the blonde as she returned to the dance floor alone. Calmly, Damien wove his way back to the sofa to find his bottle of water. The blonde was about twenty, he reckoned. She was very cute, but she had a boyfriend. And it wasn't her fault she looked like his dead twin sister. He had to leave her well alone.

'Hey, Dames, wanna share a cab home?' Jake slurred in his ear, and yeah, it was probably time to go. But then an ancient, way-too-loud Blur song sawed the air in two and the blonde was prancing right in front of them, promising to do all the boys . . .

'That's your cue, buddy,' Jake snickered.

'Nah,' Damien muttered, but Jake gave him a wicked sidelong smile and a shove.

He staggered into the blonde's arms. She pushed him off her. They made eye-contact. Her glance punched him in the heart, but she just kept grinning and twirling, and behind him, Jake cackled with laughter.

The tight weave of the crowd had loosened and all those remaining in the nightclub were able at last to survey the spaces between each other, to assess the multiplicity of ways that emptiness could shift and loop and morph. Blur drowned in the oceanic currents of deep house, and the music, impure and never simple, at last attained a lustrous peace. As Damien danced with the blonde, a monumental black man, a techno-titan, shimmied around them, birthing new worlds of music and movement from the drops of sweat he wiped from his brow. A lean Korean taunted the room, two green Glo-sticks never still for a moment in his hands. A posse of skateboarding dudes kept the flow above and below, while an Indian woman in a tight black and white dress brandished her cigarette like a torch light of approval.

Chucking up had been the best thing he'd done in weeks. Damien's high was subliminal now. He lifted his bottle of water to his lips and the blonde stretched out her hand – to request a sip or to drench herself with the whole thing; he didn't care. She tipped her head back too quickly, spilling water down her chin, then she smiled and rolled her eyes and wiped away the shining liquid with the back of her hand.

'Thanks,' she mouthed, and he recovered sufficiently to smile back as she waved him goodbye, slipping back through the crowd to her barstool and her three creepy friends. Then Jake was pulling at his sleeve: time to go. Yeah, while he was still glowing, floating, radiating love, charged with awe at the amazing powers of a Universe that resurrected people, brought them back to you in all their beauty and glory. His panic ten minutes previously felt like a million years ago. And now it all made sense, why he'd dreamed about Jessica, why she'd followed him on to that Han Air flight. She'd been telling him to watch out – he was destined to meet *this girl*.

It was six-thirty and Sydney was out on the street again, blinking in the woozy light. Jin Sok flagged a taxi and offered her a ride, but she knew where she was and her flat was only ten minutes' walk away. He kissed her goodbye, jumped in and was gone.

Savouring the sight of the cotton-puff clouds in the east, she stopped for a moment on the steps of a designer clothing shop. She was just about to move on when someone slid an arm across her shoulders and stuck a small, stiff thumb in her mouth.

Her heart pounding, she twisted around. Jae Ho was behind her, chuckling. 'I sorry, Sy-duh-nee. I frighten you?'

'No,' she lied, adrenalin racing through her body. But he wasn't threatening her. He was Jin Sok's friend, his eyes twinkling as he watched her recompose herself, and as she jutted out her chin and assessed his stance in return, she felt the shock to her system transform into the slow burn of interest.

He looked good in the daylight. Fit and alert. Impulsively, she stroked his T-shirt. His stomach was broad and hard beneath the soft cotton. Laughing, he grasped her wrist and dragged her hand down to his groin; she gasped, and pulled away. He let go. Held her gaze. It was a dare. She reached for his thumb, pulled it to her mouth and bit the firm tip.

'Ni-suh, Sy-duh-nee,' he approved, pulling her to him by the waist. 'So bad girl.'

'Bad girl? Me?' She dropped his hand and placed her palms on his shoulders, her breasts skimming his chest.

'I watch you dance,' he whispered hoarsely. 'You very much alive in your body, I think.' He pushed her back a little, frankly admiring her, and she felt something secret loosen between her legs. 'And you have very detailed mind,' he continued, nudging her into the doorway of the shop.

'Here?' They were only partially hidden from the boulevard, but he reached into her dress, grappled with her bra and coaxed out one of her breasts. Her knees buckled.

'Ahh. You smell Summer Passion.' He bent his head to suck greedily on the puckered nipple.

She closed her eyes, moaned and gripped his shoulders. She wanted him to take all her weight, lift her from the ground, into his arms.

'Here?' he urged, his other hand kneading her bottom, fingers inching down towards her wet panties. 'You cannot come to my house, Sy-duh-nee. I married.'

He was getting taller, she was getting shorter, curling into his chest. He was kissing her neck. But . . . 'You married?' she repeated stupidly, pushing him away. Of course he was; he was Korean, after all.

'I married, but I want free.' He cocked his head and pressed his groin against hers. 'What you think? Do you want sex?'

Yes she did, she did want sex, quite badly as it happened. 'We can go to my place,' she said. I live round the corner.'

'Solo?'

'*Ne*, solo.'

'Is artist style,' he said, pinching her nose. He rearranged her clothes. He held her hand all the way home.

13 / Passion Show

His flight got in at eleven a.m., but Johnny didn't bother to call. Sydney would be crashed out in bed with her sexy clubbing clothes still on; he figured he'd just crawl in beneath the covers and give her a rude awakening. Then he'd whisk her back out to the airport for an evening flight to Thailand. He had a suite booked at the Phuket Hilton to start, then they'd head to a smaller island. Man-o-man, he needed some sex on the beach.

In the black cab from the airport back to Itaewon he fired off a few quick self-congratulatory emails from his MoPho – it couldn't hurt to remind people there was only one Johnny Sandman, only one key operative capable of dealing with every last bullet point on the agenda. Even Kim had to admit that no one else in Asia could have co-ordinated PAT. The multiple bribes necessary to ensure the smooth completion of Project Aid Truck had required every ounce of his considerable political and administrative expertise, but thanks to months of his bullying, account-laundering and string-pulling, thirty North Korean women had now been smuggled across the Chinese border to Beijing, taken from their villages in the false bottoms of International Aid trucks. Not one had been lost in the border crossings, where summary execution was always the outcome of capture.

And who'd flown out to meet and greet? *Who else but Johnny Sandman?* he thought, pressing Send for the fifth time. Certainly no one from that bunch of lousy pen-pushers and conference junkies had volunteered: no one else in fucking ConGlam or GRIP ever got off their asses and out into the field – except Kim, of course. That must be why she hated him so much. Territorial bitch. Well, the Doc couldn't get on his case about *any* aspect of this trip – in fact, even she would have to give him a little, heh heh, *PAT* on the back. For thanks to his logistical genius and considerable personal charm, arrangements were now in place for thirty happy peasants and their medics to travel on to a safe house in Kyonggido, an hour south of Seoul – a place he himself had sourced, if he recalled correctly.

He had also, he informed his boss in LA, gained the trust of the surrogates. With his clean-cut features and dirty-blond hair Johnny Sandman was the Hollywood face of their new future, and in this role of Western hero he had overseen the tiniest details of their care. Two of them had pneumonia, but wouldn't touch pharmaceuticals – they said it would be bad for the babies – so expensive herbalists had been engaged. Another woman needed major dental work, which had had to be booked. The rest of them had traipsed around the hotel after him, giggling behind their hands whenever he cast them as much as a stray glance. By the time he'd shown them the video, the ladies were all Silly Putty in his hands. Beijing might have been a hassle at times, but it had also been a golden test of Johnny Sandman's new powers of Empathy and Persuasion.

Admittedly, the success of the trip did away with his last excuse for not bringing Sydney into the picture yet, and it was way too late to find another girl now. He'd been thinking positive, though, during the long nights in that crap Beijing hotel. They hadn't been getting on too bad lately. Okay, she quite wasn't as down and dirty in the sack as he liked, but a guy could always play away occasionally. And sure, she'd been driving him crazy with her moods and sulks ever since she got that OhmEgo job, but between the OxyPops and his anger transformation techniques he'd managed to soothe things over – those training sessions with Andrew Beacon had been worth every red cent ConGlam had paid for them.

The taxi was crossing the river. He switched off his MoPho and leaned back in his seat. Things were on track. Johnny Sandman was moving on up. And what a journey it had been.

Of course he'd been furious when they'd ordered him to go to Vancouver for the *Moving from Anger to Passion* course – what kind of a hokey dumbass did they take him for? The Sandman didn't sit around discussing his shitty childhood with a bunch of no-hoper losers, no fucking way – but the head honchos had been firm on this matter. They didn't want him to 'lose his edge', they'd said; not lose his cool quite so often or so dramatically. He'd been pissed when they'd alluded to the Incident – which they *knew* was really just 'Natural Exuberance' – but then, just as the fumes were seeping out of his nostrils, they'd thrown in the sweeteners. He'd get a big bonus if he brought the Queen of the Peonies back with him – the Doc was demanding a girl with no social network in Seoul, so he could see it made sense to recruit her in Canada. Plus, if he came back to Korea with Beacon's certificate he'd get not only the raise but a new title: Head of Korean Operations. He'd be doing the same shit as before – schmoozing, grooving and opening up new markets – but with a hefty pay increase, and the responsibility of overseeing the two new projects for a minimum of five years.

Johnny had visualised the business card: 'Johnny Sandman, HKO'. It sounded good; he'd agreed and they'd shaken on it. And later, on the plane to Vancouver, he'd thought: why not Head of South-East Asian Ops? The current post-holder was in his sixties and had racked up luxury offices and apartments in Tokyo, Hong Kong, Beijing and Bangkok, plus a retirement package to die for. All Johnny had to do was manage his five-year profit margin to spec and keep that uppity

Dr Kim in line and then the sky was the limit. Obviously ConGlam thought he had long-term potential or they wouldn't have been investing shitloads in this top guru course, complete with five-star hotel accommodation.

He'd been surprised to discover that Beacon wasn't some tired old hippie but young, well-built and well-tailored. *Raking up the past*, he'd said on that first day, *was a discredited therapeutic method*. His technique was all about reprogramming the psyche by internalising key phrases: 'paint your big picture'; 'impress with passion, not your fist': concepts which had gradually started to make sense, even 'own your own errors', initially the hardest to accept. *Hey, the Sandman don't make mistakes*, he'd told Beacon during the *Moving from Regret to Redemption* session, *and if you say sorry for the unknown unknowns, you'll end up shitting law suits: everyone knows that.*

'Human relationships aren't all legal contracts, though, are they?' Beacon had replied. 'Often taking emotional responsibility for your behaviour is in fact disarming: it dissolves blame and lets you both—?'

He'd opened his arms and embraced the room.

'Play a New Game!' the other participants had chanted. The saddos were all clutching copies of Beacon's book; they'd obviously been up all night reading it.

'But that's not what I'm saying,' Johnny had insisted. 'I'm saying, what if you didn't do anything wrong?'

'Johnny, try looking at it this way: saying sorry doesn't necessarily mean accepting blame for a situation. It can just mean that you feel sad that the other person feels bad; or that you're angry with a general situation that caused their upset. It can be an *empathic* statement. And Empathy—' He'd pointed his finger at the group again.

'—Opens Emotional Doors!'

Johnny hadn't ever thought of the word 'sorry' like that before –

in fact, the word hadn't really ever figured in his vocabulary. But Beacon had made him spend the day saying it to people: 'I'm sorry that your flight was delayed'; 'I'm sorry you had a rough meeting'; 'I'm sorry that your grandmother died'; right up to 'I'm sorry that you're mad at me'. He sort of got the client-and-colleague role-plays; anything that impinged on business one might reasonably expect to feel annoyed about. The more personal exchanges, though, he found ridiculous: why the fuck would he feel sad that some old woman he'd never met had kicked the bucket? And the trick to saying 'I'm sorry that you're mad at me' without taking blame was, apparently, to say it warmly, and that didn't come easily at all. But that lunchtime he'd taken himself out to the park across the road and suddenly, as he was doing his power walk, it had clicked: *showing empathy was a way of getting people to trust you* – or, like Beacon said, of opening doors. And it was far more energy-efficient to walk through an open door than to kick it down. By the end of the day he'd got 'I'm sorry' down pat.

Later, when things had started getting tense with Sydney, he'd tried to put the strategy into practice. It wasn't always easy, especially if she'd really punched his buttons, and sometimes she wouldn't accept an apology unless he also took blame, but he'd been amazed to discover that if he did grit his teeth and choke the words out, she usually calmed right down. Fuck, if he'd known that years ago, he might've ended up getting hitched to Veronica instead of having a restraining order against him in two states. Looking back – as, despite himself, he'd found himself doing on Beacon's course – the end of that relationship had not been Johnny Sandman's finest hour. But hey, Veronica was fine now. He'd Googled her one night and discovered she was married with two-point-five kids and running some sort of dog boutique in Buttfuck, Texas. Clearly, Johnny and Ronnie had not been meant to be. But seeing her Facebook photo

– her with her family – a strange mix of feelings had stirred in him: a weird relief that she was okay; followed by a counter-attacking surge of conviction that she'd always been just dandy, that he'd done nothing wrong except love a cheating bitch who had fucked the whole town whenever he was off on his tours of service. Underneath both of these reactions, he realised later in a long, halting, private session with Andrew Beacon, was a new kind of jealousy.

He used to be jealous of the guys Veronica flirted with. Now, he realised, he was jealous of *her*.

'Jealous of her? Why do you think that is?' Beacon had asked.

'Fuck, man, I dunno – 'cause I want to give fucking Chihuahuas Brazilians all day?'

Beacon had waited. He was good at waiting.

'I guess because she's found someone,' Johnny had found himself muttering at last. Fuck, this was embarrassing.

'Someone special.'

'Someone who'll put up with her, more like.'

'Do you think you can do that too if you want? Find someone?'

'Look, Beacon' – he'd needed to make one thing clear – 'I never wanted to before – not after Ronnie, anyway. Out in Asia, it's sex-on-a-stick, man, hookers or girls – *women*, whatever – who are dying to swivel on a big Western cock.'

'But now you feel differently?'

'I guess – no . . . I dunno.'

Beacon had pressed the tips of his fingers together the way he did when he was about to go off on one. 'What's your big picture, Johnny?'

At least that had been easy to figure out: 'I want the jobs ConGlam is grooming me for by sending me on this fucking touchy-feely course. I want to be ConGlam HKO, and in five years' time Head of SEA Ops.'

'Good, good: excellent clarity and focus. Now, why do you want those jobs?'

'Because I want people to know Johnny Sandman isn't some thug who got lucky with a few trend-spotting predictions. I'm a fucking genius, I know the Korean markets like the back of my hand, and I want people to show me some fucking respect.'

'You want people to see that you're special.'

'Damn right I do.'

'And maybe you want a woman to see that you're special too? To recognise not just your talents, but the whole you?'

'Women? Women are a fucking nightmare. You buy them shit; you give them head; they take off with some Mexican waiter.' He'd laughed, but Beacon hadn't joined in.

'Sometimes, Johnny, the big picture has aspects that are initially out of focus, but they get clearer as time goes on. As you continue to transform your anger, you may find that you will want a female companion to share your new passionate energy with. Or you may decide that a wife might be a career asset: someone to help you with social networking. But even stay-at-home wives can be demanding, and trigger old anger patterns. I sense you're in a transition stage; you may not be ready to think about this yet, but if in the future you want to come back for our "Relationships: Moving from Difficult to Different" seminar, as you've taken this course, you or your company would get a twenty per cent discount.'

Beacon was a hustler, straight down the line; Johnny liked that about him. They'd left it there, but that night, looking down at Sydney as she was sleeping, Johnny had wondered if maybe this girl wasn't just a hot property he was importing to Seoul, a sparky stray with no family, just what the Doc had ordered. It hadn't been the easiest of assignments, but he'd risen to the challenge, asking for a girl new to the agency, and specifying no college education. *I like a girl to have some innocence about her still – real innocence, if you know what I mean*, he'd said. *Of course I do, sir, and we have just the young lady for you*, the woman had replied. And woah, he'd struck gold.

Sydney was just a kid, really; anyone could tell she wasn't a seasoned ho. No anal, no threesomes, no drugs, got drunk after three glasses of wine, and he'd had to remind her more than once to stick her pinkie up his ass during her enthusiastic but less-than-accomplished BJs. But whatever. She could learn all the sex tricks; he could teach her those. Because maybe Sydney was someone a little bit special – someone who might hang around for a change, look good on his arm at top-brass events, make the bosses feel jealous, even. If things went as planned, she'd be working with him for the next twenty years, after all.

So he'd tried extra-hard to make her laugh; he had bought her a teddy bear; cuddled her. And the day she said she'd think about coming back to Korea, he had gone back to his hotel feeling tense as a murder suspect waiting for the jury to deliver the verdict. But he couldn't beg her. No, that wasn't Johnny Sandman's style. He'd gone to the gym, worked out for hours, swum hundreds of lengths, and the answer had come to him: *serenade her*. The next night he'd sung her his favourite Sinatra song and lo and behold, she'd fallen for it. Fallen for *him*.

Vancouver had obviously been the honeymoon period. Once he was back in Seoul things had been tougher. He'd had to consult the MAP Workbook regularly, taking it out from the back of the closet when Sydney was out at her modelling sessions or the gym. Her meeting that Jin Sok character had been a real test, but it was true that the photographer was gay; he'd had him checked out. Sydney was his now. They had their ups and downs, but according to Beacon, every couple did.

As the taxi entered Itaewon he drummed his fingers on the arm-rest, trying to resolve the issue of the ConGlam contract in his mind.

The way to play it was like this: once they'd got to Thailand he'd tell Sydney about the Project, and he'd also tell her about his own prospects with ConGlam. He'd say sorry for being uptight before China, and he'd promise that things would be very different once they were both flying high in the company, both relaxed, happy and focused. The bottom line was this: they were tigers in the sack together, they looked good together in photos, and they were going to make a fucking fortune. What girl was going to argue with that?

'I love my wife.' Jae Ho was perched on the edge of Sydney's sofa, smiling as if he had just seen a fish jumping or a falling star. 'She . . . good spirit.'

It didn't sound like a passionate assessment to Sydney. She stopped fiddling with the CD player and squeezed in beside him. He stroked her thigh, almost tentatively.

Wondering if he was having second thoughts, she said nothing.

'You very soft,' he told her, his hand lingering beneath the hemline of her dress. 'Korean sophists write soft is *Eum. Eum, Yang.* You know?'

Sophists? 'You mean Yin Yang?'

'No, not Yin Yang,' he said, waving his hand emphatically, 'Yin Yang *Japan* story. In Korea, everything *Eum Yang.*' He sprang up and pointed to the florescent bulb above them. It was off – the wiring was broken, but she hated florescent lights, so she hadn't tried to fix it. 'Light now *Eum*,' he announced. Jauntily stepping over to the switch, he flicked it. Nothing happened.

'Sydney light always *Eum*,' he giggled.

She jumped up and plugged in her string of fairy-lights. The little bulbs lit up, almost invisible in the dawn light. 'Now is *Yang*?' she asked.

'Yes, but is very *Eum*-style *Yang*. Why you buy this light?' he demanded. Koreans had a way of asking why you had done something as simple as cutting your hair as they were accusing you of some unspeakable crime.

'Because is pretty,' she said, sitting back down.

'Ah.' He smiled indulgently. Roaming about her apartment, he scrutinised every postcard she had tacked to the walls. Sydney took the opportunity to admire not only him but also her new home: one spacious room with balcony windows and a long corridor lined with closets. Its primrose-yellow, verdigris and peach colour scheme had looked erratic at first, but it melded surprisingly well. She had furnished the place sparingly, buying a sofa, a round coffee table, a silk bed-mat and cushions. The sheets on the bed-mat were a little crumpled, the pillows in disarray; a fashion magazine lay opened on the floor beside her ashtray: otherwise the place was just too new to be untidy.

'This very good fortune!' the painter cried, picking up a little pink plastic pig Jin Sok had given her. You keep by bed. If you dream of pig, you go out and buy ticket for money game. Yes!'

'A lottery ticket?' She giggled as Jae Ho bowed over her bed-mat and placed the pig carefully on her pillow beside the teddy bear she had, at the last minute, decided to take with her from Johnny's place.

'Sydney.' He waltzed back over to the sofa and sat down beside her. 'I want ask you question.'

'Yes?' She pressed her leg against his.

'Self-sex?'

'Huh?' Were they going to fuck, or not?

'Self-sex – sometimes you make?'

Oh . . . 'Sometimes.' She stretched out her fingers and he regarded them with interest.

'I want watch.' He pinched her thigh, sending a quick dart of pleasure to her clit. So that would turn him on? Well, it would be easy enough to oblige.

'I want lie on bed,' she said, 'is how I always do it.'

He lit a cigarette as she rearranged herself on the *yo*. She picked the pig and teddy up from the pillow and set them on the floor, then peeled off her panties and hitched her dress up around her waist, watching him through half-lidded eyes as her fingers fell into their familiar routine. He assessed her through wreaths of smoke, his legs apart, rubbing himself through the strange fabric of his pants. The motion of his fist made a faintly abrasive sound. For the first time she noticed that, against all Korean custom, he was wearing his black leather boots in her home. She whimpered and pulled off her dress. Then she undid her bra, tossed it aside, and returned to the wet place between her legs.

He rose from the sofa and stepped on her thigh, lightly, but with enough pressure to bend it back against the bed. She strained against his weight, trying to hoist her hips into the air. He laughed and inched his foot down to her knee, then, one leg at a time, tugged off his boots, then his trousers. Kneeling either side of her throat now, pinning her arms to the bed, he threw the trousers over her face. They rustled synthetically, smelling of sweat and smoke, then, just as alarm was rising in her torso, they were gone, pushed aside, and she was gazing up at the reassuring bulge in his fire-engine-red Y-fronts.

'Good girl – you good girl, Sy-duh-ney,' he whispered, lowering himself down her body, roughly displacing her hands from her clit. He hadn't watched her masturbate at all, but whatever he wanted was fine, just fine. The edges of his shirt trailed over her skin as his cock nudged at her lips. Lost in the sensations, she spread her legs even further apart, aching for deeper penetration, impossible through his underwear, but inevitable, she could tell. He pried her apart with his fingers, nuzzling into her, a foretaste of fullness. Then he pulled off his underwear and his naked body towered over her, his torso plush muscle, his cock erect and quivering.

'Do you like my little man?' he asked.

His taut scrotum was nestled in long silky tufts of black hair and his cock was a colour she'd never seen before: a gorgeous purplish bruise-brown, entwined with thick, twisty veins blue as rivers in an ancient map.

'I like him very much,' she whispered.

The only way to stop staring was to take him in her mouth where he fit perfectly, his smooth head nudging into her relaxed throat as her tongue massaged his rigid length. But then he withdrew and, swinging his hips down between her spread open legs, entered her point-blank.

Yes.

No – not ever!

Yes, but . . .

She reached out for the box by her bed mat, 'Hey, I have—'

He paused. Touched her face. 'Is okay, Sy-duh-nee. No problem.'

No problem? Really? In the time it took her to absorb his tender tone, his slow thrusts developed a searching rhythm, and a huge, slippery sense of longing rose up in her. Was this what *real* sex was like? Without rules, without limits, instinctive; *trusting* the feelings? Being close, *so close* to a man. Why couldn't she experience that, just once? He wasn't a *client*, he was someone she *wanted*.

She couldn't think anymore. Her body was hauling her over the brink of resistance to the hot edge of tears. She flung her legs up around his back and manoeuvred her body to allow him deeper. Grunting, he pushed her knees apart, lifting his hips to gain access, and fucked her faster, then, grabbing her buttocks and hoisting her upwards, he pushed in from a new angle. Yelping, she threw her hips up to his. She'd never desired a man so much, ever in her life.

With that realisation she entered another dimension, a wet, sliding place where there was no separation between his body and hers.

When at last he grabbed her breast and devoured her nipple, something detonated deep inside her. She yowled, almost in disbelief, as the orgasm radiated throughout her body.

The sunlit peak mutated into a plateau of dazed contentment. Moaning softly, she opened her eyes. Jae Ho was smiling down at her like an elf, like a genie, like no man she had ever met before. She ran her finger up the ridge that started at his sternum and split his broad abdomen in two. His MoPho rang in his trouser pocket beside her head. Gently, he resumed his probing.

'No babies,' she ordered, forming a cross with her hands on her belly. He nodded, picked up speed, then swiftly pulled out and shot his cum all over her hip.

Afterwards they lay still and quiet in a thin sheen of sweat.

'Short, I think,' he said.

Had it been quick? It had seemed timeless. 'No,' she replied, sleepily, 'very nice.'

'Western man very long,' Jae Ho insisted, holding his hands about nine inches apart. 'Asian man short.'

In her blissed-out semi-doze it was hard to think what to say. Sure she liked big cocks, but she had to be turned on to enjoy them – and with Jae Ho she'd been so excited she'd hardly noticed his size. And now – unlike a guy who thought he was God's gift but couldn't even get it up all the time – instead of rolling over and starting to snore, he was talking to her, stroking her, sounding anxious to have pleased her. *That* was sexy.

She reached up and tickled his nose. 'Western men all different. Size not important, anyway.'

'I think you lying.' He sat up on his elbow and examined her intently.

'I am not—' She turned toward him, and he gasped.

'Sydney have belly!' he announced. 'Like Vietnam pot-belly pig!'

133

Jeez, what a way to change the subject. 'Thanks a lot!' she protested, but he was rubbing her tummy and poking his finger in her belly button.

'I like belly,' he declared. 'Very woman shape.'

Lots of guys liked curves on girls; she knew that from her escort days. She gave his hand a little slap. 'Woman, okay. Pig no!'

'Okay. Sydney my piglet,' he decided, as she twisted round and snuggled her bum into his lap. He cupped her tummy as they spooned, like Johnny sometimes used to do. It had always felt nice, comforting, until he'd started telling her to *stop fucking worrying about the fucking designers*, and they'd get into a fight. Jae Ho didn't know anything about her job issues, and he didn't need to. He was a beautiful break from all that. Stroking his fingers, she yawned and closed her eyes.

When his MoPho rang again he rose abruptly, and dressed. Before he left he clutched her breast for a moment, smiled as he had done at the fairy-lights, then kissed her lightly goodbye.

'See you soon, Sy-duh-ney.'

'See you soon, Jae Ho,' she whispered. She flopped back on her pillow as the door closed, hugging herself with glee.

She'd slept with an *artist*. He'd talked to her, asked her how she felt. He didn't even know how gorgeous he was. She was never again going to sleep with some thick dolt just because he had money. Soon she would be appearing in her first-ever runway show; soon she would be friends with designers and scientists and having a mad torrid affair with a painter. From now on she was *in charge* of her own life.

As the cab drew across the river Johnny felt the anticipation rising. He took the stairs two at a time.

'Herrrrrrre's Johnny . . .' he announced.

To an empty apartment.

The living room was silent, the bed un-slept in. Where the fuck was she? Was she fucking *fucking* somebody else? Where was all her *junk*? He flung open the wardrobe: nothing but empty hangers dangling and jangling on her side. He banged open the door to the en-suite. All her toiletries were gone.

'*Sydney*,' he shouted. He sounded ridiculous, he knew it, and shut up. She was gone. Had Kim fucking taken her? Blood pulsing in his temples, he stormed back into the living room. Half the CDs were missing, but the blanket on the sofa was mussed up and the remote lay where she usually left it, as if she might wander back from the toilet at any minute and turn the TV on.

His gut twisted and a lump bulged in his throat. Just for a second a hot prickle darted around his eyes. Fuck, was the Sandman *crying*? He wiped his face roughly with his sleeve. No, he was just exhausted – and, it had to be admitted, outmanoeuvred.

That bitch Da Mi must have stepped in. But in so doing, she had overstepped big time. He just had to let Sydney know he was back, that she could come home. He grinned. Kim didn't know what Sydney was like when she wanted something bad. There was no way she'd be able to keep the girl against her will.

He switched his MoPho back on and called Sydney. Out of service – of course she was. He'd have to call Kim, demand the new number – but first he needed a drink: Johnny Walker Black Label, a double, on the rocks.

The note was on the kitchen table beside a stack of his Andrew Beacon books and a pile of jewellery: Sydney's Gotcha Watch and the six pairs of EarRings he'd given her.

Johnny. I'M SORRY you got so mad at me all the time. I'M SORRY I don't want to work for your

stupid clients any more. I'M SORRY I hate your sicko porn. I'M SORRY things didn't work out. I'M SORRY I just want to do things MY WAY for a change.
    xx SYDNEY xx

His chest heaving, his hands shaking, Johnny poured himself a stiff shot of Scotch and sat down. Light filtered between the shutters on the windows, scoring sharp lines down the centre of the kitchen table. His Gotcha rang. He let it. He finished his drink. Then he listened to the message from Kim.

'Good morning, Mr Sandman. I gather all went well in Beijing. Congratulations.' Her voice was pointedly monotonous. 'In your absence and after consultation with your superiors, it was decided that GRIP would take over the negotiations with your Canadian candidate. She has arranged independent living arrangements and is now under our protection. Under no circumstances are you to contact her in any way. To do so would be grounds for instant dismissal. Please call me to discuss your own revised role in future proceedings. I look forward to speaking to you soon.'

So Kim *had* organised the bolt-hole. Fuck. Fuck. Fuck. *Fuck.*

Johnny threw open the shutters and hurled Sydney's accessories out of the window. Then he ripped up the note and tore the Beacon books into pieces and pitched them down to the street as well. After smashing all the dishes against the kitchen wall, destroying the chairs and slashing the mattress in the bedroom to shreds with a carving knife, he polished off the Johnny Walker bottle and passed out on the sofa for nine hours.

He woke up hungry, still monumentally pissed off, but not displeased. Fuck Beacon. Fuck empathy. Fuck *opening doors.*

Part Three

GROOMING

14 | Gene Genie

'Sy-duh-nee, Supermodel, Gentlewoman – Your eyes like green fish – You moving super-shocking tidal wave.' Tapping his chest, Jin Sok beamed over Sydney's shoulder as she peeled off her false eyelashes. 'My know-how – you style. So natural. Super Natural.' Sydney twisted round and flung herself into his arms, almost knocking a bunch of mauve roses out of his hand.

The Hyatt show had been a stunning success. The OhmEgo designers had tarted her up in strawberry and lemon-lime Lycra, strapped her feet into stilettos, ripped her hems and torn her bodices to shreds. She'd thrust her way down to the end of the catwalk for the very first time, swinging her right arm slightly higher than her left, just as Jin Sok had instructed her, and when she'd reached the end she'd leaned into the audience, her hands on hips, prying the air with her tongue. People had clapped. They had actually *clapped*. On her second and third forays she'd played it coy – winking, undoing one top button, snapping her skirt – only to return for her fourth and final appearance with a full-blown pirouette. The applause had gone on and on, rippling around the room like an ocean of love. Yes, *love*. Backstage the designers had hugged her, *Korea loves you*, they had said. Now she was glowing with exhilaration. She was also starving, but just like before the show, there was no food in the dressing room.

'Sydney. Darling. You were *amazing*. You positively *exuded* happiness up there.' A warm familiar voice gushed into the room. Sydney disentangled herself from Jin Sok's bear-hug and swivelled around into an enormous bunch of fat pink peonies.

'Da Mi! Where are you?' she laughed.'

Da Mi emerged from behind the flowers. 'Here I am, darling. Straight from the front row.'

Sydney carefully placed the frilly peonies next to the roses on the make-up ledge. 'Da Mi,' she said proudly, 'this is my best friend in Seoul, Park Jin Sok. He's the best fashion photographer in Korea. Jin Sok, this is Dr Kim Da Mi. She's a top Korean-American scientist.'

'*Pangapsumnida*.' The two Koreans spoke as one, smoothly exchanging name-cards. Then one of Jin Sok's assistants poked her head around the door and rattled off something in Korean.

'See you in lobby, yes?' he apologised.

'*Anneyong!*' Sydney blew Jin Sok a kiss, then clasped Da Mi's hand. 'I'm so glad you're here,' she whispered. 'I want to talk to you about GRIP. I've moved into my new apartment and I need as much work as possible.'

Da Mi squeezed Sydney's hand. 'How exciting. I have a great project right now that pays exceptionally well. Why don't you come round for dinner tomorrow night to discuss it?'

'Fantastic – Jeez, I'm so hungry now, I could eat a whale!'

A few minutes later, surrounded by babbling hordes of fashionistas, media junkies and Seoul celebs, Sydney was munching on canapés with Da Mi in the hotel bar. She lifted her champagne glass, about to make a toast, when Da Mi took a small plastic bottle out of her purse and squeezed a drop of clear liquid into her glass.

'What's that? Pollen?'

'An anti-diuretic – it counters the dehydrating effects of alcohol. So you can drink all you like without getting a hangover. Would you like to try it?'

Sydney stuck out her own crystal flute. 'Sure!'

Glasses in hand, she and Da Mi inched across the hotel bar to a knot of people with Jin Sok at its centre. Sydney pulled him aside. 'All clear?' she whispered.

Jin Sok grinned. 'Mr Johnny at Trance tonight, has date with drag queen. A real woman for Mr Johnny tonight!'

'My ex is back from his business trip,' Sydney explained to Da Mi. 'I'm a bit worried he might show up looking for me.'

'He come here, I kick him onto street.' Jin Sok flexed his biceps and pulled a Popeye face. Sydney rolled her eyes and took another sip of champagne. As congratulations and gossip swirled around her she relaxed for the first time since her night with Jae Ho, for, unless he was hiding behind a pillar, Johnny was not among the chic and wealthy crowd filling the Hyatt bar. Neither, however, was Jae Ho, but though Sydney longed to ask Jin Sok about the painter, she didn't dare. She'd casually mentioned him a few days ago, only to be told how beautiful, kind, and intelligent his wife was. She wasn't sure if Jin Sok knew about her escapade, or if he was simply warning her that Jae Ho was off-limits, but she had quickly changed the subject.

Maybe it was greedy to expect to see him so soon. For now, she let the Hyatt festivities fill her to the brim. It was three a.m. before she tumbled out of a taxi and entered her apartment building, carrying armfuls of flowers into the elevator and up to her new home.

Da Mi sent a black cab round to pick her up at half past seven the next evening. Grateful for the air-con, Sydney settled into the creamy leather backseat and turned her full-skirted baby-blue GrilleTex™ dress up to body-temperature and her MoPho to her favourite playlist. As the Mercedes slipped through Hongdae's maze of back alleys she nodded along to the latest Europop froth, staring through the tinted

windows at the multicoloured pub and club signs, the street-sellers'
silver chains and bracelets and the shining eyes of post-happy hour
tourists and Korean teens.

The taxi turned north, accelerating smoothly up the eight-lane
expressway towards the mountains. The music was all echoey and
industrial now, almost as if the MoPho knew she was driving between
massive office buildings and warehouses. Da Mi had told her to have
a comfortable ride, so Sydney opened the drinks cabinet behind the
driver's seat and mixed herself a dry martini. She didn't really like
gin, but martinis always looked so sophisticated, and she wanted to
train her taste buds to accept them. She managed the second sip
without flinching. Ahead, the rocky jaws of Seoul's mountain parks
chewed up the pale, blank sky.

The road followed an ancient wall between two craggy slopes and
then descended into a valley thick with trees and large, Western-
style houses, half-hidden by brick walls of their own. Finally the
driver pulled up in front of a high iron gate set into a barricade
crested with foot-long shards of glass.

Even as Sydney wondered if she'd come to the right place, a guard
stepped out of a sentry-box and walked over to the car, a pistol jutting
out against his hip. Frightened, she fumbled in her bag for her MoPho
– maybe she should call Da Mi? But before she could start dialling,
the man had peered into the back seat, given her a thumbs-up and
stepped back to open the gate.

The curved driveway led through a landscaped garden, past a pond
filled with large green lily pads to a large, traditional Korean house,
its tiled roof sheltering whitewashed walls and a dark-beamed porch.
Apart from the cab tyres complaining on the gravel, the estate was
silent, as hauntingly dignified as the palaces and monasteries Sydney
had visited with Jin Sok.

The cab-driver stopped by the latticed front doors. Despite the air-con, Sydney's palms were damp. She wiped them on her skirt, adjusted her rhinestone hair clip and reached for the door handle, but the driver turned and raised a white-gloved finger.

'I open,' he announced.

Sydney stepped into a muggy bath of night air. She'd be indoors in a moment; there was no point in cooling the temperature of her dress. Instead, she steadied her nerves with a narcotic lungful of night jasmine: the bush swarming up the porch was throwing off the scent like steam from a hot tub. Behind the foliage, Da Mi was standing at the door, dressed in a long crimson skirt and a filmy red sleeveless blouse, buttoned to the neck. Her hair was braided with red and gold silk ribbons and coiled around her head. She held out her hands and Sydney mounted the steps.

'Sydney, you look delightful,' the scientist cooed as she led her into the cool, dark interior of the house. 'So whimsical and fresh.'

'That's some heavy security you've got here, Da Mi.' A celadon cup of hangover-free white wine in her hand, Sydney mock-toasted the large antique sword hanging on the scientist's wall. They were sitting on silk cushions at a low black table filled with food. Beside them, a paper screen door had been pulled back to reveal the back porch and garden, where a bamboo grove and a row of pine trees stood guard over a bed of pale white flowers. Dusk was falling now, but the garden path was lined with solar-lamps, and inside candles cast gleaming reflections on the polished hardwood floor. The room was minimally furnished, but with beautiful stuff: a carved chest; an almost translucent porcelain vase; a scroll painted with fat pink peonies like the ones Da Mi had given her; and a shiny black lacquer stereo cabinet, inlaid with mother-of-pearl. Sydney couldn't see the stereo speakers, but the voice of Kim Min Gee, the Korean Leonard Cohen, murmured like a sad wind in the corners of the room.

'It's the only way, I'm afraid, to protect the openness of the architecture.' Da Mi gestured lightly around the place. 'As you can see, I have some valuable treasures here.'

'This room is bigger than my whole flat – Jeez, I wish I could open up my wall like this. Except I'd probably get pissed and fall out onto the street.' Sydney blushed and took another sip of wine. 'Unless I get some of your drops. It was so great, waking up bright and early this morning.'

'I'm sure your new home is lovely.' Da Mi minutely adjusted the position of a candle on the table. 'I have a feeling it's going to be a chrysalis, and the real you will emerge from it like a beautiful butterfly.'

'That would be nice.' Sydney sighed. 'Right now I still feel like a grub, especially compared to you and all the Korean models.'

'Sydney! You look so much better than when we first met. I hope you still have an appetite. Please, help yourself.' Da Mi gestured at the dishes of Korean food on the table: seaweed soup, cucumber salad, breaded fish, *kim chee*, dumplings, mushrooms with pine nuts, marinated *tubu*, fried greens, shrimp, and a dish that looked curiously like a present, wrapped in dark green leaves. Sydney didn't have a photoshoot for a week. She filled her bowl.

The mushrooms were wild, picked in the mountains, Da Mi told her, and the parcel was a traditional temple dish: rice wrapped in fried lotus leaves. It was considered a royal delicacy, and rare, even in the best restaurants these days. 'But I have so many lotus leaves in my pond, so I always serve them for my special guests.' Da Mi lifted a spoonful of the rice to her lips. Sydney noticed she'd barely eaten half a bowlful of the banquet.

'Aren't you hungry?' she asked, beginning to feel like a bit of a glutton.

'Oh, don't worry; I always nibble when I'm cooking. Please, have another glass of wine.'

Da Mi dosed their next glasses with an enzyme that neutralised the alcohol completely. The wine still tasted nice, but it was a shame not to feel tipsy, Sydney thought, though she was glad her mind wasn't cloudy as she gossiped with Da Mi about the Hyatt show, Jin Sok's famous contacts and the attractions of her new neighbour-hood. Well, most of them. She was careful not to mention Jae Ho. Seoul was a small town, and Da Mi might know the painter's wife.

'That was the *best*, Da Mi,' she said at last. Contentedly, she set down her chopsticks. 'I could eat Korean food forever.'

'What about your parents? Doesn't your mother miss cooking for you?'

That was a curveball. Sydney frowned at her empty bowl. Her parents? Short answer: fuck 'em – but that probably wasn't the kind of language Da Mi was used to.

'Umm . . . well . . .' She looked up. Da Mi's gentle face was glowing in the candlelight. The scientist was from another world, Sydney thought sadly. How could she tell her what her mother was like? Cooking? Mom had only ever served take-outs and frozen fries. And *miss* her? She'd kicked Sydney out, after months of Darren trying to flirt with her in front of his friends, drooling all over her tits and groping her in the kitchen. She'd put up with it, talking back, until that day he'd pinned her up against the cupboard and Mom had walked in. Mom hadn't yelled at him, no – she'd *defended* him: blamed Sydney, calling her a *poisonous little slut*. Darren had called her a whore too, loads of times. She'd felt like sending them a postcard when she started working for the agency: 'Making $300 a night now – how's the queue at the welfare office?'

They'd die if they could see her now, she thought: reclining on a silken cushion, talking with a top scientist in Seoul. 'I doubt it, Da Mi,' she said, brightly. 'Mom was always busy with her boyfriend, this guy I didn't get on with. That's why I went to Vancouver. I never thought I'd end up in Seoul, but like you say, hey, maybe things are going to take off for me.' Saying the words, she felt almost positive. Who cared about her mom and that jerk-off Darren?

'I'm sure your mother misses you very much.' Da Mi said firmly. 'I'm certain she'd be very proud if she knew what a fantastic job you're doing, creating a new life in a foreign country.'

'I've been lucky, that's all,' Sydney said, modestly. 'I've met such great people here – like you.'

'Jin Sok is clearly crazy about you. Very protective, isn't he?'

Sydney rolled her eyes. 'When we go clubbing everyone thinks he's my boyfriend. I'll have to tell him to get lost one of these days.'

'I hate to cluck, but you should be careful who you meet in these clubs. Most Korean men are harmless and naïve, but some can be cavalier, especially with foreign women. And they can be so backwards when it comes to using condoms. I wouldn't like you to get into any difficulties.'

Sydney turned pink at the edges. Thank God the room was dark. It *had* been pretty dumb not to use a rubber with Jae Ho. Still, it was sweet of Da Mi to care. 'These are sexy buttons,' she said, changing the subject. She reached across the table and fingered one of the irregular glass beads. Beneath it, the scientist's breast moved softly as she breathed.

'I do my best,' Da Mi purred, 'but I'm not the professional.'

'Me neither.' Sydney withdrew her hand and tucked a loose strand of hair behind her ear. 'Hey, dressing up is fun, but it isn't like what you do – well, I don't know what you do exactly, but it must be important: genes are the scene, that's for sure.'

Da Mi put her elbows on the table and placed her fingertips together at her lips. 'A lot of it is just microscope drudgery, to be honest – but it's true that we at GRIP are hoping to find real solutions for real people – and not just curing diseases. It may sound idealistic,

Sydney, but imagine if we could alter our genetic code in a way that eliminated human greed, fear and aggression – wouldn't that truly change the world?'

The evening was as warm as a duvet, but the urgency in the scientist's voice made the goosebumps rise on Sydney's arms. 'Gosh, Da Mi, can GRIP really do that?'

'Let me make you a honey drink. Then we can discuss GRIP's latest project, and how *you* can help humanity evolve.'

Da Mi took the dishes into the kitchen, and Sydney took advantage of her absence to pour out the last half-glass of wine. Ignoring the bottle of enzymes, she took the drink to the porch. The night air was still close, but she adjusted her dress to keep her skin at the perfect temperature. Sitting on the steps, enjoying the kick of the alcohol, she let her mind mingle with the shadows of bamboo leaves in the garden.

She was wearing a pair of Da Mi's guest slippers, so she decided not to walk out to the lily pond. Instead, when the music stopped, she got up to change the CD. As she crossed the floor, out of the corner of her eye she caught sight of something peculiar at the far end of the room.

Was it – a door? Yes, but it was only hip-high. How cute. At first she thought it must be a closet, but there was a woven mat beside it, and a stone statue of a tiger, as if it were the entrance to some small person's home. She took a step towards it, intrigued, then stopped. She didn't want to look like she was snooping around.

'You've discovered the *anbang*.'

Sydney started. Da Mi was at her elbow, a tray in her hands.

'I'm sorry – I made you jump. Come, sit down and I'll tell you all about my secret room.'

Sydney plumped herself back down on her cushion and waited as

147

Da Mi made two hot honey drinks. The gleaming honey drizzled slowly from the lip of the blue bottle and hung, suspended in the candlelight, like a thin gold chain.

'How much alcohol have you drunk today?'

Sydney glanced furtively at her empty wine glass. 'Just a martini in the cab . . . and, um, I finished the wine up too, it was just a bit, but I forgot to add the drops.'

'That's fine; I'll just give you an extra dollop of honey.' Da Mi finished pouring and put the bottle down. Then she untwisted the cap from a small jar on the tray. 'I usually have some colloidal gold this time of night.' She slipped a teaspoon of gold liquid into her drink and the honey water turned a shade darker beneath the surface's glimmering sheen.

'What does that do?'

'It relieves stress, balances hormones and enhances brain functions, including memory and IQ. It's excellent for late-night business discussions. Would you like to try some?'

'If it'll make me as smart as you, sure.' Sydney nudged her cup towards Da Mi and let her stir the colloidal liquid in. She lifted the cup and blew on the mixture, then took a sip. The drink slipped down her throat with a whispery aftertaste of desert sun. It was even nicer than the one Da Mi had made for her at the sauna. She closed her eyes and waited for the honey to slowly spread its wings inside her veins.

'Mmmm,' she found herself murmuring.

'I'm addicted to it myself,' Da Mi confessed.

Sydney stretched her legs, feeling the honey warming her muscles. 'So what's this secret room? The "amban", you called it?'

'The *anbang*,' Da Mi corrected, 'is the inner sanctum of the traditional Korean home, the warmest place in the house in the winter, and the room where the women spent most of their time. In past times, babies were born in the *anbang*, in front of the fireplace, and old people returned there to die.' Da Mi paused, a faraway look in her eyes. Then, with a sad shrug, she continued, 'Nowadays most people brick up the sliding walls of the outer room, the *maru*, and heat it with electric *onduls*, and they use the *anbang* as an extra bedroom. But I wanted to preserve the old ways.'

Sydney was a little embarrassed by the trembling look on Da Mi's face. She peered back at the entrance, so the doctor could recover her composure. 'Is the little door traditional too?'

'In a way.' Da Mi was calm again now. 'All over the world, ancient peoples would enter their sacred tombs through a low corridor – even the priests had to humble themselves to commune with their gods. When I started using the *anbang* as a creative space, I decided to lower the doorframe, and to pray to the threshold spirits to guide me when I worked.'

'It's like your sanctuary, huh?' Sydney took another sip of the honey and gold mixture. It was getting tastier by the second.

'Exactly. Shall I take you in there and show you what I've been working on lately?'

Sydney drained her cup. 'Yes, please!'

Da Mi took a sheet of paper and a fountain pen from a cushion behind her and placed them on the table. 'First, Sydney, I'd like you to read this. I am authorised by GRIP and our project partner to offer you the sum of one million won to ensure that nothing you see or hear in the *anbang* will go beyond the confines of this meeting.'

'Really? Wow.' Sydney picked up the piece of paper. It was a contract, basically: confidentiality required . . . in event of suspicion . . . GRIP authorised to review employment . . . monitor said disclosures . . . recover damages . . . blah blah blah.

'So basically, nine hundred dollars just to listen, and if I blab, you fire and sue me?'

149

'More or less.' Da Mi smiled.

'And what about this monitoring stuff?'

'In the event of disclosure, you relinquish certain rights to privacy and data protection. It's a standard corporate clause.'

Her body felt like a bolt of noonday sun. Sydney took the lid off the pen. 'Don't worry about that; I'm not going to be telling anyone anything, Da Mi.' She dated the contract, and signed it with a flourish.

Da Mi offered her an envelope of money, presenting it with both hands, and Sydney accepted it in the proper manner and slipped it in her purse.

'Thank you, Sydney.' Da Mi regarded her gravely. 'Now, please, it is my pleasure to show you my *anbang*.'

15 / Body Snatch

Wearing that same long coat, his fingers a shade more nicotine-stained than before, Rattail sat all screwed up in the front passenger seat, chain-smoking and getting on Johnny's nerves. 'So you're sure your contact at the hospital is safe?' Johnny quizzed again. The convertible roof was up. He wanted privacy tonight.

'*Ye, ye.*' Rattail waved his hand airily, flicking cigarette ash over the dashboard. From the back, the Scalper grunted. The guy didn't speak much English and was fatter than John Candy, but he did a damn good job, he was cheap, and he kept his mouth shut – he knew he was instantly replaceable, that was why. There were more plastic surgeons in this city than there were *dukbogee ajummas*. Every second girl wanted to get her eyelids Westernised; every rich businessman wanted to buy new tits and ass for his hot young mistress. The docs would phone each other from the operating tables and compare figures – they had it made. This guy, the Scalper, Johnny had used for a couple of ConGlam witness-protection schemes. They'd hung out drinking one night and Johnny had seen the porno collection in the guy's briefcase, black and white shit from Germany mostly – he had a real sick appetite. So Johnny had insisted they use him, despite Kim's preference for someone more upscale – the Doc seemed to think ConGlam was a bottomless money pit. It had been good to win his first battle with her since Sydney's defection.

'I telling you, Mr Joh-nee, he get the weird proposal all the time,'

Rattail continued. 'Some guys want do just anything with those girls once they cold, you know?'

'Not personally.' Johnny said curtly, though a shaving curl of curiosity ran through him at the thought. 'I like 'em warm myself.'

Rattail smirked. 'Sometimes they warm – you gotta get there quick though.'

'That stuff turn you on? That why you know this guy?'

'Too nasty for me. But he old friend of mine. You want, I set you up sometime. For you, special price.'

'Yeah, well, I'll keep it in mind.' You never know, such a service could come in handy with a client sometime. The place they all really liked, though, was the bathhouse with the girls who washed you down in the hot-tub, then took you in a little room and licked you all over, head to butt to toe. A more thorough cleansing you never had. After he'd demolished his apartment he'd taken himself off there to relax and clear his mind. The stress had drained out of his body with his cum, leaving him lying there, flat out on the bed mat listening to the girls giggling to each other. He'd never met happier whores in his whole life. Maybe the johns' BO pissed the rest of them off . . .

He dragged his mind back to the road. Where the hell was Miyari Dong? He didn't use SatNav, not when he was driving with work contacts – it made you look weak, following some computer-synthed voice around the city. But that meant sometimes you did get lost. 'Is this the turn-off here?' he asked.

'I don't know, what turn you off?' Rattail flashed a pointy little grin.

'People who don't know how to give directions, that's what.'

'Oh, Mr Joh-nee like taking direction, okay, I keep it in mind. *Ye ye*, next right.'

He might have guessed that Kim would set him up with the biggest smart-ass Korean gopher in the country.

But she was one stupid bitch if she really thought Johnny Sandman was finished with Sydney Travers. He'd contemplated his options at the bathhouse, and had decided to play things cool for the time being, bide his time. The next day he'd cleaned the apartment from top to bottom – strangely, that had reminded him of Veronica, of how he'd washed the blood from her face after he'd punched her that time, how he'd styled her hair to cover the patch where he'd pulled a hank out. He hadn't said sorry then, no way. He'd said, 'You shouldn't have done it, Ronnie. You shouldn't have made me so mad.' And she'd agreed. He remembered how she'd sobbed, 'I know, I know. I'm sorry, Johnny – I'm so sorry.'

Now *that* was the way a woman should talk to him. When he thought about Sydney Travers and Dr Kim fucking Da Mi, that was his new Big Fucking Picture.

Miyari Dong was smack-dab in the middle of the neon wastes of Northern Seoul. Despite the national clamp-down on the sex trade, thanks to corrupt local cops, the Dong still had a red light district: Texas Town, a hopeless labyrinth of alleyways, each grimier and more garish than the next. Johnny had taken a few clients there over the years, to see the girls sitting out in windows, dressed in gauzy, traditional *hanbok*, lifting their skirts to display their panty-free zones. Miyari hospitals saw a lot of girl-flesh, and not all of it got patched up and sent right back out where it came from. Some of it got sent ten foot under – unless, that is, Johnny Sandman got there first with a fistful of won. Johnny turned off at the hospital, a squat, stained grey building with no signs of life, death or near-fatal accident. The green neon cross mounted over the front doors was the only thing that distinguished it from a block of offices.

'Where's Emergency? How do we get in?' Johnny clenched his jaw. It was past midnight now and they were already behind schedule.

'Is round back – but we go underground parking. You turn here.'
Johnny pulled into a narrow bay in front of the car elevator. Rattail
hopped out and activated the code, then climbed back into the car
as the horizontal metal doors yawned open. Johnny drove into the
elevator and the doors closed silently behind them.

'What floor?' he growled.

'B4.'

Ratty was enjoying giving directions now, he could tell. Johnny
unrolled the window, pressed the button and the descent began.
What creeped him out about these things, aside from the paranoid
thought of earthquakes, was the way you had to face the back while
the cement foundations of the building rolled up behind you. Plus
there was barely room for the car doors to open. Being trapped
inside a metal cube with a shrivelled-up Korean wise guy shedding
dandruff all over his seats in the front and a grunting sack of lard
in the back was not Johnny's idea of big-time fun on a Saturday
night. He didn't breathe easy again until they reached the bottom,
the doors opened and he had backed the convertible out into the
garage.

The man waiting for them in the car park was short, fat and bull-
frog-ugly. He, Rattail and the Scalper shared an unfunny joke in
Korean while Johnny unlocked the trunk. The Doc's precious hatbox
was in here, the contents kept on ice. The Scalper looked interested,
but Johnny wouldn't let him carry it – he was in charge of this gig.

'Right. Which way's the morgue? I could use some cooling down.'

The morgue was chilly, all right, and saturated with that unmistakable smell of weird chemicals, the usual low note of putrefaction
lurking underneath. Shiny instruments were laid out on drab green
cloth, ready for the next round of autopsies. There was a sink, a
stand with a row of empty hangers; a couple of bins in the corner

for used latex gloves and cotton smocks. And in front of him: the grid of drawers, six-foot trays of clammy goods.

Let's get this over with, Johnny thought.

Bullfrog rolled a covered gurney out. A pair of brown feet, toenails painted bright red, peeked out from under the wrap.

'She just come in today,' Rattail said. 'Stab wound in abdomen. Very clean, out of sight. You want see?'

Dead hookers in and of themselves had long ago ceased to interest Johnny, but he was paying for this one. No way was he forking over for a body even one inch off-spec.

'She'd better match the profile.'

'*Ye, ye.*' Ratty threw back the sheet.

The body was about the same height as Dr Kim; they'd be able to share a wardrobe, no problem. The hooker would probably look better in the clothes; she wasn't as fucking bony as the Doc, who looked positively ghoulish some days. Even Sydney had more flesh on her than Kim. This woman's tits might be sagging now but they were big and cushiony, and her hips had seen a bit of squeezing too. Casting a professional eye down the body, Johnny noted with appreciation the tuft of black pubic hair shaved in a vertical line.

For a moment, Johnny felt almost nostalgic, remembering his first time licking Korean pussy – but hey, no time for that now. Anyway, this woman was roadkill. There was an ugly red gash in her left side, about three inches long, stitched up with black thread.

'So who was she? You sure she's got no next of kin?'

Rattail conferred with Bullfrog. 'No,' he eventually replied, 'she here two times before, broken ribs, black eye. Only pimp come, pick her up. Maybe pimp knife her, who knows? She in here late afternoon, die before she tell anyone what happen. Anyway, my friend get pimp phone number from file; he glad make money from dead girl. He gonna come in here six a.m., sign for release of body, no question, no problem. Everybody happy.'

'Great. Then let's get to it.'

Bullfrog wheeled over a high-powered lamp and a metal trolley. The Scalper opened his bag and started lining up his knives. Johnny, standing next to the tray of morgue instruments, found his eye attracted to their glinting blades and quickly, when no one was looking, he pocketed one. *What the hell; just a little souvenir.* The Scalper turned around and grunted at him, Johnny hoisted the hatbox onto the trolley next to the surgeon and lifted the lid.

Fucking hell! It was real disturbing, seeing Kim's eyeless, expressionless face right there, an island of flesh resting on a fibreglass mould surrounded by ice. The lips were blue, the skin pale. Without make-up she looked – maybe not older exactly, but blander, flabbier. He had to give Kim credit though; otherwise the thing was the spitting image of her: same mole, same eyebrows, same lips. Apparently she'd grown it from a cell culture – like beansprouts on a piece of wet paper in a Petrie dish, Johnny thought, dimly recalling his high school science class.

The Koreans crowded in, overawed at first, then cracking vulgar jokes. He stepped back and regarded the three men suspiciously. He'd have preferred the surgery to take place at GRIP – these clowns would never manage to come up with any funny ideas individually, but together? You just never knew, did you? The germ of some prankish notion could pass through the intestinal tracts of their collective mind and shit could end up flying God knows where. But Kim had said there was a government inspection of the lab due this week, and insisted they do the job at the hospital: she obviously wanted to make extra work for him after he'd vetoed her choice of surgeon.

'So how long's it gonna take?' he demanded.

Rattail conferred with the Scalper. 'Three, maybe four hour.'

'That long?' He grimaced. 'Can your buddy there hand the Scalper the instruments? I got a sensitive stomach for this kind of thing.'

'*Ye, ye*. He very interesting to see how it work.'

'Is there a sofa I can crash on? You can wake me when it's done.'

'*Ye, ye*, right through here.' Rattail pointed at a grey metal door which led into a pleasant enough staffroom, for a morgue. The sofa was a bit short, but hell, he was the Sandman. He could sleep anywhere.

16 | The *Anbang*

'Precious Threshold Spirit: please bless my guest Sydney and honour us both with your wisdom as we pass into the heart of my home.' Kneeling on the mat in front of the door to the *anbang*, Da Mi bowed low and touched her forehead to the floor.

Sydney did the same. The dark floorboards smelled lemony and the grainy wood was uneven beneath her fingertips. Closing her eyes, she added her own thoughts to the prayer: *Please help me to not let Da Mi down.*

When she sat back up, Da Mi was taking a shank of Korean silk knotwork from a hook beside the door. Hidden in the folds of ribbon was a small brass key. Da Mi turned the key in the lock, grasped the door handle and pushed.

The blackness of the *anbang* seemed to swell into the room. A fingertip of anticipation shivered up and down Sydney's spine.

'Follow me,' Da Mi whispered, and her tight red skirt disappeared into the darkness. Once her toes had crossed the threshold, Sydney shuffled on all fours after her.

Da Mi closed the door behind them. It was pitch-black. A floorboard creaked. Then there was the tearing sound of a struck match and the smell of sulphur, and Da Mi was lighting three tall white candles on a table against the far wall.

It didn't seem right to speak. Sydney remained silent, on her knees. Floating like a net behind Da Mi was a tall patchwork lattice of carved wood. As her eyes adjusted to the candlelight, Sydney could see that the translucent white paper between the slats was flecked with thin pink petals.

'That's beautiful,' she whispered.

'It's a traditional screen,' Da Mi was kneeling in front of the candles. Her voice floated in the room like feathers in the air and her shadows danced up the walls. The *anbang* was tall enough to stand up in, but Sydney didn't dare get to her feet. Instead, she sat back on her heels and took in the whole effect. To her left stood a piece of furniture a bit like a black leather sun-lounger, except there was a jumble of black flaps and straps wrapped around its chrome frame. To her right was a low table with a long drawer, like a desk for someone who didn't mind sitting on the floor. A briefcase and two silk cushions, one white and one red, were tucked beneath the table, on which sat a wafer-thin laptop, a leather notebook, black padded goggles and a sleek joystick.

'That's Virtuoso stuff, isn't it?' Sydney asked reverently. 'I've seen it in magazines.'

'The best virtual gaming technology money can buy.' Da Mi slid on her bottom over to the laptop table. Pulling out the cushions, she gestured to Sydney to join her. 'Wait till you try it.'

'I thought it could still make you feel sick.' Sydney sat cross-legged on the white cushion and admired the detailed stitching on the goggles. The headpiece resembled an upside-down crown, or a black lotus, its four triangular petals designed to cover the player's eyes and ears.

'Ah, but you've been drinking colloidal gold; that will prevent the symptoms if you'd like to make a voyage.'

'*Really?*' Sydney clasped her hands together and gave a little bounce. Every kid in Seoul was longing to try a Virtuoso ride, but no gaming company had dared mass-market the product yet, in case two players out of fifty got motion sickness and fell off their scooters on the way home from the *videobang*. So that meant the technology was just for those few who could afford the $50,000 price tag – or who had friends who could. 'Wow, thanks, Da Mi!'

Tiny vertical lines formed between the scientist's eyebrows. 'Sydney, I have to let you know that what I am offering is not a game. Tonight I'd like you to enter a Satvision immersion that has inspired my present project. I don't want to spoil the impact of the ride, but it could have an emotional effect on you. Do you trust me when I say this is a vital part of your induction to the project?'

The only emotion Sydney felt was excitement, brimming out of every pore. She nodded eagerly and reached for the joystick. Da Mi picked up the goggles and tugged them down over her head. The crown got caught for a minute on her hair clip and the two women giggled. It felt like being at a sleepover, playing around with stuff they knew they shouldn't be touching. Finally, the mask was fitted snugly over Sydney's head. The two side petals covered her ears and the eye pads sealed off all incoming light.

'Okay in there?' Da Mi asked, tidying Sydney's hair. She sounded very far away.

'Great!' Her own voice was muffled now, with a faint reverb. 'Let's go!'

Sydney's mind was a vast orb of silent darkness. Her body was hidden somewhere beneath her, swaying gently like a plant at the bottom of the sea. Gradually, she detected a faint, echoey hush in her ears, then distant specks of light appeared in the emptiness around her. Remembering the joystick, she turned slowly in a circle, became a revolving point in an enormous black field. On her second rotation, the echoes grew more insistent, almost musical, and the stars got brighter but fewer. From way off in the distance a misty blue marble began rolling slowly towards her. Mesmerised, she steadily threaded her way past meteors and satellites towards the shrouded beauty of the Earth. Soon she was hovering above continents and seas garlanded with wisps and whirls of cloud. Amber lights twinkled across the land masses. It was like snorkelling above a giant coral reef.

Now she was drifting above the Mediterranean Sea. Somewhere in Italy, a red light was blinking. More red lights were flashing further east. She zoomed in closer: *wow!* These were areas with high Satvizrez. She could go down to any one of them and float around the streets, imagining all the people who lived in the dinky houses there, worked in the beehive office blocks. Where did she want to visit tonight?

Wiggling the joystick, she swung out towards Asia, passing more and more red lights as she crossed India and Thailand and swooped up over China. Mentally waving to Seoul, she entered the huge expanse of the Pacific Ocean, then pointed herself at Vancouver. In no time she was hovering above the sprawling red beacon. Sydney dived down for a closer look at the city and the red light diffused, its fiery glow sinking into familiar grid of streets and buildings. Now, strangely, just when she knew where she was, the joystick didn't seem to work any more; instead of directing herself, she was being pulled along: past English Bay, over Chinatown and into Gastown, right past the hotel where she used to work and into the new upmarket end of Hastings Street.

It's a bit freaky, not being in control any more, but maybe this is part of the emotional experience Da Mi talked about, Sydney thought. It was also sort of nice not having to make decisions. So she relaxed, just let herself surf the sunset between the condominiums and converted warehouses, and back down to the seam between the renovated district and old Gastown. In a cute touch, Christmas decorations were hanging between the antique street lamps – and wow, look: there were even people down there, just a few, hunched up in winter jackets, walking dogs or smoking cigarettes. They were all immobile statues, bathed in that weird red light.

Sydney was nearly down at ground level now and she could see that most of the shops were shut. There was a Christmas tree in the window of a grocery store, a tilted angel at its tip. Peering into the store, she could make out a calendar on the wall. *No way!* It was from last year, and all the December squares had been crossed off up until Christmas Day.

Sydney frowned. Where had she been last Christmas? Oh yeah, with Annie and Jolene: burning a chicken in Annie's apartment off Commercial Avenue and hiding Jolene's MoPho so she couldn't talk to that creepy client who liked sticking wine bottles up inside her. He paid double for the trouble, but still, Christmas Day: the freak could wait.

That had been a fun day, she remembered, drinking Baileys and brandy cocktails, doing strip-teases for each other. It would be cool to see if she could peek in at the window, see Annie twirling her nipple-tassels for the neighbours. Jeez, that had been a laugh.

Pushing the joystick, Sydney tried to lift up and out of Hastings, but instead, she was drawn towards the figure of a woman in a mini-skirt and knee-high boots, standing at the entrance to a narrow alley. A Native woman, with strong cheekbones, she would have been at-tractive once. But though the street was still bathed in red light, it wasn't making her look good. She had a big puffy bruise on her cheek, a tattoo on her neck and scabs and sores on her scrawny legs. A junkie. No wonder she was out.

A sour taste rose up in Sydney's throat as she remembered what Annie'd always told her: *You have to swear to yourself never to do needles or crack.* Or you'd end up like this hard case: living in some flop-house on Hastings instead of your own small apartment; working the stinking alleyways of Chinatown instead of doing it in clean hotel beds; taking any diseased loser who came up, instead of picking and choosing amongst nervous first-timers and loaded jetsetters who tipped a hundred bucks if you so much as stuck your pinkie up their butts. *Never do that without being asked*, Annie had told her. *Always make 'em think they're getting extra.*

For a second, Sydney wondered if she could signal to Da Mi that she'd had enough of Satviz, but then the hooker stamped her feet and exhaled a cloud of scarlet smoke into the air.

Weird. Was this a movie now, then, or still real life like she'd thought? As Sydney puzzled, the woman smiled, revealing black, gap-ridden teeth. A jowly man in a bulky overcoat had stopped to talk to her. He was a white guy, maybe mid-forties, with beetling black eyebrows that met in the middle. Sydney winced as the woman unbuttoned her jacket and let him look at her tits. He appeared to like what he saw. The pair turned down the alley, and Sydney found herself following, sucked along like a dust mote in their wake.

The alleyway was cast in blood-red shadow and lined with industrial-sized garbage bins. Sydney flinched, glad she couldn't smell the overflowing refuse, which must have come from a Chinese restaurant: despite it being Christmas, kitchen steam was blowing out of a small round window next to a loading dock. At least one rat was burrowing in the rotting piles of boiled chicken bones and mouldy egg-fried rice, but the hooker and her john just drifted through the crimson cloud to the bottom of the alley, where they stopped in front of a soggy-looking mattress, slumped against the wall. There was no doubt what it was used for: the ground here was littered with crushed beer cans, empty wine bottles and used hypodermics and condoms. Sydney grimaced as, the couple haggled, over what – twenty, thirty bucks? She shifted the joystick again, trying to back out onto the street, but she remained inside the alley, jammed between the garbage bins, staring in horror as the man suddenly grabbed the woman by the hair, pulled her down onto the mattress and punched her in the face.

Without warning, Sydney's mother's voice slashed into her head: *You keep away from Darren. We don't need trash like you in our home.*

'Stop,' Sydney whispered, squeezing her eyes tight shut, but her mom's voice rose like a chorus of bats in the darkness:

There's places for sluts like you. They're called brothels and jails.

Take that, you little whore – and don't blame me if you end up on the streets.

One day you'll pick the wrong man to tease. You'll end up six feet under, and don't think I'm paying for flowers.

The words swirled round and round, making her dizzy, sick to her stomach. She had to do something to make them *shut up.*

She opened her eyes and her mom's voice faded, washed out by the scene in the alleyway, where the greasy-haired man in the overcoat was clamping his hand over the woman's mouth and forcing her legs open with his knees while he fumbled at his belt clasp. The hooker kicked and tried to push him away, but the john had his flies opened now, and as he began shoving into her, Sydney's mom's voice screeched again in her head.

You're asking for trouble, dressed like that, you're begging for some man to rape you. When he does, don't you come running to me.

This was horrible, horrible, *horrible.* But it was a *game*, right? So did she have to do something to help this woman? Did she have to save her, protect her, show her mom whose side she was on? Her heart hammering in her chest, Sydney tried again to force the joystick forward, to get closer, thinking she might be able to pull the attacker off the woman, but she remained suspended in the picture, unable even to rotate. *It's not working, Da Mi. The game isn't working.* She tried to speak, but her lips were glued together. She closed her eyes, but the afterimage of the struggling couple was burned onto her retinas, so she opened them again, to see the woman's arms beating weakly against the man's back, and the man twisting her head sideways, as if he were about to break her neck. Now the rat was sniffing at the woman's cheap black boots. Sydney couldn't watch a moment longer. Gasping and shaking, her heart clenched tight as a fist, she reached up and tore the goggles off her head.

The *anbang* was a blur of black and white. On the Virtuoso screen Sydney could see the man was pulling out a knife, raising his arm above the hooker's head. With a click of the mouse, Da Mi blanked the laptop screen, then she turned to Sydney. A single tear was tracing a slow path down her impeccably made-up cheek. The scientist opened her arms.

17 | Blind Date

'Dr Kim want see you, Mr Joh-nee.' Rattail giggled as he shook Johnny awake. Johnny peered at his watch: just gone five a.m. He heaved himself upright and staggered back into the morgue.

The smell of disinfectant was slightly stronger than before; otherwise all signs of the recent surgery had been erased. Bullfrog was standing by the gurney. A small plastic bag, demurely tied up by the handles, was plumped by the door: discarded hooker face, no doubt.

'Where's the Scalper?' Johnny asked.

'He take cab.'

'Why?' Johnny was puzzled. 'I didn't pay him yet.'

'He say you and him go for drinks, you pay him then. He tired, had to go, and me and my friend we want clean up, make girl look pretty for you.'

'What? Oh fuck off, Rattail. I told you, I like 'em with blood pumping in their veins.'

'Yeah, but I think you want look.' Rattail placed his hand on Johnny's arm.

Johnny shrugged it off. 'I inspect work, Rattail,' he said brusquely and stepped over to the gurney. The plastic wrap was pulled down to the woman's shoulders. Kim's stern face was united to her hairline and jawbone, framed by a thick red line and clear, neat stitches. The lab would take care of the seams later, he'd been told.

As Johnny contemplated the eerie image of his arch-rival on a mortuary slab, Bullfrog peeled back the wrap that was covering her body.

It was like a 3D version of those emails you got sometimes, of Condy's head stuck on some Playboy bunny body, riding a hairless stud-muffin with the face of some grateful English toff. 'Haha,' Johnny smirked.

Bullfrog stroked the woman's thigh. The porno patch had been combed. 'Ipo, ye?' he asked.

'Pretty girl,' Rattail needlessly translated, with a transparently false sigh.

'Wa-chuh dis,' Bullfrog said in mangled English and plucked the woman's flaccid nipple between his thick fingers. He twisted it once, twice, and it hardened. The Koreans laughed, and Johnny felt a not-unpleasant twinge in the pit of his stomach.

'Is cold,' Rattail explained. 'But you don't like girl cold?'

'She's not so bad to look at.' Johnny heard himself say. 'It's the place that gets on my nerves.'

'We take her back into lounge, where you sleeping so good. Heater on. Very nice.'

Johnny hesitated. But nah, this was too gross, even for him. 'I told you, I'm not into stiffs.'

'You touch her. Smooth skin, very nice. Inside very warm. My friend, he put little heater inside, jelly too. Hot, wet, very nice.'

Rattail nudged Bullfrog, who pulled the woman's legs apart, proudly displaying her glistening snatch. Manipulating the lips, he exposed the clit and then, reaching inside, pulled out a little battery-operated hand warmer, the kind you could buy at any Seoul subway station. This one was dripping with KY.

'She's okay,' Johnny admitted, his voice a little choked.

'You want some time together?' Rattail wheedled. 'Is only two hundred fifty thousand *won* extra.'

'With you two peeking in the keyhole? I don't think so.'

'No, no: we go coffee shop upstairs. Back in half-hour. We give you key.'

Johnny paused, his eyes on the prone figure splayed out before him. His balls were aching now.

Ah what the hell: you only live once.

'I'm not paying for it, buddy. I got *you* this gig.'

The two conferred. 'Two hundred *won* only,' Rattail said. 'My friend take some trouble prepare her all nice, and he have wash her out after.'

'Hey, I'm using a condom – no way I'm fucking a dead whore without a rubber.'

The Koreans muttered to each other again.

'He have to pay guy at incinerator.' Rattail jerked his head towards the bag by the door. 'One seventy-five.'

'One fifty. Final offer.'

Bullfrog nodded. He understood numbers, evidently. They all did.

The money exchanged hands, Rattail palmed him the key and Johnny opened the door to the lounge. Bullfrog wheeled the gurney in front of the sofa and stepped back.

'Okay. Now fuck off.'

Johnny waited until the two Koreans had left the morgue, then shut the lounge door and locked himself in with the corpse.

Here she was, Kim's dream-baby avatar, laid out, legs spread. Her skin, well, her skin had an unappealing sheen to it, like sweet and sour chicken that had been sitting on the buffet too long. But he wouldn't be male if he didn't get pumped looking at that hot pussy: red and juicy, it was just waiting to be fucked – and how about that face, the face of the woman he hated most in the world. It would be something, wouldn't it? To see that body walking around in Kim's designer clothing, Kim's voice coming out of its mouth, and know he'd been there first. The Doc would be so pissed if she knew.

His cock thickened. The room was warm and sweat tickled his armpits. If he did this, he would be laughing inside every time he talked to the Doc, and she'd sense it; she'd feel uneasy, disrespected, though she wouldn't know why. The Kim box would be ticked for now, so he could turn his full attention to the question of how he was going to make Sydney Travers wish she'd never been born. Yeah, fucking a corpse might not be the crowning glory Ratty's and his chum seemed to think, but it was a step in the right direction – and who knows, maybe he *would* get a taste for dead meat: dead *blonde* meat. Now there was an arousing thought.

He unbuckled his belt, unzipped his jeans and took out his cock. It was a cast-iron bar in his hand.

For a moment he hesitated. He could just wank over the face . . .

No – well, yeah; he'd pull out and come on Kim's face later, but when Johnny Sandman opened an account, he liked to take a tour of the vaults. He shoved the gurney against the wall and pulled the body's legs up around his thighs. The head lolled to one side, the hair disarrayed on the sheet. *Sexy. Very sexy.* The tip of his cock nosed the wet snatch and he groaned. Fuck condoms; anything nasty would be dead by now, wouldn't it? Lifting the legs up into a V for Victory, he spat, a big gob, onto Kim's precious face. It landed – bulls-eye – on her mouth, a shiny oyster disappearing between her parted lips as a trail of drool slid down the side of her chin and settled in the stitches on her throat. Blood flooded Johnny's skull. 'Is that what you've been waiting for?' he shouted as he thrust into the corpse's warm slit. 'Hey, Da Mi? You want some big hard *Johnny cock*?'

18 / Enlightenment

Wailing and sobbing, Sydney flung herself into Da Mi's arms.

'I'm so sorry.' The scientist's blouse was light and silky against Sydney's cheek, but her voice was ragged with distress. 'I feel terrible. Can you forgive me?'

Oh Jeez, she was letting Da Mi down. Just because she'd been reminded of stuff in the past – stuff that was over. Sydney disentangled herself and wiped her face with her hands. What a feeb she was. 'No – no, you told me it might be intense! I'm fine now, really, Da Mi.'

Da Mi handed her a tissue. 'The immersion must have triggered some buried trauma. Is that what happened, Sydney?'

Sydney opened her mouth, then closed it again. If Da Mi knew how much she hated her mom, she'd probably think Sydney was way too screwed-up to trust.

'No,' she muttered, 'it wasn't a memory. But I saw a man attacking a woman in Vancouver and I guess I could relate, 'cause I used to work near Gastown.'

'Gastown!' Da Mi's hands flew to her mouth. 'Oh dear, Sydney. I didn't know you worked there. On the streets?'

'No. In a hotel.' Jeez, where was this going? She didn't come here to talk about the escort work. 'It was fine, really. Nothing like . . . *that.*' She gestured at the goggles.

Da Mi was still looking troubled. 'I'm so sorry. I should have suggested you visit somewhere you didn't know. But to tell the truth, some of the other red-light zones are even worse.'

'*Even worse?* Da Mi, what is that programme – some kind of global snuff game?'

'It's not a game.' Da Mi sighed heavily. 'It's real imagery, of Christmas Day last year, hacked from military satellites and edited to highlight acts of violence, misery and cruelty that were taking place all over the world. If you had gone to Africa you would have seen child soldiers being forced to have sex with each other; in Iran, victims of US chemical attacks; in Thailand, child abuse by sex tourists; in London, a homeless man being kicked to death and set on fire by a gang of teenage girls.'

Da Mi's voice was low and full of sorrow. Sydney stared at her small, tense face, images of the red lights on the Satviz globe flashing in her mind. 'But that's *awful*. Who would want to sit and watch all that? I mean, apart from some *sicko*.'

'The hackers are a group dedicated to exposing abuses of power, including the violent living conditions in deliberately deprived areas. Some of them work at very high levels in military and governmental agencies. They leaked this programme to various law enforcement and human rights organisations, but it quickly fell into the hands of an American media consortium called ConGlam.' Behind Da Mi, the candles glowed like cats' eyes. 'Sydney, ConGlam is GRIP's new project partner. They gave me the Satviz package to demonstrate its gaming potential, but really, I view the content as its most important feature. Each time I enter that programme I become more determined to use my scientific knowledge to help put a stop to the terrible events it depicts. I wanted you to see it because I hoped it might inspire you to join me on a special project that could bring an end to rape and murder and human misery forever.' Da Mi leaned forward slightly, her gleaming eyes fixed on Sydney.

Sydney frowned, struggling to fit her thoughts into the neat wood and paper boxes of the latticed wall behind the candles. You thought your life was shit, but it was nothing compared to what went on all around you every day. She'd learned that in Vancouver. Her own mom was just a stupid, jealous bitch. Annie's mom had been way worse, pimping out her eleven-year-old daughter to her dealer. And out there in the world were complete sadists, chopping people up in dungeons, torturing them just for kicks, blowing them up to make money. But you couldn't stop them. It was just the way some people were made: selfish and cruel. People like Da Mi, sitting in her perfect house, with her perfect life, couldn't understand that; they didn't know that lots of people *liked* being bastards, would never let anyone change them.

'But, Da Mi, it doesn't matter if you're rich or poor, or black or white, some people are just, I dunno, wild *animals*. That's human nature, isn't it?' Slowly the question faded from her lips, for Da Mi was beseeching her with a tender, almost radiant look.

'Sydney, I've just put you through a dreadful experience. Please, let me make it up to you, and at the same demonstrate how exactly science *can* help change human nature. If you will allow me now to belt you into the Enlightenment Chair, I guarantee it will be the most uplifting and spiritually nurturing half-hour you've ever spent.'

The scientist gestured gracefully across the *anbang* at the black leather sun-lounger, with its mysterious straps and wires.

'The Enlightenment Chair?' Sydney instantly regretted the note of doubt that twanged in her voice, but Da Mi, as always, overlooked her gauche reply.

'It combines meditation and science; Buddhism and rational enquiry,' she said. 'If I had invented it I could die now, a fulfilled woman.'

Whatever it did to your head, the Chair did look sexy, kind of like a strappy shoe. And Da Mi hadn't been lying last time, had she?

What the hell. 'Okay,' she agreed.

'That's very brave of you, Sydney. You won't regret it, I promise.'

Sydney climbed into the chair, tugged down her skirt and adjusted the pillow behind her head, making herself comfortable. Da Mi wrapped thin black cables round her ankles and wrists, attached round sticky pads to her neck and buckled a wide belt around her waist. 'These are energy sensors. They'll monitor and moderate your heart rate, balance your hormones and harmonise your qi. You could just lie in the Chair and sleep or watch TV, but for the full healing effect, you'll need to wear the goggles again.'

Sydney lay still as Da Mi pulled the goggles back down over her head. This time, instead of blackness, her vision was filled with a soft, pearly pink, and instead of echoey breathing a delicate melody, all bells and violins, whispered in her ears.

'At a certain point, you'll hear my voice asking you a few questions. Don't try to speak; just imagine you are nodding or shaking your head and the system will pick up your intention. Okay?'

Sydney nodded, and fell away into a beautiful pink dream.

At first there was the calm, swoony music, all around her, and soft colours, blossoming like flowers for what felt like forever. She could barely remember the straps and belts; all she felt was a lovely light warmth and cosiness, as if she were wrapped up in a huge summer duvet. Then – she didn't know after how long – she rose and floated above the chair until she was suspended within a subtle, flowing river of pink and orange light. Swaying in this tranquillity, beneath a glowing sun, she sensed a dancing movement in the distance, and soon she could see girls in long dresses swirling in the arms of laughing young men. Behind them she could make out fluttering

flags on the turrets of a castle on the green flank of a hill. Bluebirds
flashed above the dancers as the girls spun between the boys. The
girls' pointy features were as familiar as Sydney's own face. They
were holding pink and yellow ribbons and as the dancers drew closer,
encircling her head, the ribbons wove into a tent around her, whirling
with the girls' green and blue gowns and long blonde hair into a
blurry canopy of light. Lost in a weightless, candy-coloured dream,
her breath slowly rising and falling, Sydney knew only that she had
been missing an essential element of bliss when Da Mi's questions
began.

'Are you comfortable?'

Da Mi was there. Da Mi knew. *Da Mi cared.*

Yes. She nodded slowly.

'Good. Are you breathing deeply?'

Yes.

'Lovely. Are you happy?'

Yes. Oh yes. Yes. Yes . . .

'Wonderful. Now, can you imagine anything that would upset you
right now?'

The question had no meaning. Upset? Slowly, Sydney shook her
head, and a wave of gold rippled through around her, releasing the
scent of star-gazer lilies.

'Anything at all that would make you angry or afraid?'

Marvelling at the scent of the lilies, Sydney was baffled by the
suggestion. Again, the answer was *No.*

'Good – that's very good. I'm very pleased for you, Sydney. But just
to be sure, can you do something for me now?'

Yes. Of course.

'Sydney, please try to remember the alleyway in Vancouver, the
place you visited just now – the man and woman, in the alley. Can
you remember them?'

Dimly at first, then coming into sharper focus: the image of the man in the heavy coat and the woman with the bruised face drifted into Sydney's mind. They were walking into the blood-red alleyway, but she knew that neither of them really wanted to go there with each other. The man and the woman weren't happy or peaceful; not like her. Not like Da Mi.

'It's sad, isn't it?' Da Mi sounded compassionate. Da Mi understood.

Yes, Sydney nodded as the man punched the woman. Very sad.

'Is the man hurting the woman?'

Yes. The man was holding her down and raping her. *Yes*.

'How does the woman feel?'

Oh, that was a hard place to go. Zooming in close to the woman being raped, a woman she would ignore if she saw her on the street, maybe even cross over to avoid. A scrawny, angry junky who did what she did to numb her feelings, blot out the world. Was she numb on that mattress? Was this normal for her?

'Just open your mind, Sydney. Let her show you how she feels.'

The man shifted, and from between the woman's flattened breasts, a glass bubble emerged. Inside it was the image of a child, a little brown-skinned girl wearing jeans and a T-shirt and a beaded head-band, dancing in a field of long grass. Was that the woman? Or her daughter? The bubble hovered over the woman's body, like an emergency capsule leaving an empty space ship.

Hi yi yi. Hi yi yi. Sometimes in Vancouver Sydney had heard Native people drumming and chanting from back yards or apartments. The sound came back to her now: *Hi yi yi. Hi yi yi.* She'd liked hearing it. Native people were strong. They were always there; they hadn't gone away, even though white people kept trying to shoot them and poison them and take all their land. Annie had told her about it all. This woman was strong. Even if he killed her, she was stronger than this man because she was still dancing inside.

I'm sorry I called you a hooker, Sydney said to the woman. *I wish I knew your name.*

I'm sorry I'm scared of you. I wish I knew your story.

Something eased in her chest. Was that just her feeling better, or did the woman hear her, somehow?

'What about the man?' Da Mi coaxed. 'Do you hate that man?'

That man was very sad. Inside he was sad and angry and full of hate. No one loved that man. Someone had hurt him when he was a child. She could see the child inside his heart too, now, very clearly: a tow-headed boy with freckles and big ears, crying, and shrinking up against a wall. The man couldn't release him into the world. He was keeping the child locked up inside him. No, she didn't hate him. *No.*

'Do you feel angry with him?'

That was harder. Yes, she was angry with him – but not with the little boy inside him. The little boy needed love. And what was the point of everyone pouring anger into the world, like raw sewage into an ocean filled with golden fish and haunting songs? No, the man was doing a bad thing, a very bad thing, a sad and terrible thing, raising that knife and plunging it into the woman, into her chest and throat, but she wasn't angry with him. *No.*

'Do you feel afraid?'

No. Tears began to gather in the corners of Sydney's eyes. They slipped beneath the padded rims of the goggles and down her cheeks.

'You feel sad?'

Yes.

'Just sad?'

No.

'What else?'

Love. Yes, she felt love: warm, powerful, healing love.

'Love. How beautiful. Can you give some love to the man and the woman?'

Yes. She smiled. *Yes.* And out of her heart came a huge sphere of golden light, arching high up above the world, into the stratospheres and the stars, and then down again, down into the alley where it flowed through the hovering glass bubble and the dancing girl, and into the hearts of the man and the woman. Slowly, as if lifted by a great wave of sorrow and regret, the man detached himself from the woman, and fell back on the ground in a foetal position. Instantly, with a huge pulse of relief, the glass bubble burst into glittering fragments and the little girl was dancing freely in the air. As she spun and leapt, the little boy pushed his way out of the man's chest and climbed into the air. The children didn't touch, but for a moment they both glowed like coals. Then, in twin starbursts of light, the children disappeared and in their place two small golden birds fluttered up and up, out of the alleyway and into the sky, the red sky that was now turning pink.

The alleyway was fading now. The amber sun was still floating above the green field. The pink and orange river was still streaming gently around her. She was drifting now into an ocean of music. She was happy, calm and full of love. Love was the answer. *Love.*

'Take as long as you like coming back, Sydney.' Softly, the lounger emerged beneath her body. The music faded out, and Da Mi was stroking her hand.

'That was *incredible.*' Sydney crossed her hands over her heart, and leaned toward Da Mi. They were sitting on the cushions in the centre of the *anbang* again. 'What *happened* to me in there?'

'Technically speaking, the chair sends out signals that affect the serotonin receptors in the brain,' Da Mi explained. 'The pleasure this produces allows the mind to move beyond fear and anxiety, into what I would call a higher, more evolved level of consciousness. You could say that the chair fine-tunes our brain waves, or perhaps, as the inventors do, you could call it an Enlightenment Chair.'

177

Sydney wanted to follow the science, but she was still trying to understand what she'd just seen and felt. 'I just don't get it. I mean, a few minutes ago I was in pieces – and then I was *forgiving* that man, and I think I *understood* that woman, how she survived, how strong she was, everything. I guess it was all just in my head. But it felt *amazing*. How does it work so *quickly*?'

'It doesn't normally. The chair is a German product, a meditative tool used to induce a profound state of calm. But I have discovered that when I take the honey drink before I use it, the chair not only makes it impossible to even conceive of a whole spectrum of negative emotions, it also replaces them with a euphoric sense of forgiveness. After two teaspoons of honey, you could lie in that chair and think of people you absolutely detest, but you would be unable to feel anything but love and compassion for them.'

Sydney's body was still singing, her mind translucent as the paper in the latticed *anbang* screen. Unbidden, an image of her mom dancing in the kitchen with Darren came into soft focus in her mind. They were laughing and kissing, and then her mom turned to her. *Come here, Sydney*, she called, *come and have a hug*. Up close her mom's face was lined but pretty; her lipstick was smudged and she smelled of menthol cigarettes. She had been happy once, Sydney remembered. Darren had a beer in his hand. He ran the other one through Sydney's hair. Yeah, even Darren had been nice to her when she was little. It was only later that he changed, after she grew tits and he lost his job and started slobbing around the house and drinking all day. People were weak. Sometimes you did just have to forgive them.

She stretched her legs. 'You could be the leader of a new religion, Da Mi.'

'No, I couldn't.' Da Mi smoothed her skirt. 'The effect is temporary. Taking regular sessions in the chair does help one aspire to a certain level of emotional detachment, but they can't permanently alter the structure of the brain. I still feel annoyance, anger, jealousy, every day, in the usual petty ways. Even now, you're probably wondering if you really forgive that man.'

'No!' Sydney exclaimed, 'I do!' But even as she said it, there was an uncomfortable twinge in her stomach. Forgiving a rapist – wasn't that pointless and stupid? A guy like that didn't care how nice you were to him; he'd hurt you in a second if he could. And as for her mom . . . *You're the biggest mistake I ever made*, her mom had said to her once – did a mother like that deserve to be forgiven?

'I mean, I *did*,' she said awkwardly. 'But it's not about forgiveness, is it? You have to stop bad people, lock them up, not just sit in a chair and understand them.'

'You see? First you start using the past tense, then you start rationalising, and soon the whole experience will seem like a dream. If you read about a rapist in the newspaper tomorrow, you'll instinctively fear and hate him. Even if you were to use the Chair regularly, you would still need to make a significant, conscious effort in normal life to utilise its teachings.'

Listening to Da Mi now was like being dashed with cold water. It couldn't be, could it, that the beautiful feeling of loving forgiveness she had just experienced was evaporating, leaving the whole world cruel and heartless again?

No, Sydney thought, *I mustn't panic*. Even if she returned to a normal state of consciousness, she could never be the same. She had experienced the loss of hatred and fear, she had felt peaceful and generous, healed. She wanted to live like that forever. And if she couldn't, she wanted to keep one thing from her session.

'The woman was real, right?' she asked, urgently. 'What was her name?'

'Her name,' Da Mi replied gravely, 'was Leanne LaRue. Despite the hackers' best efforts, her killer was never found. But at least she was discovered soon after her death, unlike so many First Nations women who have disappeared in British Columbia, and her relatives were able to bury her body.'

It felt important to know everything. 'Did she have a little girl?'

'I don't know, Sydney. Why?'

Sydney rubbed the edge of the silk cushion with her fingers. 'I just wondered, that's all.'

Leanne LaRue. One day she'd go to that alley and leave flowers on that mattress for her. In the meantime, she had to help Da Mi put an *end* to this shit. She leaned forward, intently. 'Can you develop the Chair?' she asked. 'In your project?'

'Develop the Chair? Possibly. But the problem is, Sydney, you're right.'

Her, right? 'About what?'

'In fact, it's not *us* who need to radically change, but violent people. And there are so many of them: far too many to help with the Chair. Currently, there are fewer than one hundred of these Chairs in existence, and the rare orchids needed for my honey – that's just enough for me and my friends – require a huge greenhouse and constant maintenance. Even if I could work with the manufacturers to make the effects permanent, we wouldn't be able to make the Enlightenment Experience available to the population of one small prison, let alone the world.'

Oh. She got it. The Chair was a temporary high for people with money – just like the Girlfriend Experience, in fact, though Sydney wasn't going to explain *that* to Da Mi.

'What the chair demonstrates, however,' Da Mi continued, 'is that it is possible to alter human behaviour by altering our emotions. We experience emotions physically, of course, as reactions to our environment, but in fact, they are regulated by the brain. So if I can't change the world, then what I need to do is design a new brain: one that generates more love and less fear and aggression – a hi-speed broadband kind of brain, one that instantly downloads compassion and joy, skipping the tedious dial-up process that turns so many people off meditation. If I can do this, I can give birth to a new kind of person, one who will help create a new world ruled by happiness and generosity instead of greed and anger. Sydney, let me ask you seriously: is that something you would like to participate in?'

Da Mi's voice was like the candy-coloured river in the goggles. It flowed smoothly through Sydney, uplifting and caressing her, soothing her moment of fear. *Yes*, she thought, *yes*. If she could love and forgive a *rapist*, if she could experience understanding and compassion for her mom and Darren, even for a moment, then anything was possible in the world.

'Yes way, Da Mi!'

'Thank you, Sydney. I'm so glad. Please, take a look at this.' Da Mi pulled out a glossy colour brochure. *VirtuWorld* it read in a pointy, elegant font on the cover, above a picture of a castle surrounded by a daisy-chain of blond children in flowery hats.

'It's the place in the Chair!' she exclaimed.

'It is. It's also the project I would dearly love your help with. VirtuWorld is a GRIP and ConGlam co-production, a European theme park presently under construction on the banks of the Han.'

Sydney opened the brochure. The first page was bursting with pictures of hi-tech Euro-style rides. 'The Kremlin Gremlin, the Eyeful Tower,' she read. 'It looks really fun.'

'It will be a fantastic day out, Sydney, but the main attraction of the park won't be its virtual reality jousting tournaments, but the Peonies: one hundred and twenty cloned children, genetically gifted with superior musical and athletic ability and, most important of all, truly peaceful minds.'

Sydney turned the page to find a picture of an orchestra composed of sixty blond peas-in-a-pod girls and boys. They must all be Photoshopped, the same two kids, but still, it was freaky to look at.

'Clones? You can do that, Da Mi?'

'We've been able to do it for years, but only recently has the law been changed to allow us to bring these new, much-loved and inherently loving children into the world.'

Sydney leafed through the rest of the brochure, which was filled with pictures of the children: dancing, doing yoga, meditating, playing badminton, singing in a pop group wearing silver skirts and trousers. 'The Peonies is a cute name,' she said, hesitantly.

'ConGlam expects they will be a huge draw for Koreans, who value social conformity, but also admire excellence in achievement and the culture of the West. What ConGlam doesn't know is that the Peonies will also be the world's first race of truly enlightened human beings. Only you are privy to that secret.'

Sydney examined the pictures more closely. The children looked like kids at some fancy boarding school, their beautiful faces shining with intelligence and happiness. She took a deep breath and closed the brochure. 'But why are you telling me?' she whispered. 'I'm just a hick from Sticksville, BC.'

'No, Sydney,' Da Mi spoke with steady force, 'you are a brave, charming, resourceful young woman. As soon as I met you I knew you had something special to offer this project. ConGlam is looking for an egg donor, to provide fifty per cent of the Peonies' raw genetic material. I want you to be that donor, but I also want you to be the Queen of the Peonies, to be a central part of the image of VirtuWorld, and to work with me over the next decades to make a small but very real paradise on earth.' Da Mi's eyes misted, but she continued speaking, softly, almost as if to herself. 'For so long, I've been keeping this a secret. Even my most trusted medical staff know only that the children will be talented and gentle. I'm not a mad scientist, Sydney,

I'm a human being who needs to share her dreams, and after the way you responded so deeply to the Enlightenment Machine tonight, I know that I can share those dreams with you.'

Sydney hardly dared breathe, let alone speak. 'Of course you can, Da Mi,' she whispered.

'My dreams are the dreams of all people who have suffered, Sydney. I know from the little you've told me about your life that you are a survivor. You've overcome many difficulties and lonely times to arrive here tonight. Epigenetically speaking, that kind of spirit is an inheritable trait, and I want the Peonies to have it. If I can also give you the chance to thrive, that will bring me the greatest pleasure and honour.'

Da Mi bowed deeply from the waist, and Sydney reciprocated. When they rose again, Da Mi had tears in her eyes. 'Oh dear,' she said, 'you're going to think the Peonies are simply the pie-in-the-sky daydreams of a soft-hearted old woman, but I have the scientific proofs of my intentions. Here – I want you to ask every question you can think of.'

'You're not old, Da Mi,' Sydney protested as Da Mi handed her the leather notebook. It was filled with page after page of diagrams and equations, strange terminology, sets of initials circled in red ink. Sydney leafed through it, wondering if she would ever understand a single thing about 'genomes' and 'proteins', if she'd ever even be able to pronounce the words scattered throughout the pages like magic spells: 'serotonin', 'oxytocin', 'noradrenalin'. She'd had a friend called Nora once . . .

'So, um . . .' she started tentatively, 'how exactly are you going to change the brain?'

Da Mi leaned forward. 'Stem cells,' she said, with an air of quiet triumph.

Sydney nodded wisely. She sort of knew what stem cells were. Or at least she could Google them later.

'I've found a way to use them,' Da Mi continued, 'to alter the genes that govern the areas of the brain responsible for regulating love, altruism, and empathy. I'm building on decades of work by others, of course. I am just the vehicle, not the driver of this evolutionary change.'

Sydney closed the notebook and placed it back on the table. 'Won't it be weird for the clones, looking exactly like each other?' she asked. It was a dumb question. In response, Da Mi sighed.

'Science fiction has so much to answer for when it comes to the common perception of human clones,' she said. 'Twins and triplets are genetically identical and no one fears for their sanity, do they?' But the scientist wasn't expecting Sydney to answer. She was talking forcefully now, as if she were lecturing to a hall full of people. 'No, the Peonies will look alike, but each will have their own unique personalities and gifts, and they will also have loving and supportive surrogate mothers. Physically, psychologically and spiritually, the children will be among the healthiest people in the world. They might need protection from the cruelty and greed of society at first, but VirtuWorld will provide just that sheltered environment.'

Da Mi was back in the room now, smiling at her again. Sydney thought hard, trying to pick a better question this time. 'What about later?' she asked, 'when they've grown up?'

'As intelligent and confident adults, they will be free to live wherever they wish,' Da Mi assured her, and in a dreamy voice added, 'Perhaps they will start new religions, write great books, lead new political coalitions of the dispossessed and the right-thinking . . . At the very least, their own children will inherit their powerful consciousness, and spread peace into future generations. Once our "experiment" is proved successful, all parents in wealthy nations will be demanding Enlightenment genes for their own children, and if the UN could oversee the procedure in the developing world, the Peonies would multiply, like a single cell, indefinitely, until, two hundred years from now, the world will be the paradise visionaries and saints have always known it could be.'

She paused. Then, in a brisk new tone, she asked, 'Have you heard of the Mayan prophecies, Sydney?'

'Sure. They're about the end of the world – but it was supposed to happen in 2012, wasn't it?'

Da Mi smiled. 'The Mayan Prophecies foresee not the end of the world, but the end of one cycle of history and the beginning of another, far better human society. This transition is not an overnight event, but a process that will take decades, if not hundreds of years, to become fully apparent. In December 2012, there was a great planetary convergence – it marked the first day of the new Mayan Great Calendar, a new epoch that will eventually bring peace and prosperity to all human beings. The winter Solstice, December twenty-first, is traditionally a day to welcome the return of the light, and I want to implant the embryos on December twenty-second this year. Can you help me prepare for that date?'

It was all so wild and enormous, but if Da Mi thought she could help, she would try her hardest. 'Definitely, Da Mi.'

With a smile, Da Mi produced another contract from the briefcase. The terms included a sizable signing bonus, as well as large monthly payments for the next twenty years; in return, Sydney would undertake not only to provide the eggs for the clones, but to appear seasonally at VirtuWorld for banquets and feasts, dressed in the latest designer gowns. She would also be provided with an unlimited supply of honey, and she would be able to come to Da Mi's house to use the Enlightenment Chair whenever she wanted – though she would soon be able to afford one of her own, of course. *Maybe*, Sydney thought, as she took Da Mi's gold fountain pen in her hand, *Mom could never handle me because I wasn't ever going to grow up to be a wait-*

ress in small-town BC. It was hard to totally forgive all those vicious things her mom had said, but maybe one day, with Da Mi's help, she would be able to throw them out, like ugly, itchy clothes or painful, too-tight shoes. Then she'd get a brand-new outfit, one that suited her down to the ground.

She signed the contract.

Da Mi snuffed out the candles and they crawled back out of the *anbang*. It was dawn, birds were carolling in the trees, and the living room was gleaming, every polished surface offering armfuls of the golden gossamer light Sydney had been born to wear.

Part Four

KEEPING MUM

19 / The Flock

The women spent their last three days in Beijing sightseeing. It was mid-July and sweltering, but even Older Sister stopped complaining as the air-conditioned bus ferried them from The Forbidden City to Tiananmen Square, from the Ming Tombs to sprawling shopping markets. Wherever they went, Mee Hee craned her neck in all directions at the city swarming around them. Sometimes Beijing was homey as a village, people squatting, washing, cooking and sleeping on the sidewalks. Sometimes, with its massive office towers and their scalloped, angled profiles, the city was marvellously strange.

Su Jin was the only one not impressed. 'America is more modern,' she sniffed as the bus passed a group of construction workers smoking beside a huge crater in the road. 'In America, cigarettes are illegal, so the air is clean and no one has wrinkles any more. Soon, in America, people will live until they are two hundred. Then they can choose to be frozen until something new and exciting happens, or they'll move to Mars and meditate for peace, like the ancient monks in all religions of the world.'

'What rubbish,' Older Sister snorted in the seat opposite. 'You've been reading too many of Dr Dong Sun's trashy magazines, girl.'

Mee Hee reached out for her friend's hand. 'America must be a wonderful place if Dr Kim was educated there,' she said softly before Su Jin could snap back. 'Let's go one day and see for ourselves.'

Su Jin squeezed her hand, then let it go as the bus pulled into the parking lot. Soon the women were hiking along the Great Wall, exclaiming over the views from the endless, ancient rope of stone. Walking back, they passed other Koreans, laughing and taking photos of each other on the parapets: real South Koreans, in big black sunglasses and sparkly jewellery. They made Mee Hee feel very shy. Would she ever look as glamorous?

'Seoul has a big American influence,' said Su Jin knowledgeably, back on the bus. 'I can't wait to go there.'

'We won't be in the big city much,' Older Sister pronounced. 'We don't have to change our ways. I was born a country woman and I will die a country woman. Just give me a garden to tend and children to raise, that's all I ask.'

Yes, Mee Hee thought, *that's all I want too. But just to see Seoul, not to live there, just to visit, surely that wouldn't be beyond me?*

The bus left from Beijing the next morning with the Doctors Che sitting up front behind the South Korean driver, dressed in blue suits – like tour guides, they said. The journey to the coast took hours on the pot-holed highway, but the women were enchanted by the scenery – the emerald shoots of rice poking up in the paddies, farmers pushing their carts, the golden roofs of temples hidden in the hills. When they weren't looking out the windows they amused themselves by memorising their new passport names and making up stories about their pasts in South Korea. Mee Hee was now Cho Min Hee, a seamstress in a village in Kyonggido; she had won the trip to China in a lottery. It was the first time she'd ever left home, and her husband was very worried that she would stay in Beijing with a Chinese tailor. Everyone knew how nimble Chinese tailors were. But no, she'd bought her husband a piece of jade from the Forbidden Palace and was coming back home to live with him for ever.

At the ferry docks, the doctors handed over all their passports to the Immigration official. He rapidly thumbed through them and stamped their 'return' visas with a pounding rhythm. Thereafter, no one gave them a second glance.

They spent the night huddled in their bunks on the ship. Younger Sister was seasick and Older Sister stayed awake with her, holding her head and cleaning her mouth with a wet cloth whenever she threw up. Su Jin slept curled up tightly in a ball, but Mee Hee lay quietly for hours. Her photograph of Dr Kim was down at the bottom of her bag, but she didn't need to look at it to summon up her saviour's kind face. Usually that serene image would be enough to help her float off to sleep, but tonight she hovered in a half-dream, imagining her first meeting with the beautiful Dr Kim; wondering if she could ever dare to give Dr Tae Sun a present; allowing herself to remember, for the first time without crying, the feeling of Song Ju's head in the crook of her arm.

In the morning she drank coffee with the other women in the boat café. The ferry arrived in Inchon at noon. The women clung together on the deck, staring at the shoreline, then sat silently on the bus as it grumbled off the boat and into the busy port city. Even Su Jin could find no words to express the feeling of being in South Korea at last.

Everything was breathtakingly familiar, and yet so horribly different. The mountains visible behind the tall buildings were the same beloved shapes as the mountains in the North. The signs were all in Hangul; they could read the advertisements and the names of all the shops and *yogwans*; when they opened the bus windows they could even understand the cries of the vegetable salesmen, though the accents clanged in their ears. But the streets were zooming with cars and the air was heavy and sooty, and the narrow sidewalks were chaotic with people: jostling, hustling, well-dressed, blank-faced people with no thought to say *anneyong haseyo* to anyone at all. There were no bicycle lanes here, and only spindly ginkgo trees poking at odd intervals out of the pavement. The bus felt as comforting as their grandmothers' hearths compared to the snarling streets of Inchon.

All too soon, the bus pulled into the parking lot of a large hotel.

'You are going to spend the afternoon in the *mog yuk tan*, to recuperate from the journey,' Dr Tae Sun announced. 'Just bring your day-bags, please!'

How thoughtful he was. Mee Hee, her head still pulsing from the rollicking sea trip, was one of the first to get to her feet. She gave him a shy smile as she disembarked.

Outside, the women stood in a straggly clump on the tarmac. Shuffling to the safety of the luxurious bathhouse was about all they were capable of. They scrubbed and bathed as if in a trance, barely able to recognise themselves in the steamy mirrors behind the showers.

Later, they had seafood for dinner, right on the waterfront in an outdoor restaurant. With the help of a little soju, some of the women became giggly at last. At the foot of the table, Older Sister loudly told the waitress the correct way to stun and slice open a wet, wriggling eel. She had visited her sister once, on the coast, and learned exactly how.

Mee Hee and Su Jin sat beside the doctors and Che Dong Sun proudly explained life in the Republic, while his brother sat quietly at his side. Mee Hee gazed at Dr Tae Sun tenderly, understanding his inability to speak. He too was dumbfounded, being here at last.

As dusk fell, they got back onto the bus. As it coughed and purred its way down the highways and through the towns of Kyonggi-do Province, Mee Hee fell asleep, her head against the window.

She dreamed of eels and octopuses until she was awakened by a sharp poke from Su Jin, who was hissing, 'Wake up! We're here!'

The bus had stopped and her sisters were gathering their belongings from beneath the seats and from the racks above their heads.

Looking out of the window, Mee Hee could see a perfect, twinkling village spread out in front of her like a vision. Everything – the low thatched houses, the Meeting Hall, the trees, the two mountains rising behind the buildings like protective spirits – was exactly as it had been in the framed photos, except now, in the middle of the night, warm, honey-coloured light was shining softly through the *maru* walls of the houses, and each spiny curved tile on the roof of the Hall was etched silver in the moonlight.

Mee Hee emerged from the bus. Above her head the stars formed a graceful canopy, bright as a length of queenly silk. The air was vibrating with the sound of crickets in the paddies and beneath their insistent ticking she could hear animals rustling in the grass, a stream dancing past, her sisters murmuring as they too absorbed the beauty of the scene.

'Come now,' said Dr Tae Sun, gently taking her elbow. 'Let me show you and Su Jin to your new house.'

Mee Hee whispered, 'I am back in Korea. Thank you.' His eyes crinkled, and for a moment she thought he might speak. But he just leaned down to pick up her handbag.

'Dr Tae Sun and I will unload the luggage from the bus,' his brother announced loudly. 'Come now, you all remember which houses are yours from the photos, yes? Older Sister, please help me direct everyone correctly.'

Dr Tae Sun patted Mee Hee's arm. 'Just a moment,' he whispered, and went to help his brother. Mee Hee found Su Jin and reached for her hand. Soon they were following Dr Tae Sun as he carried their bags past three carved Spirit Posts into the village and up a narrow stone path to their new home.

20 / King Bling

The squeal of brakes and the stink of burning rubber seared the air. Startled, Damien looked up from his iced latte as a foreigner in a white convertible hurled a phat-looking watch into the gutter in front of him, where it smashed into bits. The car tore away. With a nibble of anxiety, Damien watched it go. Back in London, in twelve hours' time, England would be playing America in a World Cup semi-final at Wembley Stadium. He'd been on edge all day; no matter how much he'd tried to ignore the competition, how nonchalantly he'd taken England's stuttering progression through the group stages and early knockout games, how understated had been his celebration of the dramatic 2-3 quarter-final victory over Spain, not even a die-hard Collapsenik Hammer junkie could pretend he wouldn't be demolished if England were denied a World Cup final on home soil by the Yanks. This semi-final had Potential Psyche-Crusher stamped through it like Kiss Me Quick in a stick of Brighton rock.

But it was like the Somme: you just had to starch your upper lip and soldier on and up into your doom. Coffee finished, he headed over to the Samsung Apartment Block to teach his next lesson. His students were a couple of rich brats who refused to do anything but play dolls and compare Sailor Moon brandware. Eight-year-old Korean females, he'd concluded, were both the original Material Girls and the ultimate dialecticians: they only wanted something if it was (a) disgustingly expensive *and* (b) everyone else had it. Capitalism and communism would have melded long ago if they ran the world.

That day he watched Yoon So, cool as a sadist's cucumber, take a pair of plastic-handled scissors and chop her purple Happy Face eraser into tiny bits. Why not? She had a Hello Kitty pencil case with nine more like it inside. In spite of his better judgment, Damien was impressed. With two major earthquakes in the last month, famine in four African countries, massacres of protestors in Pakistan and Taiwan, the third Maldive atoll under water and Hurricane Rita swamping New York, what was there to be happy about? Sure, all his *hagwon* students were going crazy about the England–America game, planning to get up early to watch it before their morning lessons. But *they* weren't facing total emotional annihilation. If it wasn't for the fact they'd be terribly disappointed in him, he'd rather sleep right through it. When it came to world news Damien much preferred the recent item, so small you almost missed it, that Climax, Saskatchewan was officially the safest place on the planet. Now *that* had put a rare smile on his face.

'What the fuck do you mean, I'm not *suitable* as a donor?' Johnny shouted. 'That was the first clause in the deal: Johnny Sandman: King of VirtuWorld.' So much for being one up on Kim. The heat didn't help. A volley of forty-degree sunlight was thudding down on the Caddy, not cooling his temper. Jabbing at the dashboard, he raised the roof and started the air-con. Global warming had really screwed up the whole point of convertibles.

'I'm sorry, Mr Sandman' – Kim's insincerity oozed out of his Gotcha – 'but that clause was conditional on the health of your sperm and testing has indicated an abnormal tri-nucleotide repeat in your sample: one hundred and twelve copies of the sequence. While not dangerous in itself, this quantity risks transmitting an even longer repeat to your children, the so-called Fragile-X syndrome: the most common cause of autism and a range of other intellectual disabilities.'

Fragile-X Syndrome? What the fuck was Kim up to now? 'Recheck your figures, Doc,' he snorted. 'There've never been any retards, fragile, agile or otherwise, in my family. I'd appreciate a second opinion before I take any more of this *horseshit*. Where the fuck are you going!' He slammed on the brakes, just in time, missing some asshole on a solar-powered scooter. *Fucking rats on wheels. Someone should melt them all down into toaster ovens and stick the fat heads of the drivers inside them.*

'I know this must come as a shock.' Kim was enjoying this, he could tell, more than she'd like being roasted by a couple of No-balls fucking Prize winners, he bet. 'But I can assure you our lab results are the best in the field. I understand your disappointment, but we cannot use your genetic material in the production of the Peonies. The risk is far too high.'

Pedal to the metal, Johnny exited Hannamdaegyo Bridge and careened on to Olympic Expressway. To his right, pastel-painted LegoLand apartment blocks shimmered woozily in the heat. On his left, the Han River glittered like a blue rhinestone belt. Behind his Police sunglasses, an impulse of brainlight crackled at the edges of his vision. *A fucking migraine: what else did he need?* 'Look, Doc, I don't buy this for one teeny tiny minute,' he warned, digging in his pocket for his OxyPops. 'If you're such a fucking scientific genius, why don't you get in there and erase those nuclear tricycles or whatever the fuck they are?'

Kim launched into a longwinded excuse, sounding, as usual, like she'd stuck a thesaurus in the blender with honey and lighter fluid and mainlined the result. Why couldn't she just say, 'I've got it in for you, asshole, and I'm not going stop 'til you're back on Venice Beach, panhandling like the dirty junkie bum I know you are'?

Johnny tipped back his head and gulped down two pills. As the oxygen started its soothing chain reaction first up to his fried synapses, and then down his tense vertebrae, he experienced a swift, cold surge of logical deduction. Could the Doc possibly know about what had happened at the morgue?

No. If she'd found out about that, she'd do more than just ditch his sperm, and she wouldn't be giving him any nicey-nicey warnings, either. No, he knew what was really happening here. Breaking a personal promise to himself not ever to talk to Kim about Sydney, he growled, 'The girl's behind all this, isn't she? She's got you twisted round her little finger, just like she screwed me blind.'

'Miss Travers is completely unaware of our involvement, Mr Sandman.'

'And that's the way you want to keep it, isn't it? When are you going to tell her I'm going to be the King at those fucking banquets we've been designing the menus for, hey? Or are you going to get some other joker for that job too?' Grinding his jaw, Johnny overtook a Hyundai people carrier with 'Lucifer's Hammer: The Rapture is Coming!' stickers plastered all over the back window. Inside, a bumper crop of happy-clappy Jesus Freaks were making fish faces in unison: singing hymns or practising their sucking-off-the-Pope technique: who knew, and who cared?

'That's something else I need to discuss with you. Recent market research has indicated a strong preference among Korean women for dark-haired, pale-skinned Englishmen. I am sorry to have to break it to you, but ConGlam have initiated talks with the actor Hugh Grant to play the role of the King.'

What? Johnny practically choked. 'You don't know what you're doing, Kim,' he sputtered. 'You don't have a clue how much you owe me. All ConGlam ever wanted from GRIP was the ProxyBod prototype. Who backed you one hundred per cent on VirtuWorld? Johnny

Sandman. Who recruited Sydney? Johnny Sandman. Who's done all the footwork, all the dirty work? *Johnny Sandman.* If you think you can sideline me in my own company, you're thinking very wrong indeed.'

Up ahead, the broad, ribbed dome of Chamshil Stadium bulged out of Sports Complex Park, a giant woodlouse waiting to be trodden on by a cruel, relentless god. Johnny accelerated as Kim blabbed on, thanking him for his instigating role in the VirtuWorld project, hoping he would stay on as liaison officer, assuring him he would still maintain his excellent salary and expense account, praising his expertise, financial acumen, blah-di-blah blah blah. 'With time,' she concluded, 'I'm sure you will appreciate the rationale behind my decisions.'

'With time,' he mimicked her, then turned up the menace, 'you're going to regret this very deeply, Kim.'

'Are you threatening me, Mr Sandman?' Her voice was tight and icy as a polar bear's asshole. Johnny paused. He'd been on a knife's edge at work since Sydney left. On the one hand he wanted to march into meetings with an AK47 and blow the entire GRIP board away; on the other, upon his return from China he'd started negotiations with Han Air and the Korean National Tourist Board and he was halfway to convincing a senior government official to subsidise off-season return flights from Europe and the States. LA was very pleased; he'd been assured a big Christmas bonus if he signed the deal by December, plus a spa holiday in Malaysia. In another year or two he'd be in a position to fuck Kim up, big time. Then there'd be no one to protect little Sydney any more.

'Excuse me, Doc, I was talking to some selfish maniac on the road,' he replied, syrupy with sarcasm. 'I do appreciate your concern for my future offspring. Thank you very much is what I'd like to say.'

'That's what I thought. Again, thank you very much for your assistance last night. And I'm sorry to have been the bearer of bad news.'

Johnny clicked off the Gotcha. His stomach was eating him alive. It hurt talking about Sydney – *physically* hurt. It was painful even to think about her – he'd remember that time she got a goofy spot of soup on her chin and the lopsided smile she'd cracked when he'd rubbed it away, or how she used to wander out from the bathroom in her panties and ask him to moisturise that spot between her shoulder blades she couldn't reach. Then his guts would contract and he'd feel like chucking up. And this morning he'd dreamed about her: that she was back, walking in the door, her little tits brushing against his chest as she leaned towards him for a kiss . . . then a tangle of worms and a cloud of ashes spilled out of her mouth, the room exploded with cackling and hissing and he'd woken up, his eyes hot with tears.

Yeah, *tears*: not good; *not good*. Even in a dream, no one made the Sandman cry. Those bitches deserved everything that was coming to them, but right now, he was going to step on the gas, turn up the speakers and blast 'My Way' so loud it would break every plate-glass window in Seoul. Then he was going to smash a few squash balls into the eye-sockets of his opponents at Sports Complex. And later? He'd be taking some quality time to fine-tune his long-range plans for Sydney Travers and Dr Kim Da Mi.

'I'm so sorry to drop in on you like this, Sydney. I just don't know what to do.' Da Mi set her cup of pollen-water down on Sydney's coffee table and massaged her right temple. Even her silk blouse was quivering with distress.

'That's no problem, Da Mi – what's going on?' Sydney tried to sound reassuring, but it was weird having Da Mi at her place. Normally they met down at the lab, where they were doing all kinds of tests to make sure Sydney could safely donate her eggs. Then they'd drink honey-water and Sydney would play with the white kittens Da Mi was cloning for the top department stores. It had been a real surprise today when the scientist had called to invite herself round.

'The King of the Peonies, Sydney, has become a major headache.'

'I thought you said he was all ready to go?'

'He was – but now you're on board, things have changed. Our first choice was a light-haired man like you, but of course it's highly problematic to be creating a group of exclusively blond super-children.'

'Really?' Sydney said brightly. 'Wouldn't it make up for, like, a hundred years of dumb blonde jokes?'

Da Mi didn't laugh. 'I'm sure you'll remember, Sydney,' she said firmly, 'that the Nazis tried desperately to create a dominant race of blond people. They exterminated anyone who didn't conform to this stereotype, and in the process gave us geneticists a terrible legacy to struggle against.'

Sydney screwed up her face. 'Oh yeah, right. I forgot about that. I know about the concentration camps, Da Mi.'

Da Mi patted her hand. 'I know you do, darling. Young people today aren't taught properly about the Nazis' wider programme, but I am determined not to feed into their lingering myth. ConGlam's vision of exotic blond Peonies has always troubled me, and so I've finally convinced them to support different colourings. I've also commissioned some market research, and it appears that a dark-haired King would be more appealing to the average Korean woman.'

'It's a great job; I bet loads of guys would want to do it,' Sydney said encouragingly, stirring another dollop of honey into her *cha*. It was fantastic not having to worry so much about calories. She didn't want to get fat, of course, but as soon as she was the Queen, she wouldn't have to fit into sample dress sizes any more.

'It's a bit more complicated than that, I'm afraid. This is top secret, Sydney, but I'm very pleased to tell you that ConGlam are approaching

Hugh Grant to play the King.'

'Hugh Grant? – oh yeah, that British actor. But isn't he a bit old for me?'

'He has a lot of fans in Asia, especially since fathering a half-Chinese child. And his age would be an asset here. But there's no question of him donating sperm; the inheritance laws would make his fortune vulnerable to future claims. And in any case, he wouldn't be suitable as a genetic donor.'

'How come?'

Da Mi rubbed her forehead. 'He can't sing, and our Peonies must be musical. As you're not especially gifted in that department, we need to find a Hugh Grant look-alike with a good voice – right away.'

Sydney put down her cup. 'Don't worry, Da Mi; Hugh Grant's pretty ordinary-looking really. There must be loads of guys that look like him, and lots of them who can sing.'

Da Mi clicked open her briefcase. 'In fact, Sydney, there are exactly three young men with documented singing voices who closely resemble Hugh Grant living in Korea right now.' She passed three photographs to Sydney. 'A friend of mine at Kimpo Airport provided me with these,' she said. 'They're all young men who've arrived in Seoul in the last year. I know their names, but it's been hard to trace them. I was hoping you could keep a look-out in the nightclubs while I try other methods of detection. There'll be a healthy commission if you find the right person.'

More money? Sydney tried to look honoured rather than delighted as she flipped through the photos. They were all of guys with dark hair, standing in an airport queue.

'Hey – this guy.' She peered closer. His name and nationality were written on the bottom of the picture. 'Damien Meadows, UK – I've met him.'

'Really?' Da Mi reached for the photo. 'Where?'

'In Hongdae – in a nightclub.'

'Sydney, that's wonderful – he's perfect. Very *About A Boy*. And' – Da Mi riffled through her briefcase again and pulled out a sheet from a file – 'he apparently has real musical talent.'

She passed the paper to Sydney. It was a printout from an English newspaper website: a photo of a little boy in a white dress with a red tunic-y thing over it. Apparently, Damien Meadows, at the age of eight, had won a choirboy competition.

'No way! That's so cute, Da Mi!'

The scientist took the sheet back. 'Wouldn't it be perfect if the Peonies had the voices of angels? Do you think you could find him again?'

'Yeah, sure – all the foreigners end up in that club on a Saturday night.' Sydney tried to remember when she'd met the guy – oh, right, it was the night she'd met Jae Ho. Come to think of it, Damien had been into her. She giggled. 'I think he liked me. I'm sure I could have his pants down around his ankles in no time!'

Da Mi indulged her with a laugh, but replied in a serious tone, 'Sydney, I am extremely anxious that nothing further goes wrong with the selection of the King. If any of our competitors get wind of this, before you know it copy-cat VirtuWorlds will be springing up all over Asia. If you *are* able to contact Damien, I would prefer him to think of himself as simply an anonymous donor for an infertile ex-pat couple.'

Sydney saw tiny lines at the corners of Da Mi's mouth and eyes. Jeez, it must be a nightmare, having to organise all this as well as the science stuff in the lab. And yeah, dragging some cowboy in off the streets was pretty risky; most guys in Seoul were just here to get paid and get laid. They couldn't be trusted to share Da Mi's vision of the Peonies.

'Anonymous donors usually don't care about seeing the kids,' she offered. 'It would hardly matter to him if he was helping make one kid or five hundred.'

Da Mi relaxed into the sofa. 'I knew we'd see eye to eye on this.'

It was so good to make Da Mi happy. 'Hey, you're just trying to make something wonderful happen and all you need is a bit of raw material.'

'It will take him ten minutes – and he'll be very well paid. I'm sure he'll thank you for the opportunity. Now, here: I have a present for you.'

She handed Sydney a small package wrapped in gold tissue paper. Inside was a top-of-the-market, new-range Gotcha Watch: a sleek silver bracelet ridged with elegant buttons, its LED display embedded in a dark green comma-shaped face.

She was silent. She couldn't even say thank you. Da Mi, with her perfect manners, filled in the gap. 'I'm sorry if it seems extravagant,' she said, lifting the watch out of the box. 'But Gotchas can be very useful. Look: it's set up to one-button call my MoPho. You just press here – I don't want you going into nightclubs without immediate back-up.'

Her mouth was dry; she was barely listening to Da Mi. 'Where did you get it?' she whispered.

'I got it wholesale, actually. From a ConGlam contact. Why?'

ConGlam distributed Gotchas? It took Sydney a moment to find her voice. 'I had one before,' she said at last. 'With a matching EarRinger. Johnny gave them to me. He said they were exclusive to his supplier.' Her voice fell to a whisper. 'Da Mi, do you think he works for ConGlam too?'

Da Mi met Sydney's gaze. 'That is another thing I have to talk to you about, Sydney. After what you said about Johnny at the Hyatt, I was worried about your safety. I got a friend to look into him for me. It turns out he *is* doing some commercial fieldwork for ConGlam.

No, wait—' She raised her palm as Sydney groaned. 'That would explain how he got his hands on the Gotcha. But I can assure you he has nothing to do with VirtuWorld. The park is highly classified, and I have total access to the employment files.'

For the first time in weeks, Sydney felt a skewer of fear. 'Jeez, Da Mi, do you think if he found out about my contract he'd try to hurt me?'

'He's not bothered you so far, but on the other hand, he's petulant, jealous and childish. If he does hear of your involvement with ConGlam, he might feel you're treading on his patch. Honestly, darling, I'd feel so much better if you wore this.'

Sydney picked up the Gotcha again.

'The design is based on comma jade.' Da Mi's voice was melted caramel. 'It was highly prized in Ancient Korea. Look, this button shows the time, and this one activates the phone. The Gotcha will call me directly – you can speak into it, and listen by holding it up to your ear. I think that earring design is a little intrusive, don't you?'

Sydney slipped the Gotcha over her wrist. The comma was like one half of the Korean *Eum-Yang*: connecting her strength to Da Mi's. Johnny didn't know who she had on her side now. Let him try to hurt her – just let him try.

'It's beautiful,' she said. 'I'll never take it off.'

After an hour's muggy bus ride and two hours at his evening *hagwon* job, Damien trudged back up to his flat, past ripe piles of rubbish, broken furniture and an abandoned refrigerator. *Ajashis* and *ajummas* sat on the steps lining the steep road, cooling their weathered faces with bamboo fans while their grandchildren strutted around sucking on Freezies. The Dong had its own ways of dealing with the heat.

Back home, Damien had a cool shower, and took a beer, his laptop and his electric fan out on the roof. With no air-con, the flat was impossible – not that the patio was much better. But he had a lounge-chair to flop on and the sunsets were great, thanks to the pollution. Once it got dark, he'd surf the net, plug into the pre-match build-up.

In a previous life, this would be a dope-smoking occasion, but Damien no longer bothered with the odd toke, not even a free E. It was weird, but since dancing with that blonde model he'd been more relaxed than he could ever remember – as if her brief, melting appearance really was a sign from Jessica to tell him he was on the right track here in Korea, with his vow of clean living and punishing schedule. And if that was just superstitious nonsense, well, what was the point of getting to know her to find out the truth? Nothing about the blonde's real life could be nearly as significant as her chance resemblance to his dead twin.

The sun was floating like a skinned peach in a bowl of pink and orange smog and the crescent moon was just visible, a pale lemon rind in the cocktail of the sky. Lying in the warm dusk, listening to the random sounds of the city, a breathy, early synthpop tune came to mind . . . Thomas Dolby? 'Airwaves'? Then he was remembering a game he'd once played with Jessica, something she'd invented when they were banished to their room for squabbling over the radio. He was the moon and she was the sun and they were going to punish the people on Earth by leaving the solar system and rolling deep into space. Like footballs, he'd said; no, like bowling balls, she'd told him. They were going to knock down anything in their way – space-ships, comets, asteroids – until they found a planet that needed them, then they'd orbit it forever, feeding it sunlight and moonlight, so plants could grow, tides turn, and the people and animals could come outside from the caves where they'd been hiding. And then they'd open a disco, Jessica had said.

They'd danced around the room, clambering over the beds and

climbing on chairs, singing The Human League and Thomas Dolby songs at the top of their lungs, leaving everyone and everything behind . . . He'd had a pure, high voice, better than hers – Mum had forced him to sing in the church choir and Jess had been so jealous when he'd won that award. After she disappeared he'd quit. He hadn't sung again, ever. He'd tried a couple of times, but nothing came out except dust and creaking hinges. Mum had been really sad about that. Every now and then she'd ask him if he wanted to try again, but he'd always shaken his head. He couldn't say anything, but Dad had understood.

But now, at last, being Jessica's twin felt okay again: not like being a freak with a fucked-up past, or walking around with no coat in a rainstorm, but like having a secret ally, someone not even death could snatch away.

'Dah dah dah-dah dah dah dah-dah dah dah daaaaah,' he ventured, under his breath. Not bad. Then the girl's part – 'I' – a high note . . . *No, shut up, Meadows*. It was bloody ridiculous, singing classic crap eighties pop duets to himself. As the moon bit into the darkening sky Damien fired up his laptop. Time to check into Hotel Reluctant Patriot for an hour or so.

He didn't last long. The febrile pre-match hype and his long working day both conspired to fatigue his very soul. In a few hours all that hope and excitement would have turned to greasy ashes in the mouth of a once-proud footballing nation. And if he was going to wake up at five a.m. and work solidly until eight p.m., he should get some kip. He shut down the PC, reset his MoPho alarm, stretched out and closed his eyes.

The MoPho alarm warbled into his consciousness. He stretched, stiff from his night on the lounger, and powered up his laptop. *Right, Meadows*, he told himself, *do your duty, be an Englishman for once. It's time to join your countrymen worldwide in a ritual immersion in failure, self-castigation and utter loathing of the Yanks.*

The headlines hit him like a lorryload of ice.

Shivering, he could do nothing but read helplessly on, devouring online broadsheets, racing through blog after blog. Jake texted, the *hagwon* rang, but he ignored his MoPho, ignored his growling hunger, his growing thirst, his need to piss until, at seven o'clock, he paced to the edge of the roof and stared out unseeing over the blaring, oblivious city, thinking, *Holy fuck, holy fuck,* holy fuck!

And then, rubbing his sore shoulder and taking in a lungful of smog: '*Snukes?*' What the hell kind of kiddie telly word was *snukes*?

21 | The Beloved Leaderess

Her first morning in the village, Mee Hee woke early and stretched in the gauzy summer light. She gazed happily up at the rafters. There was so much space beneath the thatched roofs of the houses: a large *maru* room, a kitchen, a bathroom, and *three* bedrooms: one for each woman and a bigger one for the children later, Dr Tae Sun had said last night. Or the women could share and let each set of twins have a room. Mee Hee and Su Jin had pulled their *yos* into one room within ten minutes of arriving at the house.

Now Mee Hee sat up, smoothed the sheets and bowed her head towards her photograph of Dr Kim, which she had placed on a low table beside the *yo*. Last night she had decided that every day she would give thanks to the doctor for her beautiful new home. Now she prayed she would be worthy of the honour and luxury Dr Kim was bestowing upon her.

Across the room, Su Jin stirred, blinking in the light.

'Good morning,' Mee Hee chirped.

'Nyuhhh.'

Su Jin often took a few minutes to fully awaken. Mee Hee got up and washed, then pulled on the pink linen trousers and shirt that had been waiting for her in the house. They were a traditional country design, cut for comfort. Su Jin had a set too, in beautiful spring green.

Su Jin sniffed, though, when she finally got up and dressed. 'These aren't very stylish, are they?'

'They're lovely, Su Jin. Look at the care that's gone into the stitching.'

'They make us look shapeless,' Su Jin complained, but she ran her hands over the fine weave and fingered the twisted cloth buttons.

'There'll be lots of time to dress up later,' Mee Hee said dreamily. 'Dr Kim wants us all to be like princesses in her new world.'

Su Jin pointed her nose in the air and put on a haughty voice. 'Princess Mee Hee! Princess Su Jin! You've been digging for carrots again – clean your fingernails at once!'

'Oh, Su Jin, she's not like that.'

Su Jin sat down on her *yo* and began to brush her hair. 'We don't know what she's like, do we?'

'We will soon. Dr Tae Sun said she would visit *this week*.' Mee Hee picked up her photograph of the doctor. 'She will probably look even more beautiful in real life.'

'She's had a lot of work done on her,' Su Jin said knowledgeably.

'Work done?' Mee Hee frowned. 'What do you mean?'

'She's no spring chicken, is she? Dong Sun told me she's nearly sixty, but she looks about forty, so unless she made those videos years ago, she's had plastic surgery or Botox injections – or else she wears about eight layers of make-up.'

Mee Hee put the photograph back down on the table so it faced away from Su Jin. 'It doesn't matter. You can tell from her eyes how caring she is. Look what she's done for us already. We should put your photo of her in the living room, with flowers and a candle.'

Su Jin gave her a saucy look. 'That would make Dr Tae Sun *very* proud of us.'

'Oh, you!' Mee Hee picked up a pillow and threw it at her friend and Su Jin squealed and tossed it back across the room. It hit Mee Hee on the arm and bounced off on to her *yo*.

'Stop it!' She stamped her foot. 'We have to go for breakfast now.'

'You started it,' Su Jin said piously. 'Give me five more minutes. I want to do my nails.'

'Okay, but give me your photo. It's only right to show our respect, Su Jin.'

Rolling her eyes, Su Jin reached for her suitcase. The photo was down at the bottom, wrapped up in a bag of laundry she'd been too lazy to get done at the hotel.

'Our Beloved Leaderess.' She handed the photo to Mee Hee, then unzipped her make-up bag and took out a bottle of bright red nail polish. Her fingernails were growing well now, and she liked to do her toes too.

Mee Hee went into the kitchen to shine up the glass and the frame. Then she set the picture on a cabinet in the living room, beneath a scroll depicting birds and bees hovering around a rhododendron bush. Today she would gather some flowers in the woods and place them with a bowl of fruit beside Dr Kim.

It was a short walk down a grassy path to the Meeting House, where the women were gathering for breakfast, sitting around two long black tables set beneath a high timbered ceiling. The doctors were already there, each sitting at the head of one of the tables. Mee Hee stole a glance at Su Jin. Would she want to sit near Dr Dong Sun? But Su Jin was scrutinising the room, its empty bookshelves and large wall-mounted television screen. Without waiting, Mee Hee scurried to Dr Tae Sun's table. There were two places free near the top. She plumped herself down on a cushion and patted the other, saving it for Su Jin. The smell of newly cooked rice drifted out of the kitchen.

When all the women were present, the doctors stood up.

'Welcome Sisters,' Dr Dong Sun greeted them. 'This is your Meeting House. All our meals will held here together. In the evenings you can watch DVDs and relax, and during the day there will be pleasant tasks to accomplish – sewing, weaving and food preparation, and later, looking after the children together.'

'The fields outside are our garden.' Dr Tae Sun beamed. 'We will grow our own vegetables there. Some crops are already growing; later you can walk around and see them.

'Soon we will organise kitchen, garden and craftwork committees,' Dr Dong Sun continued, 'but this week the village cooks are preparing your meals – and it smells like breakfast is ready, so enjoy!'

Soon the women were eating egg rice and *kim chi* and small chewy fish, chattering excitedly about their wonderful new home.

'Our houses are blessed,' Mee Hee said quietly, to no one in particular. 'Good spirits look over them.'

'That's why we placed hemp cloths over the beams in the *maru* rooms.' Dr Tae Sun smiled at her from the head of the table. 'To honour the Kyonggi-do god and ask his protection for you all.'

'There are no outhouses,' Older Sister announced. Her neighbours tittered at this coarse observation, but she continued in a louder voice, 'so the outhouse gods cannot come and disturb our happiness!'

The women burst into laughter. As Mee Hee set down her chopsticks and pealed with merriment, she caught Dr Tae Sun's eye. He was smiling at her with such fondness that for a moment it felt as if he, not Dr Kim, had arranged everything – the trucks, the hotel, the ferry, the village – arranged it all to rescue her, to see her laugh until her stomach hurt, not with hunger, but with joy. Her face crimson, she looked away.

'Yes, there *is* an outhouse,' Dr Dong Sun declared to the raucous room, 'at the back of the vegetable garden. Make sure you always cough before you enter, to frighten the outhouse god away!'

The women laughed and talked on as the village cook and her helpers cleared the dishes and wiped the tables so they gleamed like ebony again. As the cooks refilled the teapots, Dr Dong Sun stood up to make an announcement.

'Today is for relaxing. Tomorrow, though, you must wait here after breakfast,' he said. 'Dr Kim Da Mi is driving down from Seoul for a very special meeting with you all.'

There was a twittering rush of excitement as the news sank in. Mee Hee hugged Su Jin, but her friend was stiff in her arms.

'Aren't you happy?' she whispered, suddenly frightened.

'Yes, yes,' Su Jin muttered. 'Of course.'

Mee Hee let go of her friend. Then, without knowing how she had summoned the courage, she raised her voice. 'We should decorate the Meeting House for her, with flowers from the garden.'

'What a wonderful idea.' Dr Tae Sun applauded. 'I hereby nominate Mee Hee as Head of the Flower Committee.'

'Oh!' Her hands flew to her mouth. What had she done?

'I second the nomination,' Dr Dong Sun boomed. 'Sisters, those who want to help Mee Hee plan for Dr Kim's visit can stay in the Meeting House. The rest are free to do as they please until lunch.'

Nearly half of the women stayed, but Su Jin gave her a peck on the cheek and disappeared.

The next morning the doctors were late for breakfast. The cooks served the food, but wouldn't speak to anyone. One of them was crying. Mee Hee lowered her eyes. Maybe the woman was grieving someone? Perhaps the wildflower arrangements in each corner of the room would help her feel better. It had been wonderful to pick the bouquets of sweet-smelling plants, feel their stiff stems in her hands, stroke the shiny blades of long grass.

Beside Mee Hee, Su Jin set down her tea cup with a clatter. 'I wish we could watch TV, not just DVDs' she complained to the table. 'The gardener said there's no radio or Internet because of the mountains. And we're not allowed to go to the shop to buy magazines.'

'You just got here!' Older Sister cut in. 'Why do you want to walk twenty miles to read some trash?'

'I wanted to read about our countrymen in the World Cup,' Su Jin hissed. 'The gardener said South Korea reached the quarter-final – against *Brazil*. They lost, but they played with honour. And the England–America semi-final was on television last night. That was a *historic* occasion.'

Older Sister snorted. 'Since when do you care about England and America?'

'We are citizens of the *world* now,' Su Jin hissed. 'Or at least *some* of us think we are.'

'Shhh.' Mee Hee hushed her friend. 'Here they are.'

Dr Tae Sun and Dr Dong Sun had entered the room. Their peas-in-a-pod faces were both pale and drawn. They'd been working so hard, Mee Hee thought; perhaps they hadn't slept well? The brothers took their seats and the breakfast began, but it was not the chatty meal of the day before. The doctors were silent, and the women spoke quietly to their housemates, not happily across the tables to each other.

Finally, as the cooks cleared the dirty plates away, Su Jin lifted her teacup. 'I wish to propose a toast to our football team in London,' she said loudly. 'To the Red Devils, who do both North and South Korea proud in every international competition.'

The doctors exchanged glances. Dr Tae Sun cleared his throat, but Dr Dong Sun rose to his feet. 'To the Red Devils. And to Mee Hee and the Flower Committee. The room looks beautiful.'

Mee Hee ducked her head as her sisters applauded.

'We did it together, for Dr Kim,' she stammered. But her voice was lost in the growl of a car engine and the sharp crunch of gravel outside.

'Sisters!' Dr Dong Sun rubbed his hands together and stood up. 'She's here. Quick, let's form a half-circle in front of the door. Come, there's plenty of room.'

Mee Hee felt so light and tingly she thought she might float up into the rafters. She held her breath as footsteps sounded on the wooden entranceway and bit her lip as the carved doors swung open. She wanted desperately to stare, but that would have been dreadfully rude, so like everyone else, she bowed her head and peeked through her lashes at the small woman in a green silk dress who entered the room.

Just a fluttery glimpse of the doctor revealed that she was far more beautiful than her image on the DVDs, or even in the photo. She was as glamorous and poised as a woman in her prime, as delightful and sparkling as a young girl, and as wise and loving as a grandmother. Now, before Mee Hee could sneak a sideways look at Su Jin, Dr Kim was flowing like a mountain stream into the Meeting Hall. She paused in front of the crescent of women, letting out a sigh of approval that brushed Mee Hee's heart like a breeze against a chime.

Beginning, as was right, with Older Sister, the doctor greeted each woman with a low bow and a few words of welcome. She knew everyone's names, and the names of their home villages. She took each Sister's hands between her own and thanked her gravely for coming to Kyonggido. When she came at last to Mee Hee, though, she stopped for a long time, her soulful dark eyes searching Mee Hee's face.

Mee Hee's heart beat rapidly. Was she not right? Did she not belong here after all?

'Lee Mee Hee,' Dr Kim said at last, her voice as rich and supple as warm milk. 'You are the one from my mother's village.'

'I didn't know—' Mee Hee lowered her head and tried to focus on her own clasped hands. Was it true? Was this honour truly hers?

'Dr Che came twice for you. Please, tell me: do I look like anyone you know?'

Mee Hee raised her chin, blinking back tears. With the greatest of difficulty, she forced herself to look directly into Dr Kim's enquiring face.

The doctor's skin was so refined, her mouth so perfectly painted, her hair so immaculately arranged, it was impossible to imagine her family being farmers or shopkeepers, people who spent all day sweating in the sun or crabbily counting goods in dark storehouses. But her soft, sad eyes were filled with a longing Mee Hee knew only too well. It was the blood-longing, the sorrow felt by all those who had family somewhere in the South. The hard war that had driven so many from their homes was decades ago now, but no matter how many new babies came, the blood-longing never left the eyes of the old people who had lost brothers or sisters, cousins or children to the South.

Swallowing hard, she lowered her eyes again and said, 'Perhaps you are descended from the Kims who ran the schoolhouse. I know they had a girl. Kim Hyun Woo, the man who is perhaps your uncle, he spoke often of his older sister, Kim Young Mi, thinking she must have done well for herself in the South. She was so beautiful and intelligent, he always said. Yes, perhaps you are the descendant of the teachers. They are a very good family. You have a *yangban* look about you. I think that must be so.'

Afraid, she raised her eyes again. Doctor Kim's face was lighting up slowly from within. One solitary tear slipped down her cheek like a pearl, gleaming as if warmed by her longing. And with the tear, some of the terrible yearning in her eyes was also slipping away. Mee Hee could see there was a new clearness in her gaze, the clearness of new knowledge that she, Mee Hee, had given. For a moment, as their eyes met, Mee Hee dared to imagine that perhaps she and Dr Kim might one day come to feel like real sisters . . . be there for each other, provide comfort, and share secrets, and Su Jin too . . .

But no, what was she thinking? She bowed, trying to make herself as small as possible, but Dr Kim reached for her hands and kissed them and clasped Mee Hee's hands to her blouse. Mee Hee's heart cried out in her chest.

Then Doctor Kim released her and stepped back, speaking loudly for the benefit of all the women, 'My mother's name was indeed Kim Young Mi, and now I know my uncle's name as well. Thank you, Lee Mee Hee. I am forever in your debt. I only wish I could affirm my uncle's dreams about his sister, but my mother did not survive the long march to the South. She died on the road, shortly after I was born. I was taken by the Red Cross and was fortunate to grow up in America, free from hardship and hunger, but thirsty always for knowledge of my birth family. Kim Hyun Woo? He is living still?'

Doctor Kim was addressing her again. Mee Hee straightened her back and tried to speak as calmly and clearly as possible. 'Kim Hyun Woo is old and very thin and weak, because he gives most of his food to the young ones, but he is hardy like a weed. Even though his own son died without giving him grandchildren, he says we must not let the ordeal of life defeat us. He still plays *baduk* every Sunday in the village square, and he teaches the older boys as well. He is famous for his laughter when he wins, and when he loses too. The magpie, they call him, because his good humour brings us luck.' Choking on emotion, Mee Hee stopped.

At the top of the line Older Sister was sobbing noisily, while many of the other women were wiping their eyes.

Dr Kim, however, remained still. 'You have my bottomless gratitude, Lee Mee Hee,' she said, in a voice that everyone could hear.

As Dr Kim turned to greet Younger Sister, at last, Mee Hee felt her toes leave the ground. Floating on a hazy carpet of light, she realised that she would die for this woman.

But she didn't have to die. She had to give birth.

22 / Womb Raider

It was two days after the World Cup bombing, and the centre of Seoul had been cordoned off by the police for a massive peace rally. Jin Sok had insisted Sydney come and march with him and his friends, so she went along, holding hands with the Korean models, chanting slogans and keeping an eye out for Damien Meadows. Da Mi was driving back from meeting the North Korean surrogate mothers in the mountains, but she'd called twice to see how Sydney was. She'd also suggested the rally might flush Damien out of hiding. But if it had, Sydney didn't see him in the heaving sea of people, flags and banners. At least the real Hugh Grant hadn't been at the football game like so many other celebs.

Da Mi had arranged to take her out for iced coffee in Apkuchong after the rally, so Jin Sok dropped her off in his location van, promising to see her again soon.

Da Mi was waiting in the elegant French café; she rose to give Sydney a hug as she entered. 'Darling, how are you?'

Sydney plopped herself down on a seat. 'I dunno – I didn't see Damien. And some of the people on the rally were saying Britain wants to bomb North Korea now.' Her lower lip began to tremble. 'I'm scared, Da Mi.'

Da Mi squeezed her hand. 'I know, darling. Lots of people are. But you're perfectly safe in Seoul. North Korea only ever uses its nuclear facilities as bargaining chips – it's a complicated game of bluff with the Americans. I very much doubt they sold raw uranium to the terrorists – and even if they had, North Korea's weapons-grade plants are far too close to Seoul to be targeted by the West.'

'Really?'

'Really. It's far more likely Great Britain will step up its campaign in Pakistan, where the terrorists were probably trained. Though,' she continued sternly, 'if they keep targeting Muslim countries and religious leaders, and continue to kill civilians with their callous and bungled operations, the British Armed Forces will unfortunately make future attacks on the West more likely, not less. But darling, do you want a flavour in your frappé?'

'More attacks?' Sydney wailed. 'But the whole world will be radiated. We'll all die of cancer, Da Mi.'

Da Mi was speaking in Korean to the waitress. She turned back to Sydney and stroked her hand. 'No, no, darling. Honestly, future attacks won't be nuclear – snukes are the gold dust of terrorist weapons; it's almost impossible to obtain the raw uranium to make them. And Britain won't be in a hurry to escalate a nuclear war. No, this bombing is their equivalent of the World Trade Center demolition: a powerful statement by those who are, nevertheless, ultimately powerless to affect the course of history.'

'Are you sure?'

'Absolutely, Sydney, never mind the fearmongers on the march; we have to stay calm and prepare for a new kind of future. Yes, it's turbulent right now, but both the Mayan and the Hindu calendars predicted that this would be an epoch of seismic transitions. A five-thousand-year-long age of militarism is coming to an end. Alpha males will fight tooth and claw to maintain their power, but like the dinosaurs, this macho posturing is doomed to extinction. Humanity is finally outgrowing violence, and the forces of peace and cooperation will at last prevail.'

'I dunno, Da Mi.' Sydney sniffled, 'aren't we just getting way better at blowing each other up? Maybe this really is the end of the world, like all those Lucifer Hammer people keep saying.'

As the waitress set their coffees down, Da Mi smiled at her, then said, 'Sydney, did you know that before the Mayan Great Day of Creation, human beings didn't make weapons?'

Sydney frowned. 'No.'

'It's true. In all the early settlements and towns – Çatal Hüyük, the Orkneys, Knossos, Hussuna – we find ample evidence of cooking, playing, agriculture, worship, but no artefacts of war. There's nothing inevitable about killing each other.'

Sydney struggled to follow Da Mi's argument. 'But before, you said we were aggressive because of our brains?'

'Yes, that's correct, I did. Our hormones and our serotonin levels certainly have a profound affect on our behaviour. But equally, our environment and our social conditioning affect our hormone production levels – you might even say that our violent, competitive global economy *forces* us to be aggressive and fearful and jealous in order to survive. That's why I've insisted that the Peonies grow up in a mountain village, governed by the principles of mutual aid and respect for all creation.' Sydney opened her mouth to say that she knew the Peonies would be perfect, it was the rest of us who–, but the Scientist raised her palm and swept on. 'Sydney, I have dedicated my professional life to the goal of advancing human evolution at all levels – physical, social and spiritual – and if there's one thing the Mayan prophecies and my own Korean heritage have taught me, it's that right now we need to go back to the ancestors in order to move forward. We need to live and work together in small groups, but in ways that are globally connected with others. Lucifer's Hammer isn't a meteor; it isn't even this bombing: it's a metaphor, a symbol representing our last chance to stand together and work cooperatively again. I'm not afraid, because I know that the Hammer is knocking some sense into us all at last. Look at how the whole world has joined together in sympathy and support for London right now.'

Da Mi was so smart, Sydney thought; she knew all about history as well as genes. Sydney couldn't begin to argue with her. It was just hard to see a nuclear terrorist attack as a step on the way to world peace. Sydney gazed around the café. To the background noise of tinkling coffee spoons and the trippy sound of a French pop song, people were staring at the plasma-screen TV replay footage of the Wembley detonation. There was the pink and orange stadium all lit up for the evening game, then, with first one terrible white flash, then another, it was sucked up into two towering mushroom clouds that filled the screen and smothered the night sky.

Sydney couldn't look at the next images, the survivors. She pushed away her coffee. 'I'm sorry Da Mi. I guess I know what you're saying, but still, everything's a total nightmare right now. How can people just sit and *eat* while *that's* on TV?'

'Koreans have just watched Japan endure Fukushima, and many of them remember Hiroshima. To them a nuclear bomb is not unthinkable. Sydney,' Da Mi said firmly, 'life goes on, and we must all do what we can to make it better for future generations. And you and I are creating the Peonies, yes?'

Sydney fell silent. That was true, and if Da Mi was right, it was super-important. At the very least, it was something she had promised to do, a steady, secure job in a world where nowhere was safe any more. 'Yes,' she said, in a small voice, and then, in a rush, 'You know I'd never let you down, Da Mi.'

'I know, sweetheart – so you must stay strong and have fun finding Damien Meadows. I'm sure he'll appreciate a new friend right now.

Now here.' Da Mi took a paper bag out of her purse. I want you to try this special *dukk*. It's filled with honey-syrup.'

Sydney took a piece of the doughy rice cake. It was chewy, and filled with delicious runny honey.

'Ummm,' she gurgled.

'Do you like it? Oh good; have another piece. Now, darling, when does your next period start? We need to get that ultrasound done.'

A week later Sydney started bleeding. She called Da Mi right away, then rang off and skipped to the bathroom to shave her legs, wax her bikini line and think about what to wear to the lab. Perhaps an A-line linen skirt and her new Calvin Klein panties? That would look professional. Fingers crossed, her ovaries would also look good, then she could donate on Day Fourteen. Luckily, because her eggs were going to be frozen she wouldn't have to take the ovulation suppressants and stimulants normal egg donors had to inject to synchronise cycles with their recipients. Instead, on Day Twelve and Thirteen, Da Mi would dose her up with fertility hormones and her ovaries would then make loads of eggs which would be sucked out of her by a long needle. It would only take twenty minutes. Then, once she'd found Hugh Grunt and got the eggs fertilised, Da Mi would do her genetic mojo on the blastocysts – whatever a blastocyst was – in time to implant them on December twenty-first.

The ultrasound room smelled like her mother's favourite air-freshener: antiseptic pine needles. And the bed had stirrups. Great. She should have worn jodhpurs.

'I'm sorry it's so clinical.' Da Mi spoke in Korean to a young nurse, who pressed a button on an iPod in the corner. Traditional flute music wafted across the room as Da Mi and the nurse stepped outside and Sydney slipped off her sandals, skirt and panties and climbed up onto the bed. Lying on a thick white towel, she pulled a sheet across her stomach. Da Mi rejoined her and turned the ultrasound monitor so Sydney could see it. At the foot of the bed, the nurse greased up something; Da Mi called it a 'transducer'.

Sydney opened her legs.

The plastic wand nudged into her, a cool, foreign presence, provoking just a hint of 'ouch', Then Da Mi was pointing out her uterus on the screen and she was lost in the grainy wonder of the lopsided cushion inside her, that spermatozoan Shangri-la where, she could proudly say, no cum had ever been. Well, except for pre-cum maybe.

The transducer shifted position and the Koreans started cooing at the screen.

'Fantastic.' Da Mi patted her hand. 'A healthy endometrial lining in the womb, and at least twenty antral follicles between the two ovaries. You are a very fertile young lady, Sydney.'

'Really? Maybe I should get a hormone patch.'

The scientist smiled. 'We'll provide you with the very latest in birth control, never fear. But for the next two weeks you shouldn't take any chances: condoms can break, and if you were to require an abortion, it would hold us up at least two months, not to mention the distress you might be caused.'

'Don't worry, Da Mi' – Sydney crossed her fingers – 'can't you see the dust-bunnies up there? I've got way better things to think about right now than men.' It wasn't exactly a lie, she reasoned as the nurse removed the transducer. She didn't know if Jae Ho would ever come over again.

'Still, people, especially Westerners, will be having a lot of panic sex right now. It always happens after a disaster. I'd prefer you didn't visit the nightclubs until we harvest the eggs, darling. We can look for Damien Meadows again after your hormones have calmed down.'

Raging hormones and panic sex? It sounded a shame to miss out. But she didn't want to disappoint Da Mi. 'Sure, I promise.' Sydney sat up and towelled her thighs clean of blood. It was a beautiful colour, dark as pomegranate juice.

By Day Fourteen, she was horny as hell, jacked up on fertility hormones and bored to death by the four walls of her apartment. She couldn't get to the GRIP clinic fast enough. Da Mi held her hand as some male doc extracted her eggs with a long needle, and in an hour she was back out on the street with a purse full of cash even three hours' shopping couldn't dent.

As she dumped the designer bags on her *yo*, Da Mi called. 'Sydney,' she purred, 'your eggs are *marvellous*. Now I want you to just relax and enjoy looking for Mr Good Genes!'

Fantastic. That night she was back in Gongjang, looking for the English guy, Jae Ho, a trio of squaddies, she didn't care who she took home. Jae Ho, however, did. She'd only been dancing twenty minutes before he caught her eye and nodded at the door.

'Are you climbing again?' he murmured, later.

'Sort of. Gently,' she explained, wondering if she was lying, and if he understood her anyway. Then she leaned back and he twisted and buckled, the tip of his cock sharp as a star inside her, and suddenly, unmistakably, she was coming again, her cries as vulnerable as his voice.

'*Eum Yang*,' he said into her ear when they awoke. He reached down her arm and fingered her Gotcha. 'Very good. Sy-duh-nee, Olympic bomb is *Yang*. Make love is *Eum*. We need much *Eum* in world now.'

'Yeah?' She cuddled him drowsily as his hand pattered down her belly.

'*Tong gul*,' he said, pulling at her pussy lips. 'Cave.'

'*Tong gul.*' She felt hypnotised. Maybe that's why having a native-speaking lover was the best way to learn a foreign language. After sex, your mind was wide open.

'Do you know Tang Gun?'

'Tang Gun? No. What is Tang Gun?'

'What? *Who!* Tang Gun First Korean! Before, only animals and God. Animals want to be man, fight, very bad. So God make cave for two animals – bear and tiger, for one hundred days. He give them only *manul—*'

This one Sydney knew: 'Garlic!'

'—yes, only garlic to eat. The tiger, not happy, not eat, but bear love garlic, eat all. So God make bear into woman. She have baby. Tang Gun.'

Weird. She'd just donated her eggs and here he was, telling her a baby story. But something was amiss. 'So why Tang Gun first Korean? Why not bear woman?'

'Okay, okay, Western woman, Tang Gun first Korean *King.*' He ruffled her hair. 'I sorry, very sorry, first Korean is *woman*. Now you like my story?'

'I like very much.' She stroked his cock as it drooped on its plump brown pillow. What was the word for mushroom? Oh yeah – 'Does bear woman eat *posot*, too?' she asked.

'Bear woman eat mushroom man! What mushroom man eat? I hungry!' he declared. She checked the clock. Eleven a.m.: not a bad time for brunch. She got up and had a look in the fridge, but except for some milk and a jar of hot sauce, it was empty

'I very bad wife,' she smirked.

He picked up his pants, fished about in the pockets for some money and passed her a *man won* note. 'You buy some food?' he asked sweetly.

If Johnny had ordered her to go shopping, she would have hit him.

But she was Jae Ho's hostess, and stretching her legs and getting some free groceries sounded like a great idea. She pulled on leggings and a T-shirt dress, some flip-flops and sunnies, and headed down to the corner shop. When she got back Jae Ho, still naked, was putting the finishing touches to an ink drawing in his sketchbook. She had never seen an artist working before, and she hung back, nervous of disturbing him. His muscles taut, he exuded concentration like a smell. With a pang, she suddenly wished she could draw *him*, but she could only do cartoon characters or stick-figure doodles. There was no point asking if she could take a photo. She would just have to remember him forever. Or make sure he wanted to come back.

He clapped the book shut. 'I give you picture. After eat.'

Pleased, she unpacked the groceries: eggplant, Korean zucchini, *udong* noodles, garlic, onions, *kim chee* and a tin of weird rubbery sea creatures she wanted to try. It was silly to be wearing clothes in the cocoon-like warmth of the apartment, so she undressed and cooked naked. *Udong* were usually served in soup, but she liked them in a sloppy, spicy sauce, which she spooned out of the soybean tub. She was careful not to let the hot oil spit, or to splash herself with hot water draining the noodles.

The room filled with the rich aroma of sesame oil. Jae Ho cleared off her bedside table and placed two cushions on the floor. She was anxious presenting the big bowl and chopsticks to him, in case the food was all wrong, but he slurped up the noodles greedily, chasing everything down with crunchy helpings of *kim chee*. Afterwards, when she'd cleared the dishes away and wiped down the table, he tore the drawing out of the book and laid it on the table.

'Is for you.'

She gazed at it in silence. He had drawn her blonde hair streaming into the corners of the page, her face thrown back in rapture. It looked exactly like she felt when she came.

'It's beautiful, Jae Ho.'

He impressed his name in the corner with his carved wooden *do jang* and wryly surveyed the result. 'Now you blackmail me. But I know nothing; is only drawing of big explosion Canadian model.'

'Is your wife jealous of your models?' The question just popped out, but Jae Ho didn't appear to mind.

'My wife very professional woman. She make big profit from my models!' He returned his art supplies to his bag and checked his watch. '*Aigo!* I go! Mousie, I go to Taegu now, to visit mother-in-law. I see you soon, I promise.'

So that was why he had stayed so long. 'Does your wife know you with a woman now?' she couldn't stop herself from asking as he hurriedly dressed.

'Maybe.' He shrugged.

'Will she be very angry?'

'Maybe.' He paused. 'Sydney, in Hongdae, we must be very careful, okay?'

'Jae Ho.' There was something she suddenly, desperately needed to know. 'Why you make adultery with me?'

'Adult-ery,' Jae Ho zipped up his pants. 'What is adul-tery?'

'You know, cheat, have an affair.'

'Cheat?' She couldn't tell if he was just pretending not to understand. She grabbed the bi-lingual dictionary she had bought and found the word. He studied the entry intently.

'Ah! Adultery.' He winked. 'I make adultery because I am adult?'

'No! Why? You love your wife, why make adultery?'

Jae Ho sat down on the sofa. 'Sy-duh-nee, in Korea, we say: love is song.' Nodding wisely, he stretched out his hand. 'First take knife, cut every finger. Open. So is blood. Then pull hand over paper, make five lines.' He mimed this action in the air. 'Is music lines. With

227

fingers then, you make the notes.' Poking at the air, he scored his marriage on an imaginary stave. 'This song is my love with my wife.'

Sydney stared at the air between them, trying to understand. 'I don't know, Jae Ho. It doesn't sound very happy to me.'

'Happy not important in Korea love. My wife, very good to me, every day she try to understand me. Very nice for me. I very lucky man. But every day, also, my wife, headache, or heart ache.' He smiled ruefully, pressing his fist first to his temple then to his breast. 'Headache, or heart ache,' he repeated. Then his face shuttered up a fraction and his tone grew tighter. 'And I, always in my life, I must think first about myself.'

That was the remark he left on. The one she tried to instantly forget.

23 | Pebbles

Johnny switched off the TV and flung the remote into the corner of the couch. This round-the-clock coverage of the snukes was getting on his nerves. Why hadn't al-Qaeda, or whichever mutts were responsible, managed to take out Hugh Grant? Instead they'd just created more work for the Sandman. There'd been immediate domino panic in the global security sector, and Johnny's new contacts at Han Air were now desperate for ConGlam's advice on beefing up their tech packages and staff training. He'd spent hours at the airline's head office this last week, stretching his empathy skills to the limit. 'It must be terrible for our colleagues in London'; 'I understand your fears, Mr Lee'; 'I appreciate your anxiety, Ms Park'; 'I'd feel the same as you if I was in charge of airport X-ray machines, sir'. Fuck, that shit was taxing. No sentimental Korean office worker wanted to hear Johnny's real opinion of the attack: that London had it coming. Had the British government been sleeping in a fucking teapot for the past twenty years? Instead of reducing their *army*, they should've cut their insane funding for all that multiculti shit, and banned the burqa like the French. At least he saw eye-to-eye with LA on that front.

As well as generating and managing the new hardware and protocol consultancy contracts, now ConGlam wanted Johnny to produce a report on the bombings' likely effect on British long-haul travel plans, so he'd had to spend an age researching tourism stats after terrorist attacks, earthquakes, tsunamis, toxic spill catastrophes, and nuclear events. Still, it had to be said, working full-tilt and impressing the fuck out of LA had taken his mind off Kim and Sydney. In fact, some days it felt like the old Johnny was making a comeback. He got up and stretched. It was time for some Sammy Davis Jr. 'Climb Ev'ry Mountain' would do it – who knows, he might even sing along.

He was just loading the playlist when his MoPho clattered on the glass coffee table.

That had better fucking not be Kim, he thought, but no, when he checked the screen, it was the cherry on the cake at last: the call he'd been waiting for. *Fucking yes*: fuck those gimmicky kiddie clones – flash-in-the-pan, novelty items, who needed 'em? Project ProxyBod was where the action was; that was why ConGlam was bending over ass-backwards for Dr Kim and her ragtag bag of sci-fi tricks and treats. *This* shit was gonna be scary; this was gonna rake in the megabucks, pull up the red velvet curtain on the future of the species. With a grim surge of purpose, Johnny picked up.

'*Anneyong haseyo*, Mr Cho.'

'Job done.' Cho spoke Korean like it was his second language.

Johnny checked his watch. 'I'll be there at two-thirty.'

'With cash?'

'*Ye, ye*, no problem.'

'Good.' With a Bakelite clunk, Mr Cho hung up and Johnny grinned. Naturally, a taxidermist would take a cut-and-dried approach to conversation. Why mince words when . . . well, who wanted to think about the mince that Mr Cho had to deal with every day?

Scrolling through his MoPho address book, he fetched up the number of GRIP's biotech engineering lab at Yonsei. This Sunday was circled as delivery day for Pebbles, as everyone now called the PB prototype; there'd be no nosy students milling around, and only a skeleton caretaking staff to avoid as he dropped her off. As long as

Mr Cho had done his job right, the boffins would soon be getting some up-market hardware inserted into that beautiful body of hers. He made the call, then returned to Sammy. Yeah, it was 'That Great Come and Get It Day'.

It was stifling, but what the hell; at least he wasn't in London, wearing tinfoil. In his new Gucci shades, Johnny drove along Chongno with the top down. Waiting at a traffic light, he checked out a group of chicks in mini-skirts. Catching the eye of the cutest one, he revved his engine and she screamed and jumped up and down. Yup, he was back in the Zone again: turning Anger to Passion. Beacon would be proud.

As he pulled into the narrow alley behind the livestock market, he began to feel queasy; he put it down to the smell of chickenshit and the yapping of dogs about to be beaten and slaughtered. Koreans thought pooches tasted better if they had adrenalin running in their veins just before they kicked it. And maybe they did – Johnny had never eaten unbeaten dog, though he'd been forced to chow down on the supposed delicacy of the penis more than once, or risk losing very lucrative contracts. Did ConGlam care what he did for them, though? You had to be careful which joker in middle management you complained to about shit like that, or before you knew it the rumour would go round his clients that Mr San-duh-man positively *loved* doggie cock.

Johnny backed carefully into the space behind the workshop door. Parking always steadied his nerves. Slamming the car door shut helped as well, but as he rang Mr Cho's bell, there was still an acrid taste in the back of his throat.

Cho was as taciturn as the morning they'd first met. 'You're late,' he complained as he bolted them inside the long room.

The sunshine was filtered through sheets of old newspaper taped to the window. Johnny's eyes adjusted to the sepia light. The stooped, grizzled old man in front of him reeked of BO and formaldehyde. Trying not to breathe too deeply, Johnny took the envelope of *man won* bills out of his pocket.

'Traffic's bad today,' he said by way of apology. Cho didn't rate – or ever seem to need – an 'I'm sorry.'

Cho turned away as if disdaining the offer of cash. 'You see first.' He steered Johnny through a narrow maze, between shelves and tables, past rows of stuffed magpies and weasels, stacks of plastic tubs, jars of what looked like preserved foetuses, brains and hearts. Sprawled on a platform in the musty centre of the labyrinth was the carcase of a deer, surrounded by a neatly arranged collection of tools. The antlered head lolled over the edge of the platform as if trying to nip at Johnny's leg. But Cho hurried him past, to where a makeshift curtain was strung up across the width of the room. The taxidermist gestured at Johnny to step forward and tugged at the fabric.

A small, voiceless part of Johnny was afraid that the stiff would sit up and point her finger accusingly, but Pebbles was lying still on a table, her body covered with a thin blanket, and she seemed at peace. Her hair had been neatly combed and swept back off her face; there were no foul liquids drooling from her lips, and a clean, lemony scent had replaced the subtle blend of stale sweat, cheap perfume and putrefaction she'd exuded as he fucked her in the morgue. In any case, she now had no eyes beneath her flattened lids; she couldn't pick him out in a line-up if she tried.

As Johnny assessed Pebbles, he began to feel calmer. That it had been her last screw was an accomplishment. Aspects of the experience had been revolting, sure, but to cross another threshold in life? That was always worthwhile. And the knowledge that he had porked Dr Kim's priceless body double had been a source of some consolation after she'd kicked him off the Peonies project. *Maybe I should have let Ratty video it,* he thought, *what wouldn't I give to play it back to Kim sometime?* But no, that was just an indulgent fantasy – and anyway, he didn't need a video to recall how he'd felt when he'd come on her face. It was like he'd climbed an electric pylon, spat on his hands and grabbed hold of the wires. Strangely, he remembered, it had been Sydney's face that had flashed up in front of him then. Well, that slut would be next.

Cho shuffled beside him, his plastic slippers hushing against the concrete floor.

Johnny slipped back down to earth. 'Hey, baby,' he drawled, giving vent to a low wolf-whistle.

With a sound that could almost have been a chuckle, Cho pulled back the blanket. The GRIP engineers would insert a mechanical skeleton along with the microchips, so the body lying before him was simply skin and stuffing. Pebbles' breasts were larger than before, but her pussy had been shaved and demurely sewn up – Kim's orders, no doubt. Johnny could also make out rows of tiny stitches along the insides of her limbs, but the stab wound in the stomach had been invisibly mended, somehow, and the only slit left in her – apart from her mouth – was a long gash from chest to pubic bone, where Cho had sewn a zip. Johnny could see the seams around the hair and jaw-line where the Scalper had performed the Faceplant, but on the whole Pebbles looked much less like the Bride of Frankenstein than he'd expected, more like a large, harmless doll.

In fact, with all the silicone and preservatives injected into her, Pebbles looked a lot less dead than before. Her skin wasn't oozing MSG any more, but looked dry and smooth. And though she was obviously still lifeless, her body was simply an inanimate object now, no longer invested with the dense, fascinating sense of *vacancy* that clung to a fresh corpse like an aroma. Now she was merely a hollow dummy: a Kim Da Mi dummy, Johnny thought with a smirk.

The ProxyBod Prototype team would fit Pebbles up with stainless steel bones and a circuit-board brain, programmed with Kim's particular facial expressions and gestural tics. They'd also enlarge her head and eyes slightly – giving them not quite Betty Boopish but more child-like proportions in relation to her body: this, Kim had said in her Powerpoint presentation, would offset the so-called 'uncanny valley' effect that made near-human replicants so creepy to look at. Eventually, of course, GRIP and ConGlam would be moving into bona fide cell-for-cell clones of human hosts, concentrating on achieving perfect epidermal verisimilitude, but for now, Pebbles was an impressive start, even he could admit that.

'*Kamsahamnida*, Mr Cho.' Bowing, Johnny handed the old man the envelope.

This time he took it and counted the contents rapidly in that slick backwards way Koreans had, holding the bills between the fingers of one hand and flipping through them with his thumb. Grunting his approval, he stuffed the payment in his pocket and nodded once at Johnny. 'I get you a bag. Don't worry. Included in price.'

Johnny grinned. Mr Cho appeared to have made a joke.

Without the clammy glaze that had troubled him in the morgue, Pebbles was much nicer to touch. It was almost too bad her uncanny valley had been stitched up, Johnny thought as he helped Cho wrap up the body. Together they bundled it, light as a fairground prize, into the trunk of his car.

24 / Su Jin

The women had spent the morning in the garden and the afternoon setting up looms in the Meeting Hall. Dinner had been delicious as usual, big yellow *pajon* with squid, followed by barley tea. Normally, Mee Hee had no difficulty falling asleep after a busy day, but tonight she was lying awake, thinking about Dr Tae Sun. He was always touching her – on the arm, on the shoulder – and offering to help her in her tasks, bringing her books he thought she might like. She was embarrassed by how badly she read, but she was improving; he told her so, and it was true. She wanted to read Korean folk tales to her children, and stories from the books of European fairy tales that now lined the shelves in the Meeting Hall.

Lying on her *yo* in the darkness, Mee Hee clasped her hands to her breasts. She also wanted to kiss Che Tae Sun.

Across the room, Su Jin shifted on her own *yo*. Mee Hee let out a long, quiet breath and lowered her hands. There was a footfall on the floor. Su Jin must be going to the toilet. But instead Su Jin patted her way along the wall to the wardrobe, carefully opened the door.

'What are you doing?' Mee Hee whispered, sitting up.

Su Jin froze, her profile a grey outline in the moonlight creeping through the window. She was holding her day-bag. It was full. 'I thought you were asleep!' she hissed.

It was like a dream, shocking and strange. 'Su Jin? Where are you going? Why have you packed your bag?'

Su Jin knelt down beside her and fixed her eyes on Mee Hee's face. She was silent for a minute, then at last she said, 'I didn't know if I should tell you.'

'Tell me what? I don't understand.'

'I'm leaving,' she said quietly. 'I don't want to have babies for Dr Kim. I want to live my own life.'

'But Su Jin—!' Mee Hee sat bolt upright and gripped her friend's arm. 'You didn't have to come – she said you could stay behind in China. It will be very dishonourable to run off in the middle of the night, Su Jin!'

'I don't want to live in China,' Su Jin retorted. 'I want to live in Korea. Dr Che – Dong Sun – is helping me. He told me a place to go in Pusan where I can get work sewing and he gave me money for a bus. It leaves at five o' clock in the morning from a village down the road.'

'Pusan?' Mee Hee was trembling now. She let go of Su Jin's arm. 'That's a big city. Why do you want to go there?'

'It's a nice place, with beaches and mountains. I can work and save money, meet a man of my own. I don't want to be a farm animal here, breeding a litter of children for the Americans to profit from! We weren't even allowed to watch the World Cup, the cooks don't tell us anything – we have no idea what's going on in the world.'

'But that's not— Su Jin, this is our *home* now. The doctors, Dr Kim, they've done so much for us – look at our houses, and the food they give us. They just don't want anything to upset us, that's what they said—'

'No,' Su Jin hissed, 'we're being drip-fed, like when we got off the trucks. We're being hooked up to a big fairy tale, all sugar and milk, and if we stay here we'll be like children forever; we'll never grow up – don't you see that, Mee Hee?'

'But Su Jin, what's wrong with a fairy tale?' Mee Hee pleaded.

'You've seen what the real world is like. Inchon was terrible, so dirty and busy; Pusan will be horrible too. You'll be exploited by *capitalists*. They won't care about you like Dr Kim does. It's—' She tried to think of the right word. 'It's *unusual*, I know, what she wants from us, but her heart is pure, anyone can see that!'

'My mind is made up,' Su Jin said firmly. 'I want my own hard life, my own challenges. I don't want to be a mouse in Dr Kim's laboratory, giving birth to children who will never love me most of all.'

'You're wrong, Su Jin – they *will* love us. And we'll love them. It will a big family, and we'll all take care of each other.'

Suddenly, swiftly, Su Jin kissed Mee Hee on the cheek. 'Shhh. Maybe everything is perfect here, Mee Hee, but I'm not – I'm like a weed, I grow better when no one is looking after me.'

Mee Hee pulled her friend into her arms and held her close. 'I would miss you too much, Su Jin. You can't go.'

But Su Jin's body was unyielding in her arms. 'If you're lonely, ask Younger Sister to move in here,' she instructed. 'She's always praying and annoying Older Sister. But you wouldn't mind.'

'Oh, Su Jin, please—' As she realised Su Jin was not going to change her mind, Mee Hee loosened her embrace. 'What shall I say to everyone?' she whispered.

'Tell them I wasn't here when you woke up. That's true. And please, whatever happens, don't say anything about Dr Dong Sun. Especially to his brother. Promise?'

'I promise,' Mee Hee said doubtfully as Su Jin stood up. The grey light in the room was seeping into her heart. How could she ever be happy again without her sister Su Jin?

Bag in hand, Su Jin quietly left the house.

Mee Hee lay awake all night, terrified that Su Jin would be dragged back to the village by the husband of the head cook. Whenever the women joked about running away to the big city, they all agreed there was no point because he would surely stop them, being paid, as far as they could see, to do very little except sit around and smoke and watch them all. But rain pattered on the roof, the cock crowed, the sun rose, and no one came back to the house.

'I'm sorry,' Mee Hee whispered to her photograph of Dr Kim. 'I tried my best.' The photo looked serenely back at her, but Mee Hee could no longer return its gaze. Feeling pale and weak as *tubu* milk, she got up and went outside.

The Buddhist sisters were sitting in a circle in the courtyard, meditating. Younger Sister, she could see, had slid open her *maru* door and was praying beneath her crucifix. The rains had cooled the air and there was a breeze coming up from the lake in the valley. Avoiding the others, Mee Hee wandered to the edge of the plateau on which the village stood. She stopped at the three Spirit Posts and leaned against the friendly one with the tall black hat. Beneath her, emerald green rice fronds were poking up through the paddies. Against the horizon, the tender rays of the sun caressed the bristling cheeks of the mountains. Each tree radiated its own halo of light.

Her heart trembled like a dewdrop at the thought of her shameful inadequacies. She had let Su Jin go; she had failed Dr Kim. But no matter how little she deserved to be here, Mee Hee knew she would never want to leave the village. Every day it greeted her with the sparkling tapestry of birdsong, the bracing scent of pine, the glowing promise of another dawn. The village was her entire world.

25 | Oasis Boy

'Hey, Day! Long time no see!'

Jake flicked Damien's shoulder with a tea towel. Sam, standing by the cash register, nodded greetings. He had a new haircut, a number one round the sides, and it suited him.

Jake, though: he looked like some backwoods Canadian–Asian wild man. He'd started a few dreads, and a bear's claw stuck out of his left ear.

Damien slid onto a barstool, feeling a bit of a crap mate. He should have seen Jake before now. They'd talked, of course, but they had opposite schedules, and the last thing Damien felt like after one of his epic teaching days was dragging himself to Azitoo and immersing himself in the hysterical aftermath of catastrophe. He'd much preferred being fussed over by the mothers of his private students, who fed him cake every lesson and showered him with presents: socks, cologne and fancy soaps he'd sold on eBay. But most *hagwons* closed the last week in August, and with three envelopes of cash steadily getting fatter in his wardrobe, he'd finally felt he should come out to play. 'It's nothing personal, mate,' he said. 'I've been working my bollocks off, that's all.'

'I hear ya, buddy.' Jake shook his head. 'I guess Canada's looking even better than ever right now.'

'No shit.'

'Man, it's still freaking me out – I mean, snukes, floods, the four Brides of the Apocalypse . . . What didn't you guys get?'

'What Jake mean,' Sam interjected, 'is we hope everyone you know okay.'

Even though he had no ties with anyone in England now, Damien was touched by Sam's sympathy. 'My mum was in Scotland, thanks,' he said. 'And Brighton's still just outside the evacuation zone.'

'At least the third bomb didn't go off.' Jake rested his elbow on the bar and began polishing a pint glass. 'I still can't quite believe security was that lax – okay, so maybe MI5 didn't organise the whole thing, but there must have been someone on the inside helping those gals, doncha think?'

Damien shrugged. 'I dunno. They didn't even have to enter the stadium to vaporise it. And if women want to strap nuclear bombs under their skirts, I don't know what you can do to stop them.'

'True, too true,' Jake conceded.' I could never get my ex to quit.'

'Jake! Is not joking matter,' Sam said sharply. 'Damien, we very sorry for your city.'

'Sam loves disasters,' Jake told him. 'He gets all misty-eyed, can't tear himself away.'

'Time of many heroes,' Sam said solemnly. 'Korean athletes and fans told: go home, but no, stayed, helped evacuate, tend to survivors. We have World Cup Spirit of Dunkirk too.'

Jake rolled his eyes. 'Damien, buddy, what can I get you?'

'Thought you'd never ask. Seeing as it's my birthday, I'll take a cocktail.'

'Your *birthday*? You dark horse, Dames.' Jake snapped his fingers. 'But perfect timing. Tonight we launch our Disgusting Drinks menu – here, first one's on the house.'

Damien perused the list. The Bloody Anus – Vodka, V8, Tabasco, chilli pepper and brown M&Ms: *Hurts more coming out than it does going in* – sounded too much like smuggling drugs. He lingered over the STD: *soju*, tomato juice and crushed Doritos, *You won't believe how fast it's catching on.* But in the end, only one appealed.

'Make it a "Miracle on the Han", boys,' he ordered dryly.

Jake double-checked the ingredients. 'Coffee, Baileys, spare tyre, rubber boot, cigarette butt and gummy octopi. Do we got it all, Sam?'

'We all out of spare tyres.' Sam lit a cigarette. 'Jake sell them to recycle man for personal profit.'

'These are lean times.' Jake shook his head in sorrow.

Damien put the menu down. 'I'll just stick with a G&T.'

'No, no.' Jake rummaged in a drawer. 'I know what to make you. Sam, where's that Oasis CD?'

Sam found the disk and as the hoary old classic spun out into the bar, Jake mixed him a champagne cocktail. Damien watched the lump of sugar dissolve in a starburst at the bottom of the flute. *Happy Birthday, Jess.* He raised the glass to his mates and took a sip. The hit rushed to his brain, a brandy, bitters and fizz supernova. He was on the verge of humming along to the song when Sam stopped the CD. 'Jake, this song very bad taste,' he complained. 'No one want hear about explosions in sky.'

'Sure they do!' Jake objected. 'Mama Gold's "Clouds of Change" is a massive YouTube hit right now.'

As the cousins squabbled, the bar began filling with people, a few Damien knew slightly, others strangers, but all directed by Jake to buy him birthday drinks and offer 27/7 commiserations. Gradually, Damien started to have fun; it was good to be out again on a Saturday night, especially one that ended with a 'disgusting drinks Olympics'. An Ozzie bloke imbibed a glass of spit mixed with scrapings of mud and hair off the dance floor, only to come in second to a self-proclaimed hoser from Toronto, who downed a shot of female urine donated by one of the staff. It was two o'clock when Jake and Sam locked up. Damien floated after them into the alley. He'd had a toke for the first time in yonks, and while he might be another year older, the night was still young.

'You guys want to head into Hongdae?' he asked.

It felt like everyone left broiling in Seoul for the last weekend in August had gone to Gongjang with a brutal determination to make the night out-sweat the day. So where was Damien Meadows? Sydney, dancing with Jin Sok, kept flicking her eyes back to the steel door. Da Mi had called that day, anxious about the King. If they didn't find Damien soon she'd have to use some blond sperm she had hanging around in the fridge. Sydney was on the lookout for Jae Ho too; she had bumped into him three days ago in Apkuchong, and he'd hinted he would be out dancing again soon.

'Strawberry Soda! You like?' Jin Sok rolled a cold can down the nape of her neck.

'You're frisky tonight,' she teased. He had been incredibly flirtatious on the dance floor. 'What happened?'

'Today I make self-therapy.' He giggled. 'Today I happy-cry!'

'You what?'

'I cry for happiness. For world peace. For five hours I cry!'

'Jin Sok, I love you – you're crazier than me!'

The rhythms of the music fizzed and foamed around and through them and they danced again and got parted in the madness and when she finally washed up in the corner by the bar, Jae Ho was sitting on the stool by the white teddy and Damien Meadows was standing with his friends behind the tree.

He couldn't believe it – and yet somehow he had made it happen: he had summoned her up for his birthday, the slender candle on his cake.

No, that was ridiculous – but still, there she was, dancing ten feet away from him, and he felt . . . well, lovely. Serene, even. *At one.* Everything was in motion, like it always was. The universe was bringing people together, pulling them apart, destroying all hope, then creating life anew . . .

'Day.' Jake stuck a bottle of beer in his hand, then returned to his conversation with a Korean Elvis impersonator.

Damien sidled round the edge of the dance floor, past the painting on the wall. Under the influence of two Champagne Supernovas, four G&Ts, a joint and one blonde dancer, the canvas looked almost good. But not as good as the model, who was dancing right up to him, beautiful, radiant, smiling . . .

His body was throbbing, his spirits soaring. *Go for it*, a voice said in his head, and he stepped onto the dance floor. It was easy to half-smile, move closer and closer to her, until they were laughing hello like old mates and stepping back by the sofa to talk.

'I haven't seen you for *ages*,' she said into his ear, her breath a soft caress on his neck. 'I was worried – I thought you might be back in England.'

'Nah, just working too hard.' He shrugged modestly. This international pity business had really been working for him tonight. She pressed against him, her insistent hip unexpected, but far from unwelcome. 'Yeah? I've got an easy job for you, if you like. A scientist I know needs someone, a guy, for a project she's working on. It pays great.'

Ah, the old, 'I got an angle on a job' chat-up line. 'Sounds interesting. Tell me more.'

She put her hand on his forearm. 'It's a bit complicated to explain. We could meet up tomorrow? Go for tea in Insa Dong?'

Her accent was definitely Canadian, and so was the way she exaggerated her questions, with that little uplift at the end. Couldn't hurt to get to know more Canadians, could it? And Jake said Insa Dong was nice: a leafy downtown strip of traditional tea-houses, art galleries and antique shops: touristy, but quaint, and a must-see before you left the country.

'Sounds good,' he heard himself say.

'Great! I'll meet you on Chongno, at the Park entrance, at three. You can call me Sydney, by the way. Coz that's my name.' She stuck out her hand.

'I'm Damien,' he replied lamely as her slim fingers slithered out of his.

He was about to ask if he could buy her a drink when the DJ threw on some wailing Sephardic drum and bass concoction and her face lit up. 'Oh fuck, I love this track,' she declared as she wiggled back onto the dance floor, giving him a little *bye bye* wave.

It wouldn't be cool to follow her. No.

'You all right, Day?' Jake poked him in the ribs

'*Ye, ye.*'

'We're going now. Do you want to stay?'

Yes. But always scram while you're ahead. 'Nah, I'll hop in the cab with you.'

He glanced around for Sydney as they left. She was laughing with her Korean geezers at the bar, but she gave him another wave and smartly tapped her watch. He replied with a discreet thumbs-up and headed out the door.

'Does Birthday Day got a *new friend*?' Jake grabbed him round the ribs as they exited onto the street.

Damien pushed him away, grinning. 'More like a job interview.'

'She's gonna pay ya for it? Sounds good to me, buddy!' Jake whooped.

At six-thirty, the DJ brought the sparse crowd back down to earth, spinning Bob Marley's 'No Woman, No Cry'. A broad-shouldered, dirty-blond guy in a Tibetan T-shirt requested a waltz and Sydney turned lightly in his arms as he hummed along to the song. Jae Ho and Jin Sok sat smoking at the bar, Jae Ho's eyes following her every move.

The stranger bowed to her as the last notes faded. The night was over. The dozen people left in the club broke into applause.

'So long she dance, Superwoman!' Jin Sok teased as she tumbled back to the bar.

'I old!' Jae Ho laughed. 'I go home sleep!'

She felt her smile freeze. *What else is he going to say?* she urged herself, and forced a polite response. He left as she and Jin Sok were gathering up their belongings and was nowhere in sight when they emerged into the light of the new day. Jin Sok rode her home on his new motorbike, kissed her on both cheeks and left to shower before church.

Sydney wandered around her apartment, still wide awake. Everything was so still and pretty, all her things touched gently by the dawn, but all she felt inside was a dull, empty ache.

Don't be stupid, she told herself ruthlessly, putting the kettle on to boil. *Of course he's got to go home to his wife. He can't stay out every weekend.* Besides, she had get up soon to call Da Mi and head down to Insa Dong. She should put on her sleep-mask and get some sleep.

The doorman buzzed.

She hurtled down the hallway.

Three minutes later Jae Ho strode in off the elevator and pressed her up against the wall.

26 / The Bluebird

'Where's Su Jin?' Dr Tae Sun cast an anxious look down the table to the empty place beside Mee Hee. 'It's not like her to be late for breakfast.'

At the next table Dr Dong Sun was counting heads, lips moving, head nodding as he scanned the room. Her hands hidden in her lap, Mee Hee dug her fingernails into her palms.

'I haven't seen her this morning,' she said, hoping her voice wasn't quavering. That was true, wasn't it? She hadn't seen Su Jin since the sun came up, had she?

'Maybe she went for a walk,' suggested Young Ha.

'That's not like Su Jin either,' Older Sister guffawed. Some of the other women tittered, but Dr Tae Sun shook his head with a worried sigh.

'There's no use everyone's food getting cold,' Dr Dong Sun said firmly, getting up from the table. 'Eat, everyone. I'll take a look around the village.'

The other women tucked into their egg-rice, chatting about the new looms, but the space at Mee Hee's side chilled her whole body, and her heart felt as empty as the brown bowl next to hers. She looked up at Dr Tae Sun for comfort, but he was pale and distracted, his forehead crumpled, his mouth pinched. She kept her head down after that, barely able to chew, concentrating only on her throbbing palms. She wanted just to melt away, to become invisible. She would work nonstop in the garden all day, weeding, digging, doing the most back-breaking tasks.

But as the cooks were clearing away the dishes, Dr Dong Sun returned and came over to her side. 'I couldn't find her,' he said, not unkindly. 'Let's go back to your house. She might have returned there after I checked.'

She nodded mutely and together they left the meeting hall and walked down the path. The morning was warm and humid, but the chill in her left side was beginning to numb her whole body. In contrast, her mind was spinning and clattering like a bobbin running out of thread. What on earth was she going to say to Dr Dong Sun when they reached the house? He must suspect that she knew he had helped Su Jin escape from – no, *leave* – the village.

With every step, Mee Hee felt colder and dizzier. Of course she would never tell anyone that Dr Dong Sun knew where Su Jin was – she had promised Su Jin, and besides, Dr Dong Sun would just deny it. Who would Dr Kim believe, after all: a peasant woman, or her treasured doctor? But she couldn't tell him that his secret was safe with her without revealing that she knew what he had done, and that could be very dangerous. If Dr Dong Sun thought for even a moment that Mee Hee might betray him, he could blame her for everything – he could say that she and Su Jin had stolen the money for the bus fare.

No, even if it meant she never had word of Su Jin again, it was better that Dr Dong Sun thought she was as ignorant as all the other women. Feeling calmer, Mee Hee mounted the steps to her veranda. Dr Dong Sun's tread crunched behind her on the twigs she had neglected to sweep away before breakfast.

'Su Jin?' she called out tentatively, as they crossed the threshold, half-daring to believe that she might have changed her mind and returned, but the *maru* room was just as she had left it: tidy and, apart from a ladybird crawling busily over the azalea, lifeless. As Dong Sun poked his head into the kitchen, the ladybird spread its shiny black-spotted red wings and flew away.

'She's not here,' Dong Sun announced, looking up at the rafters as if Su Jin might be hiding above their heads like a vengeful spirit.

'No.'

'When was the last time you saw her?'

Mee Hee lowered her eyes. So far she hadn't had to lie. 'Last night.'

'What time?'

'When we went to bed.'

'And you didn't hear her leave?'

Dr Dong Sun was as still as a gecko, his eyes steady and quiet behind his glasses. 'I was dreaming,' Mee Hee heard herself say. 'I heard her getting up in the dark. I thought she was going to the bathroom. When I woke up she was gone.'

Dr Dong Sun nodded. 'I expect you thought she was out walking, that you'd see her at breakfast.'

Her heart gulped. *Yes*, she tried to say, *yes, thank you. That is what I'll tell Dr Kim.* Dumbly, she nodded.

'That's fine, Mee Hee,' Dr Dong Sun said warmly. 'I know you're upset – but don't worry, Su Jin has a strong character; we both know she can take care of herself. Come, let's see if Dr Tae Sun's found her in the garden.'

But Dr Tae Sun was standing sadly at the gate, his hair in disarray, sweat patches staining the armpits of his shirt. 'She's not here, and the gardeners haven't seen her,' he blurted to his brother.

Mee Hee turned away from the neat rows of carrots and stared into the dark gaps between the trees that spread for miles, up to the top of the mountain and down into the valley. Su Jin was gone, and she was never coming back.

Before the weaving session that afternoon, the doctors called a meeting of all the women. Su Jin hadn't returned from her morning walk, Dr Dong Sun told them, but the women were not to panic; the woods were perfectly safe and there had never been crimes or violence near the village. Probably she had tripped, perhaps broken her ankle. Search parties had been organised, the gardeners and the cooks' husbands would look for her. For the time being the women should stick close to the houses. There was no use someone else getting lost.

'It's the outhouse spirits,' Older Sister loudly declared. 'She didn't believe in them, and now they've sucked her down head-first into the compost!'

'Please, Older Sister!' said Mee Hee's next-door neighbour, Cho So Ra. 'Can't you see Mee Hee is upset?' She put her arm around Mee Hee, who wasn't the only one crying.

'We must all pray for Su Jin,' Younger Sister said softly.

'Yes,' chipped in Young Ha. 'After weaving, we can pray or meditate together in the Hall. Would you like that, Mee Hee?'

Mee Hee's tongue was as dry as straw. Her sisters were so loving and kind, but she was a traitor, deceiving them, letting them all worry that Su Jin was dead or captured by bandits or lost and frightened in the woods. Still, Su Jin did need their prayers, out there alone, on her way to that big roaring dragon of a city.

'Yes, let's do that,' she whispered.

The doctors smiled.

'That's a wonderful idea,' Dr Dong Sun said, 'and just what Dr Kim would like you all to do. She is fully aware of the situation, and she is also praying for Su Jin.'

'Can we return to the looms later, Dr Dong Sun?' Young Ha asked. 'I think we should ask God to help us right now.'

The women divided into groups, sitting in circles to pray or meditate. Mee Hee sat next to So Ra and tried to breath slowly and deeply. *Please, Household Spirits*, she asked silently, *please Buddha, please Baby Jesus, please Virgin Mary. Let Su Jin come home. Please let Su Jin change her mind and come back home.*

Supper was subdued. Rumours had begun to circulate, about a strange man in the forest. Older Sister swore he had exposed himself to the cook's daughter a year ago – tried to entice her into a cave, even. Some of the women spoke in praise of Su Jin, her intelligence and fearlessness, but Mee Hee sat silently, stirring her noodles with her chopsticks. If only she hadn't woken up last night, then she wouldn't be experiencing this intolerable pressure in her chest, this terrible feeling in her stomach like a hundred little knives trying to slice their way out of her. She could so easily comfort her sisters, but instead she was protecting someone who didn't care about any of them.

Mee Hee put her chopsticks down. Under the table, she felt with her fingertips for the small red-crescent ridges in her palm. As the day went on, terrible thoughts had been growing in her mind: Su Jin hadn't been going to tell her, Mee Hee, that she was leaving. Su Jin wouldn't have minded if Mee Hee thought she was dead. Su Jin had never loved or trusted her. Su Jin had thought she was a stupid, backward peasant. Su Jin was laughing at her now. As her fingernails bit again into her palm she broke into a cold sweat.

'Mee Hee isn't well,' So Ra said.

'Do you want to go and lie down?' Dr Tae Sun asked in concern, and when she nodded, he said kindly, 'Go and rest. I'll come and check up on you later.'

Bowing to the table, Mee Hee excused herself and left the Hall.

Back at the house, she lay miserably on her bed, half-listening to the drilling chorus of the crickets in the paddies, fingering the bluebird pin that Su Jin had given her in Beijing. *Hope*, she had said it meant hope, but Mee Hee felt drained of hope, of life, of all sensation except a dank, clammy feeling of dread.

She forced herself to sit up and look at the bluebird, caged in her fingers on her lap. When she opened her hands, the brooch caught the light from the bedside lamp and the enamel glinted like Su Jin's eyes when she was excited or insistent, shone like her blue-black hair after she had washed it and was letting Mee Hee comb it out. The bird was beautiful, but now it was meaningless. It was a joke, a cruel joke, a false bird, made of lead, that could never fly, never sing, never make a nest.

Reaching over to the table by her *yo*, Mee Hee turned the photograph of Dr Kim so that it was facing Su Jin's bed. Then she undid the clasp of the pin. The point was sharp as a needle. Swiftly, she stabbed it into her forearm. A sizzle of pain shot up her arm. She removed the pin and a tiny liquid ruby rose to the surface of her skin. Quickly, before the heat in her veins could evaporate, she jabbed herself again. She was just lifting the pin to bring it down into her flesh for a third time when there was a knock on the front door.

'Mee Hee,' Dr Tae Sun called out, 'are you awake?'

She pulled her sleeve down over the droplets of blood. 'Coming. Right away.'

27 | Independence Park

Tae Hung Dong was under attack. Noise and glare ricocheted off the buildings and down the street; metal gates clanged open and shut, cocks were crowing, *ajummas* clucking, kids shrieking. A psalm was blasting from the church on the corner, competing for volume with a strawberry salesman in a blue Hyundai truck, blaring his prices out from a megaphone. Damien winced and put on his sunglasses. Sundays in the Dong: sheer cacophony. Normally he stayed home, cocooned in his expensive-but-essential-present-to-self sound-reduction headphones until he had to leave for his evening privates.

At least it wasn't raining. It had chucked it down for most of August, like it did every year, according to Jake, but today should be nice for a stroll in the park. If he was going to make it that far he needed more caffeine. He stopped at the Nescafé machine outside the DVD shop, plugged in a thousand won and pressed *milk coffee*. The recycled paper cuplet dropped down and an instant later the whiz of pre-mixed instant java hit the bottom. Brilliant. He reached in and grabbed the cup, remembering too late that there was always a pause and then a second stream of water. The extra jet rushed, wasted, through the grate. Shit. There were barely two centimetres of caffeine in his cup, a pathetic insult to his system.

He shoved his cup back between the plastic pincers and fed in another couple of coins – and watched as another paper cup was ejected down into his. *Fuck.* The twin jets of boiling water pushed it further in, at an awkward angle. Then the two cups jammed in the pincers.

It was impossible to retrieve them through the sliding plastic door.

His knuckles scraped for his efforts, his foot sore from kicking the machine, a vein throbbing in his forehead, Damien finally had to concede failure: once again a ruthless mechanical process had triumphed over simple human needs.

No. He would *not* be beaten. By forcing the second cup down to the bottom of the first, he finally managed to extricate them, spilling hot coffee all over his hands in the process. *Fuck. Fuck. Triple fuck.* He set the cups on top of the machine and stepped into the convenience store to ask for a tissue. Fortunately, this was one of the Korean words he knew, *hyu-gee*. As in *hyu-gee* Grant. And *hyu-gee* pain in the arse.

For his labours and burns he got an extra half-centimetre of coffee. At least he'd stopped yawning by the time the taxi let him off in front of Pagoda Park.

Sydney was squatting in front of an old man sitting cross-legged on the sidewalk, cooing over a cardboard box full of fluffy yellow chicks. For a moment something like panic twitched in his gut. He hesitated. *Get a grip*, he told himself fiercely, *she's just a girl you've met in a club – and she has some work for you.*

'Hi Sydney,' he said.

'Aren't they *adorable*?' She turned to face him, pushing her sunglasses up on her head. She didn't appear to be wearing a bra beneath her pink halter-top.

'They're mutants,' he warned her. 'Seconds from the chicken factory. Fucked-up clones, or males – one of my students told me. The runts will die in a week, and the males all get killed anyway – that's why this old geezer has them.'

'No, I don't believe that. Look – they're perfect.' She seemed younger than he'd thought, maybe just twenty?

The *ajashi* ignored them and raised his arm to attract the attention of passing Koreans. Sydney stood up. She looked a bit peaky, with dark rims beneath her eyes, but at the same time she was almost quivering with that unreal animation hard-going party girls often got the day after, a sort of spaced-out second wind when they wanted to fuck all day and you just wanted to smoke dope and listen to Japanese experimental music.

'*Kamsahamnida, agashi*,' she said to the old man, then took Damien's arm. She smelled of vanilla and oranges, and no, she definitely wasn't wearing a bra. 'Well, I wish I could have one, even if it was a psychopathic serial-killer rooster without any claws. But I wouldn't know how to take care of it and I'd be too sad if it died.'

'Better start off with a Tamagotchi then. They're coming back in.'

'Really, for like the fourth time?'

'They have Korean ones now,' he told her, 'rock stars you have to send to rehearsal and keep off drugs or else they fail to climb the charts. Psychologists thought that killing off electronic babies was too damaging for middle-school girls.'

She laughed, and put her sunglasses back on.

What was he doing, thinking about her breasts when she was about sixteen and her mouth was the spit of Jessica's? He had to go steady, have a cuppa, then get on to his evening class.

They walked to Insa Dong along chalky paths that wove around patches of grass and trees in Pagoda Park. The intersections were studded with statues of imaginary beasts, crosses between wild cats and armadillos. Under trellises in the shade, old men moved black and white stones across *baduk* boards, read newspapers or just sat quietly, their hands resting on their canes, a glassy, faraway look in their eyes. Most were wearing suits that had seen better days, the material thin and fading, like their faces. Two barbers had set up chairs in a corner and were busy trimming and shaving the elders.

Sydney pressed up against him. 'Free haircuts for Korean War Veterans,' she told him. 'My friend Jin Sok told me.'

Damien couldn't stop himself. 'Is he the bald guy? At Gongjang?'

'Yeah, he's the photographer on my main modelling contract.'

Was he just imagining it, or was she casting him an amused look? Christ, how bloody pathetic was he, interrogating a girl he'd only known ten minutes about her friends?

'Hey, do you smell pot?' She was whispering now – and yeah, there was a whiff of something herbal in the air. 'Where the hell is it coming from?' She took a few steps down an avenue of stunted pine trees and Damien followed, glad of the shade. Ahead of them stood the stone pagoda that gave the park its name. Centuries old and crumbling, surrounded by scaffolding, it resembled the fossilised spine of some ancient Gentle Giant. Indistinct images of Buddha were carved between the vertebrae.

They stood at its base and sniffed.

'There?' Damien gestured at a circle of tables set up by the back wall of the park. They ventured closer, to where Korean acupuncturists were treating elderly men and women, inserting dozens of small steel pins into their hands until they stood proud, metal harvests springing from gnarled, leathery soil. Crumpled tissue swabs blotched with brown blood stains littered the tabletops.

'This place is a bloody geriatric amusement park,' Damien joked.

'Whoah!' Sydney gasped. 'Look at that.'

Beyond the tables, a small group of patients were standing around a grill where sheaves of herbs were burning over the coals. The Koreans were braising their hands, thick with needles, over the heat, turning them slowly to allow the smoke to penetrate the rows of tiny perforations on both sides.

'Barbecued flesh,' Damien said. 'I had no idea it smelled so much like pot!'

'Are you from London?' Sydney asked, abruptly.

Images from the news flashed into his head: people with no skin, or covered with tattoos in the patterns of the clothes they had been wearing. He shoved them aside. 'No, Brighton, on the south coast. They're getting fall-out, but hey, the government says it's within the health and safety limits.'

'Lucky you're here, hey?' she said, quietly. Then she slapped his arm lightly. 'Let's go celebrate that fact.'

Sydney took him to one of Insa Dong's famous teashops, a place with rounded walls and a log roof. The windows were obscured with dark green potted palms that reminded Damien of Mexico; the tables separated by an old railway track, complete with signal lights. Secluded in a cushioned booth, they ordered ginseng tea. As they waited, Sydney launched into tales of excess in the Apkuchong fashion world, where other models would scratch your eyes out soon as look at you, and Jin Sok, who turned out to be gay, was 'her rock'. He was tired, and let her prattle on. She'd been scouted in Vancouver, she said, but was from a small town on the British Columbian coast, not far from a pig farm where some whacko had murdered a zillion prostitutes.

What would Sydney think, he wondered, if he asked her birth date?

Christ, he had to drop it, right now. *She's not Jessica*, he told himself fiercely, *so get that fucking ridiculous notion out of your head*. She was a cute, glitzy starlet, and maybe the reason she'd come into his life was to reassure him that Canadian girls could be sexy as hell. 'Are you planning to go back soon? I've heard BC's great,' he ventured.

'No way – oh hey, wow!' The waitress set down two celadon cups of pale tea. Bits of ginseng root were floating on top. Sydney blew on the steaming tea, then opened her purse.

'Here's Dr Kim's card – the scientist? She's *kyopo*, so there's no language problems.'

'Genetic Research International Productions,' Damien read out loud. 'Sounds dodgy. So what's she after, then?'

Sydney pursed her lips. 'She's not dodgy. She's doing really important work, trying to stop diseases.' There was an awkward pause.

Damien was on the point of apologising when she leaned over the table. Her voice was a little husky now, confidential. 'But she also does fertility treatments. I donated some eggs last month to help foreigners in Korea have babies. She's looking for sperm too. She pays half a million *won*, but I bet you could talk her up.'

Damien whistled silently in his head. So she was a real Canadian after all: save the whale, save the baby seals, save the Rocky Mountains, save the infertile foreigners in Korea. Examining the card, he thought through the offer. Half a million would be a nice chunk to add to his fund . . . but no, it would be crazy to squirt his genetic identity into some test-tube – especially right before he got his new passport. Still, he didn't want to hurt Sydney's feelings.

'Sounds like a lot of money for a wank,' he joked.

Sydney was looking up at him from beneath her lashes, like a cross between Darla the Vampire and a cockapoo puppy. 'It's not just a – a *wank*,' she pouted.

He pocketed the card. 'Well, who knows; maybe I'll give her a call.'

'It's really easy work,' she persisted, 'especially for guys.'

She was just a kid, and she was just trying to be nice. But Christ, he had to get her off his case. 'Look, Sydney, it takes just one tiny change in the law and all those stray sperm are wiggling right back home to Daddy. I've got nothing against helping people; I just don't want some spotty kid turning up on my doorstep nineteen years from now demanding I put him through university.'

'It's not like that here – Da Mi is totally confidential.' Scarily, there was a touch of Nurse Ratchet creeping into Sydney's expression.

Damien lifted his teacup to his lips. He felt like biting the translucent green china. Jessica had always put on her heavy-duty face whenever she wanted him to do her bidding.

Abruptly, Sydney changed the subject. 'Are you teaching English here?'

'Depends who's asking.'

'Sorry, I didn't mean to pry.'

There was another strained pause, and Damien realised he might have offended her. She was just making small-talk, after all. Apart from Jake, Canadians didn't always get his sense of humour. Though, to be fair, he had sounded snarky. Christ, he had to lighten up.

'I'm just taking the piss. Yeah, I'm teaching, kids mainly.'

Sydney perked up. 'Do you like it?'

'Sure, what's not to like? Half the time it's just a big love-fest; the other half I play the heavy and they have to obey my every command. I should have started doing it years ago.'

That made her smile. Her eyes were an amazing shade of green, like limes with gold pips. They looked extra bright when she smiled.

'Aren't you worried about Immigration?' she asked.

'Nah. I've only heard of one kindergarten getting busted, and my privates are all in Chamshil. The heat's off there now, so I'm just getting on with it really. What about you?'

'Oh, I have a work visa. My modelling agent got me a contract.' She thought a moment, then said, 'Hey, Chamshil – do you ever swim at the Olympic pool?'

'I get there too late. My Chamshil jobs are from five to nine and the pool closes at six. It's a bit of a pisser, really. I used to go in the sea in Brighton.'

'Do you think you still would? I mean, do you believe the government about the radiation?'

He didn't want to think about Brighton. 'Who knows?'

'I'd like to go to London.' Sydney asserted. 'When it's safe again.'

Why were people so fucking desperate to visit London? Maybe the Mayor *had* organised those bombs. 'London's just a maze of over-priced shops and overrated museums filled with tourists, terrorists and riot police,' he told her, tetchily. 'And it rains all the time. Total mono-season. You'd be far better off back in Canada.'

'Canada?' Sydney wrinkled her nose. 'I'm having way more fun here.' She nodded dreamily. 'Umm. I love these bits of ginseng in the tea.'

Damien chewed on the bitter root and found his mouth puckering. This lunch was fizzling out. But then again, he was exhausted.

Sydney yawned. 'I gotta get home and crash. Wanna swap numbers? We could go to a movie sometime maybe?' She sounded eager now, a little vulnerable, as if he might refuse.

She must be lonely, Damien realised. She's kooky, definitely; bossy, a bit; but pretty and lonely and mostly the right kind of nice. She hadn't said anything about high school or poker, after all.

'Sure,' he said, getting his MoPho out of his pocket. He slid it next to hers on the table and they watched in silence as the phones coupled, waiting for the flash and burble of a small 'successful upload' fusion tone.

Sydney followed Damien along the narrow sidewalk of Insadong's main drag, passing antique shops and galleries, mulberry paper vendors and calligraphy shops dripping with brushes as big as her head. She was feeling irritated with herself. The meeting had hardly gone to plan. She'd felt ridiculous in the tearoom, earnestly discussing ovaries and sperm – Damien clearly thought she was an idiot. And now they were heading towards Jae Ho's wife's gallery; on this street, Jin Sok had said. She'd invited Damien to Insa Dong partly so she could see it without having to walk past it by herself, but right now she was in no mood to confront Jae Ho's perfect wife and perfect life, let alone him. She'd left him still sleeping in her apartment, but who knows, he could be down here already, helping his wife, or even having coffee with Jin Sok. She just wanted to get home as quickly as she could.

Damien didn't know that, of course. He stopped in front of a large grey and white canvas hanging in a window. 'Hey, isn't this by the same guy who hangs in Gongjang?'

Sydney's heart floundered in her chest. 'Yeah, must be,' she said, as casually as she could manage.

The canvas was emblazoned with a tarry black cross, a plus sign to balance the minus sign at the nightclub. The background was an aerial map of Seoul, roughly painted over with thick, viscous brush-strokes. Jae Ho had scratched at the paint, scoring the outlines of buildings, bridges, streets – and the occasional suggestion of people drowning in a sick and rotting sea.

'Ground Zero. Floods.' Damien remarked. 'I wonder if he painted it since London.'

'Looks like a dirty window to me.' Sydney peered past the painting to the gallery within, all gleaming hardwood floors. There were some ink drawings on the walls, and a tall Korean woman in a sleeveless dress was talking on the phone behind a desk, her face obscured by a huge bouquet of flowers.

'He's a friend of yours, isn't he, the artist?'

She had thought about that question already. 'He's a friend of Jin Sok's. Cool guy – doesn't speak much English.'

'Do you want to go in?'

'I'm bushed. Maybe another time?'

Damien was heading over the river to teach, so they parted company at Chongno with a quick kiss. Sydney got a cab back to Hongdae. It was an uncomfortable ride. Damien thought she was a freak and wouldn't return her calls; Da Mi would be disappointed in her, and the start-date for the Peonies would be delayed. Plus, it had been horrible, looking into the gallery, wondering if that elegant woman at the desk was Jae Ho's wife. She got stomach cramps just thinking about it.

But there was nothing she could do about any of that right now. She was dog-tired. She wanted only one thing now, and that was her bed.

She wasn't expecting Jae Ho to still be in her apartment, but his boots were lying in the hallway where he'd kicked them off the night before, and inside the studio room, he was still asleep. She slipped off her clothes and curled around him on the *yo*. He stirred, opened his eyes, ran his hands over her body. She waited for him to ask where she'd gone, but he just yawned, picked up her alarm clock, frowned and said, 'Oh, late.'

She laid her head upon his chest, listened to his heart. 'Jae Ho?' she whispered.

'Umm?'

'Do you want to go out for dinner with me this week? Not in Hongdae.'

He ran his fingers through her hair. 'Sy-duh nee. I no like appointments,' he finally replied. 'Appointments give me . . . stress. Today I had appointment with my wife, for lunch, promise. But I sleep. I here. Now I worried.' She raised her head to look at him. The aperture of his face closed in on itself like it had done when he was talking about the blood-song.

There was another long silence as her stomach turned.

'Piglet, I playboy. I *married*,' he said, apologetically, his voice lifting on the last word, as if he was alarming even himself with this reminder. Soberly, he continued, 'I want free, but I *not* free. I don't want you get too in love with me.'

'No,' she said firmly, desperately, sitting up, 'I free! I only want to see you sometimes – special times. Like *giseang*.' *Giseang* were traditional Korean courtesans; they were cultured and intelligent, and they entertained their clients with more than just their bodies. She hoped the reference would make him smile, and it did.

'You play guitar?' he teased.

'I learn!'

'Okay, okay!'

But it wasn't okay, she could tell.

He got up and began to dress, not looking at her, checking he had everything he'd left strewn around the flat.

Suddenly she felt angry with him – and with herself. Was she really such a simpering idiot? 'Maybe I'll get another boyfriend,' she said, airily. 'As well as you.'

'Ah, good idea.' He smiled. 'Who? Oasis boy?'

'Oasis boy?' She didn't get it.

'Black hair boy. I think you make date with him last night.'

'Oh, him. Maybe.' She tried to sound indifferent, but her stomach was doing back-flips. What was wrong with Jae Ho? Why didn't he give a shit if she fucked someone else?

'Very nice. He look good with you.' His tone was light and approving – but surely he must be feeling *something*.

She tossed her hair. 'Actually, I just went out for tea with him. I'll have to see.'

Jae Ho nodded sagely, and buttoned up his jeans.

After he left Sydney lay down on her *yo*, curled into a tight little ball. Everything was all wrong. Jae Ho was a heartless jerk, trying to get rid of her – or pimp her out to other men. Or maybe he wasn't. Maybe he was just insecure. Maybe he'd decided that she really wanted a Western boyfriend and was just trying to get out of their relationship with his pride intact. In which case she'd just done the stupidest thing in the world – why had she taunted him? She should have reassured him instead. Had she just fucked everything up?

Just as the tears began drooling down her face her Gotcha vibrated on her wrist: Da Mi, calling to see how it had gone with Damien. They'd agreed to talk as soon as Sydney got back from Insa Dong.

She clamped her hands between her legs, but the Gotcha just buzzed against her thighs, saying *Da Mi is your friend. Da Mi has always been way kinder than this selfish bastard who only wanted to fuck you.* Da Mi had given her so much, and so far all she'd done was fart about, paying nothing but chapped lip service to the tiny favour Da Mi had asked in return.

Taking a deep breath, she wiped her face with the sheet and picked up. 'Hi, Da Mi,' she said in a tiny voice into the Gotcha.

'Sydney. Are you all right?' Da Mi's voice vibrated faintly from the watch.

'Yeah.' She sniffed. 'I mean, no, I guess not.'

'Oh, darling. Did Damien upset you?'

She fought back the tears, trying to think of a plausible story, but nothing came to mind. 'No,' she gulped, 'not him.'

'Who then, sweetheart?'

'I feel so bad. I should have told you ages ago.'

'Told me what? Sydney, calm down and tell me what's wrong.'

Sydney struggled to control herself. Through her weeping hiccoughs she tried to explain. 'Oh Da Mi, I've been trying to be good, to be enlightened, but it's so hard without the Chair. I didn't mean to, honestly, but I . . . got *involved* with this married guy, an artist I met at the club. It felt so beautiful sometimes, I thought he loved me, but now I know he doesn't. He was so horrible to me today. I'm sorry, I wanted to tell you . . . but I didn't do anything during the donation cycle, I promise.' She wiped her nose again on the sheet. God, what would Da Mi say?

'Darling, it's just what happens in these clubs. I know you didn't do anything to jeopardise the Peonies. Your eggs are perfect. Now we just have to get you sorted out too.'

'But how?' Sydney wailed. 'I'm in love with him – I can't stand it that he doesn't care about me at all. It hurts so much, Da Mi.'

'Shhh. It's love pain, not cancer, my darling. Just an excessive attachment, that's all. You can easily cure it in the Chair. Have you been taking your honey recently?'

'No,' she admitted.

'You have some in the apartment, don't you? So after this call, make yourself a double dose and get an early night. I have to go to Kyongiddo tomorrow to deal with an emergency, but I'll be back by the evening. Why don't you come up to my place for dinner? I'll send a taxi.'

Her heart was a rock-hard ache between her ribs. *No, it's hopeless. Nothing can help me*, Sydney wanted to sob. But she hesitated. Maybe she *should* try the Chair again. It had been so amazing last time. And at least she'd be getting out of the apartment.

'That would be really nice, Da Mi,' she sniffled.

'Perfect. We'll give you a booster tomorrow, then you can start having regular sessions. No man is worth all this torment, Sydney.

You don't have to give up romance to be the Queen of the Peonies, but when you're closer to Enlightenment, you'll be able to choose someone who's good for you. Someone who shares our values.'

Sydney sat up, and pulled the sheet around her. 'That's what I want, Da Mi – I guess I thought because Jae Ho was an artist he was special, but today he was so *casual* and . . . *mean*.'

'Trust me, sweetheart, he doesn't deserve you. Look, why don't you make yourself a cup of honey drink now?'

Yes, she should really. Sydney got to her feet and, still wrapped in the sheet, headed over to the kitchen and opened the cupboard.

'Good girl,' Da Mi cooed from her wrist. 'But tell me, how did it go with Damien?'

Sydney clattered about the kitchen, filling the kettle, dipping a spoon in the jar of honey. 'I don't know, Da Mi. I was feeling bad about that too. I passed your card on, but I don't think he'll call. He said he didn't want some kid showing up in twenty years. Maybe I just didn't sell it to him well enough.'

'It's not everybody's cup of tea. We might have to try another angle. Otherwise, do you think he'd be a good choice?'

'I think he'd be *fab*. He's really smart – the way he talks about things, it's very . . . English. But he doesn't want to go back there. I mean, who can blame him?'

'That might be a way in.'

'If I haven't blown it already. I think he thought I was a nutcase, Da Mi.'

Da Mi chuckled. 'I'm sure he thinks you're lovely. We'll just have to keep trying. I have a biotech project coming up he might be more interested in.'

'I've got his MoPho number. He said to call.'

'You can do that soon – just remember, don't mention singing unless he does. Now, look, don't worry any more about this artist; get some sleep tonight and I'll send a taxi round tomorrow.'

Da Mi said goodbye, leaving Sydney to lie back in bed with her honey drink. She drank it slowly, feeling its restorative powers. She knew it was dumb to get all worked up about Jae Ho when the whole VirtuWorld project was only just beginning. Maybe a few more sessions in the chair would make her less emotional, more accepting of this situation? By bugging Jae Ho about his wife she was only driving him away. Fucking Damien to make him jealous would be stupid too. Anyway, soon she'd be famous, with queues of men to choose from. But right now she was 'knackered', as Damien would say.

Giggling to herself, she slurped down the last of the hot honey drink and rolled underneath the blankets.

28 | Carving Knives

Sunday afternoon, and he'd finally finished the first draft of his post-snukes British foreign tourism projection report. Johnny fancied a cigar and a big snifter of Courvoisier. He strode down to Churchill's, a new Itaewon gastropub with a North African menu and backroom humidor. The glassed-off antechamber was comfortably furnished with wing-tipped leather chairs and copies of the latest *Financial Times* on long wooden newsgrippers. Today it was empty; maybe the place was too new to have caught on yet.

He'd savoured three puffs of his Cuban leaf when his MoPho buzzed in his jacket pocket.

Withheld number: that had been happening lately, calls he'd miss, and no left messages. He'd no time for games like that – but then again, it could be the lab.

'Mr Joh-nee?' A voice he hated whined in his ear.

'Look. I said *I'd* call *you*.'

'I sorry, very sorry, but emergency. You can talk? Private?'

Johnny took a swig of his cognac. 'Better make it snappy, Ratty.'

'Okay, okay, I talk quick. My mind trouble, Mr Joh-nee. I need thirty million won in cash very soon, or else I have show sexy sexy video to a friend of ours. I don't think Dr Kim gonna be happy when she see what happen at hospital.'

Johnny checked over his shoulder. The tall Moroccan waiter was still flirting with some Korean chick in a skimpy dress. He must do

267

well here, one of a kind. There might be an escort angle to follow up on later . . . But for now, Johnny had to concentrate on this fuck-up. Like, was this unrefrigerated shrimp trying to *blackmail* him?

'Did I hear you right?' he murmured. 'Did I hear you say you want to *extort* money from me?'

'Oh, excuse my English, I don't know.' Rattail tittered. 'All I know is I watching very interesting video, on the Internet already.'

'Well, if it's so fucking *interesting*, why did you wait so long to tell me about it? It's been a while since the hospital. Maybe it took you that long to cook up this story, Ratface, or hire a couple of actors to make some bad porno flick?' Johnny kept his voice low, with one eye on the entrance to the antechamber. No one was within earshot.

'Oh no, no, I was phone you before, you no answer. I don't want leave message. I want talk to you. Video is real. Camera was inside air-con unit. Colour beautiful – red James Dean innerwear, I like very much. You please tell me where you buy them. And sound excellent quality. I think Dr Kim going to be very upset when she hear you calling to a dead prostitute her name.'

Shit. Those were his underpants all right – and there *had* been one of those tall air-con units in the corner. Still, this deep-fried runt and his plug-ugly cronies could just have been peeking.

'So are you going to send me this link then?' he asked, dry as a Bond martini. 'Or am I going to have to come over and drag it out of you?'

'Oh no. No worry. We meet Hollywoods. I show you on my MoPho.'

Meet this whiny schmuck? This human *mosquito*? Johnny took a draw on his cigar and blew a perfect smoke ring across the room. It sailed between the upholstered chairs before warping and dissolving in front of a framed photograph of Winston Churchill. Old Winnie the Poobah hadn't said anything about fighting 'em in the humidors, on our *afternoons off*.

'What makes you think I care if Kim sees it, Ratface?' he countered, not quite able to hide his irritation. 'She's not my girlfriend – or my boss.'

'No, you right; I think maybe you like Kim to see it, make her mad. But I think you don't want her tell your people in LA you losing your temper, doing bad things – *illegal* things. Things embarrass company. I heard your boss pay big money for you learn how treat people nice. I heard he say you go on course or you fired. I think you job not so safe, is it Mr Joh-nee?'

Kim. It could only be fucking Kim who'd told him all that. Johnny stubbed the cigar out. 'Listen to me very carefully, Ratface. I don't know who you've been talking to, or how long you've been plotting this little scheme, but let's get one thing straight: I'm not giving anyone my money. Assuming this video in fact exists, I want you to *erase* it, and any files of it *anywhere*, or else my people are going to find you and when they're done with you there isn't going to be much left. Do you understand?'

'I understand, but I have friends too – friends who send Kim the website and call police if anything happen me. I don't think you want go jail in foreign country. You only want website erased, memory card destroyed – and price is thirty million won.'

'So you can turn up with another website address and double your price? Yeah, okay, let's meet. So you can show me the website and we can talk about your options. See: my course worked. I treat you nice, Ratty; you treat me nice too.' Johnny made his voice sickly-sweet, though irony was usually wasted on Koreans. As for Ratty's so-called friends, Bullfrog and co. were easily dealt with, and the Korean police made the Keystone cops look like a crack unit of the Presidential Guard.

'Good, good. We meet tonight? You bring cash?' You could almost hear Ratty licking his lips. Fucking amateur.

'Tonight? Tonight, Rattail, is my night off. I'll see you tomorrow, ten p.m., at Hollywood's. Bring the camera too.'

'*Ye, ye*. No problem. We talk then.'

'Don't be late.' Johnny ended the call and downed the rest of his Courvoisier. Who would know Rattail, and also know enough to keep his mouth shut if the creep went missing? TJ, that was it. TJ owed him from way back.

Monday night he pulled up at Rattail's apartment building at nine, parking in the back, away from the building supervisor's office. He was dressed in black, and had taken the precaution of wearing glasses, a false moustache and a hat – but still, the fewer people who saw him the better. Before getting out of the car he pulled on a pair of latex gloves and double-checked that the scalpel was in his coat pocket. He was proud of this touch: the blade was the one he'd picked up at the morgue.

Ten minutes later he was in the stairwell on the ninth floor. His plan was simple: just hang out by the elevator. Koreans never walked up or down – they were too afraid of robbers, which they pronounced 'lovers', funnily enough. All this was assuming that Rattail was home, and would leave his apartment alone. If not, he'd just have to meet him at Hollywood's and take it from there.

The stairwell was just out of sight of the open walkway that connected the apartments. It was dusk now, which made it easier to lurk in the shadows. If another tenant appeared, he could just duck up a step or two. Finally, he heard footsteps approaching, and peering out from his corner, he saw Rattail, standing in front of the elevator, pressing the button. Bingo. Swiftly, scalpel in hand, Johnny stepped out of the shadows, grabbed the taller man in an arm-lock from behind and whipped the blade up to Rattail's throat.

The swift attack had the desired effect: the Korean crumpled like a puppet with cut strings. Quaking, he sputtered a few words in Korean as Johnny dragged him into the stairwell.

'Who do you think I am, asshole?' Johnny whispered. Patting down Ratty's grubby beige trench coat, he discovered the camera, and the Korean's MoPho. 'Now be quiet and share your toys with Uncle Johnny.'

The digicam was a tiny Japanese model. He shoved it into the pocket of his own coat, along with the MoPho. The sweat was rolling off him: it was way too warm for this shit – and way too exposed. Anyone could walk by at any minute.

'Right, take me to your apartment,' he ordered.

His breathing rasping and shallow, one arm twisted behind his back – a hold Johnny had always found very effective – Rattail led the way. At the door to number 932 he fumbled with his keys and finally let Johnny into a sparsely furnished studio apartment. Despite having hardly anything in it, the place was a dump: dishes were piled up like tower blocks in the sink, and the faded linoleum floor was caked with ripples of grime. A fuggish aroma of dirty socks and stale cigarette smoke hung in the air, while a pile of dirty laundry in the corner, skid marks clearly visible on a pair of grey underpants, added a rich, almost tangy top note to the stink.

'How can you live like this, Ratty?' Johnny muttered. 'I'm going to have to call you Pigshit from now on.'

The computer monitor on the table in the corner was off, but the green light on the keyboard indicated the hard drive was still running. Johnny forced Rattail into the chair in front of the screen and turned it on.

'Okay. Now you show me the file, you erase it, then you show me the website you made and you delete the video. Understand?'

His thin shoulders trembling, tears now greasing his face, Rattail nodded.

Johnny stood behind him, looking over his head as he opened up the file. It was entitled, in English, *Mr Johnny's Blind Date*. Johnny watched it for ten seconds, then pressed the scalpel a little more firmly against Ratty's throat. The Korean clicked his way through the process of deletion and then opened up the website. It was nothing special, Johnny was relieved to see, just a cyber-holding bay – no pay-per-view or download buttons.

'What about your buddy down at the morgue?' Johnny kneed Ratty in the back. 'What about the Scalper? Do they know the password? Have they downloaded the file? How many times have you three jerked off to it, huh?'

'No, no, they don't have.' Rattail twitched. Johnny had no doubt that he was lying. Well, first things first.

'What's the code for the car elevator at the hospital? Quick!'

'73281,' Rattail sobbed.

'Good boy. Relax. I'm nearly done with you now.' Rubbing his own neck, Johnny had one last think about his options. He'd deliberately left this part of the evening's schedule open to the whim of circumstance, but now was the time for that whim to be guided by a little practical application.

On the one hand, he really was trying to put his hitman days behind him. Indiscriminate butchery was fun, of course, but it didn't fit easy into the new Johnny Sandman HKO, future Head of SEA Ops, big picture.

On the other hand, could he really trust this scummy weasel not to try and take revenge?

Ratty's hands were clutching the edge of the table. His fingernails were filthy. Because he spent his life *wallowing in dirt*. Look at the way he lived: bleach had never touched that kitchen sink; soap had never graced the back of his neck. Would he take Johnny's kind intervention today as a message to clean up his act? No: he'd just find some new pile of disgusting muck to throw at his superiors as soon as he could.

Sadly, the Sandman's latex gloves would be getting wet tonight.

But this decision brought up some serious logistical issues. It was against his principles to kill Ratty anywhere near his flat. That could get some over-zealous police officer interested in 'a personal motive', might get the computer hard drive checked over. Hustling the Korean down the stairwell and across the car park this early in the evening was also far too dangerous an option. Bumping off Ratty and taking the hard drive down with him would also be conspicuous, and the computer was way too big to conceal about his person – plus its absence in the flat would scream 'investigate me'. Too bad Rattail didn't use a laptop; that would have been a no-brainer: simple to hide under his coat, easy to dispose, and an obvious target for an opportunistic burglar.

The Korean was breathing more normally. His fingers twitched in the direction of a packet of cigarettes beside the computer keyboard. Obviously he felt the wrath of Johnny Sandman had passed.

'You have other porn videos on there?' Johnny asked, casually.

Rattail's shoulders relaxed a little. '*Ye, ye.* You want see?'

Johnny waited as he clicked open an Mpeg and a badly lit image of a tubby Korean being pissed on by a pre-op tranny filled the RealPlayer window.

'You like?' Rattail asked hopefully. 'I have plenty I show you.'

'I think it's *fag shit.*' Johnny took a swipe at Rattail's head with the flat of his palm, releasing a small cascade of dandruff. 'I want you to erase it, and every other sick, fucking video you have on there. One by fucking one.'

Ratty sniffled as his life's work began to disappear, but Johnny watched the general obliteration with a growing sense of security. One trashed file reconstructed by computer forensics was evidence.

A dozen, though; that was just a guy getting bored. All gone, though: that might look a little strange.

'Better leave a few,' he growled. 'I need to go soon. Show me your favourite one that's left, get it up and running.'

'Okay, thank you, Mr San-duh-man, thank you.' Rattail sighed and opened up another video. Johnny grimaced as a ginger-haired US soldier appeared on screen, fucking a goat in a cellar while his buddies stood round in a big circle jerk, their dog tags glinting against their bare chests.

'You're really sick, you know that, *Pigshit*?' With one deep incision he cut Rattail's gulping throat. A jet of blood from the jugular spurted over the keyboard, the monitor and the wall. The body jerked briefly, like a fish on the end of a line, then, with a satisfying gurgle, slumped to the floor.

Johnny stepped back from the pool of blood spreading over the lino. Checking his hands, he was pleased to see only a few crimson smears on the latex fingertips. He could always pick up a few shifts at a Halal butcher's if he ever quit working for ConGlam.

There was a plastic bag in his pocket. He took it out, peeled off the gloves and stuffed them and the scalpel inside it. He'd throw the knife into the Han later, and burn the latex along with his cheap new clothes. For now, he pulled on another pair of hospital gloves. There wasn't a mirror in the room, so he ducked into the bathroom to make sure no flecks of blood had splashed his face. All clear – but fuck, that shower was a high school experiment in how to grow mould. He resisted the temptation to pocket Ratty's Hugo Boss after-shave. Taking trophies from a murder scene was strictly for psychos and retards.

Back in the main room, he erased the video from the digicam and set it beside the computer. Instinct told him not to rough up the apartment or make it look like a robbery. There'd be plenty of people with a grudge against that sleazy bastard; best just let the police scratch their heads over which one had had the guts to even the score. With any luck no one would discover the body for days. It hardly appeared Rattail had been in the habit of socialising at home.

Now for the smart part. He sat down at the desk, took Ratty's MoPho out of his pocket and went through the text messages. Reading HanGul was not his strong point, but he forced himself to concentrate. Yup, the inbox was full of chats with Scalper and Bullfrog: Ratty crowing about the success of his plan, telling them he'd be at Hollywood's at ten; to call him at midnight. Well, that carelessness had saved their sad lives. Johnny switched the MoPho into camera mode, took several arty photos of Ratty's drenched corpse and sent them to his little gang of would-be cyber-criminals. They'd be fucking insane to pass any copies of the video onto Kim after they'd seen the guaranteed results of such insubordinate behaviour.

He switched the MoPho off; he'd ditch it in the Han with the knife. Now he had to get back to his business report. Listening at the door, he heard only the muted sound of traffic below, so he slipped back out onto the walkway and strode quickly across to the stairwell. The air was dusty, but compared to the apartment, fresh as a Wisconsin breeze. He sucked a deep breath of it into his lungs. The sun had set now and the night city was sprawled out below him, bright lights gleaming like a vast orchard of money trees.

Humming a blockbuster show tune of his own devising, a little ditty about a guy called Ratty, getting Internet chatty, now as flat as chapatti, never gonna see Cincinnati, Johnny jogged down the nine flights. *All in all, an excellent night*, he thought as he turned his key in the ignition. Like the convertible revving into life, the beast in Johnny Sandman had re-awakened, its appetite keener than ever.

Maybe Andrew Beacon wouldn't have approved of his empathy levels tonight, but it would sure save ConGlam some coin if their Head of South East Asian Operations could bump off the opposition with his own bare hands.

29 | Dr Tae Sun

Mee Hee pulled out the Western-style armchairs. She and Su Jin had never used them, but they seemed appropriate for the gravity of the situation.

Dr Tae Sun perched on the fat-cushioned seat. He looked as awkward as she felt. Over his shoulder, the shrine to Dr Kim was lost in shadow. How could she have neglected it tonight?

'Please, excuse me. I must light a candle, for Su Jin and for Dr Kim.'

He waited patiently as she fumbled in the drawer for the matches. The candle lit, she sat opposite him, hands folded in her lap.

'Mee Hee.' He leaned forward, his eyes bright. 'I have important news. After supper, I spoke to the driver of the bus to Pusan. He told me that Su Jin was one of his passengers this morning.'

Relief swept through Mee Hee, followed by a swift rake of tension. Su Jin's whereabouts wasn't a secret any more. But did that mean she would be chased and punished? 'That's good, isn't it?'

'Yes, it's very good, of course, to know she isn't lost in the woods. I wanted to tell you, to put your mind at rest. But before we tell the others, I need to ask you, do you know why she would want to leave us?'

Mee Hee's arm was stinging. She rubbed it underneath her sleeve. A few feet away, a large flying beetle was batting against the window. Normally, she and Su Jin would have chased it outside, but with Tae Sun looking at her so intently, she didn't dare stand up.

'She likes those women's magazines,' she said at last. 'Maybe she just wanted to see the city for the day?'

'I don't want to frighten you, Mee Hee, but Pusan isn't like those women's magazines,' Dr Tae Sun said gently. 'It's a rough town, full of sailors and prostitutes. Su Jin doesn't have any money, and we're worried about where she'll be sleeping tonight. Mee Hee, if you know anything at all, please say. You won't get yourself or Su Jin into trouble. We only want to help her, to make sure she's safe.'

Dr Tae Sun reached over and placed his hand upon hers, loosening her fingers. His palms were dry and sure. She searched his eyes for a sign of anger, a hint of disappointment. But his square, pale face, as always, looked on her only with kindness.

She took a deep breath. 'She has money,' she heard herself whisper.

'How did she get it, Mee Hee?'

She paused. She mustn't tell on Dr Dong Sun; she had to lie – not for Su Jin, but for herself. 'She found it, in a purse, in Inch'on. She told me last night, when I woke up; she made me promise not to tell.'

Dr Tae Sun was smiling at her, his hand stroking her own, his warmth spreading up her arm. 'You only wanted to help her, I know that. But helping us find her is the best way to do that, isn't it?'

Yes, she thought, *Su Jin might be in danger. She might have disregarded Dr Dong Sun's instructions; she might have been followed by a sailor. Anything could have happened.*

And if something bad had happened, it would all be Mee Hee's fault. In a small but steady voice, she continued, 'She said she was going to get a job sewing. I tried to stop her, but she wouldn't listen. I felt so terrible all day. I lied to Dr Dong Sun. I'm so sorry, Dr Tae Sun.'

'No no, I understand. But don't worry about telling us. If we can find her, we can help her get the kind of life she wants. No one is going to force her to come back. That wouldn't be good for the babies, or for anyone.'

'I never want to leave,' Mee Hee blurted out.

'We love having you here too. Now, let me look at your arm. You must have a mosquito bite, it's bleeding.'

Reluctantly, Mee Hee held out her arm. The two spots where she had stuck the pin were red and swollen, smeared with blood. Dr Tae Sun examined them carefully.

'It's been a hard day for you, hasn't it?'

She nodded.

'Shall I give you something to help you sleep?'

'Yes, please.'

'And tomorrow, do you want to move into another house, with your other sisters?'

His lips were slightly parted, wet; his eyelashes delicately curling upwards behind his glasses. She had never noticed that before.

'No, no,' she stammered. 'I like it here. I won't be lonely. I promise. Maybe you could . . . come and visit me sometimes?' Aghast, she dropped her head. 'Or my sisters could come and keep me company.'

Dr Tae Sun rolled down her sleeve. 'I'll tell Dr Kim that you're happy to stay here alone. And of course I'll come and check up on you. That's what I'm here for.'

Ten minutes later he was back from the dispensary. He gave her two herbal sleeping pills and watched her take them, then rubbed a soothing ointment onto her arm. He was so close to her she could smell the fresh soap-powder scent of his shirt, and beneath it, the light musk of his body.

'Sleep well, Mee Hee,' he said, softly. Then he stepped out again into the humid, chirruping night.

After he had gone, she turned off the lamp and sat quietly in the living room, praying for Su Jin's wellbeing and for Dr Kim's forgiveness until the candle sputtered out.

The next day, Dr Kim arrived at the village. The women gathered in the Meeting Hall, sitting on the cushions Dr Tae Sun had set out. Mee Hee sat beside So Ra in the second row, trying not to look at the three doctors. There was a grain of rice from breakfast caught between the floorboards. Later she would gouge it out with her fingernails, but for now she must keep still.

'My sisters,' Dr Kim began, 'I have good news. Su Jin is probably in Pusan. At least, we know she took a bus there yesterday.'

So Ra squeezed Mee Hee's arm as a ripple of whispers ran through the room.

Beside Dr Kim, Dr Dong Sun cleared his throat. 'It's a shock to everyone that Su Jin has left us without saying goodbye, but everything possible is being done to find her, so we can help her settle in a new life.'

Dr Kim stepped forward now. In her green silk jacket and floor-length skirt, she moved like a shimmering flame in the morning light. But her presence could not warm Mee Hee. She fixed her eyes on the hem of Dr Kim's skirt, the pointy satin tips of her shoes.

Her sisters nudged each other, and the room fell silent. 'I am very sad, of course,' the scientist said, 'to think that Su Jin wanted to leave. As you all know, much care has gone into making this village your home. Please, I beg of you, if there is anything that makes you anxious, let me or the Doctors Che know your worries and concerns.'

'Is there anyone here unhappy about our village life?' Dr Dong Sun asked. 'If so, please, speak now.'

The silence was unearthly now. As if everyone one in the room had stopped breathing. In front of Mee Hee, Chin Mee slowly raised her arm. 'Please, I'm sorry,' she said, in a voice as tremulous as a reed flute, 'I love it here – but I know that Su Jin wanted to get married one day. Maybe that's why she ran away. I think some of us would like to get married too. Would that ever be possible, Dr Kim?'

Dr Kim beamed down at Chin Mee. 'You are beautiful young women; of course you're all thinking about husbands. But please, let me reassure you that as soon as you have given birth to the Peonies, you will be introduced to fine men from the local area. These men will be offered jobs in the village, and anyone who wants to get married will have complete freedom to do so.'

Now Older Sister stuck up her hand. 'Excuse me, Dr Kim, but will they want us? Why would they want to look after our children?'

Some of the women gasped. Dr Kim raised her hands. 'Older Sister, have you ever read the Bible?'

'Not myself, but Younger Sister talks about it – all the time.'

The women laughed, but Dr Kim shushed them. 'Ask Younger Sister to read you the story of the birth of Jesus. He was the Son of God, but his earthly father, Joseph, cared for him and his mother as if they were an ordinary family, joined by love and blood. Isn't that right, Younger Sister?'

Younger Sister, beside Older Sister, flushed with pride. 'That's true, Dr Kim.'

'All the men we introduce you to will be honoured to help raise the Peonies. And of course if you want to have children with them, you'll be able to do so.'

Around her, Mee Hee's sisters admonished each other. *See, I told you so. How could Su Jin leave?*

'Now,' Dr Kim continued, 'I want to ask a very special lady to come to the front of the room. Lee Mee Hee?'

For a terrible moment, Mee Hee felt as if she might empty her bladder on the floor. It was coming now: the denouncement, the shame. She had lied to all her sisters and now she was going to be punished. Her face burning, she stared at Dr Tae Sun.

'Don't be afraid, Mee Hee,' he said softly. 'Come.'

Somehow, Mee Hee got to her feet and stepped in front of all the women. Reaching out her silk-clad arms, Dr Kim hugged her. This couldn't be happening. Mee Hee held herself stiffly, conscious only of the scientist's perfume, the intoxicating scent of night-flowering jasmine.

Finally, Dr Kim released her and turned to the women. 'It's very hard to lose a special friend,' she said. 'Mee Hee will be lonely over the next few days and weeks, but I want to ask all of you to help make her feel supported and secure.'

Mee Hee couldn't let this continue. She had to speak. 'No, no,' she said. Her tongue stumbling over the words, she gestured at her sisters. 'I'm not lonely. I have so many special friends. My sisters give me all the love I need.'

The women broke into applause. Some were crying, their faces shining.

Dr Kim herself wiped away a tear as Dr Tae Sun placed his hand on the small of Mee Hee's back. 'Thank you, Mee Hee,' he whispered. 'You may sit down.'

The floor was solid and the cushion was soft beneath her. Mee Hee felt her spine lengthen. There was nothing to fear. Dr Kim had forgiven her. And she hadn't even had to confess.

30 / Pig Bar

Sydney entered the *anbang* feeling weak and humble and incredibly grateful to Da Mi. Anyone else would have been furious with her for taking such stupid chances with a married man when she was supposed to be a role model for the Peonies. But Da Mi just kindly and firmly strapped her into the Chair, explaining that it might take two weeks or more to fully move beyond her attachment to Jae Ho. To start with, they would work on calming her nerves and helping her to feel in control of her emotions once again.

She put on the goggles and floated for a long time in the healing pink and orange river of light. At the corners of her vision she sensed the Peonies dancing around her, their gentle presence making her feel peaceful, safe, secure. Then Da Mi began to speak, voicing positive thoughts that Sydney echoed in the chamber of her mind: *I am strong and beautiful. I let go of people who belong in my past. My future is filling up with love.* Finally, when she was glowing and feeling invincible, Da Mi's voice brought her slowly back into the room.

She felt fantastic that night, but the next day she went into freefall. Words were just words: her future *wasn't* filling up with love. When she got home and closed the door of her apartment, her life was empty, empty, *empty*. Crying bitterly, hating herself for being a needy fuck-slut, hating Jae Ho for his selfishness and silence, hating everything in her apartment for reminding her of him, she peeled his drawing down off the wall. She couldn't quite bring herself to rip it up, but she stuck it face-down in her junk drawer, beneath a tangle of recharger cables and a sheaf of papers she needed to hire an accountant to sort out. Then she collected all the clothes Jae Ho had ever pulled off her body, stuffed them into a black bin bag and dumped the bag out on the street.

Good girl, she heard Da Mi say in her ear, and for a second she felt a surge of power. But this momentary relief quickly faded. She bought a bottle of white wine, and went back up to her apartment to drink it. She woke up with a headache. And shit – she had to pack an overnight bag for a photoshoot out in the countryside with a new photographer. She pretended not to understand his English and nearly got fired; but the other girls were sweet to her, and at least she wasn't in Seoul for a couple of days.

On Friday she had another session. This time Da Mi talked to her first, for a long time, about secrets. How powerful they were; and therefore, in the wrong hands, dangerous. The secret she and Da Mi shared was like a seed in fertile earth, that one day would blossom into a marvellous flower for everyone to see. But the secret of an extra-marital affair was like a seed buried in toxic soil, watered by betrayal, lies, vulnerability and selfish greed. The flowers it bore were stunted, distorted, discoloured. Often, they never even budded at all. In the Chair, Sydney repeated the old affirmations, and one new one: *I choose my secrets wisely*.

When she woke up Saturday morning she felt lighter, free of rage and self-pity for the first time in ages. She spent the weekend pottering about, tidying her flat, and shopping for new clothes to replace the ones she had thrown out. Monday she had another session and felt even better afterwards, so when Jin Sok called on Thursday to suggest going out she enthusiastically agreed. She was going back in the

Chair the next day. That was practically two weeks, wasn't it? What could go wrong?

She met Jin Sok in Hongdae at a new basement place, Hong Gum Dwae Gee, or Golden Pig Bar. It was a 'Techno-Opera Lounge', though with its black walls swathed with purple plastic sheeting it looked more like a goth's bedroom. It was empty apart from the DJ and a young couple sitting at a table nursing beers and prawn crackers, but even so, the place had a certain something. A French singer was warbling from the speakers as Jin Sok led Sydney across a metal dance floor that trembled and boomed beneath their feet.

'Look.' Jin Sok pointed to the wall behind a crushed-velvet sofa. 'New painting Jae Ho.'

Jae Ho. Her first test. Sydney faced the painting.

The canvas was large, nearly six feet tall, and unusually, oval-shaped. No, she realised, it wasn't a canvas: it was a piece of chipboard, the kind you might see lining a construction site. It had been painted with a swarm of rapid red, orange and gold brushstrokes, the textured board beneath adding to the fiery effect. As if going back to the construction site, though, over the flames Jae Ho had sprayed the black outline of an erect cock and balls. It was a crude, stencil-like image, but it also seemed odd: like a visual puzzle. The balls were shaped like a horizontal figure eight for some reason, and the head of the cock was tipped by a black almond-shaped flame. The whole painting was framed with a twisting length of barbed wire, spray-painted gold.

Her stomach felt fine, her heartbeat remained normal. 'Is candle?' she teased.

'Is Buddha!' Jin Sok laughed.

What? Oh yeah. The cock did look like a guy meditating: the tip was his head, the figure eight his crossed legs. Despite herself, she smiled. Jae Ho was such a joker.

The puzzle was solved: or was it? As she shifted her attention to the gold paint gleaming and gliding in the background Sydney felt a flicker of wonder, a strange dawning sense of familiarity, and then, slowly, something almost like pride. For hidden in the brushstrokes, she realised, were the flick of her hair, the twitch of her signature smirk, the slow stirring motion of her hips upon Jae Ho's, the long arc of her arm stretched upon her pillow in the morning. Like the drawing he had given her, the background of the painting was a burning map of her own rhythms and curves.

Was a sense of awe a strong emotion? She didn't know, but it couldn't be bad, surely.

'Is Korean toilet sex!' Jin Sok guffawed. 'Is from his last show – wife's gallery. Many people upset. Pig Bar owner pay big money. Jae Ho very happy man.'

She dragged her eyes away from the painting. He hadn't told her about the show – well, why would he? He wouldn't want her there. She had been his dirty secret, that was all.

But that was okay. *Everything was okay.* She let go of people who belonged in her past, and she chose her secrets wisely now.

'So, can only artists get a drink in this place?' she complained, plopping herself down on the sofa. Like a genie appearing from behind a purple curtain, a young woman in a short skirt and chunky space boots flounced across the dance floor, a tray jutting out from her hip. Her shoulders were set square, her hair pulled back from a flat, freckled face.

'What do you want, motherfucker?' she barked at Jin Sok.

'New waitress!'

They both pealed with laughter, and Sydney was introduced to 'sculptor and international artist' Kim Moon Sun.

'I go to Canada soon,' Moon Sun told Sydney. 'To Toronto – to study.'

'Great. Your English is excellent.'

'Thank you. I study hard. I can say, "you lousy asshole" too.'

'What about "you racist scumbag"?'

'"You racist scumbag"? No, I don't know. What does it mean?'

'Racist means someone doesn't like you because you are Korean, or black, or whatever,' Sydney explained. 'Scumbag is, like, used condom. Is good expression. In Canada I use it a lot.'

'"You racist scumbag!" Thank you very much. Please, Sydney, what are you drinking? My service.'

Sydney ordered a beer and Moon Sun spun back to the bar.

'Chartreuse Fish Eyes, everyone in love with you,' Jin Sok told her.

'Chartreuse?' Jin Sok's vocabulary was so wild. He knew more colours than the iPod people, but they still had trouble sometimes arranging how to meet.

'Chartreuse green Paris drink.' He leaned over and flicked an eyelash off her cheek.

The French singer drowned in an oncoming wave of No-Funk. Moon Sun returned with two beers, the club door swung open and a short, plump Korean woman wearing a pirate's headscarf and a Lucky Strike T-shirt sailed in. Behind her, smiling and laughing, was Jae Ho, arm-in-arm with a woman in a long white crocheted dress. Her face was still and smooth as stone, but her eyes flitted about the room like black butterflies. Sydney recognised her right away.

'*Anneyong haseyo!*' Jin Sok roared, rising to greet the party.

Jae Ho winked at Sydney and pulled up a chair. Sydney froze as his wife squeezed in beside her on the sofa.

'Sy-duh-nee,' Jin Sok said expansively, 'I want you meet my little sisters.' With a courtly gesture, he indicated the pirate queen, who was perched on the arm of the sofa. 'This Hae Lim, special woman in Korea. She owner of Pig Bar and Trapdoor. Her husband Song P'il you meet – owner Gongjang. They Hongdae mafia.'

Everybody laughed. Sydney nodded at Hae Lim.

'And this please is Noh Eun Hee. She wife my little brother. He painter, she gallery owner, they perfect couple, yes?'

Sydney forced a crooked smile as Eun Hee took her hand. 'Small En-gli-shee. So-ree.' Caressing Sydney's bare arm, she said something in Korean to the others.

'She say you have beautiful skin,' Jin Sok translated, solemnly.

'*Kamsahamnida*. I sorry no Korean. I very sorry,' Sydney babbled.

Eun Hee intently scanned her face. 'You know my husband?'

Sydney's stomach was crumpling like a ball of tinfoil. She could only hope the weird lighting in the club hid her red-hot cheeks. 'I know his painting, in Gongjang,' she managed. 'And this one here.' She lifted her head briefly towards the furnace on the wall. 'He is a very good artist, I think.'

Jae Ho grinned and translated. He seemed perfectly relaxed, clapping Jin Sok around the shoulders, helping Hae Lim place the drinks order with Moon Sun.

'Ah.' Eun Hee leaned back on the sofa and spoke rapidly in Korean to Jin Sok.

'She say you have very interesting face,' he told Sydney. 'She think maybe you Russian. Or Spanish.'

Sydney couldn't look at her. 'You are very beautiful,' she blurted, guiltily.

'Oh no.' Eun Hee shook her head and hid her mouth behind her hand.

'Too many beautiful women. Photo please,' Jin Sok demanded, pulling his Leica out of his case. Hae Lim obligingly squeezed in beside Eun Hee, then Eun Hee's hand was in Sydney's hair, pulling her head into the shot, and the women's cheeks pressed together, temples touching, as Jin Sok took the picture.

'How old?' Eun Hee asked when the camera was put away.

'I am twenty.'

'Are you married?'

She shook her head, and swallowed. Right now, not being married felt like being a total failure.

Hae Lim bubbled up with a comment and the Korean women had a spirited conversation, apparently in agreement.

'They say young Korean women today, they losing what it means to be wife,' Jin Sok explained. 'For older generation, is important care for husband, be gentle with him, serve him well. But for under-thirty, not the same. The new Korean woman, she always putting herself first. They are sad about this.'

Moon Sun was striding purposefully towards them, a tray of drinks in her hand. Jae Ho beckoned her impatiently, and Sydney felt a flash of contempt. Did Eun Hee wait on him hand and foot? Then Jae Ho said something flirty to Moon Sun and the waitress responded by snatching his beer bottle away and thrusting it at Jin Sok.

Jin Sok and Hae Lim doubled over in laughter as Jae Ho shrugged mournfully and gazed fondly at Eun Hee.

There was nothing she could do. Sydney sat back and let the Korean jokes and conversation swirl around her like the DJ's tragic arias and Eastern European folk disco. Finally Jin Sok invited her to dance, and she made the sheet metal floor crash and rumble with her heels. When she returned to the table, Moon Sun was setting down a massive pig's head on a golden platter. The Koreans gasped in unison.

'Is from opening party,' Hae Lim explained. 'I want photo, Jin Sok, please.'

Jin Sok unpacked his camera from his bag and hovered above his subject. The pig's head was a pallid rose colour and rubbery-looking, like a faded, plastic flower, but it was glistening as if it had just broken out in a light sweat. The eyeballs had been removed, leaving two tight slits.

On a whim, Sydney took a half-burnt cigarette from the over-flowing ashtray, reached over to the pig, prised open an eyelid and stuck it in. The red tip glowed bitterly at the end of its white dagger. Hae Lim screamed with laughter and when Jin Sok cried, 'Another, another!' she donated her own cigarette.

The company fell silent as Sydney poked it into the other slit. Ashes from the first fell softly onto the pig's cheek, a small slagheap of regret. With both eyes now lit up, the pig was no longer victim or trophy, but an edgy, cruel-looking monster, staring its persecutors into a state of guilty unease.

'Sydney is artist,' Jae Ho said, softly. Everyone applauded. The pig's moment of glory was over.

'Is portrait of my last boyfriend,' Sydney said, to another hysterical outburst of laughter. She meant Johnny. Or did she? Right now Jae Ho was stroking Hae Lim's thigh.

The party left Moon Sun to close up and moved on to Gongjang, the women tripping on ahead, arm in arm, the two men hanging back to talk and smoke underneath a streetlight. As usual on a weeknight, the atmosphere in the club was low-key. Song P'il was piling TVs on top of each other in the corner. Hae Lim wobbled over to him, leaving Sydney sitting on a sofa with Eun Hee. Finally Jin Sok and Jae Ho joined them, and she chatted with Jin Sok, trying not to watch Jae Ho lighting Eun Hee's cigarette with a flourish, tickling her shoulder, nibbling her earlobe. Finally they made their excuses and left, and Sydney waved goodbye, a grin plastered on her face.

'He very lucky man,' Jin Sok slurred. 'She very beautiful, warm heart woman.'

'Yeah.'

Sydney got up to go to the bar, but Jin Sok pulled her down again beside him. 'Sy-duh-nee, I know he go to your apartment,' he sorrowfully announced. 'Is not for married man to do. He not treat you right; he not respect wife. He my little brother, she my little sister, you my friend. I don't want you food for playboy. I must tell him stop. Is my duty.'

Her face was on fire. She couldn't look at him. 'Jin Sok – please don't say anything to him,' she begged. 'He'll be very angry if he thinks I told you.'

'No, no; I tell him now. On way to Gongjang. I tell him, is not right what he does. He very ashamed. Don't worry, he not angry with you.'

Jin Sok's lack of interest in English tenses had often led to confusion and frustration, but never more so than now. Sydney slowly absorbed the enormity of what he had just told her. '*He's* not angry with *me*?' Her fingers drilled into the sofa; her jaw was a solid mass of bone. 'What about *me* being angry with *you*? Why did you do that, Jin Sok?'

'I sorry Sy-duh-nee, but *she* hurting. I know. He has child. He must stop now. I tell him.'

He had a child.

Sydney swallowed hard, then grabbed Jin Sok's arm. 'But he was hurting too,' she hissed, 'and me – I was so lonely, but he was close to me, so kind. It was *private*. No one knew! I didn't want to tell his wife.' She was close to tears, talking in the past tense already, her mind reeling. 'How could you interfere, Jin Sok? How could *you* know what's best?'

'You don't have lonely be. Many friends for you in Seoul,' he said kindly. 'Your Miss Kim, Da Mi, she call me, she very worried for you. She not want you fall in love with Korean Casanova. She want only best things for you.'

A croaking white noise filled Sydney's head. *What*? What had he just said? '*Da Mi* told you about me and Jae Ho?' The words disintegrated the second they passed her lips. She could see Jin Sok's mouth move, but she couldn't hear his reply. She backed away from him on the sofa and fumbled between the cushions for her purse.

'I sorry, Sy-duh-ney – you want me take you home?'

She shook her head, dumbly lurching to her feet.

He reached for her hand. 'I call you tomorrow. You be okay. Everything better be.'

Turning her back on his sympathetic face, she stumbled out of the club, up the stairs and back out onto the street.

A bloated moon hung over the city. The sidewalk was greasy with the exhaust fumes that had built up during the day. Her vision blurring, her legs shaking, Sydney ducked into an alley and leaned against a wall. The alley stank of splitting garbage bags and images from the murder in Vancouver flashed into her mind. Jeez, she had to get a grip.

Behind her something scuttled in the dark. Afraid of rats, afraid of Jin Sok coming after her, afraid of – she didn't know what – she peered out into the street, then, wiping her face with her hand and trying not to blubber, she trailed home through the nearly empty streets, crossing over when she saw a cluster of Hongdae regulars, English teachers and their Korean girlfriends. At last she was back inside her apartment, lying on her bed, her face a mask of tears and snot, stuffing her sheet into her mouth to stifle her cries.

When she woke up, the sky was dark with heavy clouds. She lay in bed listening to the storm break. Thunder and lightning crashed and cracked above her, the rain beat against the building and rushed down the drains, and the windowpanes thudded in their frames. When the fury had finally subsided, she got up, made a pot of coffee and went back to bed with it. The taxi for the Chair session arrived, but she didn't answer the bell. Da Mi rang on the Gotcha and she didn't answer that either. Instead, she stuffed the Gotcha behind the sofa cushions and watched romcoms on her flatscreen all day. It didn't stop raining, but she was snuggled in bed, sniffling her way through hours of misunderstandings magically transformed into perfect, happy endings.

On Saturday she woke up late again. It was still raining. *Fuck, when is this monsoon season going to end?* she thought, though the darkness of the room was comforting. She spent the day in her cave, reading magazines, watching TV, doing her nails. Jin Sok called, but she ignored him. At five, she went to the *mog yuk tan* on the corner – it was just a neighbourhood one, nothing fancy, but the shower and hot pool helped her feel better. Back home she cooked herself a stir-fry, then, as the rain finally began to let up and the clock moved closer to midnight, she rummaged through her wardrobe and got dressed to kill.

She dropped into Pig Bar just as it closed and asked Moon Sun if she wanted to go to Gongjang. Fifteen minutes later they were walking hand-in-hand down the alley to the club.

The place was heaving, and Jae Ho was propping up the bar. Sydney's heart rapped loudly in her chest.

'Asshole.' Moon Sun scowled. 'He has beautiful wife and he just chase foreign skirt!'

Sydney flinched. 'Why? The painter?'

'See my friend here, black girl?' Moon Sun gestured towards a girl dancing a few feet away. Her orange sleeveless dress clung to her full figure. 'Jae Ho, he phone her every day. He tell her every day he love her, she beautiful, everything. She hate him. She never encourage him. He thinks he has right to hassle her like that. He is Confucian pig.'

Setting her face in an expression of blank indifference, Sydney reassessed the girl: short, busty, with a bright Modette style. Obviously no one had told her that look didn't suit fat chicks. Casually, she scanned the room until she was looking back in Jae Ho's direction. Caught staring at the black girl, he shrugged and turned away.

Her blood racing cold in her veins, Sydney tore through all the possible options in her mind. Clearly, Jae Ho had only said he loved this girl because she'd refused to fuck him. There'd been nothing to gain by telling her, Sydney, the same thing. Okay, so maybe he *was* playboy. But he *had* felt for her, he *had* – until Da Mi and Jin Sok fucked everything up. A hot pulse of anger flared in her chest.

But then the girl in the orange dress laughed and waved at Moon Sun, and something inside her went limp. Maybe Jae Ho had been getting bored with her? Maybe this squashy girl with her big tits was really his type – men always wanted shorter women. It was pathetic, but true.

'What a jerk,' she said, viciously. 'He tried with me too. I told him I don't date Korean guys. Too bossy. Western women, we don't like to be pushed around.'

'George Clooney is my style,' Moon Sun announced. 'Some crazy hero! He make his own way, I make mine. We meet only in foreign country. George Clooney respect woman, he is like a stimulus to growth.'

It wasn't how Sydney would have described George Clooney, but she approved of the general outline of the fantasy.

'Yeah, that's the best,' she agreed. 'Independence.' Her stomach in tatters, her jaw set, Sydney grabbed Moon Sun and started dancing hip-to-hip with her, grinding each other into fake delirium, always aware of Jae Ho, who was prowling through the room, like her, only half-submerged in the spaced-out music of not-home, airports, limbo, voyage.

At three a.m. he winked at her, tilted his head at the door. Hating herself for her weakness, she waited five minutes, then, leaving Moon Sun on the sofa, holding hands with her friend in the orange dress, she followed him outside.

Water from the gutters was sloshing down the street. In the yellow glow of the street lamps the rain was like needles, slicing shining bullet paths through the air, nearly blinding her. She stepped into the road, and her dress was instantly plastered to her body. Her stomach felt taut and hollow. Where the fuck was Jae Ho? She pushed wet ropes of hair off her face. She couldn't go back in the club like this. She'd have to give up, go home.

'Sy-duh-ney.' The sound of her name came faintly through the cascading rain, an echo through a waterfall. He was standing on the steps where they'd first kissed.

'Jae Ho.' With a surge of exhilaration, she ran to him. 'I'm soaking!'

He was clutching a black folding umbrella in his hand like a policeman's truncheon. 'Sy-duh-ney,' he said loudly, over the rain. 'I wait last time. I tell you, I must go home. I have family I want see.'

Her nipples were hard, her dress was sticking in silky ripples to her skin. 'That's okay,' she wheedled, leaning close, stroking his arm. 'You come to my house next week. I be very good, very quiet. Like second wife.'

'No, Sy-duh-nee, second wife old Korean way. Not today. I not see you any more. I sorry. I cannot.'

Sydney took a step back. 'Fuck off then!' The words spewed out of her mouth, harsh and thin, driven into the street by the wind and rain.

He gave her a silent look, part pity, part disapproval, then shrugged and opened his umbrella.

Tears boiling up in her eyes, she watched him disappear, a stocky black figure tramping through the storm.

Shivering, she turned to start the walk home.

'Sydney! Sydney!' There was that echo again, higher and more insistent this time. A woman in a billowing black hooded cape was hurrying towards her, calling out her name.

'I'm so glad I've found you!' Da Mi rushed up to Sydney and clasped her wrist. 'I've been calling and calling your Gotcha – did you lose it? Jin Sok said you were upset with him. Oh, Sydney, you're drenched. Is everything okay?'

Sydney wrenched her arm free. 'No, Da Mi, it's *not* okay. You told all that stuff to Jin Sok – I couldn't *believe* it. I thought you were my *friend*!'

She walked on, but Da Mi followed, tugging at her elbow, shouting over the wind and the rain, 'I *am* your friend – and so is Jin Sok. Look, I'm so sorry if what I said caused any difficulties between you. Let's talk it through, okay?'

Sydney spun on her heel. 'There's nothing to talk about, Da Mi,' she spat. 'I'm wet, just let me get home.'

Beneath her hood, Da Mi's face was streaked with shadows from the street lamp and twisted in distress. 'Oh darling, I know you're angry with me – but I'm sure we can work it all out. I've got a taxi waiting. Can I at least give you a lift?'

In the yellow light, Da Mi looked washed out, almost old. A lump rose in Sydney's throat.

Da Mi opened her cloak. 'Come, we could sit in there for a minute and talk.'

Sydney hesitated. Why was everything going haywire with all of her friends? Hunching into the black wing, she let Da Mi steer her to the taxi waiting on the corner.

'Now, let's dry you off.' Da Mi took off the cloak and handed it to Sydney. The outer shell was waterproof GrilleTex™, but the lining was pearly-pink satin.

She just held it for a minute, then at Da Mi's insistence, she rubbed her face and hair, blotting up the worst of the rain. 'Thanks,' she muttered.

'I've got a Thermos with me. Would you like a honey water?'

'No.'

'Oh, sweetheart – are you sure? It would calm your nerves.' Da Mi opened the Thermos and held it out.

At the smell of the drink, Sydney's mouth began to water. 'All right,' she said sulkily.

Da Mi waited as she took a warming sip. 'Oh, dear, you really are upset with me, aren't you?'

Sydney balanced the cup on her knees. She tried to speak, but nothing came out except a strange *tsking* sound.

Da Mi sighed. 'It must have been a shock when Jin Sok told you we had spoken – maybe I shouldn't have called him, but I was so worried about you. Sometimes just a couple of healing sessions in the Chair can make you feel more confident, but it's not enough to give you the detachment you need to make a clean break with the past. Or it can stir up all the emotions, and if a trigger situation arises, you don't have a clue how to react.'

Begrudgingly, Sydney shot her a quick look. 'It felt a bit like that, yeah.'

'I thought it might.' Da Mi said consolingly. She moved a fraction of an inch closer to her, but then, as if she knew Sydney was still bristling inside, withdrew. 'Please, darling. Let me explain. I just wanted Jin Sok to look out for you. I honestly didn't mean to mention Jae Ho, it just slipped out – but frankly, Jin Sok had noticed your attraction too. I know it's all been very messy for you, but can you accept it was for the best? The sooner you can put him behind you, Sydney, the faster the Chair will work for you. Think about the future that's just around the corner. Don't you think that's worth giving up a fruitless love affair?'

Sydney leaned her head against the window. Outside in the pelting rain, a few drunken clubbers were weaving up the street underneath a pop-up umbrella: Moon Sun, her arm around the waist of the black girl, who was clinging to a blond surf-dude. He was so tall, and the umbrella so small it made no difference at all.

The little group disappeared around a corner. The girl was pretty, really, Sydney thought dully. And it was hardly like she was trying to steal Jae Ho away. It wasn't fair to hate her. Maybe she'd even done Sydney a favour by showing up what Jae Ho was really like. Just another married man, fantasising about foreign girls. It was the same every night here, and it would be the same ten years from now, twenty even, maybe: people dancing to forget themselves, to get soaked in the magic of a few sweaty hours. She'd thought she'd found something special in the mix; but it was all just a fleeting illusion.

She took another sip of the honey drink. It was sweet liquid comfort. Da Mi, though— Da Mi had only ever offered her nice things – more than nice, *amazing*: the chance to step above the crowd, to feel secure in the world, be someone everyone would remember.

'I'm such an idiot sometimes,' she said. 'You were only looking out for me. He's history; I know he is. I'm sorry that I let you down.'

'You've never let me down, Sydney. It's very hard to break a love-sick spell. Look, why don't you come back home with me now? You can have a hot bath and a good sleep – I've got new silk pyjamas in the guest room. And tomorrow we can get you back into the Chair.'

Sydney felt so tired. But one thing was clear as *soju*: she had to move on from Jae Ho. He was an asshole, and he had just walked out of her life. But Da Mi hadn't; Da Mi was right beside her, smelling of lilies and jasmine, inviting her home to rest.

She thought about her own apartment, strewn with clothes, empty wine bottles and mascara-stained sheets. It would be so good to have a long hot soak in that gleaming tub in Da Mi's bathroom, sleep on freshly washed sheets, wake up and walk around that gorgeous garden, breathing the fresh mountain air of Pyongchangdong.

'Okay,' she whispered, and Da Mi signalled to the driver and the black taxi steered out into the raging torrent of the street.

Part Five

MISCONCEPTIONS

31 / Chusok

Chusok fell at the end of September this year. The Korean Harvest Moon Festival was a time for stressed-out city slickers to head back to their home villages to eat, drink and 'honour the ancestors'. Damien's privates had cancelled their lessons and the *hagwons* were all closed. Jake had invited him to a party in the mountains, but the thought of sitting in bumper-to-bumper traffic for six hours to get there was unappealing; instead he'd decided to stay home, sleep and drink beer. After three months' hard labour he could do with some time to slob out.

Saturday afternoon he lay on the sofa with a Grolsch and his laptop. As predicted by the pundits, NATO had stepped up its campaign in Pakistan, but had so far shown remarkable restraint on the nuclear front. The hawks, playing the noble victims, were courting favourable world opinion in a build-up to taking on Russia. Considering that the snuke fallout had turned out to be far less potent than originally feared, you had to wonder if M15 hadn't decided to save English footballing pride, destroy Yankee enthusiasm for soccer and give themselves an excuse to oust not only the Taliban but Putin all in one fell swoop. What was the cost of rebuilding Wembley compared to all that?

In other news, the NHS was on rolling strike action, autumn rains had already caused the Thames to flood twice, and according to several prominent psychics, Lucifer's Hammer was right on target.

Everything was getting worse and worse, and still people weren't thinking further ahead than next week. Well, at least they wouldn't all be stampeding to Winnipeg. He opened another beer and put on Damon Albarn's new opera. The Tuvan throat-singing heroine was yodelling her way to the top of an aria, when his MoPho rang.

When he checked the display he blinked: Sydney. Well, that was a turn-up for the books.

'Hey, Sydney – what's up?'

'Oh, same same. I've got a few days off for Chusok, so I thought I'd give you a call.'

As he pictured her sharp little face, a chorus of reindeer began *hooing* and *groaking* as they thundered through a pine forest in search of their herdswoman.

'Jeez, Damien – what the hell are you listening to?'

'An opera about Mongolian tribal people. The guy from Gorillaz wrote the music.'

'You really need to get out more. D'you want to come to LotteWorld with me tomorrow?'

LotteWorld? Crikey, she really *was* just a kid. But before he knew it, he'd agreed.

Sydney met him outside Chamshil Station, brandishing a blue-and-white polka-dot umbrella. The rainy season was coming to an end now, leaving a gentle mizzle trailing in its wake. They walked through the apartment complex on the way to the park, stepping carefully around the puddles. Above them ginkgo trees were turning a buttery yellow and their fan-shaped leaves drifted in swathes down the streets. On every corner old women were selling apples, chestnuts and persimmons from carts covered with tents of turquoise plastic.

'One of my privates served me a persimmon last week,' Damien mentioned. 'How charming, I thought. A tomato served with a baby food spoon.'

'I love these dried ones.' Sydney stopped to buy some. 'They're all furry and mushy. Yum.'

Damien pulled a face. They walked on, through a psychedelic ocean of umbrellas: students with fluorescent pinks and greens, businessmen with loud checks, *ajummas* parading outrageous flowers. On the steps of the buildings girls stood chatting, twirling their ruffly pop-outs or resting them on the floor, like lap-dogs on the end of metal leashes.

'Don't you teach near here?' Sydney mumbled, her mouth full of persimmon.

'In that building.' Damien pointed out Yoon So's apartment block. 'Two terrorist pre-teens – you'd better protect me if they see us. If I don't bring Sailor Moon stickers, I'm afraid for my life.'

But Sydney wasn't listening. 'Hey, there it is!' she cried, pointing at a block of concrete looming up ahead.

Though it looked less inviting than a bowling alley, LotteWorld was one of Seoul's premier attractions: a vast indoor park filled with mountain scenery and faux Euro-style villages, funfair rides and a giant skating rink, where a lone speed-skater was practising his simian arm swing. Above the sparse crowd, skylights filtered the day's grey glow.

'Let's do that.' Sydney pointed to a circuit of mechanical hot-air balloons creaking and squeaking along the tracks fixed to the wall twenty feet above their heads. Admiring the way her orange trousers clung to her bottom, Damien followed her to the ticket booth.

Perched inside a wicker basket, circumnavigating the perimeter of the park, they surveyed the chintzy majesty of Lotte World. Sydney's bare forearm brushed his as she clutched at the rim of the basket. She smelled like a piece of warm tropical fruit.

'Up, up and away,' he said, quietly.

She gestured at the fake trees beneath them. 'Man, those leaves are dusty.'

He leaned forwards and blew gently down into the arena.

She gave an exaggerated cough and moved a half-step away from him. 'I want to go on a scary one next,' she announced.

Hidden behind a Bavarian town hall was a roller-coaster called the 'French Revolution'. It was small, but the loop-de-loop screamer made them both sick to their stomachs. Afterwards, they found a park bench on which to recover. Beside them, a life-size mechanical donkey lifted its tail and with a wicked hee-haw shot a plastic ball filled with chocolate at two yelping schoolgirls.

That cracked them both up. They spent the rest of the afternoon teasing each other, eating ice cream, ogling Korean wedding parties and trying as many cheesy rides and shows as possible. After 'The Fantastic Odyssey', a rickety light show in a cavern set to Debussy-type muzak, complete with sprinklers and dancing papier-mâché waves, Sydney grabbed Damien's arm. 'Time for the photo booth.'

A bunch of colourful wigs hung on hooks outside. Sydney tugged a scraggy green mop-top over Damien's head and chose a bright red lion's mane for herself. Squeezing into the seat behind the grey curtain they jostled for space, their hips rubbing as Sydney wriggled beside him. She inserted some coins in the slot and threw her arms around his neck. Their frozen faces were reflected in the glass over the camera.

'Say *kim chi*!' she hissed. The camera erupted in four white thumpy flashes, capturing two gleeful idiots; pouting movie stars; funhouse villains; sorrowful clowns.

They waited outside for the booth to spit out a sheet of stickers: sixteen tiny photos of a couple of nutters in wigs, surrounded by a frame of palm trees, sun and sand. Sydney stashed her half in her purse; Damien slipped his in the back pocket of his jeans.

'I'll put one in my address book,' she said. 'Next to your name.'

'Better write in pencil,' he warned.

Her smile drooped. 'Are you going back to England soon?'

'Not if I can help it.' he said grimly.

'Because of the fallout?'

He tensed up. 'That too. But I always planned to save some money and go travelling.'

'But you're going to be in Seoul a bit longer, right?' She sounded so anxious, it was flattering.

'Yeah, sure. Until December.' He shrugged. 'If Lucifer's Hammer hasn't hit by then and we're not all washed away by a world-wide tsunami.'

'Lucifer's Hammer,' she scoffed, 'that's just a scare story. Da Mi says the world isn't going to end on the Solstice; she says it's already transforming into something way better.'

'Haven't seen much sign of *that* yet,' Damien snorted. 'Sorry, who's Da Mi?'

'You know, my scientist friend.' She brightened up. 'Hey, that job is still going, if you want to make some extra cash before we're all drowned.'

This time he almost felt bad about letting her down. Her Korean friend was probably really generous to her, but super-pushy; he'd seen that kind of relationship between English teachers at the *hagwon* and their agents; he always felt sorry for the foreigners. 'Thanks, Sydney,' he said. 'I've got more than enough work lined up.'

She pouted, then cocked her head up at the skylights. 'Hey, the rain's stopped. Wanna check out the boating lake?'

'So how do you rate it?' Sydney asked on the subway home.

'LotteWorld?' Damien thought about it. The place was cheesy, but its faded grandeur had touched him with a sense of eerie familiarity.

'In a way,' he reflected, 'it reminded me of London: all grey and shabby, but still convinced it's the greatest show on earth.' He paused, then corrected himself. 'The way London used to be, I mean.'

Sydney touched his arm. 'Hey, I'm sorry,' she said.

Christ, was he getting choked up? 'Cheers,' he replied, awkwardly patting her fingers. She dropped her hand, and he looked away, up the aisle. By the doors, he noticed, the strap-hangers were parting for a legless man who was propelling himself down the centre of the train, his hands in white cotton gloves, his muscular arms hoisting his torso along the floor. He was wearing a Hammer T-shirt, its graphic of a comet with a devil's tail hitting the globe half-obscured by the tray of chewing gum hung around his neck.

'Ask him if he's selling the T-shirts,' Sydney whispered.

Stopping in front of them, the man began to chant, a droning incantation of which Damien could only make out the word 'Yonsei'. Whatever his spiel meant, it took grit to make these rounds in his physical condition. Damien dug out some change and chose a packet of Chiclets. Girls always liked them. The man nodded sagely, pocketed the coins, and moved on.

'An old guy was chanting like that on the train the other day,' Sydney said as he tipped a couple squares of the gum into her palm. 'Everyone was laughing at him. Then he turned to me and asked me if I knew why I was here. "Beautiful daughter of God," he said, "don't worry. Be happy."'

'That's all right then.'

'It's true, though, don't you think?' Her eyes were shining, her skin almost translucent in the fluorescent light of the carriage. 'What the Buddhists say? That we can be happy all the time if we want?'

Damien shrugged. 'If you don't think about the past or the future, maybe. But if you do just live in the moment, other people will run your life for you. Personally, I'd rather be a bit anxious sometimes.'

The train was drawing into Edae. Damien got to his feet. 'Nice to see you again, Sydney. Give me a call – anytime.'

She jumped up eagerly and gave him a kiss on the cheek. The doors slid open. He looked back as the doors closed and caught a glimpse of her staring into space, a fierce look on her face as if she was arguing with someone.

Suddenly he was stabbed with panic. He wanted to bang on the doors of the carriage, jump back on the train, pull her out of her seat and drag her up into the daylight with him.

I'm sorry, Jessica. The words bubbled up in his head like mud.

Christ, man, let it go.

32 / Pusan

Chusok was beautiful, so healing for Mee Hee's sore spirit. Each of the three days was filled with cooking and eating, and special ceremonies for the ancestors. The first evening the women sat together in the kitchen making *songpyon*, of course, taking great care to shape the rice cakes as prettily as possible to ensure they would all have beautiful daughters in the coming year. After many jokes and Grandmother songs, they quietly laid the sticky dough balls in big baskets on top of the pine needles they'd collected and steamed them until the scent of the needles filled the Meeting Hall. Then it was time for the first taste.

Older Sister's *songpyon* was plump and stuffed with roasted chestnut meat; So Ra's was pointy and filled with honeyed peas, and Mee Hee's was slender and sprinkled with toasted sesame seeds.

'Your daughters will be delicate and pretty, but a little bit nutty,' Dr Tae Sun teased.

'They will be like Su Jin, then,' she whispered.

'Perhaps Su Jin is making sweet and tender *songpyon* right now, to have a daughter like you,' he quietly replied.

The next day Dr Kim arrived in time for breakfast. After they had eaten, she took the women on a walk in the woods. There, in a clearing, was a turtle shrine, which, Dr Kim said, they could visit whenever they wanted to honour their ancestors. The village was far from where they had all grown up, but the geomancy lines beneath their feet were travelling back to their old homes in the North, to let the ancestors know the way. All morning the women tidied the clearing. Then they placed piles of *songpyon*, persimmons and apples in front of the shrine, praying and singing and sending all their family members love and respect.

That afternoon was filled with games: tug of war and seesaw, and a tournament of Flower Cards. Then, after they had cooked chestnuts and rice and meat and fish and had served the doctors, the women ate and washed all the dishes before putting on the long white robes Dr Kim had brought with her. They gathered in the garden and danced in a floating circle under the full moon.

This was the spirit of Chusok: the spirit of the harvest moon that swelled the earth with nourishment and abundance, and would swell the bellies of the women with good food and with babies. This was a time to celebrate being women, to be unafraid of the night, to rejoice in sisterhood. Holding hands with Chin Mee and So Ra, Mee Hee gazed up into the huge, beautiful face of the moon. Please, she asked silently, beam your blessings down on Su Jin too.

After Chusok, Mee Hee began to laugh again. As the days grew shorter and the nights colder, Dr Tae Sun started to visit her house in the evenings, bringing with him a pack of Flower Cards. Dr Kim had asked him to keep her company, he said that first night before teasing her about her studious shuffling technique. Once, Mee Hee noticed him looking at her arms, but he never mentioned the wounds she had inflicted on herself. She wanted to tell him not to worry, that ever since Dr Kim had comforted her she had never again felt the urge to repeat those harmful, shameful actions. Instead, she concentrated on making things nice for him, sewing decorative wall hangings and mats, cooking special treats.

One night he praised the *dukk* she'd made, had said that he could happily eat it every night of his life. Her own mouth was bulging with the glutinous rice dough and she hadn't dared to reply, but in the lamplight she had noticed a speck of icing sugar dusting the corner of his mouth.

That night on her *yo* she lay awake, imagining herself reaching across to brush it away.

But she was being foolish, she knew that. The doctor was only being kind, keeping her company, helping her get emotionally strong and ready for motherhood. The work helped too. All through October the women kept busy, some in the pottery shed, making vases and bowls for the VirtuWorld gift shop, others in the garden, picking and braiding cords of persimmons to hang to dry in the pantry. In the Meeting Hall, the looms filled up with bright lengths of wool: blankets and scarves for the winter.

The cold started to bite in the first week of November, and by the end of the month the *ondul* heating in the Meeting House was turned up high all day. They had to keep warm to keep well, and to sew – that was the job Mee Hee liked best, sitting next to So Ra on a cushion by the window, a needle in her hand as keening strains of *pansori* music and tendrils of jasmine incense uncoiled in the air.

'It's nearly December,' So Ra remarked one Friday at the end of November. 'I wonder if it will snow soon.'

'Pardon?' Mee Hee looked up from her stitching. She was embroidering the word *VirtuWorld* into a silk handkerchief, overlapping letters that reminded her of birds flying in the sky. The work was fiddly, but now she was used to it, she could let her mind wander occasionally to thoughts of Tae Sun. Tae Sun. He had told her to call him that now – but only at night, in private.

'I said, it's nearly—' But she stopped as abruptly as the music.

Dr Dong Sun was standing by the CD player, his face clammy and drawn. 'Sisters,' he said, 'please, put down your work. We have news of Su Jin.'

Like dried leaves in a sudden wind, hope and fear rustled through the room. But Dr Dong Sun's shoulders were rigid, his fist clenched around a pen. His news wasn't good. Mee Hee carefully folded her sewing and set it aside.

In a jostle of nervous excitement, her sisters trooped into the Meeting Hall, following Dr Tae Sun, who joined his brother at the top of the room. The women arranged themselves expectantly on cushions. Mee Hee's heart began to pound.

Dr Dong Sun's forehead was sprinkled with sweat. He cleared his throat and clicked his pen. Mee Hee willed Tae Sun to look at her, but he was staring over their heads. His face too was drained of colour.

Dr Dong Sun began to speak: Our sister Su Jin was dead. Her body had been found in Pusan, in a bad area near the docks. She had been attacked. Her neck was broken: it had happened very quickly; she wouldn't have suffered. Dr Kim and Mr Sand-uh-man were bringing her back to the village tomorrow, to lay her to rest in the mountain earth.

The news rolled across the Meeting House floor like an iron ball. The women gasped and cried; So Ra clasped Mee Hee by the shoulders. Pain burning in her chest, Mee Hee looked wildly around for Tae Sun, and at last his eyes met hers – but only for a moment. Like a helpless schoolboy, he twisted his tie, waiting, like everyone, for his brother to tell them what to do.

'There will be no more work until after the funeral,' Dr Dong Sun said hoarsely. 'You may pray for Su Jin now, or do as you wish.'

'I'll pray that no one else is so stupid and selfish as to run away!' Older Sister shouted. Several women sucked in their breath.

'Now, now—' Dr Dong Sun began, but Older Sister was determined to continue.

'We all know that cities are evil places, full of greed and suffering and dirt. But *she* called us bumpkins and yokels – well, who's still alive to breathe the fresh air and eat the carrots from the garden? I'll pray for everyone here, but I won't pray for her. She brought this disaster on her own head!'

'That's a terrible thing to say,' So Ra said quietly, holding Mee Hee close. 'Su Jin was young. She just wanted to explore the world.'

'I'm sure Older Sister doesn't mean what she says,' Dr Tae Sun stammered. 'She's in shock, like all of us.'

Her plain face pink as a potato, Older Sister hoisted herself to her feet. 'I'll help the cooks prepare for tomorrow,' she muttered. 'There'll be a lot of extra work to do now.' Without a backwards glance, she clumped into the kitchen.

'They should make her chop the onions,' So Ra snorted. 'Maybe then she'll manage a tear.'

'At least she's trying to help,' Young Ha objected. 'Su Jin was never very kind to her.'

'Everyone knows she hated Su Jin,' So Ra hissed, 'but she could still show a little compassion, at least for Mee Hee's sake!'

'Please, So Ra,' Mee Hee pleaded. She could see the doctors exchanging worried glances. 'Don't let's argue. Su Jin wouldn't like – wouldn't have liked – that.'

'No, we mustn't fight,' Younger Sister insisted. 'We should pray for Su Jin's soul.'

'Thank you, Younger Sister.' Dr Dong Sun raised his voice above the growing mutters. 'This should be a time of togetherness, not division. Mee Hee, you should not be alone tonight. We'll help you move your bed into So Ra and Chin Mee's house.'

Tae Sun shrugged, almost imperceptibly. No, there was nothing he could do, Mee Hee understood. He couldn't come and comfort her tonight.

So Ra and Chin Mee usually slept separately, but that night they pulled So Ra's *yo* into Chin Mee's room and placed Mee Hee's between them. When they returned to the house after dinner, they lit a candle, changed into their nightdresses and got into their beds.

'I hope Older Sister can sleep tonight,' So Ra said into the semi-darkness. 'Imagine not praying for Su Jin.'

'Excuse me for saying this,' Chin Mee said timidly, 'but a few of the sisters have been upset with Su Jin – because we missed her, and worried. Maybe South Korean cities aren't the hellholes the Wise Young Leader told us they were, but still, anyone could tell that Pusan would be dangerous, especially for a North Korean farm girl. You can grieve for someone and still feel hurt by them; don't you think so, Mee Hee?'

Mee Hee fingered the fold in her bedsheet. All day she had been trying to summon the right feelings, but she wasn't angry like Older Sister, or indignant like So Ra, and she wasn't guilty or afraid, either. No, she was sad, that was all. All day long it had felt as if it were raining, a heavy, slow rain inside her, but she didn't blame Su Jin.

'No, Chin Mee, Su Jin didn't hurt me. If she didn't want to stay here, it would have been selfish of me to have asked her to. I'm just sorry that she couldn't see how lucky we are to live here. Now she never will.' Her voice wavered. But, just as they had all day, her eyes remained dry. Maybe this was a sign of her 'inner strength'? Surely Dr Kim would want her to bear her sorrow with dignity?

The candle sent up a spark and Chin Mee blew it out. Mee Hee pulled her covers up to her neck. The *ondul* heating was on, but So Ra liked the window open a crack. Older Sister always said it was good to breathe fresh air all night.

'I hope they catch the murderer soon,' So Ra said into the darkness.

'Mr San-duh-man will find him,' Chin Mee declared.

'Su Jin liked Mr San-duh-man,' Mee Hee whispered. 'I'm glad he's coming to the funeral.'

Outside, an owl hooted. Perhaps it was carrying a field mouse away in its talons, Mee Hee thought. Across the courtyard, there was a creak: someone couldn't sleep, was standing out on her verandah looking at the moon. Or maybe it was the sound of the ancestors drawing closer, waiting to greet Su Jin's spirit.

Beside Mee Hee, Chin Mee stifled a sob. 'I'm sorry,' she cried out, 'but I feel afraid. Promise me you both will never leave the village . . .'

'Of course not!' So Ra sounded aghast at the very thought. 'Not even if they move me in with Older Sister!'

Mee Hee slid her arm out from beneath her blankets and stroked Chin Mee's shoulder. 'No, I never will. This is our home, Chin Mee. We all love it here.'

33 | A Hard Place

It was the last Saturday of November. The sky was the colour of a dirty dishcloth and the temperature was dropping like an anvil. Damien was in Chamshil, finishing his final class of the day with Yoon So and Young Ha. Outwardly he was reviewing English words for flowers; inside he was sizzling with excitement.

On Monday his savings had hit seventeen and a half million. He'd taken two point five and a passport photo down to Azitoo, where Jake had pocketed the envelope and promised to take it in the morning to the counterfeiter in Itaewon. On Thursday Jake had dropped round to say that the hacker in Canada had found him a ghost identity: a guy called David Harding, who had been dead for three years. If his family hadn't yet reported the fact to the SIN bureau, they weren't ever going to. *Here's to David*, Damien and Jake had toasted with a shared Grolsch. Next Friday he'd get his month's pay from the *hagwon*, another two and a half million, which would make up the twenty he needed for the Canadian passport and SIN card. He'd already told all his jobs he was leaving and would need his last pay on December fifteenth. His landlord had reluctantly agreed to give him back his key-fee a week early; all that money was extra, and would help him set up in Canada.

His plan was to be on a flight to Winnipeg three or four days before the Solstice. Jake had a mate there who'd said Damien could stay in his basement cheap – plus, the guy worked in films, knew

317

Guy Madden, might be able to get him a job. If not, there was a ton of other work in the province: the oil industry, mining – the Manitoba economy was booming. If the world hadn't been flooded or nuked out of existence by the New Year, Damien fancied working in a music or DVD shop, like he'd done in Brighton back in the day. Or he could eke out his money until the summer, then go tree-planting. Either way, he'd be alive and on dry ground. If snow counted as dry.

So this was a weekend to celebrate. He planned to hit the night-clubs on Saturday, but this evening he was going to the flicks with Sydney. He'd seen her three times since Chusok, always on a Sunday. They'd go for cheap eats, then chat over cups of tea. He told her about his working day; she babbled on about her mad world of fashionistas and spa treatment meditation courses. She wasn't a religious fanatic, exactly, but she did sometimes go off on strange spiels about forgiveness, higher consciousness, the 'detoxification of the human spirit' – basically, it sounded like she spent a few hours a week wrapped up in mud and rose petals, listening to self-help tapes. Still, if it made her smell so nice, who was he to criticise?

At the end of their dates, they'd stand around on the street like a couple of nimbies. Sydney would pause and twirl her hair, he'd mumble something about needing an early night, then she'd swipe him a kiss and hop into a taxi home. Maybe she expected him to hit on her; maybe she liked knowing a bloke who didn't. Whatever; his vow of celibacy was working for him. He had steady energy for his gruelling schedule, and he wasn't about to risk knocking everything sideways, especially not for some strange encounter with his own projections of Jessica. He'd decided that apart from that freaky time in the tube, there was something comforting about Sydney's chance resemblance to Jessica. Since he'd met her, even when they weren't together, he felt – well, more *relaxed*, somehow. He did worry about how she was going to cope when the Hammer hit, but she'd told him Da Mi was rich and lived in a gated property up a big hill, so that would give her a better chance of survival than most Seoulites.

Today they were meeting in Shinch'on at half-seven. It was ten to six now, and Young Ha was sprawling over the floor, whining 'Finish class, teacher,' when he heard the doorbell chime. This happened countless times a lesson; usually it was Mrs Lee or the household *ajumma* running errands; occasionally the Japanese tutor arrived early. He paid no particular attention until he heard strange male voices and the *ajumma* protesting; then a robotic panic began grinding in his guts.

'Yoon So, Young Ha,' he hissed, flapping Young Ha's workbook shut and trying to wrest Yoon So's from her hands. 'I not teacher, okay? I *Damien*. Friend! *Chingu*, okay? *Chingu*.'

In the scuffle Yoon So scribbled a thick pencil line over her work. She emitted a wail of outrage as behind him, the door burst open. 'Teacher not *chingu*. I hate Teacher,' she declared, clutching her copy of Longman's English Workbook Level 3 to her chest.

'Teacher, who? Teacher, who?' Young Ha shrieked as two men in suit jackets and plaid Lacoste shirts surveyed the scene with grim satisfaction.

Damien dropped Young Ha's book on the floor. He was awash in sweat and his whole body was shaking. For a long second, the only sound was his watch clattering against the edge of the table.

'We are from Immigration Office of Korea,' the taller man announced tersely. With his grooved face, jutting jaw and jerky movements he could have played a cyborg in a Terminator film. One that ran on Duracell. 'May we see your passport?'

'Passport?' Like an idiot, Damien patted his pockets. 'S-s-sorry, I don't have it on me.'

'How long you teach here?' the short, stocky man demanded.

Damien tried to think. He could maintain he was a friend of the family, giving lessons when he came over for dinner – saying you did so because you were Christian sometimes worked, he'd heard – but the details were bound to be checked with Yoon So's parents when they came home, and with Young Ha's, whom he'd never met. He'd also heard that the severity of the deportation order and the amount of the fine depended on how long you'd been working, so he could say one month, but again, if that were found to be a lie, he might be dealt with more harshly. So much rested on Mrs Lee. Oh shit, what the fuck to do?

Acutely aware that his desire to fly out the window, powerful as it was, should not be mistaken for the ability to do so, Damien opened his mouth. 'I have been teaching here' – he cleared his throat – 'two months.' The actual figure was in fact closer to five, but he could always insist he had been misheard.

'Come with us now,' Cyborg-head ordered. Damien rose, with dignity, he hoped, though his legs were still shaking and he had to press both palms on the table for support. As soon as he was upright Young Ha dove for his knees, wrapping her arms around them and pressing her face into his thighs.

'No, Teacher, don' go! I frightened, don' go! I love you, Teacher, I love you!'

'I love you too, Sailor Young Ha,' he lied, trying to unclasp her fingers behind him with one hand, patting her head with the other. Where was this unswerving devotion when he wanted her to sit quietly and draw pictures of jungles?

The shorter officer took the girl by the shoulders and spoke to her in Korean. She released her grip, and burst into tears.

'Don't cry, Young Ha,' he cajoled. 'I come back soon.' He knew this was extremely unlikely, but better to let her think he had been arrested and murdered and bear a grudge against Korean officials for ever; such dissent would do the country good.

'Goodbye, Yoon So. Tell your mother goodbye,' he said as the taller officer twisted his arms behind his back and clapped a pair of hand-cuffs around his wrists.

Yoon So was studiously erasing the pencil mark on her work. She didn't look up.

Usually the elevator came right away and was empty. Today, because he was in handcuffs and sweat was streaming unchecked down his temples, it took ten minutes to arrive and was occupied by a respectable elderly couple.

Who knows, he thought, *maybe they turned me in, and witnessing my abjection is part of their reward.*

The officers were drilling their thumbs into his shoulders and in retaliation, he flipped his hair out of his eyes, hoping that his sweat would fling into the men's eyes or spatter their shirts. But neither gave any indication of even having noticed.

Fuck, why had he lulled himself into believing the area was safe? All he'd ever done to protect himself was to occasionally vary his route to the building entrance – there were a laughable two to choose from – and to warn Yoon So's mother that if anyone came to the door, not to answer it, or to say he was just a friend. She had giggled when he explained this plan, which he had chosen to interpret as meaning that she knew more than he did and the danger was minimal. Wrong; it actually meant she was a useless nincompoop: she hadn't even briefed the *ajumma* not to open the door to strangers. Everyone knew that unless immigration officials had a warrant – which they never did on the first visit – it simply wasn't necessary to let them set foot in the place.

Damien pressed his hands closer together so the cuffs would stop cutting into his wrists. The elevator juddered to a halt. He wanted to scream. Everything was fucked now, seriously, permanently fucked.

It wasn't like these guys would just fine him, let him renew his passport and kick him out of the country, no, he knew how this worked: you weren't allowed to just leave. You were *deported*, which meant flying back to the UK, to a sea of nuclear radiation, to a big fat *DING* at passport control, a hairy-knuckled hand on the shoulder, a beige waiting room and an officer with an A4 file headed *Damien Meadows*.

The elevator disgorged him, his captors and the elderly voyeurs into the lobby. To compound his humiliation, Damien tripped as he passed the building manager, another likely stool-pigeon, who watched with an impassive air as the trio trooped by. With a brusque grip, Immigration Android steered Damien out into the parking lot, towards – not the anonymous grey Hyundai he had always imagined Immigration Officers sitting in, drinking from flasks and waiting for hapless foreigners to lope by, but a genuine regulation black-and-blue paddy wagon.

Every seam was reinforced with painted bolts. Metal grids covered the two small windows on the back doors. Shorty unlocked the back and Immigration Android roughly bundled him in. Five other foreigners turned anxious faces to greet him as the evening light briefly flooded the mobile prison cell.

'They won't keep him,' Da Mi had said firmly. 'When they pick people up they just register them on the computer and make them come back the following day with their papers. He'll be out by seven-thirty at the absolute latest.'

But now it was gone nine, and Damien still hadn't called. Looking up from the pair of jeans she was altering, Sydney glanced again at the clock.

The jeans were white hipsters, brand name *nobody*. She'd bought them from a stall at Tongdaemun Market, the all-night bargain-shopping district three miles wide and twenty storeys high. Jin Sok had taken her, their first time out together since he'd ruined things with Jae Ho. He'd translated for her, and picked out the newest trends. You weren't allowed to try anything on – how could you in the cramped aisles between the overflowing stalls? – but the salesgirl had deftly held the pair up to Sydney's throat, wrapped the waist around her neck and assured her that they'd fit, and she'd been right. The only problem with the jeans was a long piece of red ribbon stitched on the inside of the waistband. It said *nobody* all the way around, the word printed over and over, upside-down – kinda cool, but the fabric strip irritated her skin. So she was unpicking it with a vengeance. At eleven minutes past nine, her MoPho rang. Damien at last.

'*Yobosayo*,' she sang brightly, with just a hint of fake annoyance. Da Mi had said it would be good practice for her to use some acting skills. She would need them later, playing the Queen at the VirtuWorld banquets. They'd spent a whole session in the Chair preparing her for tonight's little drama. She was still nervous – she hadn't liked to tell Da Mi, but she'd got to like Damien lately. He was laid-back, kind and funny – and surprisingly into theme parks. In a way, it was a shame Da Mi couldn't just make him the offer up front. Now that he and Sydney were getting on so well, he'd probably say yeah.

But Da Mi didn't want to take any risks, and Sydney had to respect that. Also, this was her one chance to help Da Mi out, repay her for everything she'd done for her – and to help Damien out too, she reminded herself. Sure, being arrested couldn't have been fun, but he *was* going to get a big wad of money out of the deal.

'*Yo.Bo.Sa.Yo.*' Damien's voice was a grim staccato. 'Sydney, sorry I stood you up, but I got picked up by Immigration today.'

'You're shitting me!' That was a key line; she'd decided to use it, quite spontaneously, while she was in the Chair, and then Da Mi had programmed her unconscious to accept it as a trigger to genuine empathy. Now she'd said it, she wouldn't have to worry about sounding fake.

'Wish I was.'

'Oh, Damien – what happened?'

'I was at my privates in Chamshil. They only burst into the play-room, handcuffed me and frog-marched me to a paddy-wagon. My wrists are killing me.'

'You're hurt?' Sydney's stomach contracted. She shifted in her chair. Perhaps the uncomfortable sensation in her guts was just part of feeling Damien's pain.

'Yeah, well, apparently it's a serious charge, offending the Korean economy.'

That was the old Damien poking through; she grinned in relief.

'I guess.' She pulled at one of the threads attaching the *nobody* strip to the jeans. 'But what happened at the station?'

Damien sounded weary again. 'They fingerprinted me and took mug-shots – then they came back to my place, confiscated my pass-port and downloaded my MoPho.'

'Downloaded your *MoPho*?'

'Contacts, phone-log, saved texts, the works. But don't worry, if they phone you, just don't answer. They're really only interested in my employers.'

'Jeez, it sounds so scary. What's going to happen next?'

'I have to go back in on Monday. Best-case scenario, they'll fine me and deport me back to the UK.'

'Oh no – what are you going to do?' Sydney cooed. As a friend, she just needed to support Damien through this moment of uncer-tainty, help him figure out a plan.

'I've got a Korean mate in Shinch'on. I'm going to see if he's got any ideas.'

'You know,' Sydney said, pensively, as if the thought was just occurring to her, 'Da Mi might be able to help you. I could phone her and see.'

'Da Mi? Oh yeah, right, your friend. Thanks, but I think it's a bit late for me to be taking on new jobs.'

Sydney's voice rose. Too much? 'No, not that – she knows lots of people. I'll call her tomorrow. Do you still want to meet up tonight?'

'I'm knackered, Sydney. I've just called all my contacts to warn them Immigration might get in touch. Now I have to go talk to Jake. I'll call you tomorrow, okay?'

They said goodbye and hung up. Sydney yanked the tail-end of the *nobody* strip off her jeans. She hadn't expected that prickle of guilt while talking to Damien tonight, and she hadn't been prepared for him cancelling their date. She picked up the needle. Swiftly, her mind a white blank, she jabbed the tip into her palm, yelping as a hot bead of blood rose up on the mound below her thumb.

The brief stab of pain released the tension of the call. She sucked at the puncture wound, soothed by the taste of her own blood, and told herself not to be so stupid. Da Mi had said the conversation might be taxing; she had advised having a honey drink to hand. She had made one, but that had been ages ago and it had gone a bit cold. She reached for the cup anyway and took a sip. Maybe she was just upset because she would probably miss Damien when he left Korea – but hey, she could always fly out and meet him in Thailand or New Zealand later on; Da Mi hadn't said they couldn't be long-distance chums.

'Day, buddy – wassa matter?' Jake was behind the bar, a bottle of Red Stripe in his hand. He had twizzled his straggly new goatee with hair wax and tied his dreads back with a strip of black silk: going for the *kyopo* Rasta Lucifer look. A hillbilly-goth-punk compilation

CD was playing, swamping the nearly empty room with echoey voodoo guitars.

'Jake, I'm fucked.' Damien plonked himself down on a stool and cradled his head in his hands. His stomach was in shreds and all the blood had drained out of his brain and was pooling in his socks. He probably did look as bad as he felt.

'Whaddya mean? We're getting the passport next week, then it's Rocky Mountain High.'

'I'm telling you, everything's gone tits-up. Immigration hauled me in today, took my passport and my MoPho contacts. On Monday they tell me what the fine will be and if I don't pay, I go straight to jail; if I do, I get deported back to the UK.'

'Nah – no way.' Jake snapped his fingers. 'Sam, what's the story with Immigration?'

Sam was counting beer bottles. His face bleached in the light from the fridge, he rolled his eyes. 'Immigration dumb fucks. Don't go Monday; just hide out. Leave apartment and keep working, get new passport. No problem.'

Damien shook his head. 'They know about all my jobs so I can't keep working. They said this was just the beginning of a new crackdown: all *hagwons* and apartment complexes are going to be patrolled. I'll have no money; I won't be able to buy the passport or the ticket. I'll be stuck.' Christ, he was whining worse than Young Ha.

'Sam, pour this man a whisky. Look, Day, it's gonna be okay. The *hagwon* still has to pay you, right? Sam can pick up the money for you next week, no problem. So then you get the passport, and with your apartment deposit, you leave the country. Easy-peasy.'

Sam passed Damien a double Scotch. He took a hit, then rubbed his temples. He was feeling feverish. Not good. 'I dunno, mate – the *hagwon* pay's minus next week's wages, and if I want the key-fee right away, I'll have to find someone else to take over the apartment. And anyway, two million won won't go far. If I can't work before I go, I'll barely have the money for a plane ticket, let alone setting up in Canada.'

'You don't have to go to Canada,' Jake said, reasonably. 'You could skip over to Japan, get some work there. You'd be back up to speed in no time.'

'I'm *telling* you, Jake—' Damien heard himself shout and stopped himself.

Jake raised his eyebrows and stepped back from the bar.

Damien back-pedalled quickly. 'Sorry, Jake – it's just, there's some heavy shit coming down, very soon – everyone knows it. And I don't want to be on my own in an earthquake zone when it happens. I want to be somewhere far from the sea, where everyone speaks English. Okay?'

'Okay Day,' Jake said at last. 'Canada was your plan, and you've been working towards it for ages. We've been impressed, haven't we Sam?'

Sam nodded solemnly. 'Damien work harder than taxi *ajashi*. No sleep with our women, no vomit on our streets. Very good guest of Korea.'

Damien rubbed the side of his glass. Could he ask, after his pathetic outburst? But Jake glanced at his cousin and cleared his throat. 'We'd front you ourselves, Damien, wouldn't we, Sam? But we're a bit short at the moment.'

Sam sighed. 'Air-con broke. Behind on bills. Sorry.'

'What about buddies back home?' Jake asked briskly.

Damien shook his head. 'Nah.'

'Your mum?'

'Fat chance.'

Jake took a matchbook out of the oversize snifter by the till, bent the cover back and used the flap to clean a fingernail. 'And you're sure you don't want to go back to England? The fine won't be that much; you'll still have loads of money. You could go and find a mountain in Scotland for the Solstice, take your chances with the Picts.'

Sam quietly opened the dishwasher and began to take out glasses, inspecting them under the light before putting them onto the shelf. Damien could see every pore on Jake's nose, each odd, spiky hair poking out of Sam's jaw. These guys were his best mates in Seoul. Right now, they were his best mates in the world.

He took a deep breath and pressed play. 'Look, Jake, Sam – I appreciate you never asked me any questions about England. You know I never robbed any old ladies or diddled any kids; I was selling knock-off sunglasses, that's all, down by the pier. I got picked up a couple of time, given warnings – then Housing Benefit hit me with a fraud charge, going back five years – they're really tough on benefit fraud now and I could've got a couple of years inside. When I got Jake's letter, it seemed like a scheme, so . . .' He paused, then went on, 'so I decided to miss the court dates. If I get deported, the cops could nab me at the airport – and then I'm well and truly fucked.'

Jake tucked the matchbook into his jacket pocket. 'Jeez, Damien, that's rough. A wanted man – but why didn't you say so before? Instead of going on about all this Hammer guff?'

Damien rubbed his temple. Now was not the time to mention the latest news on the Hammer, hacked from Pentagon sources: the meteor was now projected to land in the Atlantic Ocean, causing severe geological, social and economic chaos in Europe, Africa, and the Americas, not to mention the global knock-on effect. Nor was he about to remind Jake that tent-towns of religious freaks and survivalist cults were already being established on Korea's mountaintops – there was one right above Yonsei. No, now was the time to hold his hand up, confess what a deep-down schmoe he really was, win back his friend's trust.

'I dunno, Jake,' he said. 'I felt daft, that's all – a real loser. You managed to be a drug dealer in Toronto, you pulled loads of scams, and I can't even sell crap sunnies without winding up in the dock – which might be better than going to jail in Korea, but I'd still like to avoid it if I can.'

Jake tried not to look sage. 'Scams, schemes; to-may-to, tom-ah-to,' he reflected, modestly. 'You just had a bit of bad luck, that's all.'

Sam rubbed at a bit of grit on a Grolsch glass. 'Korean jail not so bad.' He sounded hurt. 'Very clean. TV. Good food – okay, so not enough *banchan*, but rice, *kim chee*, *doengang jiigae* . . .'

'Oh fuck off, Sam.' Jake's gold cufflink glinted as he swung a lazy air-punch in the direction of his cousin. 'Damien doesn't wanna watch Arirang soap operas for two years. We gotta get him outa here.'

'Yeah, okay, so how, wise guy?' Sam retorted.

Jake threw Damien a 'let me handle this' look. Then he spoke in Korean to Sam. Damien could tell his reply was not cooperative. The two leaned against the beer fridge, rapidly conferring: Sam shaking his head, Jake wheedling, wearing him down, until, reluctantly, after a final burst of objection, Sam sputtered to a halt.

At last they both stepped back up to the bar. They exchanged one more glance, then Sam spoke. 'Okay. I don't do this for everyone, but you big friend of Jake. Our cut of fake ID deal is two million. Risky business dealing with mafia, and we need money for Azitoo, yeah?'

'Yeah, sure,' Damien agreed. He'd always assumed Jake and Sam would make a commission; he hadn't liked to ask how much. 'You deserve your share.'

'So, Jake say we can trust you. You did drug run, big danger; mean we owe you favour. So we gonna lend you our cut. You can send when you have it, anytime. Meantime, we going to help you get your key-money back.'

'Really?' For the first time since that doorbell rang in Chamshil, Damien could see a splinter of light in the darkness. The key-money and an extra two million would get him to Canada, buy enough time to find a job. 'That's *brilliant* – thanks, guys, so much, Sam, Jake – I'll send you the money the instant I can.'

Jake banged his beer bottle on the bar. 'Good. That's settled. Now, Dames, we'll post an ad on the usual websites, but we gotta tackle this on all fronts. So this weekend we fan out. Sam, you take Itaewon; Day, Hongdae; I'll do Shinch'on. Check notice boards, classifieds; ask everyone you meet. There's bound to be a new kid off the boat, or someone who just split up with their girlfriend.'

Sam pulled a box of Lucky Strikes out from between the Bombay Sapphire and Gordon's and offered Damien a cigarette. Damien shook his head, then took one. Jake leaned over with a light, as Sam pulled out his MoPho.

'I know student, going crazy at home. I call him now,' he said.

Damien sucked back a lungful of nicotine. His lungs burned and his brain crackled. It was a crazy plan, but what the fuck. It might just work.

When he woke up Saturday morning he had a splitting headache, a fur-lined mouth and an empty packet of Lucky Strikes scrawled with the numbers of two people who were maybe looking for apartments, or might know someone who was. One of the numbers was illegible. He called and left a message on the other, then he rang his *hagwon* and arranged for Sam to come in and pick up his pay. The secretary was sympathetic, but he knew she was just being polite. There were always people looking for *hagwon* jobs; she had a drawer full of CVs to choose from whenever a teacher quit.

Come December fifteenth the kindergarten would owe him a week's wages; the director would not be happy about him quitting with no notice, so he might have to write that money off. Thankfully, apart from Mrs Lee, none of his privates owed him anything. He didn't fancy ringing all of them, but he made an effort with the ones he liked, giving them a sob story about a family illness.

Finally, he called Jake.

'Hey, Day,' Jake chirped, 'listen, Sam's got a lead – the guy's gonna call back, so come down about seven, after you've done the campuses, and I'll take you for *kalbi*, okay?'

He was off to stick notices up on the bulletin boards at Edae and Hongdae, some in English with his number, and a few in Korean, with Sam's. Before he left he tossed a few clothes and his laptop into a rucksack, together with the five fat envelopes of cash he'd hidden in his wardrobe. If he needed to run, he just wanted the basics. Trouble was, there was nowhere to hide the rucksack. He stuffed it under the sofa, then pulled it out again, put it in a binbag, tied the handles and left it beside the front door. That would have to do.

Doing the campuses took an hour and a half and felt like an exercise in futility, so he went and played 3D vidgames for a few hours afterwards – he hadn't done that since Chusok. By seven he was drinking Grolsch in Woodstock and listening to grunge at volume eleven. As Jake slipped into the booth, Damien's MoPho heated up in his breast pocket. He checked the screen: Sydney. Shit, he couldn't talk now.

After Woodstock he and Jake went for *soju* and a Korean barbecue, and then on to Azitoo. The bar was swimming with people Damien had got high with when he first arrived in Seoul. All were filled with dismay at his predicament, but no one was looking for a place to move into on Monday. Several were planning to vacate the country by the Solstice and he gritted his teeth as they joked about the Hammer. He let a gaggle of Korean girls fuss over him, stroking his sleeve and suggesting places for their new outlaw folk hero to hide out, but by midnight, the girls' laughter was beginning to grate, the Ozzie surf boys were acting like oafs, and he was bored with spending all his energy avoiding the sloppy advances of a pissed redhead. Sam's lead hadn't called back. He made his excuses and left.

As he undressed for bed, his MoPho fell out of his pocket. Picking it up, he saw that Sydney had left a voice message.

Damien, she whispered, like a member of the French Resistance, *Da Mi can meet us tomorrow. Her office is at Yonsei. I'll see you at the gates at one o'clock.*

Well, why not? he thought as he turned out the light. If he had to walk down the tunnel, he'd like to say goodbye to her first.

34 / The Homecoming

Saturday, after breakfast, the women were sent back to their houses to rest. Mee Hee sat sewing on the verandah as Chin Mee swept the front path clean of leaves. So Ra sat beside her, polishing a set of silver cups. Across the courtyard, Older Sister was walloping a rug strung up between two pine trees. At last they heard the sound of two cars pulling up the driveway in front of the Meeting Hall.

'Dr Tae Sun said to wait until they called us,' So Ra said softly, leaning over to stroke Mee Hee's sleeve. Chin Mee put her broom back in the kitchen as Older Sister bashed the carpet one last time. A strained hush fell over the houses as they waited to be summoned.

At eleven o'clock Dr Dong Sun appeared on the path. His face was sombre, his body tensed like a bow. Wordlessly, the women rose and followed him back to the Meeting Hall.

Dr Kim, flanked by Mr Sandman and Dr Tae Sun, was standing at the top of the room, beside an open coffin. Su Jin's profile was just visible beneath its cushioned lid; her head was propped up on a pillow. The scent of lilies hung thickly in the air.

'They don't smell real,' Mee Hee whispered. Behind her, an undercurrent of excitement moved through the cluster of women at the door.

'Mr San-duh-man!' she heard someone say.

So Ra squeezed Mee Hee's hand and gave her sisters a stern look.

At the front of the group, Dr Dong Sun took Older Sister by the elbow and gently propelled her into the room.

'Please. This is your chance to say goodbye,' he murmured.

Her mouth set in a tight line, Older Sister marched towards the coffin, followed, in single file, by the other women. At first the only sound was the shuffling of feet, but as the procession passed the casket, a broken rhythm of sobs and moans built up a jagged momentum in the Hall. Behind Mee Hee, Chin Mee began crying uncontrollably and had to be supported by So Ra. As she inched forwards in front of them, Mee Hee braced herself for an awful outpouring of the grief she must have been bottling up inside her for weeks, but even when she was standing right in front of Su Jin's body, though her throat was dry and her chest heaving, she couldn't squeeze out even one tear.

The Buddhists said that each person had a destined number of breaths to draw in their lifetime. That was why in meditation they breathed so slowly, holding the air in the depths of their bodies, releasing it to the count of twenty or thirty, letting it escape in a thin stream through one nostril at a time: the longer each breath took to complete, the longer a person could remain living on the earth. Perhaps, Mee Hee thought, staring down at the beautifully dressed corpse before her, the same was true of tears. Only a few months ago she was closing the lid of her own son's coffin. Perhaps, since then, she had cried all the tears she had been born with, and now there were none left to bury with Su Jin.

Or maybe she couldn't cry because it was still too hard to believe that Su Jin was dead. The bodies Mee Hee had seen before, in her village, had been shrunken husks, the life dragged out of them like a rat pulled out of a hole by its tail, every painful moment of their passing etched on their faces as if with claws. Mee Hee had cried bitterly, looking down at those bodies, her own heart raked by memories of her neighbours' struggles to suck just one more breath into their lungs.

In contrast, Su Jin looked like an expensive doll. Her tiny body was lost in the folds of a dark green *hanbok*, her lips were painted pink and her eyes rimmed in brown pencil. Beneath the make-up, her face was relaxed, almost flattened, as if it had been poured like *pajon* batter over her skull and left to collect in tiny ripples beneath her ears and chin. Only her nose retained the character of the woman Mee Hee remembered, its pointy tip looking as if it was still sniffing at the world.

In this room, with its narcotic perfume and graceful wave of mourners, death seemed not a savage ending but a transformation. Looking down at Su Jin, Mee Hee could almost believe that her friend had at last arrived at a place of beauty and dignity, the place she had been searching for when she left the village. All that her sisters could do for her now was to wish her spirit well.

Mee Hee took the bluebird pin out of her pocket and slipped it beneath Su Jin's clasped hands. The flesh was cool and waxy, but the weight of the fingers held the brooch securely against her belly. Maybe Su Jin had no further need of hope in this world, but her spirit might appreciate the gift.

Behind Mee Hee, Younger Sister reached out for the edge of the coffin. Mee Hee took one last look at Su Jin's face and stepped back.

At the foot of the casket, Mr Sandman shook her hand, his blue eyes empty as a summer sky. 'VirtuWorld is very sorry for your loss,' he said in passable Korean.

'Thank you for finding my sister,' she replied. Though she wasn't sure he understood, he nodded. His chin was set, as though he was grinding his teeth. He must feel so badly, she thought, being their protector but still unable to stop what happened.

She wished she could hold Mr San-duh-man's hand for a moment longer, tell him that no one blamed him, that Su Jin had only ever wanted to follow her own will to wherever it would take her. But like a soldier in a military parade, his face was closed, his gaze fixed on a point floating somewhere above her head. Mee Hee made a half-bow and turned towards Dr Kim. Dr Kim would surely clasp her hands, offer words of compassion or wisdom to her village sister.

But Dr Kim was staring straight ahead, her beautiful face tense and frozen. What was wrong? Was Dr Kim angry with her? Fear throbbed in the pit of Mee Hee's belly. Her breath snagged in her throat and it was all she could do to keep standing.

Just as the floor was beginning to swirl, two strong silk-clad arms reached out and pulled her close. Dr Kim was clinging to her as a bereaved mother clings to her surviving child. 'Lee Mee Hee,' she said, her voice faint with grief, 'I have failed you.'

'No, no,' Mee Hee stammered, 'it was I who let her go. You have brought Su Jin home.' Mee Hee's cheek rested on Dr Kim's blouse. A single tear spilled down her nose. She pulled away.

'You are so dear to me, Mee Hee,' Dr Kim whispered. 'I will keep you safe for ever.'

Mee Hee stepped back into the line of women. Tae Sun was waiting beside Dr Kim to greet her, both sadness and pride in his eyes. Shyly, she touched his soft hands, then, head bowed, moved on.

35 | And A Rock

'Wow, Damien. You look like a piece of Korean pottery. Sort of green and glazed.'

Damien grimaced. 'Cheers. I'll be my own souvenir. Fuck knows I can't afford to buy any.'

'Don't worry.' Sydney nodded at the gates of Yonsei. 'Da Mi is going to sort everything out.'

Damien highly doubted it. Really, he should be checking notice boards in the universities north of the river. Trouble was, he didn't believe that would work either. And even if it did, Immigration would probably just follow him and his false passport to the airport. But if he was going to end up in the slammer, what the hell, it would be nice to have a few more memories of Sydney to sustain him.

Sydney's lips were a glossy pink today. Underneath a blue GrilleTex™ vest, she was dressed in white jeans, and a white crewel-knit sweater. 'You look great. Very Abba,' he told her.

'Thanks . . . I think.' Flashing an even whiter smile, she took his elbow and led him briskly through the campus grounds, past massive, modernist buildings, outdoor amphitheatres, and a group of students practising Taekwondo beneath some trees.

'I love this place,' she gushed. 'It's like, really classical, don't you think?'

The combination of monumental architecture and Spartan dedication to a national martial art made Damien think of the Nazis.

But why spoil his last day with Sydney by disagreeing with everything she said?

'There's a tent town up there somewhere,' he said, pointing to the forested mountain flank rearing up behind the campus. 'That's what that beggar on the tube was going on about. It's illegal, but the police let them get away with it in case the prophecies are true. If the Hammer doesn't hit on the Solstice, the dogs will move in.'

Sydney gave a mock shiver. 'Isn't it a bit cold to be camping? Hey, this is it.' They had reached a tall building with a Korean-style tile roof. 'I think it looks like that pagoda in Insa Dong.'

He couldn't help himself. 'Or a prison control tower?'

She punched him on the arm. 'Be nice.'

Sydney collected two visitors' passes from the doorman and sailed across the lobby to the elevators, Damien trailing in her wake. This place was surreal. A schmancy fountain, gold-plated railings in the elevator, and, when they disembarked on the eleventh floor, a plush pink-carpeted corridor complete with tinkling water features.

'How does the uni afford all this?' he asked.

Sydney shrugged airily. 'GRIP made a donation. Here, this is Da Mi's office.'

She stopped in front of a pair of frosted-glass doors. The long, rose-coloured handles bore more than a passing resemblance to female labia.

'Willy Wonka's chocolate factory.' Damien commented. 'Minus the willy.'

'Damien! She'll hear you!'

With a hushed woosh, as if they had in fact been listening, the doors swung open. Sydney led Damien into the room, and the doors closed behind them with a sigh.

The pale grey sky swirling beyond the wall of windows suffused the office with a moon-like glow. If you could call it an office. There were no bookshelves that Damien could see, just Korean scrolls and artworks, all in shades of white. Beneath the long windows, a glass tank housed three large white turtles. Beside it, flanked by two sculptures on pedestals, stood a gleaming white desk. From behind it, a small, immaculately coiffed and lacquered Korean woman rose to greet them. She was dressed in a red tailored tunic-thing: *great album cover*, Damien thought.

'Sydney. Damien. Please have a seat.' Dr Kim gestured at two milky-white leather flexi-chairs in front of the desk. Damien followed Sydney. The ivory carpet was soft as quicksand beneath his feet.

Sydney plopped herself in her chair and fiddled with the temp-control button on her vest. Damien sat down gingerly. He didn't like the way flexi-furniture clung to you. Like sleeping in waterbeds, or being embraced by drunk people, the feeling made him a trifle seasick. He positioned himself slightly forward. This one wasn't so bad. Not sneaking up between his thighs just yet, anyway.

Dr Kim sat down again, a little stiffly. 'Help yourself to a honey drink,' she said, gesturing to a teapot on a stand between them.

As Sydney poured, the scientist trained her gaze on Damien – at least, that was what it felt like: a train engine bearing down on him, two dark pools of light for headlamps. Up close, her eyes seemed a little large for her face; though in fact her head also seemed a little big for her body. Maybe she had some kind of dwarfism? In which case, he shouldn't be staring. Unnerved, he examined the sculptures beside the desk. One was an elongated model of a mother and child, Modigliani-esque, the other a silver double helix. There was a plaque at the bottom of it, engraved in Hangul. Perhaps it was some kind of Korean science Oscar. If his mouth hadn't felt so dry, he would have asked.

'It's good for the immune system,' Sydney urged, handing him a cup.

The honey drink was nauseatingly sweet, with a bitter aftertaste. 'Umm. Delicious,' he murmured, and lowered the cup to his lap.

'Aren't *you* having some, Da Mi?' Sydney asked, in a peculiar, pantomime-y tone of voice.

'I'd love to, darling, but unfortunately it might fuse the wiring.'

Damien shot a puzzled glance at Sydney. She was clutching her drink and wriggling in her seat, eyes shining like a child's at the circus.

'It's so convenient to be able to meet you without getting snared in traffic,' Dr Kim continued. 'Damien, I hope you won't feel uncomfortable shaking the hand of my personal ProxyBod. We call her Pebbles, don't we, Sydney?'

Damien mouthed 'What the fuck?' at Sydney, who was now vibrating with glee.

'Go on, shake her hand,' she insisted. 'It feels so real.'

Damien rose and took the outstretched hand. The skin felt plumped up, and a touch leathery. And while not limp, the fingers didn't exactly grip his. Flicking his eyes over the scientist's body, he noticed a black cable feeding out of a pocket, disappearing under the desk. Christ. That explained the creep factor.

'Pretty hi-tech, Dr Kim.' He sat back down in his chair, which remoulded snugly around his hips. 'Is that a modem cable?'

'The modem is wireless. But the batteries run out quickly. I'm plugged in today,' the Pebbles thing replied. Though of course it was Dr Kim speaking, from wherever she was. Once you knew what was going on, you could see that the mouth didn't do much more than open and shut and make the occasional pucker. The deep frown line between her eyebrows was pretty much a constant too.

'It's fantastic, Da Mi!' Sydney squealed. 'You totally fixed that problem with the lip synch. Sorry I didn't tell you Damien, but I wanted it to be a surprise.'

'Your hands are cold, Damien,' Dr Kim observed. 'Please, drink your honey. It will improve your circulation.'

Pretending to take another sip of his drink, Damien scrutinised the Pebbles creature over the rim. Its waist was very small, he realised, as if the designers had decided that a cartoon figure and doll's head might make such a freakshow more attractive. Still, the voice was very realistic, and there was a certain stately grace about the way the body moved. Though there didn't seem to be much she could do about that smile.

'So you're at home? With a cat-suit on?' he ventured.

'More or less. At the moment Pebbles can only stand or sit, but my engineers are working on an exercise machine that will enable her to walk. Can you imagine the possibilities of such a technology, Damien?'

Damien put his cup down. 'Could I get one to do a jail sentence for me?'

Just possibly, the glued-on smile broadened a fraction. 'Multi-locational appearance is indeed one marketable application. But gaming sector opportunities are my current focus. I understand you enjoy video games?'

'Sometimes, yeah.' He threw a questioning glance at Sydney. But she was glued to the spectacle of the not yet walking, but very much talking Da Mi doll.

The Pebbles thing pressed the tips of her fingers together. 'Damien, if I offered you the chance to help develop the next wave of virtual reality gaming, and solve all your legal and financial problems at one stroke, would you be interested?'

Outside, a shaft of sunlight pierced the clouds above the crawling city. In the tank, one of the white turtles blinked and drew its head back into its shell. Damien shifted uneasily in his seat, which puffed up slightly in response. This was supposed to be reassuring, he knew,

341

but it made him want to cringe. He dug his elbows into the armrests. 'Maybe. It would depend on what was involved.'

Pebbles tilted her head. 'If I outline Project ProxyBod for you, would you accept a gift of two hundred thousand *won* in return for strict confidentiality?'

The sunlight was coldly burning through the window now, coating Pebbles' face. The bloodlessness of the skin was more obvious, its taut stretch across her cheekbones mask-like in the glare.

Sydney squirmed excitedly as the ProxyBod opened a drawer and handed Damien a white envelope full of *man won* bills.

'Pebbles' set his teeth on edge. But the money was harder to dislike. The money was doing what money did best, sitting there quietly in his hand, emanating reassurance and even a whisper of joy.

'Mum's the word,' he said, more jauntily than he felt. He folded the envelope in two and stuffed it into his back pocket. 'Did you want me to sign for it?'

Pebbles' face seemed to tighten a notch. 'This encounter is being recorded through a camera in the iris of my right eye,' she said, evenly. 'If there are any problems later with the media or rival companies, our lawyers will have the best possible evidence of our verbal contract.'

So that explained the X-ray vision. Damien stole another glance at Sydney, hoping for some quick confirmation that Da Mi was mad as a bag of spanners. But Sydney was beaming blankly at the ProxyBod.

'There won't be any problem, Dr Kim,' he said, in the most reassuring tone he could muster. He could always swear Jake and Sam to secrecy too.

'Good. Now, Damien, have you heard of Virtuoso gaming equipment?'

'Sure. It simulates lucid dreaming. Unless it makes you . . . what do you guys say? . . . woof your cookies.'

It was a failed, knee-jerk attempt at being a patronising Brit, and he knew it. The Dr Kim Barbie doll sailed smoothly on. 'Virtuoso games have a negative physical effect on a few people. Perhaps we can arrange a trial session for you,' she offered.

'You gotta try it, Damien,' Sydney said excitedly. 'It's *amazing.*'

'But in the meantime,' Dr Kim continued, 'can you imagine using Virtuoso equipment not just to play in your own headspace, but to manipulate a cyborg avatar in a real room or landscape? To be hooked up to sensors enabling you to actually feel and smell that environment? An environment in which you had a perfect body, great strength, and cameras for eyes? Wouldn't it be tempting to make that not your second, but your first life?'

Cyborg avatars. The wet dreams of super-geeks. 'Not for me. But I can see that some people might go for it, yeah.'

'Some very very wealthy people are among them. I am currently working on such a project, an exclusive environment for a limited number of clients, set in a Renaissance castle and grounds. Damien, your skin tone is exceptionally white. Our client has stressed the desirability of such a shade for a game starring a Goth Princeling and Princessa. Thanks to Sydney, we have eggs from a pale-skinned woman, which together with your sperm, will enable us to meet their requirements.'

Outside, the clouds sealed off the sunlight, restoring the room's shadowless, pearly glow. Beside him, he could practically hear Sydney holding her breath. But he wasn't going to reward her with a look. No. 'Sorry, Da Mi,' he said slowly, 'I don't think I quite understood that. You're going to use my sperm and Sydney's eggs to make children that will grow up into robots?'

'Not at all, Damien. Yes, we will create and clone embryos containing a mixture of your DNA and Sydney's. But we won't incubate these into human beings. Using stem cells from the embryos and ordinary tissue engineering, we can rapidly grow adult human epidermises on a matrix of collagen fibres. The resulting forms, one male, one female, will be mounted on jointed fibreglass shells, flushed with preservatives and fused with a complex interior electronic system. Their facial features may of course resemble yours, but in no way, legal, moral, or biological, could they be considered your children.'

Was this woman, pardon the pun, for real? 'You're growing human skins in labs? Isn't that illegal?'

'Not in Korea. Here it's considered a creative response to advances in biotechnology. Think of these gaming avatars as the biological equivalents of two CGI morphed photographs of you and Sydney.'

'Do you see why I couldn't ask you, Damien?' Sydney had a giggle in her voice. 'I mean, we're not even going out.'

He'd deal with her later. 'Yeah, okay, Sydney,' he muttered. 'But Dr Kim, I'm sorry, I still just do not get this. What's wrong with plastic skin suits? Or silicon, or whatever?'

'To be frank,' Pebbles said crisply, 'ProxyBods also have erotic commercial potential. The texture of the bodies is thus of utmost importance. As a feminist, I am extremely interested in providing alternatives to the global trafficking of women. I do hope that you can see your donation as a vital contribution to a world of greater liberty for all. In return, I am sure I can persuade Immigration to drop the charges against you. And in addition, the gaming consortium has authorised me to offer you a cash incentive of twenty thousand US dollars.'

Twenty thousand bucks. Whatever currency you translated that into, it was a fat stash of readies. Damien leaned back into his chair, which gave his shoulders a subtle massage. He winced, and sat up straight again. Beside him, the pressure from Sydney's fingers was sending pink streaks through her armrests,

344

Outside the clouds were moving on the grey scale from cigarette smoke to petrol smog. Damien let the silence lengthen. In his bowels, he felt a powerful, tugging desire to get up and walk out. But he overruled the impulse. Despite her twisted mind, this woman obviously had buckets of cash – cash that he desperately needed. And even if he did decide he'd rather go to jail than sell his DNA to some warped sex gamers, he couldn't leave the office just yet. There was too much he wanted to know.

'Excuse me, Dr Kim, but when you were looking for samples before, was that also for the ProxyBods? Sydney said it was for your fertility clinic.'

Sydney jumped up in her chair. 'I didn't mean to—'

Pebbles raised a hand. 'I didn't want her to frighten you with a crude approximation of the truth. If you'd agreed, of course I would have revealed the actual circumstances of the donation. I hope you can forgive the tiny subterfuge.'

She sounded less than convincing. But then, could you expect sincerity from a ProxyBod? Damien narrowed his eyes. 'Okay. But why should I trust you now? How do I know that you won't be cloning me, or letting these embryos grow up into sex slaves, or whatever?'

'*Damien.*' Sydney hissed. But Pebbles shushed her with a finger to the lips.

'I'm glad you're asking questions, Damien. Naturally you have concerns. But let me assure you that clones of living humans have no appeal to the gaming sector. For one thing, they wouldn't want any of their products to be held accountable for any crimes you might commit. And of course you'll have a watertight legal guarantee that GRIP will protect your genetic fingerprint.'

Outside, the clouds were now charcoal-black. On the vast network of roads beneath them, drivers were switching on their headlamps, preparing for a storm. And was it his imagination, or could he see lights flickering on the mountainside, the Hammer tent town turning on its solar-powered lanterns and torches? Inside, the overhead lighting dimmed, and a couple of standing lamps lit up, casting shadows across Dr Kim's desk. Damien wiped a finger of sweat from the back of his neck. Maybe a heater had come on.

'I'd rather know what Immigration have decided before I get involved in anything here,' he said as neutrally as possible. Beside him Sydney repressed a groan. Why did she care so much? 'I don't even know exactly how much they want to fine me.'

'I have the MoPho number of the officer in charge.' The scientist reached for the phone on her desk. 'I'm sure he won't mind if I call him at home.'

With a rigid forefinger, the ProxyBod punched a number into the handset. As she conducted a rapid-fire conversation in Korean, Damien inspected the turtles. What was he hoping for? A sign? They were huddled in their shells, like moon rocks.

'*Ne, ne.*' The ProxyBod put its hand over the mouthpiece. 'They've calculated your earnings based on the schedule they found in your apartment,' she hissed. 'The fine is twenty million won. For every five hundred thousand you can't pay, they'll jail you for a week.'

Damien sank back in his chair. It lovingly squeezed his hips. Which didn't help his maths. Not that the figures took a genius to compute. Unless he could find a tenant for his flat or took up this crazy offer he'd be doing months in a Korean jail when the Hammer struck. On top of whatever he'd get back in England once he was eventually deported. If England was still there, that was, and not under six feet of water.

'How much have you got?' Sydney whispered. He shook his head. She was perched on the edge of her seat now, looking incredibly anxious, and yet also, somehow, in a state of wild anticipation. Dr Kim obviously had the girl wound around her little ProxyFinger.

Before he could wonder why, Pebbles abruptly ended her phone conversation and handed him the receiver. He took it gingerly, and held it to his ear.

'Dr Kim very important to Korea,' RoboCop barked. 'She want help you. We want you help Dr Kim, then leave Korea. No fine, no deportation. Only order to leave. Okay, bad boy? We find you two times teaching English, Dr Kim not help you. Understan-dee?'

'Understand.' Damien hung up. Sydney was looking at him expectantly. It was impossible to read the expression on the ProxyBod's face. Stay calm, he thought. Stay calm.

'I just have to promise to be good, and I walk,' he said, trying to sound nonchalant.

Sydney snapped her fingers. 'I told you Da Mi could work miracles!'

'Out of curiosity, Dr Kim, what did you offer him in exchange for my skin?'

'I didn't have to offer anything,' the scientist replied, coolly. 'I'm on the board of the National Security Commission and we know a lot about this particular office. They've been lining their pockets with portions of the fines, then doctoring the books. In general we turn a blind eye because we don't want to halt their good work, but I just alluded to the regrettable shortfalls in his total revenue and he got the picture.'

Sydney clapped her hands. 'I wish we could have seen his face.'

'The important thing is that Damien now has the chance to earn a sizable addition to his nest egg. If you can spare the time right now, I can pay you today.' With a hand-movement worthy of Elizabeth the First, the ProxyBod gestured at a door to Sydney's left.

Outside, far off at the rim of the city, behind the dark mass of clouds, a veil of watery light was floating down over the peaks of the mountains west of Seoul. All he had to do was conjure up a few thoughts of Lara Croft naked and he could take off into that pale sunset, carrying his own private tent town on his back, and never come back. If, on the other hand, he kept his dignity intact and his jeans zipped up, he'd have to go straight into hiding in the Azitoo beer cellar, dependent on Jake and Sam's cock-eyed conviction he could sublet his flat in a week.

It was a no-brainer, really. But still Damien paused. A deep intransigence, born of three decades of stealthily getting his own way, stirred in the marrow of his bones. Maybe this Kim creature did have him over a barrel; maybe he did have to walk through that door and try not to think of England . . . but he was damned if he was going to do so without at least trying to find out exactly what was going on. Sydney knew a big chunk more than he did, that much was clear, and he wasn't going to cough up his baby juice before he'd had a chance to get her on her own.

'Well, Da Mi,' he said, dropping the name like a pingpong ball on a marble floor. 'I'd appreciate a little time to think it over. Nothing against Pebbles, don't get me wrong. It's just that selling your semen isn't like getting your hair cut. To tell the truth, I feel a bit queasy about it. I don't know that I'd even physically be able to oblige.'

With grim satisfaction, he noticed Sydney's eyes dart in alarm to the ProxyBod.

'I understand your reluctance, Damien,' Da Mi smoothly replied. He wondered if she was as unruffled in person, or if they had simply edited panic out of Pebbles' operating system. 'Many people have concerns about making genetic donations. Please take all the time you need. And by all means, come in tomorrow, with your own inspirational literature if you like.'

'It'd be so shitty for all your work here to be for nothing,' Sydney blurted. 'I'd help you out if I could, but all my money's tied up in my apartment.'

Damien stood up. The flexi-chair sorrowfully exhaled. 'Thanks, Sydney. But maybe it's time for me to pay the piper, all that jazz.'

'That's a very philosophical attitude,' Da Mi said. 'But let me give you my card. If you feel your principles bending in the night, please do give me a call.'

Damien took the card and stashed it in his pocket with the envelope. She knew he was bluffing. And she knew he knew she knew.

'Do you want to go for coffee, Damien?' Sydney scrambled to her feet and tugged on her jacket.

'Maybe.' He'd been letting her get her own way for far too long.

'Cool! Here, wait up.'

'Goodbye, Da Mi. Goodbye, Pebs.' Determined to leave on an insouciant note, Damien turned to wave at the ProxyBod. She was taking a turtle out of the tank. Holding the creature by its underbelly, she stretched it out toward him. It craned its weird white head out of its shell and nodded, wisely, once.

36 / Pillow Talk

Johnny took another swig of Jack Daniel's, straight from the bottle, and cut the Sinatra CD dead in its tracks. No offence, Frank, but he didn't need to hear some mopey old song about lonesome towns. Not after Pusan Thursday, Kyongido on the weekend and now Sunday night back in Seoul, totalling figures. ConGlam was sinking a ton of dough into VirtuWorld and they wanted projections of revenue down to the last *won*. Straight after submitting the Tourism Report, he'd been asked to itemise and estimate the potential impact of the park's techno-novelty, the Peony cute-factor, the ever-increasing disaster insurance costs and the probable Christian backlash. Johnny's gut feeling was that demonstrations at the gates would bring publicity, and the park should at least break even the first year. In three years he'd be a millionaire; he'd be a billionaire in ten.

But it was a hollow victory. The spreadsheet was swimming out of focus as another blinding migraine crept up behind his temples. He pushed the mouse aside. These headaches were a bloody plague. He massaged his middle finger, just below the tip, like Veronica had taught him all those years ago, but the once-rare migraines were too severe these days. He was trapped inside the pain, inside his head, inside Korea.

He dimmed the lamp, switched off the music and stretched out on the sofa. Once, he'd been able to ride high for weeks on a hit, but the euphoria of dealing with Ratty and Co. had worn off quickly, leaving him with a lingering sense of paranoia. He should've chopped up the body. It didn't do to get sloppy, even when you only had to worry about the Seoul Police, who could be bribed for far less than Ratty had tried to extort from him. Next – and worse – he'd overstepped in Pusan, and Kim – of course – had complained. ConGlam had sent him an official reprimand; they'd referred to the Incident and even called him, asking him to 'explain himself'.

The conversation had been like a nightmare version of that session with Beacon: *What if you haven't done anything wrong?* Okay, so technically he shouldn't have finished off that skinny girl in the alley – she was just a frightened kid, running away from Mommy Kim, and who could blame her? His orders had been to knock her out and take her back to the village, but she'd bitten him and he'd got mad. He was in a stinking alley full of dogshit and fish-heads – everyone has their fucking limits, he'd yelled at LA: *I'm sorry she got to me; I'm sorry she pissed me off, okay?*

Okay, Sandman, okay; calm down. Just help out with the funeral, they'd told him – and take a couple days off, soon. First, though, they'd assigned him this punishment report – so no chance of a break when he could actually use one.

The funeral had gone well, much to his surprise. He'd thought the Doc would throw a hissy-fit when he arrived, but she'd just scoured him with an evil look and otherwise ignored him. Those peasant baby factories, on the other hand, were into American hunks; all their fluttering and giggling had taken the nervous edge off the day, made him feel like the old Sandman again. And after his carpeting, the women's admiration had given him a thin thread of hope. His success with the surrogates would be his ticket back into VirtuWorld: he needed to get a few shifts softening up the sisters, taking them on daytrips to Seoul, that kind of thing. That slut Sydney was under so much surveillance now that the only way he was going to get close to her was by being at the heart of the park operations. It might take months – years, even – but if he played it nicey-nicey, it would happen.

The headache was levelling off. There was something to this acupressure shit; steady, firm and patient, that's what Veronica had said. And if he could maintain similar pressure on VirtuWorld, who knows, things could all swing his way again. For one thing, the Doc had been strangely tight-lipped about the start-date for the Peonies. No one was allowed to discuss it, but any idiot could tell there was a problem with the King. According to Johnny's spies in LA, the fabled Hugh Grant had yet to sign; he wanted more money, of course, but also confirmation that the kids would do him credit in the image department. It was worth hanging around just to see how that played out. If Kim couldn't find some pansy-faced patsy, maybe the crown would be Johnny Sandman's again. GRIP's genetic defect diagnosis of his semen was a crock of shit, he'd bet his Caddy on that.

Johnny twirled a pencil around on his thumb and forefinger, the way Koreans did incessantly, then snapped it in two. It broke as neatly as the North Korean girl's neck.

He was stressed out, he thought as he chucked the pencil halves across the room into the garbage can. ConGlam was treating him like shit. They'd dangled all those fucking carrots to make him take that Beacon course and now he was working twice as hard for twenty per cent more in his paypacket, he was diluting his vital instincts by saying 'sorry' to every spotty receptionist in Seoul, and he'd brought home a bitch who'd teamed up with his arch-enemy to kick him in the balls: that's what. There was no *empa-fucking-thising* coming his way from Sydney or Kim, was there? Or from LA. The head honchos didn't know the prize they had in Johnny Sandman; they didn't appreciate his natural, raw ability to rule the streets of Seoul. They were trying to divert his testosterone, his wits, his *fucking genius*, into number-crunching and hand-shaking; and in the process they'd nearly fatally confused him. He didn't know who he was any more. He'd nearly botched a straightforward hit simply because he was so over-worked he hadn't wanted to hang around until the small hours to finish the job. And then he'd lost it in Pusan and once again ended up at the mercy of their precious Doctor Kim.

He was getting angry now. Good. He took another hit of whiskey. He had to focus on the rage. Rage was his rocket-fuel, always had been, since Day Dot. Veronica had once tried to get him to *talk about it* – how he must be *angry with his father* for beating him, *angry with his mother* for drinking herself to death. What Ronnie had never under-stood was that rage had jet-propelled him out of that house and into the world. Rage had thrust him into the army, and powered him through six tours of duty. Rage, in the end, had catapulted him out of *her* cheating embrace and into the ganglands of LA. There, rage had kept him honed and lethal and, at long last, got him noticed by the big boys at ConGlam. Sure, he was the Sandman: he had charm and street-savvy and a Mack truckload of smarts. But it was rage that had always buttered his bread, bounced his balls and saved his bacon. If he let his rage go – if he even just *diluted* it one drop – he might as well dig the Sandman's grave and go lie down in it with a sign around his neck saying 'please cover with dirt'.

Kim had been uppity from the beginning, but before, when she'd dissed him, ConGlam had either backed him up or told him not to worry: just ignore her and get on with what he did best. Now, though, they were fucking *siding* with her; fucking *telling him off* – who the fuck did they think they were? Was this what he had to look forward to; was 'Head of Korean Operations' just a fancy title for Doctor Kim's stooge? Was he going to have to suck up to her and her moon-faced North Koreans for years just so he could teach Sydney a lesson one day? And did he really want to slave his guts out, risking prison, for a company that gave him no fucking respect? Yes, *respect*, Beacon: *that's* what Johnny Sandman's Big Fucking Picture is all about, not fucking job titles or 'meeting someone special' – don't make me *barf* – but getting the respect that is due a fucking trend-spotting, deal-fixing, globe-trotting marketing *maestro* with bulging biceps to boot.

He realised he was slamming his fist into the sofa arm. Fuck. His head was killing him again. He switched off the lamp and lay back down on the cushions. *Breathe deep*, he told himself. *Close your eyes.*

He woke from a semi-stupor to the flashing and buzzing of his MoPho. It was Kim.

'Sandman!' she hissed, 'I'm sending you a sound-file. ConGlam have heard it already. They want you to listen to it, and then call me back immediately.'

She rang off; he'd been too groggy to snap back at her. The room was still dark and the migraine was a dull ache at the periphery of his vision. *So much for taking a break, hey, Conglam?* he muttered to himself as he plugged his MoPho into its docking station and opened STravers0286.

'Hullo, Sydney,' said some guy with a prissy English accent. 'Thanks for waiting.'

A chair scraped a concrete floor. Inane pop music dribbled in the background: a nightclub, obviously.

'That's okay. I was talking to the owner. She wants me to do a fashion show here soon.' Johnny imagined the pout on those pink lips and something sharp, a shrapnel piece of memory, twisted in his chest. Migraine or not, he was going to need a drink for this. He reached over and poured himself two fingers of Jack. In the night-club, English ordered a gin and tonic for himself and a MalibuCannibal, whatever the fuck that was, for Sydney.

Johnny took a fortifying glug of whiskey. Sydney was bragging about how she'd told the owner to turn a certain alcove into a gallery. She was such a little madam, fancying herself in charge of everything. Once he'd even promised to lend her capital for a shoe shop; the bitch wouldn't remember that now, he'd bet on it.

He lit a cigarette.

A minute later Sydney broke the ice with a chainsaw. 'I can't believe you'd rather pay that fine and get deported,' she whined.

'Sydney,' English replied, 'I'm beyond skint, and I'd supply the goods in a second if I thought Da Mi was on the level. But she just so obviously isn't.'

Johnny stiffened. Something was happening, some chance was about to present itself; he could feel it nipping at the back of his neck.

'What do you mean?' Sydney asked, all innocence.

'C'mon, there's a thousand whiter-than-white blokes in Seoul who'd donate buckets of semen and play Virtuoso games for hours if she gave them even a fraction of the cash she offered me. Why is she picking on someone who's up to his neck in shit? I don't trust her – there's got to be something she's not saying, don't you think?'

Semen? *Right*. This was Hugh Two, then, or he would be, once Kim got her fangs into him. The guy was clever, though: not accusing Sydney, but clearly wise to the fact that the girl could tell him what the Doc wouldn't. Johnny turned up the volume a fraction. Kim thought she was so fucking smart, flashing the ProxyBod card, but she'd obviously overplayed her hand if some pathetic London homo could see right through her.

Inhaling a lungful of smoke, he prepared to concentrate on Sydney's response, but a female Korean voice twittered and glasses rang softly on the tabletop.

'*Kamsahamnida*.' Sydney's Korean accent had improved, Johnny noted. 'Please, Hae Lim, this is my friend Damien. Damien, Hae Lim is the owner of Music Intelligence.'

'Damien, I very happy to meet you. Your friend Sydney, very beauty. Primitive Ice Queen. Her movement stay in my mind.'

Johnny gagged. Who wasn't that slut blowing?

Damien attempted to be gallant and pay for the drinks, but the owner refused to let him. Johnny could hear her kitten heels tapping against the floor as she left.

'*Gun bae*,' Sydney toasted. The glasses clinked gently.

There was a pause on the tape. Johnny noted his cock was getting hard. Thinking about Sydney could still do that to him sometimes. 'So,' Sydney said, a shade too brightly, 'you have suspicions of evil genius Da Mi?'

'Sydney, I want to ask you one question. Okay?'

Oooh, Johnny smirked, rubbing his cock through his jeans with the ball of his hand. *Damien's playing hardball now.*

'Okay.'

'Did you tell Da Mi I had privates in Chamshil?'

'What? *No!* What are you saying, Damien?'

'Nothing – nothing, I just think it's strange that I get picked up by Immigration at that job near LotteWorld and then *your* friend just happens to have the inside track on that particular officer. That's all.'

There was another long pause. Johnny grinned. *Wiggle your way out of this one, Sydney*, he thought. *Perhaps you'd better cry.*

And sure enough, when she did speak, it was in a wobbly voice, all misty-eyed, sulky, and vulnerable. Yeah, he knew that voice all right. A real passion-killer. At the sound of it his burgeoning lust evaporated. 'Maybe I mentioned it – I can't remember, but that still doesn't mean she set you up, Damien. There's a crackdown right now; it's been in all the papers. And Da Mi's a pretty important person, with loads of connections. You're really lucky I know her.'

'So you honestly don't think she set up that raid?'

'No,' she sniffled, 'of course not. Damien, please believe me: I thought Da Mi could help you. Look, if you don't trust her or me, why don't you just walk away?'

There was another long silence. Johnny cracked his knuckles. Something serious was about to happen, or Kim wouldn't have sent him the tape.

Damien sighed. 'Sydney, I'm sorry; I didn't mean to accuse you of anything – but you're just a kid, and it seems to me you're mixed up in something you don't understand.'

'I can look after myself.' She didn't sound so sure.

Damien spoke softly. 'Sometimes, when you don't know I'm looking, you're kind of sad and lost. You're my mate. I don't like to see you like that.'

Oh Jesus, was she crying? The sound disintegrated into a general snuffling and scraping of chairs. Johnny could hear the swish of fabric now, next to the mic. Were they fucking *kissing*?

'Ummm,' Sydney crooned.

Johnny knew what that meant. A ripe, red rage spouted up from the pit of his stomach to his throat. *Breathe*, he reminded himself. *Breathe*.

'Sorry, Sydney – I'm sorry.' Rather than grabbing her under the table, Damien pulled away, acting polite and embarrassed.

Johnny had to laugh. Typical Brit.

'No, *I'm* sorry. I feel so stupid. I've been trying so hard lately not to sexualise everything.'

What? Johnny snorted so loudly he had to stop the file and replay the next line.

'I felt *awful* after you left Da Mi's office.' She was blubbing again. 'I really like you – I was only trying to help you, honest.'

Damien's chair scraped again, bumped against hers. 'Look, you've come all the way out here by yourself,' he whispered. 'You've got into all this wacky stuff with Da Mi – but those meditation spas and whatever else she's into, I don't think they're making you happy. Why don't you tell me what's really going on?'

He was touching her; Johnny didn't have to be there to see it. English's fingers were wiping away the teardrops, stroking the fine down on her cheeks, murmuring, coaxing, trying to get Sydney to spill the secrets he, Johnny Sandman, had spent the best part of three years protecting. Would the slut fall for it, or was she playing some deep game of her own?

'I keep trying to be strong,' Sydney whimpered, 'to think about the future, everything Da Mi's promised me, but yesterday, after you left, I felt so bad. Even if you took the money, I didn't know if I could look you in the eye.'

'Why's that?'

'You'll be angry.'

'No, I won't. It's Da Mi, isn't it? For some weird reason, she's making you bring me to her?'

'Oh, Damien,' Sydney wheedled, 'Da Mi's a great person, honestly. Maybe she did have a hand in your arrest, I don't know, but she's been so nice to me; I can't tell you. I don't want to desert her; I just feel bad lying to you. And besides, if you knew the truth, maybe you *would* want to help her out.'

'The truth?'

'Yeah.'

'Okay, shoot.'

Sydney took a deep breath. 'All this stuff with the ProxyBods, it's just scratching the surface of what Da Mi can do. She *does* want our skin-tone for the avatars, but I'm also the egg donor for a massive new project, way more exciting and important. And Da Mi needs your sperm to follow it through.'

'For something more fucked-up than the ProxyBods?'

'No! It's *way* better: she wants to clone our children and bring them up to inspire people—'

Damien cut her off. 'So she *does* want to clone our children?'

'Wait, let me finish—' There was a slight shift in sound quality, a swallowed consonant, then Sydney's voice came clear again: 'It's such a beautiful vision. They'll all live at VirtuWorld, they'll be totally safe. But it's top secret right now, and because Da Mi's been screwed around so much by other sperm donors, she thought it would be better to ask you to donate for the ProxyBods instead.'

Johnny couldn't believe it. He had to press 'pause' and 'rewind' again. 'Screwed around by other sperm donors'? Yeah, well, that would be Kim describing how she fired him. And if the Doc thought he couldn't hear when she was editing a sound file, she was dumber than Pebbles unplugged. Still, no matter what Kim was trying to hide from him, the fact remained that that stupid little piece of trailer-trash had finally overstepped the mark. Her big, glossy, cock-sucking mouth was now posing a serious threat to the viability of the entire project. And as ConGlam and GRIP had discussed from the very beginning, there was only way to contain and eliminate that threat. Kim was going to have to order it, and Johnny would deliver. Then that über-bitch doctor would have to thank him – and she would, oh, yes, she would indeed, on bended knee, right in front of his royal throne.

He resumed the file. The nightclub music squiggled and bleeped. Koreans were talking. A girl laughed.

'So let me get this straight.' Damien's voice was tight. 'All the time you've known me you've been trying to hijack my sperm to create a GM breed of designer humanoids? Didn't you ever think there was something wrong with that, Sydney?'

'You said you wouldn't be angry!'

Picturing her outrage, Johnny laughed until his eyes were wet.

'That was before you told me our whole relationship was a lie!'

'I'm sorry, Damien,' Sydney pleaded. 'I thought what you didn't know wouldn't hurt you. But now I know that was wrong, because I've changed – because of all the meditations I've been doing. I'm telling you now, aren't I?'

'Probably because Da Mi told you to.' English wasn't kissing her *now*, Johnny chuckled to himself. His own cock was getting hard again though: power was an aphrodisiac, they said, and at long last power was flowing back into Johnny Sandman's loins.

'She'd *kill* me if she knew – and anyway, don't be mad. Can't you be flattered we want you? You're great, Damien: so smart, and sexy.'

'Yeah, a prime English specimen,' Damien said scathingly. 'Perfect for marketing in Korea.'

'You're twisting everything I say! Maybe Da Mi does just care about your looks, but I don't. I mean, you're one of my best friends in Korea – you know that's true, Damien.'

There was another poignant pause. Then English caved in. 'I like you too,' he confessed.

'Do you?' There was that coquettish voice again, and the small sounds of movement. She was stroking something right now, and it wasn't a cat.

Abruptly, the file ended. Johnny stubbed out his butt and drained his whiskey glass. Blood was swimming behind his eyes and his cock was bursting at the seams. She thought she'd got away with it, didn't she? It was time to call Kim and discuss exactly how to stop Sydney and her mealy-mouthed little toyboy in their tracks.

Damien awoke with a start. His mouth was full of hair and Sydney was clinging to him like a mermaid who'd failed her swimming badge. Gently, he freed his arm and without waking her, guided her head back onto the pillow. She gurgled and rolled over, drawing her knees up to her chest. Sunlight was streaming through the window, imbuing her skin with a pale wintery glow. But as he admired her gleaming spine, last night's conversation and the very peculiar events of the last few days came creeping back to him on spiky little heels. *Go now*, a little voice in his head insisted. *Vanish. Close the door without saying goodbye.*

But where would he go? To the Immigration office? The thought of it made his guts shrink. *Shit, shit, shit.* He rubbed his temples, tried to get some blood circulating in his brain. What he really wanted to do was get out of the country today. If only Jake and Sam had found him a tenant. Then he could pick up his new passport, grab his bag from his flat and head to the airport. He could wait in Japan until Sam wired him the *hagwon* money; then buy his ticket to Canada.

What the fuck time was it? His trousers were lying on the floor beside the bed. Reaching over, he dug out his MoPho. Eight a.m – and *yes!* A text message from Jake:

No luck yet. Still trying. Don't give up.

He'd sent it late last night; he wouldn't be up yet, so no point texting back. Damien slipped the MoPho back in his jeans and slumped back down beneath the sheets.

It was all too much to think about. So much easier just to lie beside Sydney, suspended in indecision and her faint scent of honey and vanilla. He slid his arm around the sleeping girl, nuzzled her fine hair. As his breathing slowed to match hers, his cock began to swell. Da Mi's conniving, Sydney's torturous thought processes, Jake and Sam's lists of homeless foreigners, the prospect of a hundred mini-Damiens becoming child-slaves or new Messiahs: all of that seemed as distant and surreal as a late-night schlock DVD.

He nestled Sydney's bottom in his lap. Maybe this was seriously wrong – sick, even. Just a few months ago he'd thought this girl was his dead sister come back to life. But whether it was the thought of prison or a combination of Sydney's wild story and helpless tears, some barrier inside him – taboo, reluctance, fear, whatever – had collapsed in the nightclub last night.

She stirred, reached for his hand and pulled it up to her chest. As he cupped her breast, memories of last night flooded his mind: pinning her against the wall, tugging at her thong, inhaling the silk of her skin; letting her push him onto the bed, unzip his jeans, gnaw at his chest as he lunged for the deepest, tightest, most private part of her; splitting her open, feeling her loosen, accept him, pour over him, crying out for him, her screaming silently for what seemed like minutes, her white body arching above his before grinding him into what felt like the molten centre of the earth. No, it hadn't been foolish or pervy getting together with Sydney. It had been like making a promise to himself.

Stiff again, he slid his cock into the cleft of her bum and she shifted, responded with pressure of her own. He gripped her hipbone, rocked her back and forth, while his other hand roamed her body, stroking her curves, squeezing her nipples, flicking her small, nubby clit. With a small throaty noise, she lifted herself up on her elbow, her backbone curving like a ladder before him. Then she slid back down, and turned toward him moaning, '*Please* fuck me . . .' She smiled and fluttered her eyelashes. 'Fuck my *cunt*—'

He grinned. She was laughing at him, at his proper British politeness during their languid post-coital conversation: *So, what do you call your vagina?* he'd asked, idly twirling her pubes. *Er, Gina?* she'd whipped back. Then they'd giggled through the ridiculous ones, from 'Foofy Bird' to 'Under-Dimple' and in the end she'd said she liked 'pussy' to get her in the mood, and 'cunt' when she was raging wet. Though she'd also agreed 'quim' was cute.

Her quim was the cutest pink seashell he'd ever smelt. Groaning, he resisted the urgent need to enter her *right now*. He reached over to the lacquered box she'd introduced him to last night, pushed away her fancy Gotcha and fumbled for another condom. She twisted towards him and watched with shining eyes as he unrolled it, then parted her legs with her hands.

Later, the latex sheath drooped off his limp cock, pendulous with his sperm.

Sydney ran her hands over his chest, her eyes sparkling like bits of green and gold glass. 'We should go on holiday,' she whispered.

And at last the kaleidoscope of the last few days stopped spinning.

Da Mi was a creep, and her Peonies and ProxyBods were about as wrong as anything could get. But he'd been working flat-out, on the run, for months – for *years*. And now he had the chance to make some serious money and get to Canada for the Solstice, exactly like he'd been planning. It was ridiculous to hem and haw. Maybe Sydney hadn't exactly been one hundred per cent honest with him, but she'd meant well, and she was more than making up for it now, wasn't she? He'd slept on it, screwed on it – twice – and now he knew exactly what to do. He wasn't going to jail, and he wasn't going to hide in Jake's gym bag, waiting to escape out of the country owing a huge debt to his mate. He was going to sail down to Azitoo with the Full Monty, buy those fake papers and leave Korea with sacks of cash – and, who knows, maybe a date to hook up with Sydney in Vancouver one day. All he had to do first was set aside some woolly moral principles and a knee-jerk first reaction, then cock-sneeze into a test-tube. Big deal. If the world went down the toilet, so would Da Mi and her Nazi experiments. But he'd be fucked if Damien Meadows was going to be her first victim.

He slipped off the condom, tied it in a knot and dangled it between them. 'Here's a deposit on the flight.'

'Yergh!' Sydney pushed his arm away, then gaped at him in astonishment as the penny dropped. 'You mean you want to help out? Really?'

Damien placed the blobby latex on top of last night's effort, in the ashtray beside the bed-mat. 'Yeah. Why not?' He stretched. 'I still don't trust your friend, mind, but as long as she coughs up the cash, I won't quiz her too hard about her recruitment methods.'

Sydney propped herself up against her pillow. 'You've got her all wrong, Damien; she's really nice. Once we can tell her you know about the park, she'll probably let you have a share of the profits.'

'Christ, don't do that,' he said in alarm. 'She can't know I know, Sydney. I don't want to play any part in her new master race.'

Her face crumpled slightly and she turned away from him. 'How many times do I have to tell you? The Peonies *aren't* a master race they're here to help people.'

'Good. Let them help people.' He snuggled up behind her. Her teddy was stuffed between the *yo* and the wall. He grabbed it, made it do a little dance on the pillow in front of her, then kissed her nose with it. She laughed, and he whispered in her ear, 'All I want is to get together again sometime with you.'

'Yeah?' She wriggled round and hugged him.

'Yeah.' Holding her close was like bathing in warm milk. He stroked her hair and kissed her forehead, hummed into her ear and pressed her to him until her necklace dug into his chest.

'Ouch.' She pulled away, sat up. 'I'm starving. Want some breakfast?'

'Sure, what's on the menu?'

Sydney picked up the tied condom and scrambled to her feet. 'Oh, the usual: dried sperm flakes and hard-boiled eggs.'

She flounced over to the kitchen and put the condom in the fridge. He jumped up after her, pinched her bum.

'*I was fourteen, she was twelve—*' he sang.

'Wha—?' She turned to him, giggling.

He placed his finger on her lips. '*Father travelled, hers as well . . . Europa . . .*'

His voice was a little thin at first, but he hit all the notes, and he remembered the whole thing, word for word. Sydney smiled and laughed as he swept her round the flat, waltzing to Thomas Dolby's epic tale of childhood lovers, cruelly parted by the vagaries of war and the demands of the three-minute pop song: Europa, who disappeared, became a famous model and film star, and then vanished again as her bodyguards dragged the narrator away from her car . . .

By the end, he was full-throated, and Sydney was roaring along to the chorus '*We'll be the pirate twins again . . . EUROPA!*'

'Yeah?' she asked as he finished, pulling him back down onto the bed mat.

'Yeah.' Burying his face in her hair, he tumbled after her.

After Damien left, Sydney put on the new Burnt Forest CD. Damien had taken the refrigerated condom down to the lab, so she chucked out the one in the ashtray, then filled the kitchen sink and washed the breakfast dishes in a haze of cello, chainsaws and birdsong. What a night. What a morning. Gorgeous sex. More gorgeous sex. Damien singing that funny song – she'd thought he'd written it for her, but he'd said no, it was by some British guy, had been a hit when he was a kid. She'd asked if he was a good singer then too, hoping to hear about the choir, but he'd shrugged, said 'nothing special', and then changed the subject back to breakfast. That had been fun too: they'd made rice and pinenut porridge from a packet and then he'd stewed some plums she'd thought were too hard to eat. His mum used to make stewed fruit, he'd said. It was easy; he'd just added water and a bit of sugar. She'd suggested Da Mi's honey, but he didn't like it. Usually he ate toast and Marmite with cucumber in the mornings, which sounded *horrible*, but he'd called that anti-British prejudice. He'd promised to make her some one day, and then she'd never eat peanut butter and jelly sandwiches again.

She put the leftover stewed plums in a bowl in the fridge, then she made another pot of coffee, sat by the window and lit a cigarette. Jin Sok had left a pack in the flat, and she liked to smoke one occasionally. Outside it was windy, grey and cold. Inside, she was enclosed in a warm bubble all her own.

Telling Damien must have been the right thing to do. Of course, she hadn't mentioned Hugh Grant; that might have offended him. No, her strategy had been perfect: he had ended up donating, and she was feeling happier than she could ever remember – better than the calm glow she experienced after a session in the Chair. She was more tingly, more promising. Maybe the Chair had helped her relax enough to go with the flow with Damien, but still, no matter what Da Mi said, there was no substitute for real-time, real-life, real-body pleasure.

She hoped he did want to take a holiday. They could go somewhere warm, Vietnam or Thailand, maybe. Her mind drifted with the cigarette smoke into thoughts of sun, sand and sex, but as she took the final drag she shivered, and not from cold.

It was stupid to pretend that everything was hunky-dory. Pretty soon she'd have to face Da Mi, having broken the very first promise she'd ever made to her. And if she didn't have the guts to confess, she would have to keep on lying, or at least not telling the truth, and that would be a real strain.

She stubbed out the butt. Everything had happened so quickly, she told herself sternly; no wonder she felt mixed-up. After all, it had never been her intention to tell Damien about VirtuWorld, never

– but she hadn't expected his refusal to play along, even when backed into a corner; and she hadn't expected to feel guilty about misleading him.

Maybe she should have told Da Mi she was feeling queasy; she could have had a few sessions in the Chair to help her keep to the plan. But if she'd confessed her doubts, Da Mi might have given up on her; to be honest, after that scene with Jae Ho she was amazed Da Mi still wanted her on the project at all. No, it was much better that she'd kept quiet, wasn't it? Shouldn't she be allowed a secret of her own?

But having a secret from Da Mi felt . . . wrong, somehow. She wished Damien would hurry up and come back. Now he was gone, everything felt infected with uncertainty.

Her coffee tasted bitter now; maybe she should have a honey drink. She wasn't very good at having two a day. *It's funny*, she thought, *how when something's bad for you, jangles your nerves or destroys your lungs, you want it all the time, but when something's good for you, you just use it 'til you feel okay, then you coast along until you feel like shit again and you're desperate for a fix.*

The CD ended and the sound of traffic reared up from the street. Across the road, the branches of a ginkgo tree were scraping against each other in the wind. With a bouncy burble, her MoPho startled her out of her trance. Private number? Who could that be?

'*Yobosayo?*'

'Sy-duh-nee?'

With a weird thrill, she recognised the coarse, lilting voice. 'Jae Ho?'

'I am fine.' He laughed. 'How are *you?*'

'Very good, thanks,' she replied coolly, though her pulse was racing. Why was Jae Ho calling her?

She opened her mouth to reel off a list of all the great things that were happening for her, but he cut in crisply, 'Sy-duh-nee, I finish

367

new painting. Painting of Canada supermodel. I want you see. You come today?'

A painting of her? She should just tell him to fuck off.

But why let him think he could still upset her? 'You can invite me to the opening,' she said.

'No, no. Opening many months. I want you see now.' His voice softened. 'Is my sorry, Sydney. I make you very beautiful, big meaning in picture. Best painting. My masterpiece.'

She thought of the drawing in her junk drawer, the painting at Golden Piglet. Was he really obsessed by her image? And was he really sorry about how he'd treated her? *Good.* So he should be.

'I don't need your sorry, Jae Ho,' she said tartly. 'I'm fine. Everything's great.'

'Good, good. So you come?'

Suddenly she wanted to do it. To show Jae Ho how well she was doing, how good she looked, how she didn't need *him* to be happy. And, yes, to see this painting of her that all of Seoul might be talking about one day. 'Maybe,' she replied.

'Seven o'clock you come. Corner building, Gongjang Street. I meet you on step.'

'Seven? I don't know.' She might be with Damien again then. 'What about now?'

'Now, no. Now I in Insa Dong. Seven only time today.'

'Look. I said *maybe,* Jae Ho. I'll see how today goes,' she declared. If she showed up, she showed up. If not, let him sweat it out.

'I hope. I wait. I very glad see Sy-duh-nee again.' Jae Ho rang off, and Sydney put the MoPho down. She had handled that well, she thought. She stood up and stretched.

Actually, it was nice to hear Jae Ho was sorry for his bad behaviour. If the painting really was a masterpiece, she might possibly even forgive him. She was going to be a major celebrity in Seoul and it would be impressive to have a famous artist as part of her set. And forgiveness, Da Mi always said, was a balm for the soul.

Now, where was her Gotcha? Da Mi would probably call as soon as Damien left her office. She would need to act as though she was hanging on the end of the line for news, excited and surprised. *If* she and Damien went on holiday, she could tell Da Mi that she was just having a little goodbye fling with him.

37 | The King

'Mr San-duh-man is the lover of Dr Kim,' Older Sister announced knowledgeably. She was shelling peas in the kitchen. It was Monday, two days after Su Jin's funeral.

So Ra scraped a long carrot peeling into a bowl. 'I doubt it,' she snorted. 'He's not the kind of man who sits in the corner while his wife runs everything.'

'You know nothing about men!' Older Sister scoffed. 'He couldn't take his eyes off her.'

'I didn't like the way he looked at her,' Chin Mee offered, shyly looking up from her own bowl of peas. 'There was a mean feeling in his eyes sometimes, don't you think, Mee Hee?'

Mee Hee stopped peeling the potato in her lap. 'Not *mean* exactly,' she said, tentatively. Who was she to judge the feelings of Mr Sandman?

'But upset about something, yes?' Chin Mee insisted.

'Maybe,' Mee Hee agreed. 'Well, yes. In China I thought he was a happy man, but here he is quieter, withdrawn. Troubled, perhaps.'

'Exactly!' Older Sister crowed, then, with a glance at the kitchen door, lowered her voice. 'He resents her power and her beauty, the way we all love her. He wants to master her, to possess her. And she lets him take control, in the bedroom only, while she dominates him in front of all of us.'

'You have an active imagination, Older Sister. I think it might be *you* who wants to be dominated in the bedroom,' So Ra teased.

The other women laughed, and for a moment Older Sister glowered. But then, a sly grin on her face, she split a pod expertly with her thumbnail. The bright green peas pattered into the bowl between her thighs.

'Yes! It's been far too long – where are the babies they've been promising us? And where are the men we get to marry in the end?'

These were the big questions that Dr Kim had left unanswered. Everything was happening according to plan, she had said yesterday at breakfast, right before she left. Soon they would be mothers and wives, soon – but no one knew exactly when. So Ra and Chin Mee laughed as Older Sister squeezed her left breast, claiming it was full of milk for pea soup. But Mee Hee's stomach ached, and she looked away.

That afternoon the doctors moved her *yo* back into her own house. After dinner she declined So Ra's invitation to play Flower Cards and hastened down the path back to her own home. Walking into the stillness inside was like drinking a glass of warm *bancha*, so ordinary, but deeply reviving too.

The wildflowers in the vase on the living-room shrine were wilting, so she threw them out. It was too dark to pick new ones; she would do that in the morning. She lit a candle and sat in an armchair, letting her mind drift, relishing the quiet touch of the air on her skin. She needed calmness around her, and she needed to be home, so that Tae Sun could join her again.

He knocked softly, as usual. It was late, just past ten o'clock, and he had a bunch of fat pink flowers. 'To welcome you home,' he said bashfully.

For a terrifying second she thought he might kiss her, but he just handed her the bouquet, then stepped neatly into the room.

She recognised the flowers from the DVDs. 'Peonies?' she gasped, then, embarrassed, buried her nose in the plump blossoms. Strangely, they had no scent. Still, no one had ever given her such a gift.

He regarded her benevolently. 'When the babies come, they will be everywhere. I wanted you to have some now, to help you focus on the future.'

Of course. How stupid she could be.

'They're Dr Kim's favourite flower,' she said. 'I must put them with her photograph.' She ducked in a little bow and retreated into the kitchen.

She expected him to wait in the living room, but he followed her and hovered at the door. 'You have to cut the stems, you know that, don't you?' he said as she laid the flowers on the counter and carefully removed the paper wrapping.

She laughed. 'Even we peasants know that.'

'Oh, I didn't mean—'

Startled by his flustered tone, she turned to look at him. His face was crimson.

'I just thought . . .'

She was mortified. He had given her such a present and already she had insulted him. 'Please, Tae Sun, I was only joking!'

'You must forgive me. I can be so arrogant.' He shook his head, his eyes downcast, their delicate lashes sweeping his cheek.

'You're the kindest person I've ever met. These are the most beautiful flowers anyone has ever given me.' Trembling, she gathered up the peonies in her arms. Anxiously glancing over the blossoms, she saw him smile at last.

'Is this the right one?' He pointed to a large ceramic vase he had given her just after Su Jin had left. She nodded and he lifted it down and filled it with water while she took the carving knife from the drawer and sliced the six peony stems diagonally on the wooden chopping board. He set the vase on the counter between them and she carefully arranged the flowers inside it.

'Once, my husband gave me a red rose,' she said quietly. 'When he was courting me. He bought it in Pyongyang. My mother showed me how to cut the stem. Otherwise, I used to pick wildflowers and grasses. I love having flowers in the home.'

'When the babies come,' Tae Sun said firmly, 'you will have the best flowers here, every day. Dr Kim will see to that – and if she doesn't, I will.'

His hands were resting on the counter near the vase, his fingers thin, yet capable and strong. He cared for her, for her safety and her happiness. Why did she dare to want anything more? 'The babies,' she said, 'when are they coming? Does Dr Kim know?'

'You mustn't lose faith in Dr Kim, Mee Hee. She wants everything to happen as quickly as possible. As do I.'

For a long moment, Tae Sun gently held her gaze. Something in her loosened and her body slowly flooded with warmth. Surely there was no mistaking his meaning?

'We are all ready, you know that, Tae Sun,' she murmured, her own face flushing now. Beneath her blouse, her breasts were full and glowing. She could feel his eyes absorb her, her readiness, her longing. For a moment she almost felt beautiful.

He paused. 'Mee Hee, if I tell you something, can you promise to keep it a secret?'

'I would be honoured to receive your trust.' Her heart was thumping now, like a wooden spoon in *pajon* batter. No, she wasn't beautiful, just foolish and lovesick. She wondered that he didn't rush over to take her pulse.

But he continued gravely, 'Dr Kim has found a wonderful young woman who will be the natural mother of the children, and the

Queen of VirtuWorld, but she is still waiting for the chosen King to offer his . . . contribution.'

The sound of water dripping into the sink was as loud as a clock. Mee Hee nodded and lowered her eyes.

Tae Sun leaned over and tightened the tap. 'It's complicated, but in fact there are two men involved,' he continued. 'The younger one will be the biological father, and the older one will act as the Queen's consort. However, neither of them has yet firmly committed to their role. If Dr Kim can't convince them by the end of this week, Dr Dong Sun and I are going to ask her to reconsider Mr San-duh-man for the job. He was our first choice, and we know you and your sisters like him very much.'

A worried expression was tautening Tae Sun's features now. He stared out the window at the blackness of the pine trees in the night. How selfish she was, only thinking of herself, when he had so many problems. 'Mr San-duh-man would make an excellent King,' she said, reassuringly.

'He's a good candidate, yes, healthy and strong. Dr Kim says he has some problems that his children might inherit, but Dr Dong Sun thinks that we should be able to successfully treat these issues.'

'He would be a wonderful father,' Mee Hee said firmly. Then she stopped herself. How could she sound so confident? Was she the one making these difficult decisions? 'I mean, we would all welcome him, if he were to agree. But I'm sure Dr Kim has very good reasons to prefer the other men.'

'The older man is very famous; he would help bring respect to all of us at VirtuWorld. And the other man is the choice of the young Queen's. She would have to be persuaded that Mr San-duh-man is better for the job.'

Mee Hee tried to imagine the lives of these foreigners, offering themselves and their sons and daughters to VirtuWorld. *Why?* she wondered. *Didn't they want to take care of their own children?* But she didn't know how to begin to ask Tae Sun about them. She would only reveal her ignorance, her naïve assumption that everyone in the world was just like her.

'I wish I could meet her,' she said, timidly. 'Do you think we could be friends?'

'You miss Su Jin, don't you?' Tae Sun said, quietly.

For a moment it felt like the walls had moved closer in around them, as if they were listening hard for Mee Hee's answer. An image of the grave mound in the woods rose in her mind. Su Jin was there now, resting in the soil, her body buried in a place Mee Hee could visit, bringing flowers, or stories, of babies, of doctors, of marriages. She would always keep Su Jin company, always pray that her friend's spirit was now journeying in a place of peace and beauty. But until Mee Hee herself joined her own parents and her lost little boy, God, or Dr Kim, had given her someone else to love.

'I have my sisters.' she quietly replied. 'And you . . .'

Stepping forward, he took her hands in his.

'However you want me, you will have me always, Mee Hee,' he said.

Beside her, imperceptibly loosening their petals, the peonies drank the water he had poured for them. The blossoms, like her heart, were full and heavy and yet at the same time light and open and bold.

'Always?' she whispered.

He released her hands, stepped back. 'Please be patient with me, Mee Hee. Dr Kim is deciding everything this week. We must wait. There must be no gossip, no complications, no questions about our dedication to VirtuWorld above all else.'

'Dr Kim has given us each other. I would do anything for her, you know that, Tae Sun.'

Fishing in his pocket he brought out a small white plastic packet.

'This is food for the flowers. Sprinkle it in the water whenever you change it. Then they'll last for weeks.'

Fingering the packet as if it were a sachet of priceless unguent, she tripped after him out into the living room. At the door, he kissed her goodbye, running his hands gently over her shoulders and letting his lips linger at the corner of her mouth.

38 | Render Unto

Her glamorous veneer couldn't mask the shrewd look Da Mi flicked Damien as he walked in the door. She was standing in front of the desk, dressed in a black tailored jacket, a white blouse and a green skirt with black trim. This, he knew at once, was the genuine article.

'So we meet in person,' he murmured, sticking out his hand. The scientist reciprocated. Her eyes were alert, her expression one of controlled amusement, but like her ProxyBod's, her small hand seemed devoid of animating spirit. He wondered if she would prefer to be wearing latex gloves.

'Where's Pebbles today then?' he asked, looking round. The turtles in the tank peered back at him. Otherwise the room was eerily still. Through the window, the sky was a monotonous blanket of cloud and the mountains looked like a flat, painted backdrop. It was well time to get out of Seoul. And the sooner he sold his sperm to the nice lady doctor, the sooner he'd be off.

'She's having her nails done.' The scientist smiled. Unlike Pebbles, she had fine lines around her eyes. 'So you've come to help us out, Damien?'

'If everything's fine down at Immigration, I'm ready and raring to go.'

'I spoke to them after you called. You have until Friday to leave. You can't return for a year, but nothing will show up on your computer records in other countries.'

'And my passport?'

She flashed open her jacket, revealing its green silk lining and inside breast pocket. 'They couriered it over. You can have it as soon as you've made your donation.'

Right. The handover. Always the edgy part of any hostage deal. The condom was in his pocket, inside a brown paper bag.

He pulled it out. 'Here's something I prepared earlier.'

Her smile was thin as a fish hook. 'Thank you, Damien. I'll take that as back-up. But we do need a fresh sample as well.'

She relieved him of the paper bag, led him to the desk and offered him a flexi-chair. He sat down, on the edge of the seat.

'This is the standard GRIP sperm donation contract.' She handed him a sheaf of papers and took the other chair. 'Your agreement is with us, not with our client. Please read it carefully. Would you like some honey drink to help you concentrate?'

There was a steaming pot of that disgusting stuff on the little table beside him. He politely declined. As she poured herself a cup, he scanned the contract. It didn't mention ProxyBods or gaming companies, but it did confirm the cash incentive, and demand confidentiality on both sides. There was a fat gold fountain pen beside the honey pot; it made a change from the chewed Biros and pencil-stubs he usually had lying around the flat. Leaning over the table, he signed the contract in glistening black ink.

'Thank you, Damien. Please come this way.' Da Mi stood up and led him to the door she'd pointed out the day before. It opened onto a short corridor. She took him down it, into an empty laboratory, then along another corridor to a small room, equipped with a leather sofa and a lamp, a couple of plants, a sink and towel and a stack of soft porn magazines. Blondes, he noticed, on the top one at least.

'Take your time.' She handed him a Ziplock plastic bag. 'You can leave your sample here when you're done.' She pointed at a sliding opening in the wall then left, shutting the door softly behind her.

This was it then: the point of no return. As if he could still change his mind, he sat down on the sofa and asked himself if this was what he really wanted to do.

Well, no, to be honest, it wasn't. But it was the lesser of at least three evils, and the sooner it was done, the sooner he was free to start a whole new life.

He checked his MoPho, just in case, but there was nothing in his message tray. Christ, it was gone one o'clock; Jake was supposed to be on a mission, not still sleeping.

But that was a useless line of thought. He'd made his decision, signed on the dotted line. He put away his MoPho, undid his belt, unzipped his fly and let his jeans slip down to his ankles. Now was the acid test: was there even anything left in him?

He didn't need the porn. He just thought about Sydney and the way she totally lost it when she came. Afterwards, he pulled his jeans back up, washed his hands and put the bag on the ledge.

When he re-entered her office, Dr Kim was nowhere to be seen. Damien went over to the window and gazed out over the cold, colourless city. People in black coats were walking through the campus, hunched over against a strong wind, clutching their collars to their throats. On the streets beyond the uni walls, silver Hyundais and Kias crawled slowly to their destinations. Damien tried to identify the roof of his flat, then picked out all the places he knew in the city: Hongdae, where the site of the new park was still a dirty brown hole gouged out of the packed pattern of shops and offices; Namsan, stubbled with leafless trees and bristling with MoPho towers; the river, a ribbon of battleship grey. Beyond the water lay Apkuchong, Chamshil, the mountains in the South he'd meant to get to but never had. There was supposed to be a good art gallery down there. Oh well, never mind.

He looked down at the turtles. They were clustered together on the gravel slopes of a shallow pool at the bottom of the tank. Up close, they were a spooky sight, their shells and wrinkled skin weird shades of stained ivory and streaky vanilla. One of them stretched out its neck and peered up at him. It resembled a wise old monk. Or a dried gob of paint.

'They're cloned albino snapping turtles.'

He jumped. Da Mi was standing at his shoulder. 'But they won't bite.' She smiled, displaying a row of too-perfect teeth. 'Look.' She reached into the tank and scratched a turtle's head. It stretched out its neck and she tickled its chin.

'Are they on drugs?'

'Not at all. As blastocyst embryos they were steeped in the stem cells of a particularly timid species of mouse, giving their brains a serotonin receptor that inhibits aggressive behaviour. Now they make perfect pets. White animals are an ancient Korean symbol of good luck and prosperity. They're selling very well.'

'So they're not natural blondes?'

'If cloning for colour is unnatural, Damien, then so is using henna hair dye or marrying someone you think would be a good parent. People have always altered and engineered their physical appearance, and they've always practised selective breeding. We are temporal beings, and it's human nature to want to help shape the future.'

He felt the urge to needle her. 'Control other people's futures, you mean?"

She raised her eyebrows. 'Do you feel as though you're being controlled right now?'

She'd obviously done Psych 101. Feeling caught out, he muttered, 'I didn't think I had much of a choice, no.'

'But your options were the result of your own actions, no? We create our own futures, surely. And whatever decisions you've made in the past, you haven't ended up in a bad spot.'

Was he imagining it, or had she undone a button on her blouse? Hating that his eye had even flicked beneath her chin, he resolutely met her droll gaze. Somehow the amusement he'd detected in her demeanour when he entered seemed less guarded now – well, of course, she'd got what she wanted and now she could afford to toy with him outright. But if she was loosening up, might she give a trade secret away?

'Cloning human beings, though?' he pressed, ignoring her personal remarks. 'Wouldn't that be taking Confucian conformity a step too far?'

Christ. Had *he* gone too far, given Sydney's game away? If he had, Da Mi gave no sign of it. 'Clones – identical twins – Koreans,' she said, smoothly. 'Every human being is unique, Damien, no matter what they look like or what culture they belong to. But have you ever wondered what the world would be like if physical appearance were truly irrelevant? What that would teach us about sharing, fair play, the true meaning of love?'

Damien felt his testy need to challenge her inaudibly escape him, like a slow leak out of a tyre. Let this woman have her freaky ideas; he had his own, involving asteroids and floods and getting the hell out of this country.

'I guess that'll be your next project, then,' he said. 'Look, Dr Kim, I've got stuff to do. If my donation's okay, could we settle up?'

'Of course.' She turned back to the desk and he followed, his feet sinking into the plush ivory carpet. Was it his imagination, or was she weaving a little? She steadied herself with a hand on the desk, unlocked a drawer and withdrew a bulging white envelope.

'You'll want to count it. Come, let's sit down.' She took her seat and gestured at the other flexi-chair. Reluctantly he lowered himself

381

into it again. 'Do have some honey drink,' she urged. 'It will help replenish your amino acids.'

He squirmed as the seat re-embraced him. 'I'm fine, thanks, honestly.'

'As you wish.' She offered him the envelope, her right hand ceremoniously tucked under her left elbow. He pulled the bills out and counted them as she sipped her drink. Two hundred American one-hundred-dollar bills.

'*Kamsahamnida*. That'll go a long way. As will I.' He stuffed the envelope in his jacket pocket. 'Spunk money' didn't have a great ring to it, but it was cash, and a lot of it.

Da Mi opened her own jacket. 'And here's your passport. It expires in a month, but I expect you know that.'

She *had* unbuttoned her blouse. He could see an expanse of faun brown skin and the black lacy crest of her bra. 'Thanks,' he muttered, slipping the document in the back pocket of his jeans. She leaned back in her chair, the folds of her blouse exposing half an inch more of her bra.

'Are you sure you won't have some honey drink? I made it extra strong today.'

This was too much. 'Cheers, Da Mi, but I ought to be going.'

Da Mi liberated a flake of mascara from an eyelash. That dreamy smile on her face, Christ, she looked almost stoned. 'Of course. But please – before you go, I want to give you a present.' She took a small box out of her pocket and passed it to him. Inside was a jade ring, its comma shape a bit like Sydney's watch.

'The Chinese say that jade stones are drops of dried semen from the celestial dragon. This is for you, from GRIP, with our thanks. Goodbye, Damien, and good luck.'

He stuffed the box into his pocket. 'Thanks, Dr Kim. You too.'

She lolled back in her chair, regarding him indulgently. He cast one more look at the turtles, baleful in their glass enclosure, and exited the office with as much dignity as he could muster. In the lobby, he tossed the ring in the rubbish bin. Then he strode out of the building as fast as he could and broke into a cantering run.

Part Six

ROYAL JELLY

39 | Getaway Plans

At last Damien was back. Sydney buzzed him up and waited impatiently on the landing. As soon as he got off the elevator she grabbed him for a hug, but he was stiff and remote in her arms.

'Are you okay? How did it go?' Nervously, she pulled him into her apartment.

His face was pinched, as if he had a headache. For a minute she thought he was going to say he'd backed out. But he took a chunky envelope out of his jacket pocket and slapped it down on the table.

'I got this. But I don't feel good about it, Sydney.' He flopped down on the sofa and rubbed his face in his hands.

'You must be exhausted. I'll make you a honey drink. It'll make you feel—'

'God, no,' he groaned. 'I'll have a tea, please – with milk. Here, I picked some up at the market.' He pulled a package of Red Rose out of his jacket pocket, passed it to her and sat silently as she boiled the kettle. She made the tea; he took it without saying thanks, blew on it and slurped.

She eyed the envelope. It was stuffed with money. Why wasn't he happy? 'Look,' she said, crossing the room to her wardrobe. She took out her own two special envelopes: one marked 'won', the other 'dollars'. Squeezing beside him on the sofa, she showed him their heft. 'How much do you think we have between us?'

He didn't look that interested. 'Enough not to work for a year, maybe two.'

He didn't get it. She put the envelopes down and stroked his arm. 'Maybe if we play our cards right, we'll have enough not to work for the rest of our lives.'

'Yeah? If I donate my liver? Or how about my left leg?'

She ignored that, let him take another swig of tea. 'No,' she said, patiently, 'of course not. But if you want a cut of the VirtuWorld profits, I could ask Da Mi – not now, but later, when the park's making loads of money. I could tell her we're still friends and I think we should pay you some royalties. Who knows, maybe you could play a part in the Banquets, be the King's younger brother, maybe.'

'Christ, Sydney,' Damien said irritably, 'you're up to your neck in confidentiality agreements. Don't blow all that for me. I told you, I'm not interested in being some corporate mascot.'

She folded her arms, shifted away from him. 'I'm just trying to help,' she grumped.

He sighed, then he reached over and pulled her close. 'I know. I'm sorry.'

His breath was warm on her neck. 'Okay,' she pouted as he stroked her back. 'But you don't have to be mean. I just don't get why you're not excited.'

'I've got a lot on my mind, that's all. I have to be out of Korea by Friday, so I should get to a travel agent's today, check out my options. Plus I need to sort a few things out with Jake and Sam.' He straightened up, fishing for his MoPho in his pocket.

Sydney leaned back against a cushion. 'Why don't you just book online?'

He was inputting the number. 'The travel agents have way better deals.' He put the MoPho to his ear and left a message: 'Hey, Jake, it's half-two. Rise and shine. I got good news. Call me.'

His sharp profile cut the air as if slicing out a hole through which he might vanish. Watching him slip the MoPho back in his jeans, panic seized her. 'Do you still want to go on holiday?'

'We should do more than that.' Damien pushed her into the corner of the sofa and kissed her throat. The envelopes of money crinkled beneath them.

'Like what?' Wrapping her arms around him, she breathed in the scent of his hair: hemp seed and liquorice, that Dutch shampoo all the foreign guys were buying this year.

Damien sat up, his hands on her knees. 'Like head out to Canada together – right away. We could buy a car, do a road trip in BC, do Christmas in Jasper or Banff. In the New Year we could check out the prairies – I heard Winnipeg's happening right now.'

'You want me to go to *Winnipeg* with you?' She was utterly baffled. 'Winnipeg's fucking *freezing* right now. And I've promised Da Mi—'

'Sydney,' he cut her off, 'I know I've sold my soul to her, but your precious Da Mi makes my blood run cold.'

She opened her mouth, but Damien raised his voice. 'Let's talk about VirtuWorld for a minute. What's it really all about, huh? Cookie-cutter people, designer babies for whoever can afford them? What's going to happen to the rest of us plebs?'

Sydney wriggled up straight. 'Damien! I *know* Da Mi. She wants to help society evolve. She's been so good to me; you wouldn't believe it.'

'She's a *witch*, Sydney. I'm positive she organised my arrest. And I don't know what's in that drink of hers, but she was knocking it back in that office like there was no tomorrow, and acting pretty strange, like she wanted to fuck me or something.'

'*Da Mi?* Wanted to *fuck* you? Are you crazy?'

'I'm telling you, it was like she was on drugs!'

'Da Mi is a *doctor*. That drink calms you *down*,' Sydney shouted. '*You* should have had some; then you wouldn't be acting like this.'

'Wake up, Sydney: she's a power-junkie. She's nice to you because you're her star exhibit! And just think about it for a minute: even if this theme park malarky turns out to be the genetic wonderland she claims it is, aren't *you* going to get sick of playing the same tired role year in year out, being ogled like an animal in the zoo?'

Sydney scrambled to her feet. 'Fuck off, Damien! I let you in on this so I could help you be part of something successful for a change, not so you could insult my friend and trash what I'm doing with my life!'

They glared at each other. Then Damien sighed and reached for her waist. 'Sydney, I don't give a rat's arse about success. I just want to spend time with *you*, not some VirtuWorld mannequin.'

She said nothing, but she didn't push him away.

'Come on.' He hugged her closer. 'Let's take off – give it a go. I've always fancied going to Canada, and you can show me around. We'd get on, you know we would.'

'I can't. I'd feel really bad about letting her down.' She spoke into his neck, her breasts squashed against his chest. He rubbed her back.

'She'll find someone else to do the banquets. Or you can visit; that'd be okay.'

Shaking her head, Sydney eased herself out his arms and sat back down on the sofa. It wasn't nearly as simple as he thought. 'She's like a mother to me,' she pleaded.

'So fly the nest.'

Sydney buried her head in her hands. 'Damien, I can't just up and leave. I've got the apartment and my modelling to think about. And Da Mi wants me to meet the surrogate mothers in December.' The envelope full of her saved *won* was beside her. She took out a handful of bills and thrust them at him. 'Let's take a little holiday in Asia –

on a beach somewhere. Or we can go shopping in Shanghai; I don't care where, just somewhere fun. Okay?'

He sat down beside her and put the money on the coffee table. Then he placed his fingers on her wrist and lightly tapped her Gotcha.

'She told me jade was made from the spunk of the cosmic dragon. Did you know that?'

Sydney laughed. 'Oh, Da Mi – she's great! See?'

Damien stroked her hand, slowly, as if he was trying to memorise it with his. 'Look,' he said, at last, 'I've been planning to get to Winnipeg for Christmas for ages. Jake's got a friend there who might be able to get me a job in film. And I'd like to see snow. How about we go to Tokyo for a few days, and if we have a good time, will you promise to at least *think* about coming with me to Canada?'

She jutted out her chin. 'If *you* promise not to hassle me the whole time!'

'I'm not trying to hassle you.' He paused. His eyes were almost stricken, as if he was afraid she was going to bite him, or laugh in his face. 'It's just – you remind me of someone who needed me once, when I wasn't around. I know it sounds stupid, but I have a feeling maybe I'm supposed to help you instead.'

She didn't need anyone's help any more. But still, it was a sweet offer. She stuck out her little finger. 'So you won't bug me or insult Da Mi, and I'll come to Tokyo and think about showing you round Canada. Pinkie-promise?'

He crooked her finger with his own. 'Pirate twins.' They squeezed each other's fingers, a deathless vow that soon became an arm wrestling match. Finally Damien let her slam his hand down into a cushion.

'I win!' she crowed, then screamed as he flung himself on top of her. He reached up under her shirt to tickle her, and somehow ended up playing with her breasts. Her face was flushed; her tummy felt

391

creamy and warm. As her left nipple hardened in his fingers she opened her legs and wrapped them around his waist. He pressed his groin against her. Something hard vibrated against her thigh.

Damien lifted off her. 'Sorry, Sydney – that might be Jake.' One hand still on Sydney's breast, Damien fumbled for his MoPho, checked the screen, and pressed it to his ear. 'Hey, Jake – did you get my message?'

'Your message? No – fucking MoPhos.' A note of panic rose in Jake's voice. 'Day, I've been calling you all morning – tell me you're not at Immigration yet?'

Damien smiled down at Sydney, who was fingering her other nipple and casting him a teasing, sex kitteny look. 'No, I'm not at Immigration.'

'Fantastic!' Jake's usual confidence snapped back. 'You gotta meet me right away. There's a guy here, sofa-surfer just got himself a university job, wants to take your flat. He's shown me the cash, Sam phoned your landlord: all this guy needs is the keys!'

No shit? So he'd sold his soul for no reason except to avoid owing Jake and Sam half a month's wages. For a moment, Damien felt sick all over. He rolled off Sydney and sat up, rubbing his temples. She pulled her shirt down, looking up at him in concern.

Oh fuck it – what was done was done. Now he'd have even more money to play with. He patted her knee. *Two minutes*, he signed, followed by a thumbs-up.

'Hey Jake, that's great.'

'Plus, he's gonna give you an extra three hundred grand for all your furniture – you still got all that stuff I left, right? Wardrobe, coffee maker, bed-mat?'

'Sure.'

'Excellentro. So if you come down here, we can take him up to the flat, then Sam and him can deal with the landlord and you and I can go down to Itaewon.'

Itaewon? Oh yeah, the passport and SIN card – Christ, it was all happening so fast.

'Yeah, that sounds good.' He could go to the travel agent's while he was running around too.

'Just hurry up, will you? This guy's waiting with his money and I don't want him to change his mind.'

'No worries, I'll be right there.'

He hung up. 'Sorry, Sydney, gotta go. Jake found a tenant for my flat. Can I stay the night here again if it goes through?'

Sydney stretched her legs over his knees and wriggled her toes. 'Oh, I *suppose*.'

Jake was wearing a Burberry trench coat and carrying a briefcase; his dreads were tied up with a velvet ribbon and tucked under a trilby. Damien watched him check his teeth in the mirror behind the bar, and exchanged an amused look with Sam and the prospective new tenant, a beanpole American called Darren. Darren had uncombed ginger hair and was wearing a fringed sheepskin jacket; just a kid from the boonies, but he seemed nice enough. He was drinking a beer, but Damien refused his offer of a drink: the clock was ticking. Jake locked up and they all crammed in a taxi to Tae Hung Dong.

'Wow, great view, dude.' Darren whistled as they reached the top of the stairs.

'Penthouse suite, what did I say?' Jake crowed. 'The sunsets are amazing. All you need's a bit of weed and that's your night-life sorted out, right, Day?'

'Jake, what I always tell you?' Sam broke in. 'Don't oversell. Let buyer make up own mind.'

They all laughed. Damien led the way to the flat and unlocked the front door. Inside, the flat was cold and dusty and there were unwashed dishes in the sink, but Darren didn't seem to care. He inspected the kitchen galley with a single swoop of his big head, stuck his nose in the bathroom and then strode into the middle of the living room.

'You can get internet here?'

'No problem.'

'Hot diggety! And no neighbours! You got yourself a deal.' He reached into his pocket and took out an envelope. 'Here's the key-money.' He looked confused. 'Should I give it to you now, or after I see the landlord?'

Damien glanced at Jake. 'I gotta get down to Itaewon. How about we swap now? I give you the keys and you go with Sam to Mr Han's?'

He and Darren made the trade. Damien stuffed the envelope in his inside jacket pocket, where it nestled beside the other two, practically a bullet-proof vest. 'I'll just clean up a bit,' he said. 'I'll be gone by the time you get back.'

Darren twirled the key ring round on his forefinger. 'Hey, no rush, dude.'

Sam checked his watch. 'You want use bathroom, Darren? We gonna sit cross-legged for half-hour, maybe more.'

'Really?' Darren's eyes widened. 'Okay. Good plan.' He tipped an imaginary cowboy hat at Damien and ducked into the toilet.

'Sam – thanks a million, mate,' Damien said. 'I'll see you later, right? Back at Azitoo?'

Sam slapped him lightly on the shoulder and headed out to the roof.

'You want me take this garbage down?' he asked at the door, pointing at Damien's hidey-hole binbag.

'No!' Damien barrelled down the hall.

Jake and Sam cackled as he tore open the bag and pulled out his rucksack. Then Sam headed out onto the roof and Jake stepped into the kitchen galley and rolled up his sleeves.

'You sort the studio out, Day; I'll do these dishes,' he said, turning the water on. 'You better collect your utility bills too, so you can call later and cancel your accounts.'

'Good point.' Back in the studio, Damien found his admin file folder and shoved it in his rucksack. He waited for Darren to leave the flat, then he rummaged around in the bundle of boxers and shirts. Yes, the five white envelopes of money were still stashed there: fifteen million won. He took them out, and from his jacket pocket added five hundred thousand of the key-money to his savings. Then he grabbed an elastic band from his desk drawer, and secured the five envelopes together. That, plus the deposit he'd already paid, made exactly enough for the passport and SIN card, less Jake and Sam's commission.

The commission. He couldn't head off to Canada owing his mates, not when he had gallons of spunk bucks in his jacket pocket. If he gave them the money now, though, he would have to explain how he got it. Maybe they should just keep his *hagwon* wages. That would be an extra five hundred thousand, but they deserved it. He could email Jake from Tokyo, say that his mum had coughed up at last. Yeah, that'd do it.

That little quisling Young Ha had given him some Korean notecards for Teacher's Day. He chose one with a photo of a ceramic flask of *soju* and two small cups and scrawled 'Skunk Buddy, Samba Sam, THANK YOU' inside. Beneath his signature he jotted down the *hagwon* address and the name of the secretary. Then he sealed the envelope and stuck it in his bag.

What else? He dug back into the wardrobe, found the long woollen scarf his mum had made for him once upon a time. It would be cold in Canada. He wrapped the scarf round his neck and was slinging the rucksack over his shoulder when Jake came back into the room with a broom.

'Kitchen's spick and span. Do you want me to give the floor in here a once-over too?'

'Christ, Jake, don't overdo it.'

'Your call, Day, your call.'

Damien held out the bundle of envelopes. 'This is the money for your guy in Itaewon.'

'Nice one, Day.' Jake raised his palm for a high-five, then clicked his briefcase open and tucked the money inside. 'Now, let's blow this ginseng popsicle stand and get this wacky little show on the road.'

They took a taxi into Itaewon and got out in front of Burger King. A Western woman was sitting in the window, stuffing her face with fries which were haemorrhaging ketchup down her arm.

'Give me half an hour.' Jake nodded at an alleyway. 'This guy's like your landlord: there'll be *nokcha* and cookies involved. If you want to sort out your flights, the travel agent across the road does the best deals in the city.'

Damien realised he was starving. 'Great. I'll meet you in Burger King.'

Jake tipped his trilby and strode off. Damien squeezed his way across a honking, bumper-to-bumper jam and took the stairs to the travel agents two at a time. It was all happening. Next stop: Tokyo with Sydney. They could check out the temples and bars, eat sushi. And once they were out in the big wide world, it would be much easier to persuade her that she didn't need Da Mi.

The travel agent was a small, boyish woman with fingers that rippled across her keyboard like a concert pianist's. She raced through eight different airlines to get him the best price possible to Tokyo: one return, one single. 'You leave tomorrow, very cheap,' she told him.

Tomorrow? Yeah, why not.

'Your flight eight a.m. Last minute always superdeal. Your name?'

'David Harding,' he remembered, just in time. 'And Sydney Travers.'

As the booking reference number printed, Damien sent Sydney a quick text:

Tokyo tomorrow a.m. My treat. Starting with dinner out 2nite. Saying gdby to m8s now. CU 7 ish. Dx

He paid for the flights out of the key-money envelope. He'd change some dollars to yen tomorrow at the airport. Sticking the printout in his pocket with the cash, he bounded down the stairs and back to Burger King.

The food was hot, greasy and North American; just what the doctor ordered. He was just washing the last mouthful down with his Coke when Jake sauntered into the joint.

'David, buddy.' Jake straddled a chair and swung his briefcase on to the next seat.

'You got them?' Damien half-rose from his seat.

Jake winked. 'Shh. Strict rules against flaunting the merchandise on home turf. Finish up and we'll head back to Azitoo.'

Damien drained the rest of his Coke. A taxi ride later, he was admiring his new identity as Sam popped open a bottle of champagne.

The SIN card was clean, shiny and functional, a piece of wallet-sized ID stamped with a nine-digit number that was his key to employment in Canada. The passport, though, that was alluring, aura-charged, a thing of beauty. It was slim and bendy, with a black and gold cover. Inside, the pages were a subtle whirl of colour, empty except for a Korean entry stamp. Best of all, right at the beginning, from behind a matte plastic film, a bloke called David Harding one year and three months younger than Damien, but just as handsome, gave him a wry look. *There's more to some Canadians than meets the eye*, he was undoubtedly saying.

'Fucking fantastic.' Jake slapped him on the back. 'Even looks like you.'

'I told our guy to ask hacker to look for a David,' Sam said, setting the three flutes down on the bar. 'So when we visit Canada, we can still call you Day.'

'Here's to the best mates I ever had.' Damien raised his glass. They downed their Supernovas in one.

Jake sucked the bubbles from his upper lip. 'So now you just need to check into a *yogwan*, watch TV for a few days. Friday we'll go to the *hagwon* for you, then you're set.'

Time to break the news. 'Actually,' Damien said, pulling the note-card out of his rucksack and laying it on the bar, 'this is the *hagwon* number here. I'm following your suggestion, going to Tokyo tomorrow. It'll be safer there, like you said.'

Sam nodded, and stuck the card in the till. Jake, though, raised his eyebrows. 'Tomorrow? Oh.' He tapped out a cigarette on the bar. 'So you want us to wire you the money?'

What wouldn't these guys do for him? At last he could repay them, just a little. 'No,' Damien said, 'you keep it. It's your commission, plus a thank-you.'

'Keep it? But you're going to need that for Canada.'

'No, I'm good; someone else lent me the money.'

'Really? You hear that, Sam? We're all square with Damien, then some. Buddy, that's great news. So who stumped up the cash?'

Now his face was burning. But he couldn't not tell them about Sydney either. 'That model, you know, the blonde at Gongjang? She's coming to Tokyo with me, in fact. She might come out to Canada later as well.'

Jake chuckled appreciatively. 'Well, well. Dames the dark *stallion*, eh?'

'Too many girls in Azitoo ask me, who that guy?' Sam shook his head as Jake lit his cigarette. 'Too many broken heart when I tell them you go.'

Damien checked his watch. It was half-past six.

'Speaking of going, chaps, I'm taking her out for dinner. This next round is on me, but then I'm going to have to say *Anyong*.'

'Ah, shit, Day, invite her down here. The Mama Golds will sere-nade you – impress the hell out of her!'

'Day in love now, Jake,' Sam reprimanded his cousin. 'Need privacy; very special thing.'

Another round of cocktails and two mighty bear-hugs later, Damien was out in the alley, grabbing a cab. Night had fallen while he was underground and Hongdae was coming into its full neon romance. He already had a million vids of Seoul-in-motion on his MoPho, so he just sat back and let it all float through him: the streaky lights and veering, sloshed Korean students, the red-and-orange roadworks signs, the glowing tableaux of mannequins in shop windows: they were all part of him now, always would be, like a dream of flying, or the colour of his eyes.

All Jake's morning texts arrived as he got out of the cab, and one from Sydney.

J Gr8 abt Japan! I gotta meet Da Mi. C U my place @ 8. x S x

Damn. It was only five past seven. Why couldn't she have let him know earlier? He checked the SMS details. She'd sent it at six, while he was underground in Azitoo.

There was no point going back to Shinchon. He could head to Skoda for a coffee, or go and browse CDs. He was strolling down the boulevard that led to Gongjang when he realised he could see Sydney in the distance. There was no mistaking that blonde head of hair, the blue vest. He was too far away to call, but he sped up his pace; just as she was within earshot, however, she ducked into a building. Confused, he slowed down.

The double doors she had entered opened onto just another grey marble lobby of just another nondescript Korean building. He stood on the step, frowning.

It was cold outside, but not enough to explain why he suddenly felt chilled to the core. Why had Sydney gone into this building? Did Da Mi have an office in Hongdae?

He wrapped his scarf around his neck. Maybe he should just take Sydney at her word, hang out in City Records. But no, if she wasn't seeing Da Mi, what was she doing – and why had she lied about it?

The blunt corners of the envelopes in his pocket jabbed his armpit through the lining of his jacket. *Detach, man*, he told himself sternly. *You've just got together with her, for fuck's sake.* If she came along to Tokyo, he'd know she was interested in him for something more than his class-A bodily fluids.

But waiting to see if she got on the plane was as pathetic as standing on this step, shifting his weight from one leg to the other. Taking a short holiday was no proof that he could trust her. Maybe Da Mi *did* have an office in this building. Maybe right now the two women were thinking up new ways to make a complete and utter fool of him. For Chrissakes – what would Doctor Who do? Bracing himself, Damien entered the building.

The door on the first-floor landing was locked. He kept ascending, as quietly as he could. The second floor was more promising, with a door that opened onto a long corridor. He poked his head through. Canvases were stacked against the wall and thin slits of artificial light fell at angles across the hall from a couple of doors left ajar. Damien trod lightly, his heart rapping against his chest, his nose twitching at the harsh smell of turps. The rooms must be painting studios. Hongdae had a good reputation for fine arts.

He could hear voices now, from behind the far door. He inched along the wall. The centre of the door was a strip of glass. Cautiously he peeked through the window into the room. There, at the far end of a long studio, Sydney and a Korean man were standing in front of a massive painting. He couldn't make out exactly what they were saying, but they were obviously having some kind of intense conversation. Sydney's vest was hanging on the back of a chair and the man's bare arm was practically rubbing hers. It was the Gongjang painter, wasn't it? The bloke who ogled all the foreign girls on the dance floor.

Shit. *What the hell was he doing?* He should knock; let them know he was here. Or just leave.

But he did neither.

'What you think?' Jae Ho gestured to the painting.

A small oil-filled radiator was warming Sydney's legs, and whether because of the chill in the air, or how close Jae Ho was standing to her, the hairs on her arms were standing on end. She wished she was still wearing her vest, but he'd said he didn't like GrilleTex™ clothes; that people couldn't look at his art properly if they were too comfortable, or thinking about changing the temperature. So she'd let him slip it off her shoulders and drape it over a chair. She did feel more alert, perhaps, but wary too. She hadn't planned to be undressed by him the instant she walked in.

'It's pretty big,' she said, playing for time.

'*Ye Ye.* You look. I shut up,' Jae Ho gallantly announced.

The massive canvas did need some time to take in. About nine feet high, it depicted the dingy chamber of a subway station. A station clock read 23:21. The last train was disappearing down the tunnel and vomit spilled over the edge of the platform onto the tracks. The whole thing looked like a cave, not least because a man in a black suit was hanging upside-down from the ceiling. On closer inspection, he proved to be a self-portrait of Jae Ho – looking, Sydney thought meanly, a good few years younger than he was. Beneath him on the platform stood a trendy Korean girl. Her eyes cold sapphires, her face twisted in irritation, she was pulling a MoPho out of her bag.

Behind the girl, a one-armed man in a faded green suit sat on a bench, masturbating. The tip of his penis was like a pink mushroom in his hand. Beside him an old woman, a huddled heap on the floor, was gathering unsold heads of garlic from a faded cloth and stuffing them back into her bag. Red light from the drinks machine blazed over her face.

Sydney's portrait was the only other spurt of colour in the painting: a peeling hot pink advertisement on the wall opposite the platform. Like the background of the painting at the Golden Piglet, the image was an impression of the traces of her motion. But here Jae Ho had taken her jutting gestures, her long hair and open mouth, and stretched them like ripped stockings over a dancing skeleton. At the centre of the portrait, a black perfume bottle in the shape of a heart sent shock waves rippling through the poster. The word 'NOW' was scrawled in gold across the bottle.

The longer Sydney stood in front of the painting, the less she knew what to think or to feel. The detail was fantastic, and the Korean faces so spooky, it was like a scene from a graphic novel, ready to burst into action. But why had he put *her* portrait in this horrible, seedy environment? Why had he given her a black heart? And why was he standing so close his arm was sending a river of heat up hers?

402

She had to say something. 'It's Chungmuro Station, right? On the orange line?'

'Is not subway station.' Jae Ho raised his index figure. 'Is Korea today: is stagnation machine, block drain system, pollution. Is bad air. But opposite also true, always true. Everything good and bad. This girl, she punky Missy generation. She have many choices like never before. Maybe she waiting to choose, waiting longer than her mother. Now she angry she miss train, she calling friend. Is Korean way. This man, he not wanted, he goblin man, but he make own joy. Is also way of Korean people. We crippled, we out-date, we have crazy business, but we do what we always want.'

Sydney laughed, but inside she felt a little sick. His English had improved so much – did he have a new foreign girlfriend? Were there any pictures of *her* in the studio?

She checked herself. This wasn't supposed to be happening. She was supposed to be so *over* Jae Ho. She was supposed to be bragging about her new boyfriend, her trip to Japan. She opened her mouth to let him know she couldn't care less about his wife, his paintings, his endless theories about Korea, but he was already talking again.

'I so glad you here, Sy-duh-nee,' he said. 'I want ask you about this painting. Why *you* think I upside down?'

He could always do that, she remembered: draw her in, make her feel valued. And she *did* have things to say. Soon she was going to be attending art openings all the time. She tossed her head. 'Because you're spying on them?'

'Spying?' He put his arm around her, resting his hand lightly on her shoulder. The smell of his skin, his breath, invaded her nostrils. She hadn't realised until this moment how much she missed his smell. '*Ye, ye,*' he praised her. 'Is artist job, to spy. Every artist redraw the map. I not *kitsch* artist.' He stressed the word as if he was proud of knowing it, and dropped his arm, trailing his fingers down her back. She should step away, she knew. But she didn't.

'Kitsch art is toy soldiers.' Jae Ho snorted dismissively. 'My art *real* army.' He gestured at the other canvases arranged around the room and she followed his gaze nervously, but she couldn't see any other pictures of foreign women. Instead, the room was full of grey battle-fields, paintings that could have been made with the sludge from subway walls. Why was everything he painted so ugly, so depressing, so gross?

'If I art make from mass produce,' Jae Ho thundered on, 'I choose pink rubber glove, glove army of Korean woman use to clean subway station. Power of my art is energy of Korean people. Not afraid to say what wrong. Not afraid of touch other people. We not like Japan.'

He slipped his arm around her waist and squeezed her to his side. She felt an overwhelming urge to throw her arms around him, to complete the embrace. It didn't matter who else he fucked, or she fucked, there was something special between them, a sizzling current that recharged them both.

But she hadn't come here for that. She'd come here to prove she could hold her own with him. With anyone. She'd spent hours in the Chair working on her self-esteem, affirming her right to be loved by someone who truly cared for her. That person wasn't Jae Ho.

His hand was straying down towards her jeans. She interlaced her fingers with his, and pulled them back up to her waist, where she placed her other hand on top of the knot. That was okay, wasn't it? They could talk like this. 'Jae Ho,' she challenged, 'you sound so proud of Korea, but most of your paintings are dark and gloomy. This one looks like a grave.' She jutted her chin at the subway station canvas, thinking she was scoring a point, but he just nodded vigor-ously and tightened his grip on her waist.

'You very smart girl, Sydney. Is grave, and is womb: old-time Korean graves always shape of woman's place, for rebirth. My painting is mass grave, for rebirth of everyone. This painting called *Cave of Tang Gun*.'

An image of him eating noodles in the nude, telling her Korean myths, sidled into her mind.

'The *halmoni* selling the garlic,' she asked, 'is she the bear? The first woman in Korea?'

Now he turned and placed his other hand on her belly. 'You remember good, Sy-duh-nee,' he said approvingly. '*Halmoni* is old-style Korea. She very old, very wise. She sitting well. I don't know who buy her garlic; I don't know who is new child of bear. I not god, only spy.'

He was rubbing her belly now. Round and round, in little circles.

She was going to Tokyo with Damien tomorrow. She was *meeting* Damien in half an hour. New energy was coming into her life. *I let go of people who belong to my past.* She should let go of Jae Ho's hand on her hip. She should remove his other hand from her stomach.

But Damien was going to live in Canada. And Jae Ho's hands felt nice. So very nice.

'Sy-duh-nee.' Jae Ho placed his free hand on her breast and, through the skimpy bra, rubbed at her nipple with his palm.

She closed her eyes and leaned limply against his side. Did she have to stop this? Why?

'You, your poster,' he whispered, massaging her breast, 'is tiger. Is tiger eating Korean economy, Korean identity. Is feeling of not wanting smell like garlic; is blue eyes on Korean girls, but also is foreign energy that inspire Korea, make Korea stronger. Like you inspire me.'

His groin was pressing into her hip. He reached into her top and gave her breast a final rough squeeze – *this is mine*, his hand said – then dropped his fingers to the waistband of her jeans. All she had to do was turn to him and he would kiss her, would slip his hand deep down into her panties, where she was already moist and pulsing for him. *Why not?* She hadn't promised Damien anything.

'I remember you secret place, Sydney.' Jae Ho's voice was hoarse now. 'You secret place very beautiful. I want touch it again.'

Her secret place.

I choose my secrets wisely.

She was in her body, in Jae Ho's arms; but at the same time she wasn't. It was like escaping from a wrestling hold, like that trick Annie had taught her: lift your arms, bend your knees, drop down to the ground – and on the way slam the guy's nuts with your elbow. But instead of dropping down, she flew up: as if a whole layer of her skin suddenly peeled invisibly away, and whooshed like a balloon to the high ceiling of the studio. *What are you doing?* it hissed down at her. *Take another look at that painting – is that who you are? Is that where you belong?*

She was exposed. Frozen cold. Shivering with shame, but also starkly aware. She couldn't hide from herself any more. Jae Ho was married. He had a kid. What they had wasn't 'special'. It was a toxic little secret. If she let him, he would just paint her into a corner, break her tar and glass heart all over again.

'I want you, supergirl.' His hand slipped beneath her waistband, found her panties. 'I miss you too much.'

The words were aimed point-blank at her, but they landed a million miles away, in the heart of some other girl, a girl in an orange dress maybe, or a yellow one, or a pink halter-top. Sydney's heart was soaring up, out of Jae Ho's grip, up to the ceiling and into the magical stream of light she remembered from all her sessions in the Chair. That was where she belonged: in a moving, flowing, ever-changing, ever-loving story. Not trapped in Jae Ho's canvas, his grubby, grasping, sunless memories of her.

With a sensation of immense relief, she wrapped her free hand around his wrist to pull his hand away, and opened her mouth to say 'no'.

Sydney was letting this bloke crawl all over her, and now he was sticking his hand down her jeans. Damien had seen enough. All the slack he'd cut for Sydney snapped back like elastic. Part of him wanted to barge into the room, to rant and rave, to shake an explanation out of her, but what the fuck was the point of that? No. *Get out while you still can.*

He whirled round, and banged straight into a huge canvas. It skidded forward, knocking a tall ceramic statue off its pedestal. The statue smashed into smithereens on the tiled floor, making a racket like resounding applause, and the canvas toppled in front of him, blocking his path. He fought it aside, sending a stack of smaller paintings clattering and slithering down the hall. Scrambling past the first canvas at last, he heard the studio door open behind him.

'*Damien!*' Sydney cried.

40 | Han Gang

Damien kicked a small square urban landscape ahead of him, sending it skittering in the direction of the stairwell. Behind him, Sydney launched herself down the hallway. Several canvases had collected in a heap at the end of the hallway and he had to fling them aside to get to the door, losing precious moments. Her heels clicked rapidly closer, then there was a long ripping sound, and a sharp '*Aigo!*' from the painter. 'Wait,' Sydney gulped, grasping at his elbow, her breath hot on his neck.

He swivelled round to glare at her. Over her shoulder, he could see the painter dragging a torn canvas into the studio. He gave Damien a little salute and smartly closed the door.

'It's not how it looked,' Sydney wheedled. 'Please, listen—'

'You said you were going to visit Da Mi! I've heard enough bull-shit to last a lifetime, Sydney.' He tried to pull away, but she gripped his arm tighter.

'You don't *understand*.'

'What's not to understand? You're running a sperm collection agency for a psycho dominatrix, you're shagging some sleazy geezer – fine, but just leave me alone from now on. I'm done with you and your bloody string of *lies*.'

'I am *not* shagging him!' Sydney wailed. 'I was telling him to *stop*.'

'Yeah, that's *exactly* what it looked like you were doing! Just let go of me, all right? Let *go!*' Still trying to prise her hand from his arm, he dragged himself through the doorway and back into the stair-well.

But she clutched at him desperately, then grabbed at his waist. They were leaning over the banister, panting and grappling, when he heard the door to the corridor shut behind them.

He twisted round to tell the painter to fuck off, but someone else, a man, not tall but broadly built, shoved him back against the railing. Something hard pressed into the base of Damien's skull. Suddenly he felt a burning desire to piss.

'Keep nice and quiet, buddy,' the man growled in his ear.

An American, Damien realised dimly as he clenched his bladder muscles. There was a metal clunk; a sound from a movie. He stared unseeing at the grey wall beyond the banister, his heart pumping like an oil-drill. Part of him felt like throwing up; part of him wanted to burst into laughter: a gunman, right. What else did she have up her sleeve?

'Johnny?' Sydney squeaked. She was frozen beside him.

He wasn't surprised she knew the guy. Under different circum-stances, Damien would have shot her a sarcastic look.

'So, you remember me, do you?' The man, Johnny, jammed the gun under Damien's armpit. Then he grabbed Sydney and pulled her in front of Damien so the muzzle was pressing into her back 'Impressive. Now, if you don't want Hugh Grant here to get instantly forgettable, you'll both come with me.'

He clamped his free arm onto Sydney's shoulder and prodded the pair of them down the stairs. Damien, wedged between the gunman and the trembling girl, registered the vanilla scent of Sydney's hair, Johnny's leathery musk, and the fact that a boner the size of a beer bottle was lodged against his arse.

A white Sonata was waiting for them in the dark alley, engine running, headlamps off. Johnny reached in front of Sydney and opened the back door. Yanking her to the side, he shoved Damien in first, jabbing the gun hard against his spine. Then he jostled Sydney into the middle of the backseat, got in beside her and slammed the door shut.

The car stank of stale sweat and hamburger. The back of Damien's skull ached, but he didn't dare lift his hand to rub it. He took a sidelong glance at the gun now investigating Sydney's ribs. It was big and black, with a groove along the barrel.

'They're child-proof locks, Hughie,' the man snarled. 'Don't even think about it.'

'My name is *Damien*.' Damien scowled.

'That's not what the ladies called you, is it, Sydney?'

There was a Korean woman in the driver's seat in front of Damien. With a sinking feeling, he met her gaze in the rear-view mirror.

'Da Mi?' Sydney sounded as though she might start to cry. 'You're doing this with *Johnny*?'

'It's Pebbles, actually,' Da Mi replied. 'The test drive was always scheduled for today.'

Damien rolled his head back against the seat, closed his eyes and took a very deep breath. 'Jesus Christ, Sydney, what kind of shit have you landed us in?' he said quietly, not expecting a reply.

He didn't get one. 'You said you were my *friend*,' Sydney sputtered as the ProxyBod turned on the headlamps and moved the car slowly down to the junction ahead.

'I am your friend, Sydney, but I am also your employer. When you told Damien about our plans you broke one of the central clauses of your contract.'

Sydney tensed beside him. 'I haven't told Damien anything,' she said, warily. 'Have I Damien?'

Before he could get drawn into a losing game, the ProxyBod shook its head. 'Sydney,' Da Mi tutted, 'I have a VoicePrint file of your conversation in Music Intelligence – and several files of your discussions after that.'

'A VoicePrint file?' Sydney sounded incredulous. 'What the hell is that?'

Johnny snickered unpleasantly. 'Kinda makes ya think twice about accepting expensive two-way communication devices from ladies you meet in hot-tubs, hey, Sydney?'

Beside Damien, Sydney stared down at her wrist.

'Gotcha!' Johnny crowed.

'You were listening all the time?' Sydney's voice was hollow, lost. Somewhere in the depths of his heart, Damien felt a stab of sympathy for her.

'It was for your own safety, Sydney,' the scientist responded calmly as the car swung into a main street. 'At first I just wanted to know if Johnny was bothering you, but, in fact, though he and I have had our disagreements, for both of us, VirtuWorld is the only future worth working for: a future you were on the verge of seriously endangering.'

'What? What did I do? So I told Damien, so what? I was just trying to get him to help out!'

Good on you, girl, Damien thought wearily. *That's the spirit. Yell at a fucking robot.* From the corner of his eye, he saw a cat run out into the road, a streak of fur and a flash of phosphorescence. The car drove straight over it. The body thumped and rolled under the chassis and was left behind to die.

'Da Mi, stop! You just killed a cat!' Sydney was outraged.

Damien wished she would shut up. 'It's a fucking dummy driving,' he groaned. Peering over the front seat, he could see that the ProxyBod was plugged into the cigarette lighter. Guess they were still working on the battery problem.

411

'My apologies. Pebbles' reaction times are not quite at optimum level yet. But otherwise she's a very smooth driver, don't you think?'

'Da Mi, why are you acting like this?' Sydney implored. She obviously still thought this woman gave a shit about her. 'If you've got all these tapes, you know how much I care about VirtuWorld. I just thought Damien might want to be part of it too!'

'You signed an agreement not to tell *anyone* about VirtuWorld, Sydney. You knew there would be strict penalties for doing so.'

'What? Like send in the *assholes*?'

Johnny cracked the gun butt into Sydney's ribs and she doubled over with a grunt. 'Why dontcha try shutting up for a change, sweetheart,' he murmured. 'Give us all a break.'

Sydney cringed. As she huddled against Damien, he stiffened. Had she really just thought of him as a Hugh Grant lookalike? But then she sobbed, and despite everything, he felt another sharp trace of pity for her. Whatever games she'd been playing, she obviously hadn't expected this nutter to show up. And the agreement *he'd* signed hadn't said anything about being kidnapped.

'Look Da Mi,' he said loudly, 'what the fuck is going on here? If Sydney broke her contract, why don't you just fire her and find some starlet to play Queen Wanna Bee? If she feels anything like I do, she just wants to completely forget about you lot.'

In the mirror, the ProxyBod flicked a glance at Johnny. 'That's what you say now, Hugh boy,' the American scoffed, 'but when VirtuWorld is raking in the cash, you'll change your tune, demand paternity tests, royalties, homecoming parades, the lot.'

'We are within our legal rights to contain the threat to our concerns, Damien.' As she spoke, the ProxyBod shifted gears until the car was gliding down the main shopping boulevard. 'You and Sydney should have read your contracts more closely. Until VirtuWorld opens, you are no longer at liberty to communicate with the world at large.'

'*What?*' Damien gripped the front passenger seat headrest and shook it. 'This is complete bullshit! There's no way we both agreed to be fucking *kidnapped*. I demand to see a lawyer!'

'Sit *still*,' Johnny roared, brandishing the gun. 'This ain't the Old Bailey, fag-boy. You'll see a lawyer if and when we like.'

Fag-boy. Damien groaned. Who wrote this shit? He sank back into his seat and leaned his head against the window, the wad of envelopes in his jacket pocket an awkward wedge between his chest and the door, the laptop in his ruchsack a hard cushion against his back.

The Sonata was passing a serpentine row of windchimes the Gu Council had erected to beautify the boulevard: steel cylinders, cut at angles, dangling from a wooden frame. Random images flashed through his mind as the car swept past: the organ at the church where he used to sing until Jessica died; that boyhood game he'd played with railings and a stick – a useless act of auditory vandalism, musical bravado. Then the car pulled out of the Hongdae shopping district and swung into the streams of night traffic, heading west. They were leaving the streets he knew, entering an endless, monotonous zone of darkened buildings and Korean street signs. Beside him, Sydney was still hunched up in a little ball. Some vital part of him disengaged.

Ahead of them, the procession of cars and taxis was a glittering river of glass and chrome. Her ribs hurt and her head was pulsing, but for a moment, faintly, the serene, untouchable feeling Sydney had experienced in Jae Ho's studio returned.

'C'mon guys,' she pleaded. 'Don't wig out, Damien. Everything's going to be fine. I just need to explain a few things. I'm sorry, Da Mi, I really am. I should have told you I wanted Damien to know about VirtuWorld – but I was never going to run away. I was going to play my part to the hilt. You know that.'

Johnny jabbed her with the gun. His spit sprayed across her cheek. 'After the way you've played us both, do you think we can trust a word you say?'

'Trust!' A blood orange sun throbbed in Sydney's head, throbbed and spread its colours. Gritting her teeth, she turned to Johnny. 'You talk to *me* about trust? When you've been spying on me for months?' She strained forward, between the two front seats. 'Da Mi! I demand to negotiate this deal so it suits my life!'

'You were going to go to Japan, Sydney,' Da Mi replied, almost sadly, 'and from there, possibly Canada. Your recent actions have seriously jeopardised the project. There will be no negotiation, I'm afraid.'

A motherload of fury welled up from the pit of Sydney's stomach. 'You *bitch*!' she screamed.

'Language, language,' Johnny admonished, clamping his hand over her mouth.

Struggling, she bit hard into his fingers. She got another rough crack of the gun in her ribcage for her efforts, but at least her mouth was free.

'—and you slimy, no-neck piece of *shit*! I am *so* glad I didn't just give you two what you fucking wanted. Just *try* and make it work without me, just *try* – you need the real mother, how are you going to get public support without me; did you think about that?' Embarrassingly, out of frustration, she began to cry. She grabbed Damien's arm. 'I'm so sorry I got you into this mess, Damien – but I'm glad I trusted you.'

'How touching,' Johnny scoffed. 'An Oscar nomination, coming right up. I'm sure knowing that you trusted him makes Hugh feel better, Sydney, considering how you were two-timing him with that Korean Casanova. Didn't tell Damien you were part of a *harem*, did you?'

'I broke up with Jae Ho *months* ago,' Sydney hissed. 'You know that – you've been listening to everything I've done all year.'

'And mighty tasty listening it's been too. Ooooh, Damien!' Johnny trilled.

He wasn't going to get to her. No way. Sydney wiped her eyes with her sleeve. ' I hope you fucking learned something from those tapes, Johnny,' she sneered. 'I had more fun with him in *one night* than I did with you in six months.'

Beside her, Damien sighed. 'You went out with him too? You sure know how to pick 'em, Sydney.'

'She bit off more than she could chew with me,' Johnny drawled. 'So I passed her on to Da Mi for some mollycoddling. She's all screwed-up emotionally, you see. Comes from being a two-bit runaway whore, doesn't it, Cindy? Isn't that your real name? Didn't like it any more after all your johns used it, did you? Or was it always just a touch too common for my little porcelain princess?'

'Johnny! There's no need to dredge up her past,' Da Mi interjected sharply.

Ignoring her, Sydney stared Johnny full in the face. He had a crooked smile on his thin lips and his blue eyes were almost colour-less in the wash of light from a big department store window. '*Some* guys, Johnny, don't have to *pay* for it,' she said.

He put his hand over her face and shoved her down into Damien's lap. 'Company account, baby,' he crowed. 'You were just *expenses*.'

Sydney grabbed Damien's arm and tried to hoist herself up, look into his eyes. 'Damien,' she babbled, 'everything we did was totally true. Me and Jae Ho – it's over; I just wanted to see his painting, that's all. I'm sorry I texted I was seeing Da Mi. I don't know why I did that. I guess I didn't want to tell you about him just yet. I didn't want you to be jealous of anyone. You're fantastic, Damien, the most incredible guy I've ever met. We sang that song and danced, and it felt like you were my brother or something. I never just had fun like that with anyone before.'

Sydney was rubbing her hand over Damien's chest. He looked down at it with disinterest. Her feverish declaration in front of these maniacs seemed in very poor taste.

He turned his head to the window. 'Take a chill pill, Sydney,' he said softly, his eyes on the road. He knew where he was again now; the car was motoring past Hapchong Station, through a mass of road-works, passing over echoing metal ramps, between long plastic cables studded with blinking red lights.

The occupants were silent as the ProxyBod swung the car out onto the expressway that ran along the river, the strong, broad Han Gang with its largely undeveloped north shore.

Damien had had a job near here at the beginning of the summer. He'd always relished the way the bus driver had floored it down this stretch, the bus rattling along before being forced by heavy traffic to inch up the ramp to the bridge. Now the car's smooth accelera-tion was fuelled by menace. Johnny gave a grunt of satisfaction and tapped the gun barrel against his window. Damien turned away. Out on the river, lit up by the lights from the bridge, he could see a string of swan-shaped paddleboats, undulating on the water. Their unlikely presence had always charmed him on his early-morning journeys, but now, ghostly-white in the dark, they were a warning, an obedient chain of flightless, soulless birds.

Picking up speed as the traffic thinned, the Sonata passed the turn-off for the bridge, and then the Lido on the riverbank, the big pool he'd always looked down on longingly in the July heat. They were heading now for the wild end of the river, an industrial zone of construction stockyards and huge sand pits: the Pyramids of the Han, Damien had dubbed them as he'd gazed on them in the distance.

Now these wastelands with their gravel mountains and building cranes loomed uncomfortably near.

Beside him, Sydney was shaking. He glanced down at her bony form and again his heart contracted. Christ. *She was just a kid.* Had she really been a prostitute? He knew some girls did sex-work or lap-dancing to pay their college fees. Somehow, in this sallow light, it seemed brave of her. Yeah, *brave*. As the streetlamps swept the car, his anger and disdain dissolved. She looked so fragile, with those pokey elbows and stray blonde hairs falling over her face, but Sydney was a chancer, a livewire, a risk machine – right now her body was twitching and tensing like a cat's about to pounce. That reckless energy, he knew, was what he had always wanted to touch in her. Jessica's energy, his buried twin . . . *like you were my brother, or something* . . . He saw now with a twist of painful clarity that if he was going to survive he would need a bolt of her electric contempt for consequences.

But equally, if they were going to defend themselves in some desolate lot, *she* would need to be in control of her emotions. He leaned over and whispered, 'I'm here,' into her hair.

Johnny reached abruptly across the backseat and jammed the piece into Damien's jawbone, wrenching his neck back so he faced the window again. '*No whispering.* Da Mi, take the next turn-off.'

'I know where I'm going,' the scientist snapped. Then her voice hardened. 'Cop alert! They're breathalysing, just ahead.'

Damien's pulse quickened. Surely the ProxyBod wasn't going to fool a cop?

'What?' Johnny barked. Tension bristling off him, he dragged his gun-hand down out of sight, around Sydney's back. At the same time he grabbed a blanket from the floor and stuffed it in between the front seats to cover the ProxyBod cable. Straightening up, he grabbed Damien by the collar, with the same arm pinning Sydney by the throat against the backseat. 'Any funny stuff when the cop sticks his head in here and little Cindy here is going to be severely punished. Got that?'

Damien nodded.

Johnny let him go. The Sonata crawled towards the traffic officer, then stopped.

The ProxyBod unrolled her window.

Cold air billowed into the car and Damien shivered. Beside him, Sydney was breathing in short ragged intervals and her body was flinching. He moved to put his arm around her but Johnny shook his head so he shrank back. The cop stuck his head in the window and rattled off a few words to the ProxyBod. Da Mi replied in an apologetic tone.

Damien held his breath. Surely the man would be able to see that what he was talking to wasn't human?

But the cop didn't appear to notice. He cupped his white-gloved hands, an impromptu bowl to capture the unmistakable reek of rice vodka; the ProxyBod leaned forwards and blew delicately into the funnel. How and why did it have breath? Did the sex clients demand it as a feature?

The cop nodded, and cast a curious glance over the foreigners huddled together in the back seat. He asked the Pebbles thing a question, she responded brightly and he replied, laughed and withdrew, and waved them on with a smile. The window slid back up, sealing the car interior again.

'What did you tell him?' Johnny asked, suspiciously.

'He wanted to know why the girl was crying. I said her puppy had died and we were going to bury it. He said he thought Korean girls were sentimental over puppy-dogs and Western girls only cried about men.'

'I didn't know Cindy had it in her to shed tears over anything,' Johnny announced.

'That gun fucking hurts!' Sydney snarled. 'Can you take it out of my back *now*, please.'

'Hard and stiff, is it?' Johnny cooed. 'Maybe it would feel better up your cunt, hmmm? Be nice to put it there, to see how easy it slides up inside. I think all this bouncing around in the back seat is turning little Cindy on. She doesn't like to admit it, now she's a famous *model*, but Cindy's really into trashy car-sex, especially gun-car-sex. What do you think, Damien? Should I give it a try, see what kind of sounds she'd make? Would that do anything for you too, Brit-fag-boy? Hmmmm?'

'Leave her alone, Sandman.' Damien's tongue was furry with disgust, but to his private horror, the overheated interior, the lulling motions of the car and the pure adrenalin thumping like a back-beat through his veins were all conspiring to give him an erection. He twisted away from Sydney and tried to concentrate on his throbbing jaw. The car had pulled off the road now and was drawing up in front of a high metal gate. He had to stay calm.

'Johnny, this is company time – don't get carried away back there!' Da Mi sounded incensed, but Damien failed to see that Johnny gave a speck of shit.

'Johnny, you repulsive scumbag, get that gun out of my pants.' Sydney's voice was quivering now, and Damien could hear the fear behind her crumbling bravado. He caught a whiff of the tangy smell of her sweat, mixed with earthier juices. For a moment he was back in bed with her.

Johnny's voice was a low rumble, thunder on a dry horizon. 'Oh no, princess, I'm real curious now. I think you like getting angry with me. I think that gets you hot. Remember all those times I let you slap me and bite me? You're a little tiger, Cindy, and the proof is in the pudding, as the British say – isn't that right, Brit-boy?'

Damien watched with helpless fascination as Johnny slid the piece around Sydney's waist and shoved it deep towards her crotch. The button on her *nobody* jeans snapped apart with an innocent ting and her zipper tore open like a long, metallic yawn.

41 / VirtuWorld

Johnny jerked Sydney's jeans down her legs with the gun. She clutched at Damien's hand. Her palm was soaking wet. His erection shrivelled like a piece of chewed gum.

'Stop him, Damien!' she panted.

'Make one move, fag-boy, and I pull the trigger,' Johnny barked.

Damien felt dizzy. The lights from a passing car briefly flooded the vehicle. The jeans were down at Sydney's knees now, and her thighs were gleaming like fish on a slab.

'Da Mi!' Sydney shrieked as Johnny struggled to part her clenched legs.

'Sandman,' Da Mi's tone was low and controlled, 'I am ordering you to stop, *now*.'

The ProxyBod met Damien's gaze in the rear-view mirror, but her face was immobile, her dark eyes message-less, her weapons invisible. Sydney's white, trembling legs beside him were no match for the thrust of Johnny's arm.

Damien could make out the blonde wisps of Sydney's pubic hair as Johnny forced her legs open. His other hand was a fist in her hair, pulling her head towards him.

'Hot and wet, eh?' he crooned, spit fizzing at the corners of his mouth. 'I think you *like* it, Cindy.'

'You. Disgusting. Fuckwad.' Sydney's speech was gargled, as if her tongue had been pushed down her throat. Damien squeezed her hand and she dug her nails into his palm. He welcomed the pain.

'I'm here,' he whispered, faintly, but Johnny was in full spate.

'Thought you'd run off on us, did you, without even saying goodbye? Not to mention saying thanks for bringing you over, setting you up in your new princess life? Well, let's say *anyong hasayo* now, Cindy, a proper goodbye fuck, for old time's sake – you owe me that, you little bitch, like you fucking owe me an apology for that note you left me, don't you? Yeah, that wasn't a nice note to leave someone who made your life a million times better, was it? Don't you think you ought to tell Johnny you're sorry?'

The gun muzzle was burrowing into the cleft between Sydney's legs. Her eyes were squeezed shut and she was biting her lip so hard that Damien could see a trickle of blood on her chin.

'Huh, you gonna say sorry, Cindy? You gonna say sorry to Johnny?'

'I'm . . . sorry . . . for you, Johnny,' Sydney rasped. 'I'm fucking *sorry for you* . . . because you're a total . . . fucking . . . *loser*.'

'You bitch!' Johnny shoved the gun inside her. She made a terrible gargling sound and her hand went rigid as metal. The car stopped and Damien lurched forward.

'Hey, Doc,' Johnny shouted, 'what the fuck do you think you're doing?'

The car had turned off the main road and pulled up by a tall metal gate. The ProxyBod was rummaging in the glove compartment, throwing maps, old juice bottles, sunglasses and OxyPops out onto the front seat.

'Just opening the gate.' Pebbles waved a remote control in the air.

'Okay, okay,' he growled. 'Take us inside.'

The entrance gates swung open. The car pulled into a vast building site. A single floodlight was mounted on a corrugated sheet metal shack by the gate; beneath it heaps of scrap materials and tools cast mangled shadows on the ground. Strings of naked bulbs, propped up by awkwardly leaning posts, lit the rest of the site, leaving eerie yellow pools on the ground. As the car rolled slowly out of the spotlight, Damien could make out bulldozers and road-rollers, and areas of swampy land with roads that ended abruptly at the mouths of gaping pits. Beyond it all, a range of sand and gravel mountains reared up in the darkness which flowed into the river; the gleaming black water and the line of lights on the opposite bank were just visible in the distance. A high chain-link fence crested with rolls of barbed wire surrounded the site for as far as Damien could see.

The ProxyBod stopped the car again, pointed the remote back at the gate, which clanged shut with a distant echo.

'Sydney, Damien, welcome to the site of the future VirtuWorld,' Da Mi said crisply. 'Johnny, you would do well to remember that you too are an employee of the park and answerable to *me*. Now put the gun in the air and let's get back to the original plan.'

'Dr Kim?' Johnny raised his voice. 'I got some unfinished business with little Cindy here, so why don't you just put a lid on it and take us to the dug-out. You don't want to get your hands dirty, you'll just have to do things *my* way for a change.'

'You've taken far too many liberties already, Sandman,' Da Mi retorted.

'I'm the fucking expert on the ground, bitch!' Johnny yelled. His face was scarlet and his eyes were bulging out of his skull. 'Now *drive!*'

Damien wanted to smash his own head against the window. Beside him, Sydney's head was rocking back and forth against the seat. A long moan escaped her. *Push*, he thought inanely, squeezing her hand again. *Just push the bastard off you.*

But what the hell could she do? Johnny's hand was shoving deep between her thighs. He watched, a helpless witness, as a tear leaked down her cheek.

'Just a minute – I'm losing connection. Just a minute . . .' Da Mi's voice was tinnier than before.

Damien's last pinpoint of hope pinged into non-existence.

'Reload. *Reload!*' Johnny screamed. 'We're too close to the road!' But the ProxyBod was inert as a crash-test dummy. '*Fuck! Fuck! Fuck!*' Johnny slammed the side of his fist against the car roof. 'Do I have to fucking do *everything* around here?'

With a gliding head motion, Pebbles returned to life, or her version of it, anyway. 'Please excuse my temporary absence. Bugs in the programme.'

Johnny was breathing like he'd just run a marathon. He smoothed back his hair. 'Don't give me your bullshit, Kim; just move.'

The car had stalled. Pebbles restarted the ignition and drove slowly down a sparsely lit passage between two towering loads of sand.

'Brit-boy, you see these sandpits?' Johnny crooked his free elbow round Sydney's neck, dragging her closer. His gun was still digging into her. 'They're going to be a beautiful beach one day; too bad neither of you Royals are going to lie on it, but you can blame this little slut for that.'

'Don't think *you're* ever going to see it, either, Sandman.' Da Mi's voice was a serrated knife blade. 'You've had your last chance to stay on board and you've blown it. I'm not having my authority under-mined by your personal vendettas.'

'Whatever, Doc. What. Ever. Don't think you're the only one with friends in high places. A lotta people on this project owe Johnny Sandman a favour, and they don't all like taking orders from a slant-eyed nun.'

Damien was only half-listening. The dark outline of something like a plan was forming in his mind. If he could distract Sandman, get him to wave the gun around, maybe he could knock it away and Sydney could poke his eyes out. Or something. Whatever happened, it was better to die trying to escape than wait to get shot at this dugout, wherever it was.

'Hey Johnny, man,' he said softly, 'why don't you take it easy a minute? If you just put the gun away, Sydney and I will leave the country and you can have VirtuWorld all to yourself.'

'Don't fucking tell me what to do, or the next trigger I pull won't be Cindy's clit!' Johnny jammed the gun harder into Sydney and she gave another unbearable cry, a cat being skinned alive, until Johnny clamped his hand over her mouth.

'Okay, okay.' Damien shrank back against the car door.

Johnny's eyes were glazed over now, his arm working methodically to hurt Sydney. 'Now pay attention, boys and girls,' he hissed. 'On the left, you will see the Global Village. Snack booths and souvenir shops will line the road, while on the right you can visit the Stock Market Roller-Coaster and the Eyeful Tower. Everything's all set to be erected. Johnny Sandman has paid all the contractors and got the best deals. Johnny Sandman has priced the flood-control banks and sourced all the finest eco-material. Isn't that right, Da Mi?'

They had reached the back of the lot. The chain-link fence continued into the river, which shone blackly in front of them. Da Mi said nothing as Pebbles drove the car along the road that curved along the shore, past a few straggly bushes and a long stretch of sand. Bits of scrap-metal pronged and coiled out of the ditch by the side of the road as if the earth were a mattress that had sprung all its springs.

But as sinister as the lot looked, it was a vision of paradise compared with the interior of the car. He and Sydney had to get outside somehow. If they could turn on Johnny, maybe they could count on Da Mi not to intervene? There obviously wasn't much love lost between her and the psycho bastard. But how to catch the fucker off-guard?

'The main attraction, the Peony Palace, is coming right up,' Johnny crowed, 'right round the bend there, nestled in the centre of the spiral, surrounding the Fountain of *Luuurve*.' Drawing out the last word, he plunged his gun hand deeper into Sydney's groin.

Beside Damien, Sydney's body was juddering, her eyes screwed shut, her breathing rapid and shallow. She seemed a million miles away, but her hand was still tucked inside his. As inconspicuously as he could, he hooked her little finger in his and gripped it tight. *Please don't believe a word I'm going to say*, he begged her in his mind. *Please*.

Lowering his voice, he said to Johnny, 'You've worked pretty hard to get this all going, I know. I can see how you'd be upset at Sydney, really.'

'You can, can you?' The tone was menacing, sarcastic, but the hand stopped moving. 'Sure,' Damien continued. Another part of his mind flashed into action and he began to rhythmically squeeze Sydney's pinkie. Three long squeezes. Then three short. 'I mean, she lied to you like she lied to me. I'm pretty pissed off at her myself – I can't say she doesn't deserve everything she's going to get.'

'Oh, you don't say?' Johnny's tone was spiced with a pinch of contempt, but perhaps curiosity too. Still squeezing SOS, or OSO, he had no fucking idea which, Damien took the plunge. 'Maybe we could take it in turns. Think about it: we're too crammed in here. I could keep that GameBoy fantasy under guard while you were seeing to Sydney, and vice versa. I've always wanted to rough up a bird with another bloke.'

'Full of surprises, aren't you, Brit-boy?' Johnny sounded amused. Was that good or bad?

Ahead of the car, a cable hung loosely from a tilting post. It thwacked the windscreen as they passed, and as if startled, the ProxyBod stepped on the gas. Little pieces of gravel tinged off the metalwork like bits of stone and glass sucked up a vacuum cleaner nozzle. Then the car revved through a puddle beneath a string of coloured lights, smattering the windows with a high, shimmering, rainbow of water.

Damien held his breath as the droplets clung to the windows.

'Take it easy, Kim!' Johnny screamed. 'I'm *working* back here!'

She couldn't feel her feet. That was something – something beautiful: she couldn't feel her feet. If she tried hard, shut everything out, let Johnny's tsunami of hatred just crash over her, let the furnace between her thighs rage until it consumed her, then maybe soon she wouldn't feel anything at all, wouldn't hear anything but a dull black roar, or see anything except stars in her head, burning lights . . . so pretty . . . like fireworks . . . celebrations . . . tiny Tinker Bell lights . . . the glowing eyes of cats . . . or fairy children . . . yes, fairy children . . . shrieking silently to each other inside her head, their little faces framed by spiky orange petals, their little mouths kissing her, biting her, fierce little fairies . . . crowding together to pull at her pinky, pull her away from the man who was hurting her, mounting and hurting, shouting and snarling, scraping and shooting fear and pain right up inside her like arrows, like knives, like . . .

The car hit a puddle.

Sydney's eyes sprang open.

A wall of water sprayed over the car in a bleary light-streaked fan.

At last she came, or something like it, a splintered, fractured, neon explosion that ripped her out of her body, out of the vision-world, into darkness and silence and then, at last, into a hurtling, white-hot scream, not of terror, but of fury.

Sydney's scream reverberated down an endless corridor in his mind: a corridor that ended in a door he never, ever wanted to open: a door behind which Jessica died every day, all alone, small and naked, while he played with sand castles and didn't care where she'd gone. That door was swiftly growing larger as he was sucked towards it by a searing, high-pitched blast of sound, it was waiting to swing open and slam him inside to a place full of maggots and rot and the smell of stale semen, the desolate howls of his mother and the empty eyes of his dad, and the high, sputtering laughter of someone who had taken Jessica away for ever, someone Damien wanted to kill but never would, because Damien was weak and stupid and frightened and worthless, and should be dead himself, should be dead, should be dead, *should be dead—*

With a huge effort of will, Damien wrenched himself back into the car. Beneath his layers of winter clothing he was cold and damp and shaking, and his tongue was a mossy slab in his mouth. It felt like a year since he'd last drawn breath.

Sydney had gone limp. Her hand was like a piece of Plasticine in his; a string of saliva hung from her lower, blooded lip. Outside, the river had disappeared into darkness. Inside the car was completely still. Even Sandman's elbow had stopped moving. The psycho was humming now – some weird, off-key tune, punctuated by fizzles of spit. Christ, was it 'My Way'?

Ahead, the road made one final curve into a large round clearing lit by a single lamppost. Beneath the light, a spade was planted between a mound of earth.

The car swung round; Pebbles braked.

A sledgehammer pounded a hole in Damien's chest.

Keep calm, he thought, swallowing back an upsurge of bile. *Keep calm. Carry On.*

Everything was happening in freeze-frame. Sydney's eyes were open, but staring vacantly ahead. She took a deep, shuddering breath.

Johnny withdrew the gun and pressed it slick and sticky, against her belly. *Grab it*, Damien thought, crazily. *Twist it out of his grasp. Break his wrist.*

But the Yank was built like a shit-house, and anyway, the thought had barely flashed into his mind before Johnny was waving the blunt barrel in his face.

'All right, English. When I hold the gun to Pebbles' very expensive head, you can tie her up. Use your scarf – and her cable. Wrap them around her arms and the back of her seat.'

'Yeah, sure, thanks, man,' he stammered. If he could grab the cable, he could whip Johnny in the face with it – or maybe he could unlock the doors and run – or at least tie the knots loose, or 'accidentally' leave the ProxyBod's hands free – maybe she could plug herself back in?

'I'm going to have to tie you up too after that,' Johnny continued.

'Hey!' Damien squeaked. 'Where's the fun in that?'

'If I want to see you get your kicks with the bitches, it's going to be when and how I say.' His voice was ugly and tarry again. His hand still gripping Sydney's hair, Johnny held the gun aloft. 'Pebbles, honey: unplug yourself. *Now.*'

Damien gave Sydney's pinky one final squeeze. She gripped his fingers tightly in return.

Now the effort of trying not feel anything, pleasure or pain, was over and the brutal new fact of the gun on her stomach was dragging her back to the interior of the car. Damien was talking to Johnny, squeezing her pinky, trying to get her to help him.

But he didn't need her help.

Sydney closed her eyes. She couldn't see the Peonies any more, but she could hear them, whistling and chattering outside, swooping under and over the car, playing dangerous games beneath the chassis, rattling the exhaust pipe, their echoes shaking the seats. She gripped Damien's little finger back. *Everything's okay*, she told him, *we're going to be all right.*

'No one is tying Pebbles up.'

Da Mi's voice slid into Sydney's mind like an icicle. She shivered as it melted away.

'You're not the one giving the orders any more, Doc,' Johnny sneered, as mean as always – but it was all meaningless now. Outside, her babies were smashing the headlights, clawing at the windows, banging their heels in the roof in a thundering tantrum of warning. It didn't matter what Johnny did or said; they would soon be on him, they would bombard him, destroy him, pull him limb from limb.

Her eyelids were glued shut, but she could see everything. All around the car endless spiral metal ladders, corkscrew slides, were shooting up like magic beanstalks between the walls of gi-normous glittering castles. These looming palaces of light were tiled with broken mirrors, their turrets made of tornadoes, double helix helter-skelters and huge swirling ice-cream cone domes, all spinning at a hundred different speeds. Glorious sunshine flooded the Vision City at the heart of VirtuWorld, throbbing and pulsing and revolving with goodness and rightness. Orange and pink flags and banners unfurled, snapped and rippled in the breeze. Everywhere she could hear the chatter of her children, the excited preparations for a battle to the death.

The ProxyBod stepped on the gas and the car revved out of the clearing and over the end of the road, dropping onto a gravel slope and hurling the passengers out of their seats. The gun rose in Johnny's fist, jerked back at a strange angle to within an inch of the roof of the car. Just for a moment Damien thought he would drop it.

Then everything happened at exactly the same time:

The car landed and Pebbles turned in her seat. The space between her eyebrows opened as if on hinges and dropped down over the bridge of her nose. Silently and smoothly, a gun barrel emerged from between her eyes, aiming straight at Johnny's head.

'Damien!' Sydney screamed, her rigid body rising in the centre of the car as Johnny pulled her into the line of fire, and Damien lunged forward. The Sonata jack-knifed, he grabbed Sydney's shoulder and a thunderbolt of colours tore through his head like a deafening Acid-Industrial non-song.

The back of the car hit the ground with a smack. Mud rained down, the windows turned to liquid and all the Peonies in the world flew in to trample and ravage and maul the man with the gun. The heavens were cracking open, trumpets were screaming, the car windows were melting and Sydney's children were swarming inside. The fish-tailing Sonata was now a spinning kaleidoscope of Peonies, chartreuse Peonies, turquoise Peonies, crimson, canary, cobalt, emerald, cherry, tangerine, bubblegum Peonies all howling for blood.

Then everything went black.

Sydney couldn't breathe.

42 | Miscarriage

All around her was the gentle, plopping sound of simmering porridge. Something warm and liquid was dropping from the roof onto the leather seat, into her clothing, slipping down the back of her neck. And Damien was on top of her, crushing her, his chin digging into her shoulder.

'Let me up,' she gargled, but her mouth was clogged with her own hair. She twisted around to push him away.

Her hands pressed against wetness. Damien's jacket was soaked with hot, black liquid. His body was inert. With a huge effort she pushed him against the door of the car. His head rocked back to hit the window, then flopped forwards on his chest. At the same time, she became acutely aware of Johnny's knees, digging into her back. Fear and fury shooting through her, she whipped round to confront him. His body was slumped back into the seat. His mouth was hanging open and there was a raw black hole in his temple.

She gasped for breath, then turned back to Damien. A dark jam smeared the glass behind his head. His forehead was a jagged red cave and his right eyeball was hanging down on his cheek.

She looked at her hands: they were slimy with blood. She closed her eyes and screamed: a shrill, escalating scream, punctuated by the slow pucker of the droplets falling, more slowly now, just one drip at a time.

'Sydney!' Da Mi's voice ricocheted into the dark space between them. 'Sydney! Are they dead?'

'*Damien's dead!*' Even while she was shrieking his name, a clear, urgent chill was rising inside her. *She had to get a grip.* She had to get out of this car.

Slowly, she opened her eyes. She couldn't look sideways. She couldn't think about Damien. She had to look straight ahead – into Da Mi's bloodless mask.

'Good.' The ProxyBod switched on the light in the roof of the car. The gun was still sticking out of her forehead. Leaning back between the seats, she tried to take Sydney's hand.

Sydney shrank back, shaking in an Arctic wind of disbelief.

Pebbles sighed as the gun slid back inside her skull. 'Sydney, you have to believe me: I only wanted to frighten you tonight. But those men would have killed you. I know it's terrible for you right now, but I had to stop them.'

It took a moment to connect the dots. '*You* shot him? You *shot* Damien?'

'He was doing a deal with Johnny – he was planning to rape you. I heard them talking. You were unconscious. I had to take action.'

'You *liar*! You horrible, *horrible* liar! Damien was *protecting* me. He was protecting me from *you*, Da Mi!' She twisted away from Pebbles towards Damien's body. Gulping, she gazed at the ruin of his face. A hot, heavy wave of grief swamped her anger. Reaching up, she stroked his good cheek. A thin layer of stubble rasped beneath her fingertips. She found his hand, clasped his little finger and lifted it to her lips.

We had a promise, she told him. *I remember our promise.*

'Please believe me, Sydney,' Da Mi said softly, 'I wasn't going to shoot you. *I'm* the one who's protecting you.'

'*Protecting* me? By *kidnapping* me? By letting Johnny *rape me* with a *gun*?' She realised she was still half-naked, swollen and stinging.

She tugged her panties and jeans up, wincing, zipped herself back in. Adrenalin was coursing through her, and in a dim corner of her brain she recognised that this silent surge of energy was preventing her from collapsing in hysterics. She also knew that however much she wanted to lunge at Da Mi's big doll and break its fucking neck, that would be a very stupid thing to do.

'You have let me down once too often, Sydney, but that doesn't mean I want to hurt you. My intention this evening was to use Johnny to get you and Damien here, then to kill him and let you two go.'

'*What?*' Again, Da Mi's words took a few seconds to compute. Sydney glanced again at Johnny's body: his oozing head wound, his gun arm dangling awkwardly in his lap. Something like relief shivered through her, followed by a wash of nausea. Swallowing back a mouthful of bile, she stared into Pebbles' glassy brown eyes.

'That was your *plan*? To kill Johnny right *beside me*?'

The ProxyBod tilted its weird, over-sized head and blinked slowly. Da Mi's most emollient, consoling voice flowed out of its magenta lips. 'He was violent and irrational, Sydney. We had video evidence of him attempting to sabotage the ProxyBod project in an extremely perverse manner. Even his superiors were afraid of what he might do next. They granted Pebbles permission to terminate him. To be honest, they would have preferred both you and Damien dead as well. I had to fight hard to save your lives.'

Sydney leaned forward. Pebbles' eyes reflected nothing human except Sydney herself, flaring in the dark irises like two tiny fires. 'You said Pebbles was a *game*, Da Mi – what the *fuck* is going on? Who the fuck *are* you?'

'Naturally the ProxyBod has military applications, Sydney,' Da Mi said calmly. 'I don't like it any more than you do – I resisted for the longest time. But ultimately I realised that cooperating with ConGlam was the only way to fund the Peonies.'

Damien had warned her, ranting at her on her sofa; Damien had *known*. 'So are they going to be monsters too?' she asked bitterly.

'No, Sydney, the Peonies are going to be everything I told you they would be: spiritual, musical, nurturing beings, and more.'

'What?' Sydney snorted. 'Are they going to have two heads?'

'Please.' The ProxyBod's voice was low and urgent. 'Let's not argue. You have to know that there is a desperately important reason for the trauma you've experienced tonight.'

'The fact that you're insane?' *Why was she having a fucking conversation? She had to get out of here.*

But she was trapped. Even if she could wrest Johnny's gun out of his hand, Da Mi would shoot her before she could use it. Shuddering, Sydney covered her eyes with her arms. Where were the Peonies now? Why had they abandoned her, dumped her back in her body again, the last place in the world she wanted to be? Her head was cracking open, every bone in her ached, and her pussy was raw and sore, like a piece of meat Johnny had bashed and banged, just because he could. Tears squeezed down her cheeks. There was nowhere to look that didn't make her want to throw up.

But even though she couldn't see her any more, Da Mi wasn't going away. 'It's not insane to ensure that humanity survives a global ecological disaster, is it?' she cajoled.

'The only disaster here is *you!*' Sydney yelled. 'I wish I'd never met you, Da Mi.' She struck her hands over her ears, but Da Mi's voice snaked between her fingers into her brain.

'Sydney, listen to me. I didn't want to tell you this – I didn't want to frighten you – but ever since I've met you I've been trying to save your life. People think we have twenty or thirty years to save the planet, but we don't. We have a month, and we won't make it. On December twenty-first, an asteroid called Lucifer's Hammer is going to hit the Atlantic Ocean. The impact will cause massive tsunamis that will hit Europe, Africa and North and South America. When they recede, the world will be devastated. Essential infrastructures will be washed away, major Western capitals will lie in ruins. The nuclear powers may well take the opportunity to settle old scores, wipe out their opponents for ever. But if the human race survives, Seoul will be protected by its mountains, and we will become one of the planet's most important cities. Korea's leaders know this; that's why they have allowed the tent-cities to flourish. And I am one of the people they most rely upon.'

She couldn't take it any more. 'Then they're *fucked*, aren't they, Da Mi?' she shouted, clenching her fists. '*I* relied on you, and look at me!'

But Da Mi just purred on and on in that low, melodious voice, like she used to do in the cafés, in the *anbang*, in the Chair. 'Darling, darling, I'm so sorry about Johnny. I stopped him as soon as I could. Please listen, Sydney: my plan was to take you to my mountain village for the Solstice, to meet the surrogate mothers. You can still come: you can survive the floods and stay safe from social chaos. If you don't, Sydney, I can't guarantee your safety. And think about it: even if global civilisation is rebuilt, in most places on the planet it will be too hot to go outside for six months of the year. Africa and India will have been half-emptied by famine and floods. Hospitals in America and Europe will be turning away millions of people dying of skin cancer, malaria, dengue fever, cholera. If you leave Seoul now, perhaps you yourself will be ill or thirsty or hungry too.'

Was there no air in the car any more? Sydney's mouth was coated with gunge, her head felt dizzy and *Damien was dead*. 'I don't care,' she choked. 'I *don't* care.'

'I care, Sydney. I want you to stay and finish healing in the Chair and be around to help the Peonies grow up. The Peonies will be strong, healthy, beautiful people – *your* children, miracle beings, created to survive even radiation and nuclear winter.'

Change the record, Da Mi. 'You're so full of *bullshit*,' Sydney croaked. 'You can't force me to do what you want, so don't try to scare me—'

But Pebbles raised her hand to continue. 'Please – let me finish. I'm not trying to frighten you; just the opposite. I want you to be excited about the future! I haven't told you half of what the Peonies can be, Sydney. Their natural lifespan will be at least two hundred years – and if you keep taking the honey drink, you can share in their longevity. Imagine being young and beautiful for decades, enjoying all the pleasures of life, all the while growing in wisdom and experience. Maybe you don't ever have to die – even if our own bodies finally collapse, in a hundred years we will be able to transplant our brains into a ProxyBod, transfer our *consciousness* itself. Can you imagine it, Sydney: all our memories, our personality, our sensual experiences, housed in an indestructible body, one that's capable of living on Mars, or travelling deep into outer space. It can be done – GRIP is halfway there already – and I want *you* to join us!'

Sydney closed her eyes. 'You want to put my brain inside one of those *things*? That's *gross*, Da Mi.'

'You're so young.' Da Mi's voice was sad. 'You still think you're immortal. Do you know how many people would kill for the opportunity I'm offering you right now?'

It was like hitting the wall in the gym, then getting your second wind. Something clicked in Sydney's skull and a dose of liquid rage coursed through her veins. She shot up from her seat, gripped the front chair backs, and screamed, '*You* would kill! You just killed *Damien*! If you think I want to hang around with you for the next two thousand years, you're nuts, Da Mi! I hate you – I *hate* you! Get *that* into your thick rubber head!'

But nothing could faze Da Mi. 'I can understand you feel that way right now,' she murmured,'but though you can't see it, I love you like a daughter, Sydney. I always have. And truly—' She paused, something suspiciously like a choke in her voice. 'I'm very sorry about Damien.'

Pebbles's bland, foundation-caked face seemed to tremble for a moment. Was that a *tear* at the corner of her eye? Un-fucking-believable.

'First you blow his brains out right beside me, and now you're *sorry*?'

The ProxyBod heaved a long, almost convincing sigh. 'Maybe he *was* just trying to help you. If I made a mistake, please, let me make it up to you. We can use the Chair to help you through the grieving process. We can find his family and help them too – did you know he had a twin sister who died? We must try to find a way to let his mother know how brave he was defending you.'

You remind me of someone who needed me once. Damien's words came back to Sydney like the faintest of echoes. She held her breath, straining to hear more, but there was only silence in the car.

'He had a sister?' She hated how tiny her voice sounded.

'Jessica. She was blonde, like you.' The ProxyBod reached over and placed its hand on Sydney's; she pulled away, but Da Mi continued in her kindest tone, as though nothing had happened, 'Jessica disappeared on holiday when they were both eight years old. Her body was found a month later, dumped in a ditch. Damien stopped singing in the choir after that. His father died, later on, and his mother has remarried; they're estranged. I expect he told you. But perhaps it would ease her grief to know that he had avenged the loss of Jessica by saving your life. Think about it, Sydney' – she spoke quickly, excitedly, now – 'we could say that Johnny and an accomplice, a Korean in a mask, had kidnapped you both, but when you got to the building site, Damien fought off the accomplice and attacked Johnny, letting you escape. You didn't see what happened next, but it looked like the accomplice killed both Damien and – for some reason – Johnny. My friends in the police would help us. You'd get some national publicity – it would all be very good for your career, and for VirtuWorld later on. We could create a shrine for Damien in the Park, make his ProxyBods your honour guard. He's a hero, Sydney: let's make sure that his spirit lives on.'

Damien was dead. *Da Mi* had killed him. By mistake, she said. And now she was telling a story to make it all better. Nothing made sense any more. 'He didn't want to be part of the park,' Sydney objected, weakly.

'No, I know,' Da Mi said gently, 'it's just an idea. I only want to show you that I'm sorry. If you can forgive me, Sydney, I'll do whatever you think is best.'

Pebbles' mouth was pinched and anxious-looking. For a moment, Sydney desperately wanted it to be true: Da Mi *had* been aiming at Johnny, and Damien *had* jumped up in the way. And now she was offering Sydney the chance to do something for him, at least to help his mother. She opened her mouth to speak, and then shut it again. Damien was *dead*, right beside her. 'I know you promised him you'd think about leaving Seoul,' Da Mi said quietly, 'but I don't think he would have wanted to you to . . .'

Sydney ripped her Gotcha off her wrist and flung it at Pebbles. 'You only know that because you were *listening* to us, Da Mi! You're *evil*: you spied on me and tricked me, and I never want to see you again in my life—'

The ProxyBod flinched as the Gotcha hit her in the face, but the expression of concern was moulded onto her features now. She reached for the flask on the passenger seat. 'Sydney, you're still in shock. Here, have some honey drink—'

'Fuck off, fuck off, *fuck off!*' Sydney lunged between the seats and knocked the flask out of Pebbles' hands. It clunked off the dash-board and dropped into the passenger seatwell. Head cocked, the ProxyBod watched it roll beneath the seat, then turned back to regard Sydney with those wide, mournful eyes. Sydney took a deep breath. 'Unlock the door and let me out of here, Da Mi.'

There was a long silence. Then, as if it were a surface that someone had wiped clean, Pebbles' face smoothed to blankness. 'I should elim-inate you, Sydney,' she said, her voice as neutral as her features.

It was like someone had turned the air-con on full blast, or opened the window in a blizzard. Sydney's skin turned icy-cold, and suddenly she was so frightened she could barely breathe, let alone speak.

'But I can't,' Da Mi continued. 'You're unique, and I care too much about you to terminate that special spark.'

There it was again: that glycerine tear, drooling down the ProxyBod's cheek, as if they were sharing a fucking 'moment'. Heat blazed through Sydney's body again. She wanted to punch Da Mi, throttle her, scratch her plastic jelly eyes out – but she clamped her hands to the edge of the seat and forced herself to stay calm. Calm, like she used to be in the Chair – strapped into the Chair, like Da Mi was now, at home.

'It's time to let me go, Da Mi,' she said. There was a crack in her voice, as if she herself were about to cry. And maybe she was.

Like a speck of dust in a shaft of light, the whole world was suspended for a second between them.

Then Da Mi snapped back into the driver's seat. 'Okay, Sydney, if that's what you want. I'm going to open the door – but I'm warning you, three things. First, don't hang around here. I ordered back-up when I saw that Johnny was out of control and the squad will be here any minute. Second, don't go back home, or to Jin Sok's. Take the money from Damien's jacket, go to a *yogwan* to clean up, then get out of the country as soon as you can. Third, don't *ever* go to the police – or the media – here, or abroad. ConGlam has contacts everywhere, and I won't be able to protect you if you surface with some crazy story about your time in Korea. If you talk to Jin Sok, you can tell him Johnny threatened you. But don't call him, or anyone, from your MoPho. In fact, that's warning number four: ditch your MoPho, and use a payphone for any calls you have to make.'

Wouldn't this woman ever stop ordering her around? 'I'll see Jin Sok if I want to!' Sydney retorted. 'And how the fuck am I supposed to leave the country if I can't go *home*? I need my *passport*, Da Mi.'

'I've got it here in my office. I'll have it sent up to the airport information desk with a credit card. If you go to Tokyo, don't stay long. Apply for visas to India, China, the Philippines, Thailand – make as many bookings as you can, but go somewhere high on a mountain or deep inland – just not Winnipeg; ConGlam might look for you there. And honestly, Sydney, don't go running to Jin Sok's studio – that's the second place ConGlam will look.'

'*Stop telling me what to do!*' Sydney thumped her fist against the front seat. 'Fucking open the door!'

'There's a tap by the security box. Wash your hands and face,' Da Mi instructed 'The gate is unlocked; you can catch a taxi on the road.' The car locks thunked open. 'I'm telling you, *don't go back home.*'

She didn't know she was going to do it until she did. Sydney reached across Johnny's corpse and opened the door. The interior light switched on and fresh air poured into the car. Crawling over Johnny, shielding his lap with her body, she dropped her hand to his gun and dug it out of his fingers. In one swift motion, she twisted round, thrust the warm lump of metal into the ProxyBod's face and pulled the trigger.

The recoil flung her backwards, thwacking the breath out of her lungs. The car filled with the smell of burning hair and electronics, and in the front seat, the ProxyBod slumped against the steering wheel. There was no blood, just singed skin flaps, torn open to reveal a glinting cluster of wiring, computer circuit boards and, right between the eyes, a stubby gun barrel.

Her ears were ringing. The weapon in her hand was smeared with her own juices, and heavy as a magnet. If she didn't move now, it would glue her to the car for ever. This fucking car. This prison. This *torture chamber*.

She had to stay calm. She wanted to hurl the gun through the windscreen, send glass shattering everywhere, but instead, she used Johnny's shirt to wipe the thing as clean as she could. Then she inserted it back between Johnny's fingers and let his arm fall back in his lap.

Her eyes blurring with tears, she groped in Damien's jacket for the cash, then she reached behind his body and fumbled for the handle. The door opened, and Damien spilled halfway out of the car.

Choking back a sob, Sydney clambered over him, stumbling into the cold, scraping her knees on the ground.

Right there, in front of her, next to a large mound of earth, were three freshly dug graves.

Goose-pimples sprang up like rivets on her flesh. The wind whistled through the wires crisscrossing the lot – a long, low note. Somewhere behind her, the river was lapping at the shore. She took one harsh, cold breath, then vomited wildly. Her guts scoured, her throat on fire, she spat until her mouth was empty. She wanted so badly to collapse, but she forced herself to get up, until, with a jerk, she was pulled backwards. Something was grabbing her legs, tugging her back to the car.

She turned. Damien's blood-soaked scarf was caught around her ankles. She tore at it frantically, trying to free herself, dragging his body fully out of the car until it hit the ground with a thump. She finally managed to pull it off, and stood up. Damien was lying at her feet, his head resting against his outstretched arm, his wounds hidden. His good eye was closed, his thin lips curved up slightly at the corner and the fingertips of his other hand gently grazed the earth. He could be listening intensely to music: one of those obscure, tuneless tracks only he could understand.

She grabbed him under the armpits. His jacket was repulsive with blood, and bits of his brain were dribbling onto her coat, making her gag again, but she dragged him clear of the car and past the grave. Her back screamed, her arms ached, her cunt burned and wept, but she kept pulling until darkness enveloped them both.

She left him curled up on a soft bank of sand, his rucksack shielding his back from the wind, his scarf folded into a pillow for his mutilated head. She left him with a dry, chapped kiss on his cold cheek. A heart of sunken footsteps encircled his body, a path that trailed off until it was lost in the frostbitten dirt. As she ran for the gate, big fluffy snowflakes began falling from the sky.

43 | Fruition

Their bellies gently swelling, the women rested in the dappled shade of the spring chestnut leaves. Mee Hee put down her history book and fanned herself. Beside her, So Ra and Chin Mee lounged on a rug playing Flower Cards, slapping the plastic cards down smartly. On the next rug, Younger Sister was doing yoga stretches, while Older Sister and her cronies were sipping iced *tubu* milk and giggling about the new guards, handsome young men who were busy building a stone wall around the village.

'What must they think of us?'

'Unwed mothers – such sinners!'

'Perhaps they'll like us better when we're slim again . . .'

Mee Hee smiled at their prattle and returned to her book. This chapter was about the first Queen of Korea, Queen Son Dok, who had unified the Three Kingdoms and then reigned long and peacefully until the end of her days. She had been renowned for her incisive prophecies, like the one she had uttered in her first year on the throne.

The Emperor of China had sent the new ruler a gift to celebrate her ascent to power: a painted scroll of peony blossoms and a box of flower seeds.

But the young Queen was not impressed. 'These flowers have no scent – is he trying to mock me because I am childless?'

The courtiers scrambled to soothe her temper. 'Your Majesty, these

444

are only seeds. How can you tell they have no perfume? Surely this gift is intended only to beautify your gardens.'

'Plant them,' she ordered, 'and in the springtime you will see.'

And indeed, come the spring, when the blossoms hung large and many-petalled on their stems, it was perceived by all that the Queen had been correct.

'But how did you know the peonies would have no aroma, your Majesty?' the courtiers asked in amazement.

'It was obvious from the scroll,' she replied. 'There were no birds or insects near the flowers, so clearly they do not have the power to attract.'

Mee Hee looked up from the book, giddy with insight. Just as the peonies of Queen Son Dok had no scent to attract bees, so Dr Kim's Peonies had been conceived without the usual fumbling rituals that bring human babies into this world. The two Peonies growing inside her were like angels, gifts from a higher power, a spirit that moved like the wind between people and places and down through the ages, bringing majesty and meaning to the humblest places of the earth.

Mee Hee shut the book and gazed down at her hands. There, on the third finger of her left hand, a small diamond ring sparkled, the ring Tae Sun had given her when her pregnancy was confirmed. They could not be legally married unless they heard word of her husband's death, but within the land of VirtuWorld, their promises to each other were everlasting.

She didn't like to draw attention to her good fortune. The other women wanted husbands too. Beside her So Ra was whispering to Chin Mee about Dr Dong Sun, and around them all the trees and flowers in the garden, like all the little homes and courtyards of their village, hummed with happiness and hope. The coming days would bring only more joy. After the births, the weddings would begin. But before that, tonight, Dr Kim was visiting, to make a special announcement.

'Mee Hee, why are you giggling?' So Ra asked, poking her legs with a finger growing fatter by the day.

'I'm happy, that's all.' Mee Hee laid down her book. 'Let me join in the game.' There was no harm in a white lie, just for this afternoon. She wouldn't spoil Dr Kim's surprise. And anyway, she had to pretend to be shocked tonight. She didn't want her sisters to think she was gloating about the fact that she and Tae Sun were going to be crowned King and Queen of the Peonies on the opening day of VirtuWorld.

Mee Hee could still hardly believe it, but Dr Kim had visited last month, two weeks after she and Tae Sun had announced their engagement. She had asked to see them privately, and there in Mee Hee's house, before the living-room shrine which she had decorated specially with roses and peonies, Dr Kim had told them that her wedding gift would be a marvellous coronation, a festival that would make the ceremonies on the DVDs look like children's games.

'But— But I thought the King and Queen would be the Peonies' parents at the Park?' Mee Hee had stammered.

'Surely their parents are those who raise them and care for them?' Dr Kim had answered.

'But they won't look like us. No one will believe that we're their parents.'

'What matters, Mee Hee,' Dr Kim had explained gently, 'is what the Peonies think. And the Peonies won't care about the colour of anyone's skin. To them, all of humanity will be one large family. That is their message, and the world must hear it, loud and clear. You and Dr Tae Sun are the first man and woman in the village to pledge your devotion to each other. You are both modest, and well-

446

loved by the others. It would give me such pleasure if you would consent to becoming the First Couple of VirtuWorld.'

Mee Hee stroked her belly as Chin Mee began to shuffle the cards. Tae Sun emerged from the Meeting Hall and waved at Mee Hee, and she blushed. It was nice to be examined by him every week – and to spend time kissing and touching, now that they were engaged. She couldn't look at him now without a warm tingle swirling over her skin.

'Here she goes again,' Older Sister roared, 'red as a beetroot, waiting to be dug!'

'Stop teasing her!' So Ra gave Older Sister a playful slap. 'You're jealous, that's all.'

'Jealous? Her doctor would snap underneath me! No, I've got my eye on one of these sturdy fellows here.' She waved at a guard, who waved back, showing off his muscles. His friend stuck two fingers up behind his head, and everyone laughed.

Mee Hee picked up her cards, glad no one was looking at her any more. Tae Sun disappeared down the path to the houses to check on the installation of more solar panels. Later, he would tell Mee Hee all about Dr Kim's plans for the village. She already knew that there were guards on the roads, protecting the gardens and houses, and that builders were going to put up a huge greenhouse soon, a place to grow hothouse flowers. They would have beehives too, so there would a constant supply of the delicious honey Dr Kim had let her try after she had agreed to be Queen.

Some of the women were getting up now, walking arm in arm to lunch in the Meeting Hall. On The Shortest Day it had been turned into their hospital, and the babies had all been planted there. In March, when the Doctors said the Peonies were all safely rooted, Dr Kim had told them about the Falling Star.

On the very day their motherhood had begun, the Falling Star had brought a terrible winter to the world, and millions of people had died. In London, New York, Washington, the streets had turned into rushing rivers, drowning old and young alike, while all around the rim of the Atlantic Ocean, whole towns and villages had been swept out to sea. Once the waters had receded, the dead had been mourned and the looters arrested. But millions more had been left homeless, and were now huddled in refugee camps, waiting for whole cities to be rebuilt.

But South Korea had been spared; their own small world, nestled between the densely forested mountains, was safe. The babies would come in the autumn, with the rich, orange persimmons and the clear vaulted skies.

THE END

Acknowledgements

I am deeply grateful to all those who nourished this book during its long gestation. In Canada, Alan Fern and Pat Vogt got me out to Seoul. In South Korea, Bhak Chezoo and Moon Kyung Sun opened many secret doors to the Hermit Kingdom, welcomed me into their hearts, and are ever-present in mine; similarly, Pascal Gerrard, Simon Kemp, Una Kim, Kaori Komura, David Lee, Julie Lee, Catherine Lupton, Chaeok Oh Asher, Glen Perice and Heather Scott also all stand at the source, along with J. Scott Burgeson, who published an early chapter in his cult 'zine *Bug*; the cyborg sculptures of artist Lee Bul, and the neon tracers of everyone who ever drank and danced all night at Azitoo and Sang Su Do. In the UK, Susi Aichbauer, Elizabeth Ashworth, John Luke Chapman, Robert Dickinson, Hugh Dunkerley, Sarah Hymas, Simon Jenner, Kai Merriott, Aidan Norton, John O'Donoghue and Lorna Thorpe made invaluable comments on the novel, as did David Swann, who heroically edited the whole manuscript one summer; Bethan Roberts, who so kindly helped me find Zeno Agency; and James Burt and John Atkinson, who freely shared with me their respective scientific and IT expertise (but cannot be held responsible for any warped results). I would also like to thank my Goldsmiths College MA tutors Stephen Knight, Susan Elderkin and Maura Dooley for their critical feedback; Thomas Dolby and his management company OpticNoise, who so generously gave permission to quote from 'Europa and the Pirate Twins'; and my agent, John Richard Parker, who delivered me safely to the spectacular Jo Fletcher and her dedicated staff.